DOWN CHANNEL

Other Sailing Classics

DOWN CHANNEL

R. T. McMULLEN

GRAFTON BOOKS

A Division of the Collins Publishing Group

LONDON GLASGOW
TORONTO SYDNEY AUCKLAND

Grafton Books
A Division of the Collins Publishing Group
8 Grafton Street, London WIX 3LA

First published 1869
This edition published by Grafton Books 1986

British Library Cataloguing in Publication Data

McMullen, R. T.
Down channel.
1. Great Britain – Description and
travel – 1801–1900
I. Title
914.1'0481   DA625

ISBN 0-246-13040-7

Printed in Great Britain by
St Edmundsbury Press, Bury St Edmunds, Suffolk

CONTENTS

LIST OF ILLUSTRATIONS

DOWN CHANNEL

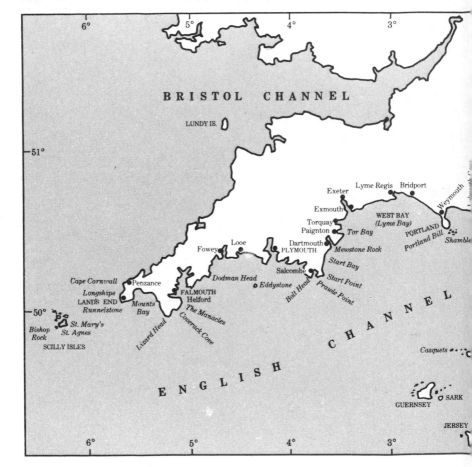

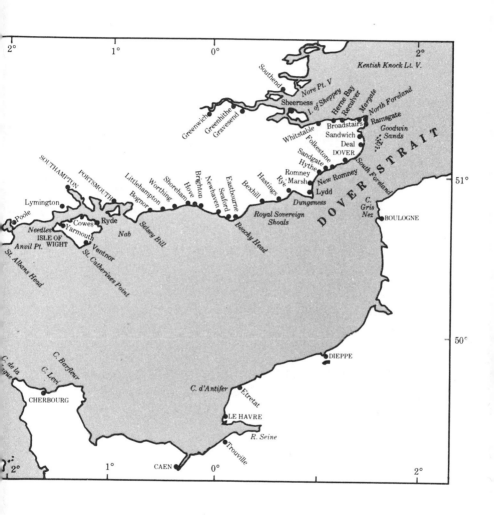

RICHARD TURRELL McMULLEN

BY ARTHUR RANSOME

For a long time now *Down Channel* has been a book not easily
to be obtained. Private owners of it do not lend it. Those who
did long ago ceased to be owners of it at all. It is to be found
only in a few exceptionally well-equipped libraries. Many a
man has, for these reasons, known only by repute, or been
able to read only late in his sailing career, a book that should
have been introduced to him when, with sore finger-tips, he
was working his passage for the first time through the elements
of knots and splices. No man who has read this book ever
forgets it, and those who know it think of it with an affection
that promises it a much longer life than is likely to be given to
much more widely famous works of much more obvious
literary merit. It is as alive to-day, forty years after its author's
death, as it was when it was written. Thanks to the initiative
of Mr. H. J. Hanson, O.B.E., the Honorary Secretary of the
Cruising Association, it is at last republished, to remind old
men of one of the inspirations of their youth and to stir young
ones to an enthusiasm for sailing which is almost enough to
ensure a man a happy life.

The virtue of this one among the thousands of books that
record cruises in yachts and small boats does not depend on the
magnitude of the feats accomplished by its writer. The actual
voyages made by McMullen seem almost humdrum in comparison with those of O Brien and Muhlhauser, both of whom
took yachts round the world; or of Slocum and Gerbault,
who did the same thing single-handed; or of Voss, who, when
he had invented a good sea-anchor, sailed the three oceans in
a forty-foot dugout canoe, looking for great storms in which his
sea-anchor should have a worthy opportunity of showing its
merit. The feat on which McMullen most prided himself was
not even the prodigy of sheer labour that he performed when,

after paying off two grumbling hands, he brought the exceptionally heavily sparred and canvassed *Orion* (19½ tons) home from Cherbourg by himself. It was his Jubilee year circumnavigation of Great Britain and Ireland in the same ship with two professional sailors and an amateur mate to help him. Of this he wrote in a letter partially published in the *Field* after his death: 'I cannot conceal the intense pleasure I derive from the thought that she (*Orion*) was not sold at the time she was last advertised, which was two years prior to the sail over the Jubilee course. Whether I should have taken her to sea again would probably have depended upon as sudden a fancy as the last; at all events my determination was never by an inferior performance to lessen the effect on my own mind of that most perfectly organised and successful cruise. My first cruise, in 1850, which then seemed to me very formidable, was round the Nore, and my last, in 1887, round the British Isles; and there I am content to leave it.' In that reference to the 'effect on his own mind' of a 'perfectly organised' performance lies the secret, or one of the secrets, of McMullen's eminence among those who, not being professional sailors, have written of the sea. He set himself a much higher standard of efficiency in amateur sailing than had ever been set before. The sea (in spite of the common belief that a special providence cares for fools) does not distinguish between the amateur and the professional. It makes no allowances. Neither did McMullen. He expected from himself all that he would have expected from a professional seaman. This was a new tone to take, and no one who has read McMullen can listen without impatience to amateur yachtsmen trying to impress young ladies by talking of the unnecessary risks they took, the haphazard character of their navigation, and the careless way in which they looked after their gear. I do not believe that any other book exists from which a man can learn so much of good manners in the presence of the sea, and good sea-manners are among the surest signs of the good seaman.

Besides setting a higher standard in amateur seamanship than had been set before, McMullen freed small cruisers from the fetters and dangers of too close dependence on the shore. He, first, proclaimed that it was an error to suppose that large vessels were by reason of their largeness safer at sea than small. He was the first to insist that the danger most to be apprehended by the skippers of all sailing vessels, large or small alike, was (after screw-steamers) not water but land, and to urge that at the first sign of bad weather the small-boat sailor should either make sure of shelter or put so far out to sea as not to need it. He emancipated the skippers of small vessels from the snapdragon style of cruising which consisted of spending every night in harbour and scurrying from one place to another during the day. 'I have always preferred the sea,' said McMullen, 'to the risk of entering or the misery of lying in a bad harbour.' What we owe to him for this has been said for all of us by Mr. Claud Worth. In *Yacht Cruising* (a book to set beside McMullen's) he tells how in 1887 he was in Greenhithe Creek cutting down the mast and turning in new splices in the rigging of a much over-canvassed ship's boat, his first yacht, and McMullen, who was fitting out *Orion* there (for the Jubilee cruise mentioned before), came over and spoke to him, and, hearing that he proposed sailing down channel, encouraged him, as an old sailor to a young one, and remarked, 'If it looks like blowing hard on shore, get in somewhere in good time, or else give the land a very wide berth.' Nearly ten years later, in the great gale of September 1896, which found him single-handed at sea, Mr. Worth 'read a few pages of *Sirius* (to be found in this volume) and hardened his heart.' He says, and many another can echo his words, 'I first learned from McMullen's writings and personal example that the deep sea is reasonably safe in bad weather, even for the smallest craft—a secret which otherwise one might only have found out after half a life-time of timid dependence upon harbours.'

McMullen is the best of teachers. There are plenty of efficient seamen whose very efficiency is (from a defect of character) disheartening to those who have all their experience still before them. Efficiency in some men seems to flower in a horrid kind of spiritual pride. The modest recruit to a delightful but exacting art, seeing such men, is given to understand that seamen are born, not made, and is naturally inclined to suspect that he may as well at once give up all hope of ever attaining even reasonable efficiency for himself. The modest recruit, humiliated even further by a short and unhappy lesson from one of these born paragons, should read McMullen and take heart once more. Nothing could be franker and therefore more encouraging than the manner in which McMullen describes the dreadful messes that distinguished his own novitiate afloat. Down it all goes: how his first boat, the *Leo*, sank the very day of her launching; how on his first voyage he nearly sank her again by getting her mast mixed up with the bowsprit of a brig; and, worst of all, the horrible accident that would have driven most young men to leave boats alone, when a flapping sail caught him in the eye with one of an unmoused pair of sister-hooks and all but lifted him overboard. He confesses that after that he could neither get under way nor bring up in a crowded anchorage without 'a taste of brimstone in the mouth from excessive anxiety.' And then follows his simple plan, which was, 'to persevere in sailing by day or night in all weathers, and never to let want of confidence stand in the way.'

At the same time, while McMullen was a living criticism of the merely playful spirit in going to sea, holding that such flippancy implied a ridiculous assumption that the sea was going to be merely playful too; while he set an example of first-rate practical seamanship and tireless attention to detail; while he built his vessels and rigged them to stand those moods of the sea which are not playful at all, no man who has written of sailing has more infectiously expressed the pleasure that he found in it, pleasure of a finer kind than had been found in it before. In his writings, for the first time, yachting ceased to be a sort of social ceremony dependent largely on the presence of spectators, but an affair between man and nature, a series of trials in which the prize to be attained is that a man shall stand well with himself. No winning guns or spectators' smiles matter in the least. In these contests a man is his own judge, and, in secret at least, a strict one. Among the motives of his own sailing McMullen mentioned 'a lively interest in natural objects and phenomena, observed to greatest advantage on the sea,' and also the favourable effect of sailing on his health; but both these motives seem unimportant in comparison with 'an insatiable pleasure in the art of sailing, which, especially in strong weather, offers such an endless variety of problems for solution that there is always something fresh to engage the attention, as well as experience to be acquired.' He is able to share pleasure, problem, and experience. With no sort of literary fuss, he makes his readers hear what he heard, see what he saw, and feel what he felt. Remember, for example, his account of getting into Fowey in the dark and hearing the church bells there ring a long tune. Or this: 'To be continually running to leeward is like living on dry bread.' Or this: 'There is a wonderful difference between being outward bound for pleasure, and homeward bound of necessity.' Or listen to this, written of meeting a 'towering sea' while alone in the little *Procyon*: 'I encouraged her as one does a horse, and, not for the first time, found she understood me well.' Only men who have never felt a small boat working herself to windward will wonder why we love McMullen for such words.

    .   .   .   .   .

Of McMullen's life it is already hard to discover much beyond what is to be learnt from his own writings, and that is very little. He was born about 1830, became a member of the Stock Exchange in 1853, lived chiefly at Greenhithe, and died in 1891, in mid-Channel, sitting in the cockpit of the *Perseus* on a bright starlit night. He was married, and his wife sailed with him on many occasions, though, as she was not actively concerned with the navigation of his vessels, he did not think it necessary to mention her in his logs. Already there are not very many who remember him. One who saw him in the *Orion* says that he was a 'little man, but a terrible worker.' 'Everything had to be done as perfectly as possible, irrespective

15

of bad weather or previous fatigue.' He 'disliked profanity and loathed any kind of slang.' The *Field*, in noticing his death, said: 'Mr. McMullen was unlike any other yachtsman we ever met: we have known men just as fond of the sea as he was, but never anyone who regarded it with such reverential interest. Yachting and yacht racing in the ordinary sense of the terms had no charms for him.' Always it was his character that impressed people more than any details of his personal history.

Like most men who are supremely good at any one thing, McMullen held decided opinions on a number of subjects besides that one with which his name will always be associated. For him to hold an opinion strongly was to express it. At school in France he had been known as 'John-Bull-Dick,' and the downrightness which that nickname suggests was his throughout his life. It by no means diminishes the interest of *Down Channel* to spend some time in the British Museum going through the various books and pamphlets that are there catalogued under its author's name. There is the original *Down Channel* of 1869; *'Orion': How I came to Sail Alone in a* 19-*ton Yacht* (1878); *An Experimental Cruise Single-handed in the 'Procyon'* (1880); *Infidelity: its Cause and Antidote* (1879); *Whither did They Ascend?* (1881); and *Priestly Pretensions and God's Word* (1885). In all these works he speaks with the same independence and force. In the *Orion* volume he followed an account of his voyage with twenty short chapters on all sorts of things, and he opened that book with a preface 'intended to be read' in which, in the course of an attack on compulsory education, he remarked: 'When our lads—who in the course of time will have to keep the look-out at sea, or clean our boots on shore— are well-grounded in Music, Drawing, and Algebra, at the Rate-payers' expense, there will at least be a chance of improvement.' He had no misgivings whatever about the divine rights of the rich, whose boots, of course, would have to be blacked by someone. He foresaw ruin and starvation as the result of trade unionism, as an antidote to which he proposed the study of the Bible. He thought that men 'strike that they may

16

work less time than industrious men ought to work without
suffering diminution of pay.'

At the same time, though he described his paid hands as
'insolent' because they smoked while washing down, he asked
nothing from them that he was not willing to perform himself.
On one of the few occasions when he raced, on a passage to
Ireland, a man refused to go out on the gaff to reeve the topsail sheet which had gone adrift, and indeed, if McMullen
had known that his rival had given up, it would have been
natural to lower the sail and reeve the sheet on deck. Mc-
Mullen rebuked him by calling the mate to the tiller and going
aloft and out on the gaff himself. A similar motive prompted
him to the single-handed sailing of *Orion* home from Cherbourg, when he noted in his precise manner, just as he used to
tick off used stores on the lists which he kept on the inside of
every cupboard and locker door in the ship, that he lost
'between two and three pounds' in weight during the
laborious performance by which, as Frank Cowper admitted,
he was 'the first to show how one man could handle a large
boat.'

But the relation between employers and employed was only
one of the many things on which he had something to say.
He was a stout, pugnacious Protestant. In *Infidelity: its Cause
and Antidote*, a pamphlet published in 1879, and embellished
with laudatory notices of the original *Down Channel* and an
advertisement of a 3*d.* pamphlet on the *Rule of the Road*, he
expresses his loathing for the men who, while subscribing to
the Thirty-nine Articles, did in their teaching seek to introduce
a new Popery and a disguised return to 'the idolatrous
Churches of Eastern Europe and of Rome.' Prayers for the
dead he described as 'an odious invention of priestcraft to
extort money from sorrowing relations' while encouraging
people to 'defer the most important duty of their lives until it
was too late.' In *Priestly Pretensions and God's Word* he returned
to the subject with further argument against what he considered was a dragging down of the Protestant Church to a
level at which, being no better than the Roman and the Greek,

17

it could unite with them. He ingeniously defended the inaccuracies of 'Genesis' on the ground that 'all but the faintest outline of the history of the first two thousand years was purposely consigned to oblivion—buried with the wicked inhabitants by the Flood.'

From such high matters as these he could turn to express his hearty dislike for 'unmanageable screw steamers' and the infant motor-car, and, in 1878, described flying as 'an art which some have rashly essayed, but which there is no probability will ever triumph over the art of sailing to windward at sea.' To illustrate his ironic manner in argument I will quote from his remarks on collisions:

'If large steamers only ran down small vessels, it might appear to gentlemen of advanced opinions as if only small vessels were in fault; but, in fact, large steamers exhibit a commendable spirit of impartiality and fair play by running down each other, so that the blame for these disasters may properly be attributed to the faults I have pointed out. . . .' and from his appeal for the prohibition of all mechanically propelled vehicles between the hours of 8 a.m. and 8 p.m., where he says, 'I make no apology for introducing this subject even into a semi-nautical book, since it is quite as bad for Her Majesty's subjects to be run down on land as to be drowned at sea.'

In his Conservatism, Protestantism, and dislike of the screw-steamers and mechanically propelled vehicles, he was in excellent company and would have small difficulty in finding supporters to-day. He was probably more lonely in his speculations as to the physical whereabouts of Paradise and Hades. Throughout his life he had a passionate interest in the stars, to which the names of all his vessels bear witness, *Leo, Sirius, Orion, Procyon,* and *Perseus.* Again and again he mentions his pleasure in a starlit night. But astronomy had for him a further interest of a kind it can hardly have for us. In *Whither did They Ascend?* he gives his reasons for supposing that the sun is 'the probable abode of the blessed.' It is not, he thinks, so hot as it appears. He supports his views with references to the Bible and

18

to the writings of Sir William Herschel. An instinctive knowledge that the sun and Paradise are identical is, he suggests, common to all mankind and explains the mournful feelings with which we watch the sun sink below the horizon and the rapture with which we welcome the dawn. Examining the conditions likely to prevail on others of the planets, inclining, I think, a little towards Jupiter, he discusses their horrid suitability as places of eternal punishment. Even in these speculations he is still a seaman and, with a touch that goes straight to every sailor's heart, he confesses his inability to believe that in 'the heavenly economy' there will be no more sea. Heaven without sea would be no heaven for him. The sea must be there too, if only from 'the presumed necessity of the ever varying and wonderful clouds.' One who, as a very young man, met McMullen a few years before he died, says that even to mention these strange beliefs of his is to give a false impression of him, because he did not talk of them. He may not have talked of them to young acquaintances, but that he himself wished them to be remembered is sufficiently proved by his writing his pamphlets and printing them at his own expense. And, after all, Columbus hoped to sail his way up the stalk end of a pear-shaped world, but that did not prevent him from discovering America, or lessen his place in history. And I think that for most people the very great interest of *Down Channel* will be not diminished but enhanced by the knowledge that this hard-headed Victorian stock-broker, this first-rate, practical seaman made his voyages round the English coast in what was still, in some respects, a mediaeval world, within actual physical sight of the glowing ramparts of Heaven and Hell.

NOTE

Down Channel in its final form contains, besides much new matter, what McMullen most wished to preserve out of his three earlier books about sailing. The book was ready for publication in 1891, and McMullen had written his preface to it before he sailed on his last voyage in the *Perseus*. His friend,

Dixon Kemp, the famous yacht-designer and author of the standard *Manual of Yacht and Boat Sailing*, saw it through the Press, adding the last log of the *Perseus*, the account of McMullen's death and a short introduction. The book is here reprinted from the edition of 1893, with a valuable additional illustration. None of the earlier editions of *Down Channel* gave the lines of any of McMullen's vessels. Plans and sail-plans were shown, but nothing else of the sort. Now, as McMullen tells us, all his vessels (with the exception of the *Procyon*, a shallow-draught boat with a centre-board) had a close family likeness to the *Leo*, his first little ship. They had long keels, straight stems and short counters or none. They were sound, healthy vessels, capable to some extent of sailing themselves, and not crotchety or fickle when hove-to. Mr. Worth, writing in December, 1930, set down what McMullen had told him of their design:—

'In the autumn of 1849 a revenue cutter was on the hard at Rotherhithe. Measurements and midship (Approx.) section were taken from her and divided by 3.

'That was the origin of the 18 foot L.W.L. *Leo*.

'*Sirius* was *Leo* with all measurements increased 50%.

'*Orion*, cutter, was the same model (more or less) with dimensions further increased. Later *Orion* was lengthened six feet by opening out the planking aft and rebuilding the after half of the vessel. Then she was rigged as a yawl.

'For *Orion* a half model was cut and sawn in sections but the other two boats were built entirely by eye with the help of a midship mould and battens.'

In the 1931 edition the lines of *Orion* were printed for the first time. For this thanks are due to the owner of *Orion*, to the Cruising Association, who, with his permission, laid her ashore for measurement, and to Captain O. M. Watts.

ARTHUR RANSOME.

1931. 1949.

INTRODUCTION

MR. McMULLEN, in the preface to the first edition of *Down Channel*, stated there is no royal road to a knowledge of yacht sailing; but a perusal of his various logs will convince anyone that there is a common road to such knowledge, and, although it may be a rather laborious one to pursue, it has many pleasures and delights, and, in some cases, presents features of absorbing interest. These logs are unlike most things of the kind, as they do not present a picture of the mere social life on board a yacht, but recount the incidents and operations of sailing under a great variety of conditions. Indeed, Mr. McMullen so far abstained from the social aspect of his many cruises, that he barely alludes to the fact that Mrs. McMullen was his companion on many occasions, notably in his stirring cruise of 1868. Mr. McMullen's *Down Channel*, to the amateur yacht sailor, will be all the more valuable and interesting for this characteristic; in fact, it forms quite an instruction book.

He began his expeditions with little or no experience, feeling his way at first, but finding everything out for himself, and, in the end, acquiring so much confidence in his own skill and endurance that the most congenial form of prolonged recreation was, to him, 'sailing alone.' For this kind of sailing very fine qualities are needful; a man must have a strong nerve, great patience, quickness of resource, endurance, and untiring industry, and, above all, an ideal of perfection to strive for in every description of work undertaken. The passion for single-handed sailing, and belief that if carried out with great effectiveness and thoroughness it formed an agreeable pursuit, developed themselves very strongly in Mr. McMullen's case. In 1880, after his 'Experimental Single-handed Cruise in the "Procyon," ' he wrote to me as follows in reference to a companion he had with him for five days: 'The advent of my young friend was a most enlightening experiment, since it showed, beyond doubt, that in such a boat an expedition of the nature I had been engaged in was safer managed alone. As regards actual work, nothing throughout the day was advanced a minute. The knowledge that every detail depended on myself no longer operated in securing the complete order and regularity which had previously reigned on board—in fact, one's thoughts being interrupted by conversations and numerous instructions, things almost essential to safety were overlooked as they had not been before. Hauling on ropes was lighter, and a hand at the helm sometimes a convenience; but the advantage previously enjoyed, of perfect order and routine, so far outweighed the assistance one less accustomed than myself to the sea and the hauling of heavy canvas could render me, that I am convinced that it was (under the exceptional circumstances of such a cruise), in the main, safer for me to be alone.'

It will be gathered that a character like that of Mr. Mc-Mullen, capable of so much concentrated energy, would make its mark in other directions besides yacht sailing; and so it was. He published a large number of pamphlets on a great variety of subjects, all showing originality and clearness of thought, and a desire that everything should be done by exact methods.

He was a staunch Conservative of the old type, a firm Protestant, and a devout believer in individual responsibility. He wrote strongly against the modern system of Trade Unionism, which he denominated the 'Idlers' Union'; and his preponderating ideality led him to denounce the 'iniquitous rules of "Trade Unionism" which punish a man of superior intelligence and industrious disposition for conscientiously making the best use of his talents.'

It can easily be believed that the end of Mr. McMullen was exactly as he would have wished it to be—when alone upon the sea. It was peaceful, and not the result of any disaster or misadventure due to human failing. The sea had for him just that

Mystic spell
Which none but sailors know or feel,
And none but they can tell.

INTRODUCTION

And he died upon the sea, sitting in the cockpit of the little 'Perseus,' his face towards the sky, whilst she was sailing up the silver path of the moon, which seemed to unite heaven and the sea. After his spirit had gone forth the little craft sailed herself to the French coast, as recounted at the end of this volume.

DIXON KEMP.

AUGUST, 1893.

AUTHOR'S PREFACE

IN reproducing my first book with additions and corrections, I trust it will be apparent that there is no disposition to abandon the simplicity which originally characterised it.

As I craved indulgence from the reader then, so must I now, for the many deficiencies in the style of the book—a style which was contracted in earlier days when publication was not contemplated, the notes being in fact only of the rough kind that, from the commencement of my ventures beyond the Nore, were made simply for my own reference and amusement.

The notes are made, not on a printed form like a ship's log, but in a blank book, which may be called a log, but is, strictly speaking, a log and diary *composite*. The frequent mention of the hour and the weather—remarks which may be troublesome to some readers—are important to me, as by their help I am able to recall to my mind the events of any days' sailing for the past thirty years.

It may be objected, that there is too much 'salt,' and too little 'spice,' for pleasant reading, which perhaps is true, as the book is not intended to trespass on the ground occupied by Murray's handbooks, nor to form an addition to the numerous accounts of domestic life on board a small yacht, which have already been published, but is little more than a bare record of sailing. For this reason Mrs. McMullen and other visitors, who never added strength to the crew, though they were occasionally on board in very trying times, are not mentioned in the book. If they had the opportunity of speaking for themselves, without doubt they could supply a few reminiscences of a strictly personal nature in reference to the gale of Aug. 22nd, 1868, on the Devonshire coast, and of more than one severe brush off the coast of Ireland. But, battened down below, striving to maintain one's position in the berth by clinging to

25

the leeboard or clutching at the shelf overhead, where little can be heard but the shouting and trampling on deck, the flapping of the canvas 'in stays,' the sea rushing along the deck and over the skylights, accompanied by the ceaseless roar of the wind, affords very little opportunity for making observations of general interest, or such as might be deemed encouragement to others who may some day be similarly circumstanced.

Amongst some of my non-sailing acquaintances, the crudest notions of an amateur sailor's life prevail. Because the vessel is called a yacht, they think there is a royal road to every place, where the sea is neither rough, salt, nor deep—a sort of Elysium, where you anchor when you please, eat and drink when and what you please, and live for the time being in perpetual enjoyment of the sun, moon, and stars. A glance at the following pages will convince them that they have formed too high an estimate of the pleasures of yacht sailing, and perhaps save them the vexation of fitting out a yacht under a misapprehension.

For years I have been accustomed to hear remarks implying that a yachtsman's time must be heavy on hand, and hard to kill. It may be so in yachting proper, which consists chiefly in promenading on quays, esplanades, and piers, in suitable attire, of course, and in passing to and fro in a steam launch or gig, with colours flying; a delight indulged in only by the extremely affluent, or by those who ought to be so.

Yacht sailing, however, is a very different affair from 'yachting,' and when carried on with spirit, as it is sometimes in large yachts as well as small, is anything but an idle recreation. It is always healthful and exciting, though not always a source of unalloyed pleasure. But even when the work is heavy and continuous, as it must be occasionally, more than ample compensation is found in the contrast of a pretty and quiet anchorage, which no one who has not been buffeted about can appreciate and thoroughly enjoy. If I may compare sailing with equestrian sports, I should say that yacht sailing stands in about the same relation to 'yachting' as the hunting field does to Rotten Row. The comparison is inadequate, but those who know the delight of being well and comfortably housed after a long and hard day's hunting in bad weather will understand the compensation to be found by the yachtsman in a quiet anchorage.

The cruise of 1868, in the 'Orion,' was so exceptionally heavy that it is necessary to remind the reader that, after an unusually long drought, with little wind, the weather changed early in August, and set in wet and windy. This violent change, with intervals of fine weather, culminated on August 22 in a gale, said to have been more destructive to shipping than any since the 'Royal Charter' gale of October, 1859. That the losses were not more numerous in the month of September was due to the frequent storm-warnings issued by the Meteorological Department of the Board of Trade, and to the fact that gales followed each other in such quick succession that the ports and roadsteads were crowded and the seas proportionately clear of ships. Thus on September 28 and 29, in a run of fourteen hours, we saw only one vessel at sea. The gale commenced on the night of the 24th, and, with short intervals, continued until the 30th, during which time the barometer was in a most agitated state, rising or falling for every little shift of wind, rising for S.W. and W., and falling for S. and S.E.

As, with the single exception of the Jubilee cruise round the British Islands, my crew consists of only two hands, it is evident that when under way day and night, sleeping and light reading were luxuries necessarily little indulged in. What time was found for reading was generally devoted to the study of charts, books of sailing directions, and an occasional newspaper.

When on long passages, if the weather were not too dark and strong, my custom has been to allow one hand below from eight p.m. to midnight, the other from midnight to 4 a.m., and both of them from 4 a.m. to 6. After the morning scrub down, which would be completed about seven or half-past, one went to prepare breakfast and the other relieved the helm, while I went below to wash and dress—my mode of commencing a new day—by which time their breakfast was ready.

When they had breakfasted the mate took the helm and the other attended upon me. Thus they had each six hours below, and I reserved my 'turning in' until the end of the passage, which has frequently averaged five days, and more than once has extended to seven consecutive days and nights. My nights were all passed on deck or below as need required, but always in readiness for the deck, having every circumstance reported to me, such as ships' lights, land in sight, alteration in force or direction of wind—the latter often occasioning much work. Then, what with the chart and the log, and the helm to be relieved for re-trimming lights after midnight, &c., &c., there has usually been sufficient employment, unless the night was calm, and we were sailing 'easy,' or drifting with plenty of sea room.

In port, or at anchor, on the coast, weather permitting, a great deal of time was passed in the boat, sailing up rivers, or into sandy coves, or rowing amongst the rocks, and into caverns—an amusement to which I am extremely partial. My first intention was to write of the 'Orion' only; but, thinking that an account of my former vessels would not be altogether uninteresting, as showing how progressive and growing a taste for sailing is, I have commenced at the stage next to toy boats, viz., the first day in the 'Leo.'

R. T. McMullen.

1891.

NOTE

The distances mentioned in this book are not the actual distances between the places named, but the number of nautical miles sailed in making the passage.

DOWN CHANNEL

'LEO'

'Leo,' 2¾ tons, builder's measurement.
Built of pine, by J. Thompson, of Rotherhithe, 1850.
Length between perpendiculars, 18 feet; over all, 20 feet.
Breadth moulded, 6 feet 1 inch; extreme, 6 feet 3 inches.
Draught of water forward, 2 feet 6 inches; aft, 4 feet.
Area of mainsail, 144 square feet; topsail, 67 square feet.
Weight of ballast, 23 cwt.

		Geographica Miles sailed
1850.	In the Thames	600
1851.	Do. and to Ramsgate	850
1852.	Do. and 6 passages to Ramsgate; greatest distance Dover	1,450
1853.	Do. and to Dungeness	1,070
1854.	Do. do.	900
1855.	Do. and S.E. coast; greatest distance Hastings	772
1856.	To the Isle of Wight	1,200
1857.	To the Land's End	1,380
		8,222

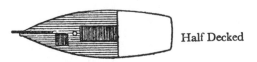

Half Decked

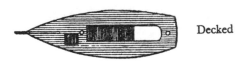

Decked

THE 'LEO'

THE 'LEO', 1850-57

NOTHING could seem more ill-omened than the first incident related in the log for 1850, at the very commencement of my novitiate.

The day the 'Leo,' 3 tons (described on a previous page), left the builder's yard, she was so carelessly moored by the man who had charge of her, that she grounded during the night on the edge of a camp-shed at Charlton, between the Marine Society's ship and the shore. Being a deep boat, only half-decked, and heavily ballasted, the tide flowed into and filled her. Words will not describe the intense feeling of disappointment and mortification I experienced when I went down the next morning to try my new boat, and saw only a few feet of the mast above water.

With assistance kindly rendered from the Society's ship, she was got up at the following low water, and taken to Greenwich to be cleared of the mud and filth with which she was well plastered inside.

Since that time I have launched two new vessels, and took the precaution to have them christened in due form; my neglect of that ceremony in the case of the 'Leo' being, no doubt, the pretext for Father Thames taking it into his own hands.

The first sail was as far as Gravesend and back, with a waterman in charge, and this was the only apprenticeship I served. A confiding kinsman, whose judgment was almost equal to my own, accompanied me, and, his opinion coinciding with mine, that there was nothing to do which we could not easily do ourselves, I resolved to dispense with pilotage services from that day as a waste of money.

My first attempt, with only the boy on board and a chart for guide, though a very mild and unambitious little cruise from Charlton to Erith and back, was not concluded without a narrow escape. Passing between the collier brigs off Charlton

33

at 10 p.m. to anchor for the night, I made allowance for the two I wished to pass ahead of, and then discovered a third vessel at anchor by itself, upon which we were helplessly driven by the tide. Our mast-head fouling his bowsprit, the 'Leo' was beginning to fill, when the crew of the brig got the mast clear and she righted.

The second cruise was regularly planned and more pretentious. It was voted a jolly thing to drop down to Gravesend on the afternoon of the one day, and start early next morning for a sail round the Nore, my confiding kinsman to do duty as mate upon this grand occasion.

Great was our rejoicing when the anchor was let go at Gravesend, after having providentially passed safely inside the ships to the anchorage below the Custom House. After tea, which was made in a bachelor's kettle on deck, all hands turned in—the boy, the bachelor's kettle, and sundries occupied the forecastle, in which there was just room for all when properly packed. We, the quarter-deckers, of course occupied the cabin. Though the boat was only 3 tons, each had a properly constructed berth 6 feet by 2 feet, with bed and leeboard complete. Nothing could be more comfortable, if you could only remember that the deck beams were within 6 inches of your head. What with glorious anticipations for the morrow, bright ideas that would not keep, but must be communicated immediately, and what with laughing and giggling, being too hot and too cold, and the novelty of the situation generally, there was not a wink of sleep got all night.

At last the day broke on which we were to make our mark in the sailing world. O dear! I shall never forget that day, though a veil is thrown over it in the log-book, where it is mentioned in these suspicious terms: 'Sailed out the first season in the Thames, &c., &c., &c. Once venturing to the Nore; but in this adventure got into such trouble that there was no chance of repeating the attempt until the recollection of it had quite blown over, which was not earlier than the following year.' Nevertheless, as an act of penance for unpardonable rashness, I will confess a few scrapes.

34

After washing and dressing in the sharp air of an early June morning, with a nice breeze from the westward, we got the anchor up at 5 A.M. This was no sooner done, and the jib set, than we fell athwart a yacht, about ten tons, which brought out two wrathful and unlucky wights in their night shirts, who, with chattering teeth and much bare flesh exposed to the fresh wind, worked well and successfully to get us clear. Having given us a parting benediction, they dived precipitately below, and no doubt drank health and success to us in a well-earned glass of brandy. I must further confess that, being in a state of bewilderment on account of the getting athwart hawse not being in the day's programme, we did nothing whatever towards clearing the vessels, nor even thought of thanking the gentlemen for their exertions until they had probably fallen into a sound sleep again.

It is usual, I think, after a confession to find, if possible, some excuse for the fault you have confessed. Now my excuse for getting athwart hawse was this: after much cogitation I made up my mind to cast the boat's head to the northward, but happening to spy a swell on board a yacht close by, with a gold band on his cap and a great many gilt buttons on his coat, I was greenhorn enough to think he knew something, so modestly asked his advice, and followed it to our grief and confusion.

Since then I have grown older, and have learnt one or two little secrets which I will disclose for the information of brother greenhorns. When you hear a man talking so loudly that you are in doubt how many yachts he owns, be sure his nearest approach to ownership is knowing a friend, who is or was an owner. Therefore be careful not to ask the name of his yacht. And when you see a yachting gilt-bespangled dandy, trust rather to your 'Seaman's Manual and Vocabulary of Seaterms,' and do not disgust the gentleman with awkward questions before company unless you wish to make an enemy.

Running down the 'Hope' under all sail on a beautiful sunny morning was such a delightful novelty, and so exhilarating, that confidence was restored sooner than might have been the case if we had not been able to charge our first misfortune upon the lubber with the gold band and gilt buttons. After a good breakfast we were in high spirits, and every fresh gust of wind was answered with an inward chuckle of satisfaction.

All went merrily as a marriage bell until we were about a mile below the Nore, when our enjoyment was at its height, and it was thought time to turn back. Finding, on coming to the wind, that it was necessary to take a reef down, we ceased all at once to see beauty anywhere, had misgivings, and secretly began to 'wish we were at home.'

A nasty short sea having got up, I had sense enough to keep the weather-shore, but quite forgot there was a Nore sand until frightened out of our wits by the vessel bumping on it. Our hair had scarcely time to stand on end before she came off again, having crossed the sand from the inside into the rough water of the fairway. Now began another trouble. The sea in the tideway was so violent, and the wind so strong, that sail was shortened to close reefs, which, though indispensable to our safety under the circumstances, would have been un-necessary, had I known how to sail the boat. In this hampered state we just managed to fetch above the Chapman Head at high water, when an accident happened which, but for presence of mind on my part, and a sudden conviction that there was no time to lose, would have been attended with horrible consequences to myself. The mainsheet was attached to the sail in two parts, viz., a single block and a pair of sister-hooks. To prevent the block from striking our heads I put it in the upper cringle and the hooks in the lower. The hooks not being moused, as they should have been, one of them, un-observed by me, shook adrift while the boat was in stays. The sail in passing over to leeward happening to hit my face, the hook caught me in the right eye, and would have dragged me over the lee gunwale if I had not seized the sail with both hands and extricated myself as soon as possible. It could not have dragged me overboard if I had chosen to resist with the weight of my body, but anyone who has had a cinder or other foreign substance under the upper eyelid will understand that, the hook having got all the eyelid in the deepest part, its leading was irresistible. My companions were horror-stricken when I told them what I thought was the matter and called for help. However, before they could get to me, it was all over. Never before or since have I felt such a sense of joy and thankfulness as when, having applied a handkerchief to the wound, I caught a glimmer of daylight. As the mate had only seen a tiller and never handled one, we were compelled to hail a schooner for assistance. There happened fortunately to be two Greenwich watermen on board, who left in their boat, which had been towing astern, and boarded us after a little hesitation. There is no doubt that the 'Leo' looked dangerous in a sea, and was dangerous, being at that time only half decked and deep with ballast. She had a shifting wash-board to keep water out, but it was a very imperfect arrangement. The men, finding her better than they expected, shook out a reef and ran for Yantlet, where we left her heeling over on the ground, and walked up to the village of Allhallows to dry our clothes, which were wet through, and to get, if possible, a hot dinner. Though very anxious to see a surgeon and get relief for my wound, which was extremely troublesome, I had to bear the pain and the doubt as to what injury was done until the next day. Having supplied our necessities at a decent little inn, we all walked down again and went on board to wait for the tide; the men lashing their boat to the 'Leo's' gunwale to assist her in rising, about which we had doubts.

Shortly after midnight, with two reefs down, we started again, towing their boat with our little punt stowed inside it, and arrived at Gravesend about 4.30 A.M., where the mate and I landed very wet with spray, cold and miserable, to take the first train to Woolwich. During the day, the men took the 'Leo' up to Greenwich. A few days later she was sent back to the builder's yard to be made safe and seaworthy, by having the deck carried aft, leaving only an open steerage 5 feet by 2 feet. A very convenient little galley was also made to accommodate

37

a Redpath's cooking apparatus, which answered well and was a great improvement.

On landing at Gravesend we certainly did not find *terra firma*, for everything seemed to be in motion. For several hours on the previous day we had been greatly annoyed by a stone bottle full of beer rolling about on the cabin floor. After the boat began to jump about, I wouldn't leave the helm, and the mate didn't care to be groping about securing things below, because I must have battened him down the while to keep the water out, and his health, though good in the open air, might have taken a sudden turn down there. For nothing is more calculated to ruin one's sea legs than crawling on hands and knees in a heavy sea, in a space so confined that it was like crawling under a table. Besides, they say it is the last straw that breaks the camel's back, and he had a suspicion that *that* would be the last straw for him. Therefore we let the bottle roll and bang about all day.

While dozing in the train up to Woolwich and in our beds the following night, we were both pitching and rolling about, the sensation of motion being accompanied by the wretched sound of the rolling bottle. We have since had many a laugh over this.

The mate having qualified for sea so far as he considered necessary for passing an examination at one of the Inns of Court, resigned his appointment and has never been seen on board a yacht since.

Upon submitting my wound to surgical examination, the eye was pronounced not to be injured, though its escape was a miracle. It was closed, however, for a fortnight, and nearly a month elapsed before it could take its turn of duty and be properly considered a 'weather eye.'

After being so badly handled at the first venture, I could not get under way or go in amongst the ships to bring up without having a taste of brimstone in the mouth from excessive anxiety. I envied the bargemen their coolness and evident self-possession, and looked forward to the time when I should feel the same confidence. My plan was to persevere in sailing by day or night in all weathers, and never to let want of confidence stand in the way. In this manner, getting into scrapes and getting out of them, I learnt more of practical sailing in a few months than I should have learnt in several years if I had hired a man to take the lead in everything.

Although the 'Leo' after being decked was an excellent sea boat, I did not venture again below Hole Haven in Sea Reach until the following year (1851), when I not only visited several times the scene of my former disaster, but ventured to Ramsgate and the South Foreland with only charts, compass, and lead for guides. Nothing could have seemed more cross and unlucky than a foul wind all the way out and home, which quite upset my plans, elaborately drawn out on paper, for running from one mark to another, and, instead, compelled frequent reference to the charts and constant use of the lead. But really nothing could have been more advantageous, though at the time the difficulties seemed insurmountable. Twenty fair-wind passages would have taught me nothing in comparison, so that in the end it was most fortunate.

In 1852, contemplating longer passages, I gave 'Leo' a topmast; and in 1855, wanting more sail for running before a light wind, I invented a sail which for want of a better name I called a *studding-sail*, but which was known about twelve years later as a *spinnaker*, when it came into use amongst larger yachts for match-sailing. It is made of very light material in the form of a jib, and sets from the topmast head to the deck where it is boomed out like a squaresail. (See Plate facing p. 33.) As it is a sail that endangers the topmast, except in the lightest winds, I discarded it in 1865.

Having given a short account of my first sail round the Nore in 1850, and my first attempt at sea in 1851, I will pass on to the last cruise of the 'Leo' in 1857. Having had a very rough season in 1856 on the South Coast and Isle of Wight, I thought it necessary, before going to sea again, to put her in a state of thorough repair. Besides refastening, she had a new deck, and a new suit of sails; the mainsail and foresail being of stout 24-inch canvas split. In fact, nothing was wanting, as far as I remember,

39

when, on the afternoon of June 10, my friends accompanied me to Greenwich to see the start for a destination known only to myself. There were two good reasons for being reserved on this point. One was that in case of being prevented by unforeseen difficulties from carrying out my intention, I must have seemed a silly boaster; the other, that, instead of receiving encouragement, I should probably have heard forebodings of ill that would have been ringing in my ears at inconvenient seasons, to my great discomfort and annoyance. The lad who accompanied me, George Chason, of Gravesend, was also judiciously kept in the dark, though he knew he was going to sea for several weeks.

At 3 P.M. Set sail and ran down to Mucking-Bight at the top of Sea Reach, where we anchored for the night.

June 11.—Sailed at 6 A.M. under all sail with a fair wind.

Noon. Off Cliff-End, near Margate, hove to in a squall from the N.W. Housed topmast and made snug. The event of the day, for which preparation was made by lowering the foresail and trussing mainsail, was a terrific squall off Broadstairs, in which the 'Leo' was on beam-ends for several minutes, until with great difficulty the mainsail was taken off her, when she righted and flew along under a small jib only. Ships lowered their topsail yards upon the caps. The cruise was so nearly ended in the squall, that I was quite *hors de combat* for the day, and had to put into Ramsgate to regain self-possession.

June 12.—From Ramsgate 7.30 A.M., wind E. 10 P.M., anchored for the night in Seaford Road, near Newhaven, Sussex.

June 13.—Under way at 7 A.M., wind E. light and fine; 5.30 P.M., anchored at Cowes, Isle of Wight.

June 17.—Wind N.E. 1 P.M. Sailed from Cowes with a reef down. At 7.45 P.M., ran into Poole, Dorsetshire, through the swatchway, and anchored off Brownsea Castle.

Though all was new to me, and the passage intricate, I had no great trouble to find the way in, there or anywhere else. The charts, according to my custom, having been carefully prepared, with the bearings and distances of different objects in coloured inks, the particulars required at the time were copied on a slate and taken to the helm with me. By this means I was able to recognise the land and the buoys, &c., without leaving my post at inconvenient times. The anxiety of sailing upon a strange coast and entering strange harbours is great enough, however well prepared one may be beforehand. To have to hunt up all the information at the last moment, is not only confusion and misery, but very dangerous.

June 19.—From Poole, 11.30 A.M.; wind E.S.E. strong and fine. Ran before a rough sea to St. Alban's Head. 3 P.M., coming on to blow very hard, had to shorten sail considerably; 5.30 P.M., heavy thunderstorm travelling up fast from S.S.E. Took bearings of Bat's Head and Weymouth Church before losing sight of them in the rain, which shortly afterwards came on like a waterspout. Having further reduced canvas, we watched the approach of the storm with anything but feelings of confidence and pleasure. While it lasted, the wind was fierce and the thunder and lightning terrible, the clouds being so low that they seemed to be almost on the sea. Fortunately it lasted only about three-quarters of an hour, and then left us tossing about in Weymouth Bay, close to the harbour. Not having steerage way, some men came out in a boat and towed us in. A model yacht only 9 inches out of water at the quarters was a strange sight off the town in such heavy weather, and attracted a little crowd of people, who walked alongside while she was being towed to moorings. 'Where is she from, Jack?' was the question many times asked of one of the men in the boat. For three days the 'Leo' was the Lion of Weymouth. Being moored close to the quay, we were under the constant inspection of a greater or less number of people, so that I felt rather hampered in the domestic arrangements.

After putting back for one day for want of wind, I put her aground to have the bottom black-leaded and give her a coat of paint outside.

June 24.—Went out and anchored in Portland Roads, where there was then no harbour. Neither were the beautiful heights appropriated by the Ordnance Department, so that it was a delightful and exhilarating scramble of nearly 500 feet, for a youth with good lungs, which I enjoyed to the uttermost.

June 25.—Sailed at 3 A.M. Passed Portland Bill at 4.45 A.M., and running before a light easterly wind with large topsail, large jib, and spinnaker set, managed to make Dartmouth at 6.30 P.M.

June 26.—Sailed from Dartmouth at 9 A.M., wind N.E.

Desiring to see the Eddystone Lighthouse, steered for it from Prawle Point, and passed close to the southward of it at 4.45 P.M.; then laid a course for Fowey in Cornwall, which we made at 11 P.M. Being unaccustomed to high black cliffs, and having no other means of ascertaining their distance—for mere appearance is very deceptive—I resorted to a powerful copper whistle, and estimated the distance by the echo.

In the entrance between the cliffs, where the night was black as pitch, the wind failed entirely, and left us rolling on a lazy swell. The sound of the sea booming in the caverns had a most depressing influence; and, overpowered with a sense of miserable loneliness and uncertainty, I had a lantern hung out and withdrawn, in the hope of bringing off the coastguard. Two fishermen happening to row in at the time, came alongside and towed us into a berth off Polruan. Soon after anchoring in the open part of the harbour, where it was very still under the starlight night, the clock of old Fowey Church struck twelve and played a long tune. I shall never forget the jolly feeling that came over me at the time.

June 27.—Inspected the harbour; then sailed for Falmouth with a light wind E. under all sail, including the spinnaker. 6 P.M. encountered Lloyd's boat, the occupants being much exercised as to what so novel looking a little craft might be. 7 P.M. anchored off the town.

From *June* 28 to *Aug.* 8.—Passed the time on the coast and in the harbours of Helford, Falmouth, Fowey, and Plymouth, &c., making frequent passages.

Though the scheme of going to the Land's End had been abandoned, the thought of returning without accomplishing it was so vexatious that at 9 A.M. Aug. 8, we sailed from Plymouth, and turned to windward against heavy squalls, determined to succeed if possible; 7 P.M. anchored in Fowey Harbour, having had enough hail, cold rain, and sea for one day. This was a very severe sail, though accomplished without accident of any sort.

Aug. 19.—From Fowey 9.30 A.M., wind W.N.W., fresh and cloudy; 1.30 P.M. passed Falmouth; 4 P.M. anchored in Coverack Cove.

Aug. 10.—Sailed from Coverack, 7.30 A.M.; wind S.W., fresh and fine. 11 A.M., with best topsail set, went into the Race off the Lizard Point. Having been advised by pilots to avoid the Race as much as possible, by keeping close to the rocks, I endeavoured to follow out their instruction, but took fright at the breaking sea and bore up into the middle of it. As it had been blowing hard from the westward for three days, a great swell was rolling in from the Atlantic, and in the Race there was such a tremendous sea that neither the boy nor myself could look outside the boat after the first few minutes without turning giddy. Sitting on a deck 9 inches above water, with a rail only 4 inches high interposing, the nakedness and insignificance of the boat were so apparent that the effect was overwhelming to the senses. I felt, besides, the wretched weakening sensation in the spine which most people feel when tossed in a high swing against their will.

It was a relief to get out of the Race into the long regular roll of the Atlantic, which is more seen than felt in a small vessel. 3 P.M., hove to off the Runnel Stone, upon which the sea was breaking high and green. Having had a good look at the Land's End and the Longships, we bore up and ran for Penzance, arriving at 6 P.M.

In one of the Harbour books, containing an account of dues received, may be seen under date of August 10, 1855: 'The "Leo," 3 tons, of London, McMullen, master and owner, 6*d*.'; which sum was not demanded of me, but was paid by the quay-master, and entered for curiosity.

There is a wonderful difference between being outward bound for pleasure, and homeward bound of necessity: a remark that will apply to many things besides sailing. The first being voluntary, and the second in a measure compulsory, the pleasure is proportionate to the conditions.

At Penzance, it struck me forcibly that we were a long distance from Greenwich, in a very small ship, and that the sooner we got on the other side of the Lizard the better. After leaving Penzance there is no harbour for 35 miles, and, though I knew there was a great swell up, and dreaded the Race, it was in my opinion better to go through it at once, than to wait and run the chance of worse—especially as the days were drawing in and long nights coming on. I could have spent a week very agreeably in Mount's Bay, but dared not linger longer than was necessary to get provisions and water.

Aug. 11.—Sailed from Penzance 11 A.M., and turned against light baffling winds to the Lizard, which, with the swell rolling the wind out of the sails, delayed us so much that it was sunset when we got into the Race off the Point. As there was not wind enough to give steerage way in so great a commotion, we had to get oars out to keep before the sea, which invaded the deck several times, and tumbled and roared, so that I feared we were amongst the rocks. The tide being nearly spent it was pretty certain that we should be driven back through the Race in the dark unless an anchorage could be found. Not having contemplated such a contingency as being benighted in a calm at the Lizard, I had taken no pains to make myself acquainted with the details of the chart, and was therefore utterly unprepared with any plan except that of keeping the sea, which I should have been content to do but for that horrid Race. The prospect was anything but cheering, when, chancing to see a cutter helplessly plunging and rolling about half a mile off, we pulled towards her, and asked the men to direct us to an anchorage. It was delightful to hear that they were going in shore to bring up, and that we had only to keep company. Having got out their long oars we rowed in side by side at the distance of one sea apart, now in full view of each other, and now out of sight, with a sea between, when only the masts were visible. A conversation carried on under such circumstances

44

was, necessarily, of a desultory nature, and full explanations had to be deferred until anchors were let go in Perran Vose Cove, and our new acquaintances came alongside in their boat.

I then learnt that their vessel was a tailor's cutter belonging to Falmouth, and their business was boarding homeward-bound ships to supply clothes to those who preferred walking ashore in a new suit to being seen in sea-stained garments. In fact, their business was to steal a march upon advertising Moses and Son, in which I hope they were entirely successful, for a more civil set of men I never chanced to meet.

With great regret I heard of the death of the Captain in a gale on the 22nd August, 1868, a day referred to in the log of the 'Orion.' They were at anchor in Coverack Cove (where I have just mentioned having passed a night in the 'Leo'), when the wind setting in furiously from the S.E. compelled them to run for Falmouth. Off the Manacles a sea broke on board, and swept the Captain from the helm. At the time this occurred, which was early in the morning, we were in great alarm in Tor Bay, where the wind likewise blew on shore.

I well remember the Captain's parting injunction, when pushing off from the side of the 'Leo.' 'If the wind should come from the S.E., get under way as soon as possible and go out to sea.'

Aug. 12.—Got under way early in the morning, and spent the day in getting to Falmouth, the weather being almost calm, with a burning sun.

Aug. 15.—Sailed from Falmouth 1.30 P.M.; wind light and variable between W. and N.; 10.30 P.M., anchored in Fowey Harbour: the last two hours being so dark that sailing was very difficult.

Aug. 16.—Wind N.N.E., blowing hard and fine. 8.30 A.M. sailed from Fowey with two reefs down; 10 A.M. reefed foresail and shifted to storm jib; 1.30 P.M. shook out all reefs; 4 P.M. anchored at Plymouth, at which port there had been little or no wind all day.

Aug. 17.—From Plymouth to Dartmouth; A.M. wind N. by E. strong and fine; P.M. light and variable.

Aug. 19.—Dartmouth to Torquay; wind N., light and fine.

Aug. 20.—Sailed from Torquay 6.30 A.M., and commenced turning to windward round the great West Bay; wind N.N.E., a nice breeze and fine. The distance to Portland direct being 44 miles, it would have been extreme folly to attempt a direct passage without a fair wind, as in the event of its coming on to blow hard, there is of course no shelter, and no possibility of getting rest to enable one to carry on the struggle in a boat of 3 tons. Working round the bay with foul winds is a task severe enough for a small boat, considering that the last passage from Lyme Regis to Weymouth is 32 miles, with Portland Bill to round, and that Lyme Regis and Bridport are bad harbours to fall back upon when the weather is too strong to round the Bill.

The distance from the Start Point to Portland Bill, the two points of the bay, is 49 miles; measured round the shore of the bay, 70 miles; a perpendicular from the shore to the centre of the line joining the two points is 20 miles, which is equal to the width of the Channel at Dover.

A stranger coasting down Channel, who depends upon harbours for safety, will find the West Bay the most formidable *hiatus* in the cruise. From whatever quarter a gale comes on, unless the vessel happens to be well to windward and to have the land for protection, she must be exposed to it for several hours. The only harbour available for a stranger in gales between South and East is Dartmouth, and to make that would require considerable skill and judgment. Unless well acquainted with the coast, and certain of making a correct landfall, it is better to face the gale, however small the vessel, than to run for a lee-shore. I am convinced that unless a small vessel, especially an open one, can be got into harbour before the sea becomes very heavy, there is more safety in keeping the deep water and in not attempting to approach the land at all; where, owing to shallow water or currents, the sea will generally be found more dangerous.

In the majority of cases when fishing boats are lost, they are swallowed up near the shore, and often at the harbour's mouth.

Two notable instances of this great danger are in my recollection. The 'Unity,' a very fine lugger, belonging to Margate, was engulfed on Broadstairs knolls, when going off to the wreck of the 'Northern Bell.' The other case was that of a fine Deal lugger, which foundered with all hands on the Panther shoal, outside Plymouth breakwater. Whether the men were crossing it in ignorance, or whether—which is much more probable—they saw no danger in doing so, of course could not be known. In both instances vessels so large as to be twice the draught of these luggers would most likely have crossed in safety.

It is very common, amongst a certain class of men, but nevertheless an absurd and dangerous fallacy, to suppose that because a vessel is small and of light draught, she can go anywhere without risk. In sea sailing the contrary is the case, because, as a rule, the difficulties and intricacies of navigation are not in the fairway, but out of it, and masters of small vessels presume upon their light draught to take short cuts that require far more vigilance and attention to the charts than is necessary where leading marks are placed for guidance. In heavy weather at sea a large ship may cross a sudden shoal of 5 to 10 fathoms, or pass through a race with impunity, when it would be highly dangerous for a small vessel to do so.

Aug. 20 (*continued*).—11 A.M. Put about off Exmouth; 2 P.M., the wind being strong from E.N.E., we bore up near Budleigh Salterton and ran for Exmouth, anchoring there at 3 P.M.

Aug. 21.—Sailed from Exmouth 7.15 A.M.; wind E.N.E., fresh and cloudy, with rough sea. After a short calm, 1.30 P.M. wind shifted to S.E.; 9 P.M. ran into Bridport Harbour (Dorsetshire), but not seeing a soul there to give directions what to do, it was so uncomfortable that we left it again, and moored to a buoy in the roads, preferring to roll outside all night, to being bumped against the pier. Moreover it struck me as being a dangerous place, and very like a mousetrap in the event of a heavy sea setting in.

Aug. 22.—Slipped from the buoy at 6 A.M.; wind E.N.E., strong; 6.40 A.M. bore up for Lyme Regis, the weather being too violent to round the Bill.

Aug. 24.—Sailed from Lyme Regis at 9 A.M., and commenced turning to windward in long boards; wind S.E., fresh and fine; 11 A.M., shortened sail; 9.30 P.M., rounded the Bill close in, avoiding the Race as much as possible. The wind dying away, we had much trouble to reach Weymouth.

Aug. 25.—2 A.M. anchored in Weymouth Roads; 10 A.M. wind S.S.W., strong breeze and fine, sailed from Weymouth Roads. Meeting the tide at St. Alban's Head, we ran close along the cliffs, to avoid it and the sea, which was violent. 2.10 P.M. passed Anvil Point, closer than I intend ever to pass any point again; the breakers there were high and dangerous, causing us considerable alarm; 2.45 P.M. set the spinnaker and ran before a fine breeze and moderate swell. 9.30 P.M. anchored at Cowes, Isle of Wight; wind very light. While lying here a terrific gale set in from S.W. in which many fine fishing boats belonging to Brighton and Newhaven were lost with all hands. In their ill-judged determination to make the land at all hazards they were overwhelmed in shoal water.

Aug. 28.—Cowes to Ryde.

Aug. 31.—Wind W. by N., a fresh breeze and fine; 3.15 P.M. sailed from Ryde, bound up Channel. Resolved to make the most of a fair wind, we set the best topsail and spinnaker, under which sail the little 'Leo' flew along in good style; 6.30 P.M. cleared the Looe Channel off Selsea Bill, and lay a course E. by S. for the night, rolling boom ends in the water. About 10 P.M., the young moon having gone down, the spinnaker was handed, as we were afraid to carry it in the dark.

Sept. 1.—12.30 A.M. passed Brighton about 6 miles out. The night being dark and cloudy, the lights of the town looked very pretty. Off Beachy Head at 4 A.M. it was a great relief to see a streak of light in the East. The 'Leo' being so small that in case of collision the damage must have been all on one side, we were compelled to keep a painfully anxious look-out for several hours. A look-out of this sort is so trying, that before daybreak phantom ships are seen in all directions. 9.30 A.M. passed Dungeness Point; wind S.W., fresh. 11 A.M. handed topsail with difficulty; 12.15 (noon) gibed, and ran into Dover for letters; 2.15 P.M. set sail again for Ramsgate, arriving at 7 P.M. This passage was the longest ever made by the 'Leo' without a break, the distance from Ryde to Dover being 105 miles; time, 21 hours; 5 knots an hour—a good average for a boat 18 feet long.

Sept. 3.—6.30 A.M. sailed from Ramsgate; 7.30 P.M. anchored in Mucking Bight in the Thames.

Sept. 4.—Wind S.W., squally. Turned up to Gravesend, and went into the Canal Basin.

Sept. 10.—Laid the 'Leo' up for the season at Greenwich, completing a long cruise of 1380 nautical miles.

THE 'SIRIUS'

'SIRIUS'

'Sirius,' 11 tons, builder's measurement.
Built of teak, by J. Thompson, of Rotherhithe, 1858.
Length between perpendiculars, 29 feet; over all, 32 feet.
Breadth moulded, 9 feet 5 inches; extreme, 9 feet 8 inches.
Draught of water forward, 4 feet; aft, 6 feet.
Area of mainsail, 391 square feet; topsail, 171 square feet.
Weight of ballast, 7½ tons.

		Geographical Miles sailed
1858.	Thames, S. coast and Land's End	1,816
1859.	Do. and Isle of Wight	1,183
1860.	Do. S. coast and Harwich	1,085
1861.	Scilly Islands and S.W. coast of Ireland	1,750
1862.	Thames and Isle of Wight	1,467
1863.	Round Great Britain	2,640
1864.	Thames and Isle of Wight	1,752
		11,693

THE 'SIRIUS', 1861

THE 'Leo' proved such a good sea-boat that in 1858 the 'Sirius,' 11 tons, was built on the same lines, with two feet added to the bow.

Having experienced the great discomfort of riding at anchor in rough weather in a boat with a long counter, I had the 'Sirius' built with a round stern, which, although it was at the time considered an ugly innovation in yacht-building, has since become common. The long overhanging stern is undoubtedly more ornamental, and is useful in match-sailing yachts with very long booms; but in my opinion it is an excrescence and a nuisance in sea-going vessels, where comfort and safety are of more importance than elegance.

Being desirous of seeing the Scilly Islands and the south-west of Ireland, I set sail for that beautiful country on June 12, 1861, leaving Greenhithe, Kent, at 3 A.M. My crew consisted of Christopher Bingley, sixty-four, of Greenwich, North-Sea fisherman, and James Giles, sixteen, of Greenwich. 10 P.M. anchored in the Downs in a calm.

June 22.—Undecided whether to visit the south or the west coast of Ireland first, I resolved to sail 100 miles, N.N.W., and then to be guided by the weather, which had a thundery and unsettled appearance, and made all particular forecast impossible. 8.15 A.M. sailed from St. Mary's under all sail, and passed out of the group of islands by the North Channel with a light breeze S.S.E. 5 P.M. shifted topsails to a small one, which we carried through a thunderstorm with strong wind from 7 to 8 P.M., and then handed in a calm, being frightened by the appearance of the clouds, which hung like a pall over the sea, and seemed to threaten mischief. Our anxiety was presently relieved by a strong breeze, which, springing up at W.S.W., broke the clouds and gave us a glimpse of the rising moon.

The sight after the storm and the splendour of my long night watch alone, from 10 P.M. to 3 A.M., made pleasant impressions that will always be remembered. Great masses of cloud occasionally obscuring the moon, made it the more beautiful when it broke out again and lighted up the sea, which had just sufficient motion to make it look impressively grand. Two or three times I lashed the helm while I went below to fetch up a lighted pipe of tobacco—'a most irregular proceeding.'

June 23.—6.30 A.M. Fell calm, distance 90 miles from Scilly. Decided to make the land between Kinsale and Cork, in order to have the choice of two harbours. 2.30 P.M. saw land ahead. 7 P.M. made out Kinsale Lighthouse, bearing W.N.W. about 6 miles. Midnight, entered Cork Harbour with a light breeze from the northward, and anchored in White Bay. The night was beautifully fine and moonlight. Distance sailed, 149 miles.

From *June* 29 to *July* 9.—Visited the following harbours: Kinsale, Courtmacsherry, Baltimore, Skull, Glengariff, Castletown (Bearhaven), Valentia, where I was hospitably entertained by the Knight of Kerry and Dingle.

July 2.—Sailed from Baltimore through Carrignane, Goat, and Long Island Sounds to Skull. Weather fine, with rapidly falling barometer. 9 P.M. heavy gale set in from N.W. to S.E. round W., with deluge of rain. The only yacht fallen in with on this coast was the 'Windward,' Sir Jocelyn Coghill, which also rode out the gale in this harbour.

July 3.—6 A.M. barometer at lowest point 29.1, having fallen from 30.25. Noon, wind S.S.E. The gale having moderated, sailed from Skull under the whole mainsail, foresail, and third jib, and turned out of Long Island Sound, through Goat Sound, against a high sea in which the 'Sirius' could scarcely get enough way on her to stay. From off Crookhaven, round the Mizen Head, and a long way up Bantry Bay, the sea was enormous, wind S.W., strong, and cloudy. 9 P.M. raining heavily, and very dark. 10 P.M. passed through the rocky entrance to Glengariff Harbour, and anchored in a calm.

July 11.—Sailed from Castletown (Bearhaven) 10 A.M., and returned to the same anchorage 2.30 P.M. Raining in torrents, with very threatening barometer.

July 12.—3 A.M. the wind shifted suddenly from S.W. to N., and blew a terrific gale. Three vessels were blown from their anchors alongside the 'Sirius,' though the water was smooth. Had the warning of the barometer been neglected, we should have encountered the full force of the gale on a lee shore open to the Atlantic.

July 19.—11 A.M. sailed from Dingle with a light wind W. bound to Penzance.

July 20.—1 P.M. off the Mizen Head in a long swell, saw a large black whale at the distance of about half a mile. 11 P.M. becalmed in heavy rain 15 miles S.S.E. of Cape Clear.

July 21.—2.30 A.M. strong wind W.S.W. Shortened sail. The long swell was so quickly heaped up into a great sea, that at 5 A.M., shortly after turning in, my hammock-hook was drawn at the head, and I was thrown on the floor. The drop from the top of the sea into the trough was so great and so sudden, that in the hammock I experienced the same sensation as in the Lizard Race in 1857. 7 A.M. furled the foresail. 10 A.M. took two reefs down. 1 P.M. Bingley (who had had fifty years' experience of the sea) went below to dinner, but returned in a few minutes with a bit of biscuit in his hand, remarking that if he had remained down there any longer he should have been sick. No adequate idea of the violent motion felt in the cabin of a small vessel sailing six knots in the trough of a heavy sea can be conveyed to the reader, and there is nothing in the world to compare it with. 8 P.M. wind W., a gale. Set foresail with sheet to windward and hove-to. Took third reef down, set storm jib, and then had tea and a clear-up below. 10 P.M. bore up on the course again. The weather being squally, two 'rain-dogs' and a complete rainbow were seen about sunset, and at night a beautiful lunar rainbow.

July 22.—The last two hours of my watch on the third night I was dreaming at the helm, but at the same time steering the course. The reason of my having three consecutive nights at the helm was this: my old mate had grumbled at the work on the passage down channel, and I said he should not have the helm at night again, but should turn in, like the boy. At 4 A.M.

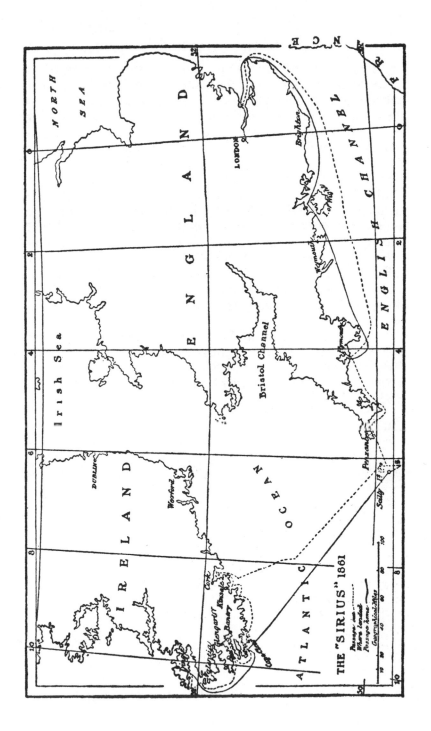

THE "SIRIUS" 1861

Passage out ......
Where Landed ----
Passage home .....

Geographical Miles

I told Bingley that if my calculations were correct we ought to see something of Scilly at seven, and directed him to call me. Exactly at that hour he did so, and informed me that two objects like ships were visible on the port bow. These, upon examination with the glasses, were found to be the Bishop Rock and St. Agnes Lighthouses partly visible above the horizon, just where they should appear if we were sailing according to the plan, which was to pass the Scilly Isles 6 miles to the westward. Shook two reefs out and set third jib. Noon, sighted the mainland, wind S.S.W., blowing hard, with rain, and such a tremendous sea on the quarter that we had many times to bear up and run off the course to avoid it. 1 P.M. passed three miles to the southward of the Wolf Rock. Settled the main halyards and furled the foresail, not caring to lose time in reefing. 4 P.M. ran into Penzance Harbour, drenched with sea above and below. Time, three days five hours. Distance, 269 miles.

After a month's stay at Penzance we sailed on the 23rd August for the eastward, calling at the Lizard, Falmouth, Plymouth, Isle of Wight, and Ramsgate.

Sept. 5.—Anchored at Greenhithe, Kent. Cruise 1750 miles.

THE 'SIRIUS', 1863

June 12.—10 A.M. sailed from Greenhithe for the North, my crew consisting upon this occasion of George Millest, twenty-four, and Richard West, sixteen, both of Gravesend.

June 21.—10 A.M. hove-to off Aberdeen, nine days out from Greenhithe. The weather during the voyage was unpleasantly cold, with much rain and some fog. The winds generally light from all quarters, with a long swell from the N.E. The best topsail was set off Yarmouth on the 14th, and was not handed until it fell to leeward of the mainsail on the 21st, the halyards being chafed through. Noon, went into Aberdeen Harbour, in want both of provisions and water. Distance sailed, 420 miles.

The most curious sight of the passage was an immense shoal of porpoises, or small whales, fallen in with on the afternoon of the 17th, when out of sight of land off the coast of Northumberland. They had a patch of greasy white on the side of the head, and another under the dorsal fin, which, instead of curving rearward as in the ordinary porpoise, stood up straight and appeared to be about three feet in length. Though to observe such a number blowing jets, tumbling, and jumping out of water, was a grand sight, extending for miles all around, we did not enjoy the company of those that were near. Being about 20 feet long, and in a sportive mood, it was impossible to avoid thinking that a miscalculation of distance by one of them would have been anything but sport to us; so that we were not sorry to get clear of them before dark.

Another curious sight was before sunrise on the morning of the 19th, when the glasses revealed to us the upper part of the canvas of two vessels below the horizon, which, owing to the intense clearness of the atmosphere, and the long swell, we had previously mistaken for small black buoys near at hand.

June 22.—After a hard day's work provisioning, repairing rigging, &c., we left moorings at 7 P.M., the evening being very wet, with a strong southerly wind, and reached out of Aberdeen Harbour with a single reef in the mainsail and topmast on end, expecting to bear up outside and run to the north.

Opening Girdleness the 'Sirius' was borne over by a succession of terrific gusts from the S.E., and encountered such a high breaking sea that I dared not put her on the course and bring the sea abeam.

Though greatly overpowered, there was no alternative but to face it, until sufficient offing could be gained to enable the vessel to be hove-to and canvas reduced. Struck by one sea after another, the lads had to sling themselves into the rigging, and I had to let go the helm and cling with determination to the weather bulwark to escape being washed overboard. Momentarily expecting to be altogether disabled by a catastrophe to the spars, but compelled to go on, the situation until 8 P.M., when we hove to, was most critical. To recount all the incidents of that night, the state of the cabins, the heavy work to be done, and the difficulty of doing it, would fill several pages. The boy was helplessly sick, and altogether useless. George, too, was sick, and I was expecting to be so. It blew a fierce gale on all the coast of Scotland that night. 10.30 P.M. wind S.S.W., bore up under close reefs, and ran before a great and hollow-looking sea.

June 23.—3 A.M. shook out three reefs. The cold was intense. 5.30 A.M. passed through Kinnaird Roads off Fraserburgh, where eight schooners were lying-to under very short canvas, waiting, as one of them informed me, for better weather. I invited one that was bound to Thurso to come on, but the master declined, saying he should wait for the sea to go down. Having a strong wind from the S.W., they were soon left out of sight. Passing Wick, the northernmost town on the east coast of Great Britain, we anchored at 7 P.M. in Sinclair Bay, 11 miles from John o' Groat's. Off Noss Head spoke a brigantine from Liverpool. The master said they had passed the previous night lying-to under the close-reefed topsail only, and that a schooner near them was thrown on beam-ends, and had to cut her mainmast away. After 24 hours of such rough weather, the change to the quiet anchorage of Sinclair Bay, with the wind off shore and the sun shining, was most charming. 9.30 P.M., in high spirits, I sat down to a good dinner of roast mutton. 11.30 P.M. twilight was so strong that I was able to read small print on deck.

June 24.—Sailed across the Pentland Firth into the Orkneys, and anchored in Quoy Bay, Hoy Sound. 8 P.M. locked up the cabins and, accompanied by the lads, made an ascent of Hoy Hill (1500 feet of rugged climbing), from which there was a fine view of all the islands. 10 P.M. returned on board.

When off Duncansby Head in the earlier part of the day, we saw a large flight of gannet in the Pentland Firth hovering over a shoal of fish upon which they made such an onslaught, descending in a continuous stream of 20 or 30 at a time, that, what with the birds from above, and an equally vigorous attack carried on by porpoises below, the sea was lashed into foam and spray.

The gannet, when diving for its prey, mounts in a spiral curve to the height of 150 or 200 feet, then collapsing its wings, descends head foremost, like a rocket-stick, with such amazing speed and force as must enable it to attain a great depth without further effort. The pretty little tern, whose plaintive 'call' is much like that of the peewit and the curlew, feeds in a manner similar to the gannet, but from a lesser height.

Razorbills, guillemots, and the like, flying with great swiftness, sometimes enter the water diagonally and at a long angle. Continuing the action of their wings under water, they reappear at a long distance from the point at which they dived, and emerge from the sea still flying, as if their rapid progress in a right line had met with but a slight temporary check. If disturbed while resting on the water, these birds never attempt to rise, but paddle a few strokes in great trepidation, and then dive perpendicularly, disappearing with a 'flop' like a stone.

Gulls, on the contrary, always rise when disturbed. Not being divers, they seize their prey in a very elegant manner by stooping for it on the wing. If an unhandy morsel, they carry it to a distance from their robber comrades who have very indistinct notions of the rights of property. On the Atlantic coast of Ireland I once saw a gull resting on the water, with a long eel in its bill, held by the middle, which it manœuvred in a curious manner to get the head into a favourable position for swallowing; then darting its head forward several times, as our blackbirds and thrushes do when swallowing big worms, the eel gradually disappeared.

June 25.—Wind W.S.W., fresh and fine. After experiencing great delay in Cantick Sound becalmed by the lofty hills, at noon, with one reef down, we passed out of the islands too late on the tide, and, to avoid being driven eastward round Duncansby Head, had to seek shelter, 'lying-to' in the eddy of the Island of Stroma, in the middle of the Pentland Firth, until the flood tide eased sufficiently to enable us to proceed. Once, getting too near the terrific rush of tide at the southern point of the island, we were hailed and waved off by a man standing there. The extensive eddy formed by this island affords comfortable shelter with a commanding breeze, if a good look-out is kept and it is quitted at the proper time; but I should not recommend it to strangers, nor repeat it myself except under strong necessity. Spent the remainder of the day in getting to the westward; midnight, anchored in Scrabster Roads. Sea heavy; boy very sea-sick.

June 26.—From Scrabster 1 P.M.; at 7 P.M., when crossing the entrance of the Kyle of Tongue, a fine view presented itself of mountains lighted up like gold by the sun, such as I had only seen before in pictures, and erroneously believed to be exaggerated. Shortly after, it came on to blow hard from W.N.W., with a rough sea. 10.30, anchored in Hoan Island Road.

June 28.—9.15 A.M. sailed through Hoan Island Sound; 11 P.M. rounded Cape Wrath.

June 30.—10.30 A.M. anchored in Loch Staffin, Isle of Skye, and, with a boy of sixteen as guide, ascended 1500 feet to the famous 'Rock of Quiraing,' accompanied most of the way up and down by a crowd of good-natured little urchins in tatters, who could not understand a word of English, and whose bodies and garments emitted such an odour of stale peat that it was sickening. 6.30 P.M., anchored again close under 'Storr Hill,' and made another ascent, chiefly up a watercourse, to the 'Old Man of Storr.' Afterwards filled up water from a little cascade tumbling down on to the beach; and, at midnight, anchored in the harbour of Portree. That the weather must have been very inviting for such a day's work as this, after two tedious days and nights at sea, speaks for itself.

From *July* 1 to 6.—Called at Lochs Sligichan, Carron, Alsh, Duich, Hourn and Scavig.

The visit to Loch Scavig may perhaps be considered curious enough to deserve special notice. July 6, wind S.E., fresh and fine. 7.39 A.M., sailed from Loch Hourn under all plain sail and jib-headed topsail. Excepting that at 3.30 P.M. we got becalmed for a time about three miles from our destination, all went smoothly until abreast of a mountain 3000 feet high on the western side of the Loch, when, at the shortest notice, we encountered a strong and increasing westerly wind, and, as fast as the work could be performed, had to shorten sail to three reefs, and let the jib in a few feet to ease the strain on the bowsprit. In this condition, keeping a sharp look-out for the rocks, which, though numerous, are fortunately for the most part visible, we worked our way up, being frequently taken aback with eddying puffs of extreme violence, which hove the 'Sirius' gunwale down, first on one tack and then the other. I thought it was an uncanny spot we had come to, and began to wish we had stayed away; particularly as the head of the bay showed nothing but a rock-bound shore with no appearance of shelter. Keeping the vessel under way with the lad, I sent the mate in the boat, who shortly returned and reported 'no entrance'; whereupon we let go the anchor in five fathoms, and as our position accorded neither with the book of sailing directions, nor with the account I had heard, proceeded in the boat to search for it myself. The result of the exploration being satisfactory, we weighed anchor again, and sailing to the western end of a long and low brown rock, passed through a narrow gut with a half-tide rock in the middle of it, into a basin of still water about a cable and a half in diameter. In this snug, but most dreary and lonesome little berth, we brought up with a large scope of chain, and carried a hawser to the rock to keep the vessel from fouling her anchor.

For the moment my anxieties were relieved; but they pretty quickly returned with the recollection that, about two years before, a yacht of 50 tons, in charge of a pilot, had passed ten hours on the half-tide rock in the entrance, having been taken aback at the moment of attempting to pass out.

The knowledge acquired in gaining the anchorage was quite sufficient to prove how excusable an accident this was, so that the thought of how to get out again, with nothing but little eddying puffs of wind from the mountains to rely upon, was constantly in my mind. Nor was I at all relieved when rambling on shore next morning, and having climbed to a height of about 500 feet overlooking 'Loch Cornisk,' I had to hold on firmly to the rocks during a squall with clear sky overhead. Of all the solitary spots in the world, I can imagine nothing more dreary or depressing than this little Loch in the Cuchelin Mountains. With neither a tree nor a shrub to relieve the monotony, the eye encounters nothing but rocks, bare and rugged, culminating in peaks from two to three thousand feet high all around. It is of this scene I think when viewing through a telescope the mountain ranges on the moon's surface, which can be only a shade more barren.

While away on this little excursion, the crew were getting ready for a start, and preparing for their dinner and my luncheon a fine big fish we had hooked forty fathoms deep in Loch Hourn the previous day. But when it was ready I desired it to be kept back, feeling it was impossible to swallow a mouthful of food until it was decided we should get safely out of so difficult a position. There was very little space to get way on the vessel after the anchor was hove up, but by plying an oar vigorously at the critical moment, we managed to clear the rock, 'all shaking,' and, after making a few short tacks, gained the open sea. Then we hove-to with the foresail to windward and did justice to the fish, which had suffered nothing by keeping.

Glad as I was to have been there, I was more glad to have got free, and determined that no amount of curiosity should tempt me into such a prison of shrieking little whirlwinds again. Whatever it may be now, at the time of my visit there was not the slightest prospect of assistance arriving from any quarter if anything had gone wrong.

From 8 to 10 P.M. we were beating past the lofty islands of 'Rum' and 'Egg,' blowing strong from S.W. with a rough sea, and at 9 A.M. of the 8th anchored at Tobermory, Isle of Mull.

July 9.—Sailed south, passing between the Treshnish Islands, which are long, narrow, and straight, steep-sided like the inner side of Plymouth breakwater, and quite bare of vegetation, and then reached in past the Isle of Staffa to get a view of Fingal's Cave. Having no proper chart of this little digression from the course, I 'conned her' from the masthead, from which rocks under water would be visible, and was careful to return as nearly as possible on the same track. On the 13th, after four days of tedious drifting and contention with light baffling head winds, and a narrow escape from the outlying rocks of the Isle of Tiree very early on a misty morning, we arrived at the Isle of Bute, in the Clyde, 31 days out, of which only 3 days and 7 nights were spent in harbour.

From *July* 13 to *August* 15.—Sailed about the Clyde, visiting all parts of the Isles of Arran, Cantire, Rathlin Island, and Port Rush in Ireland, &c.

Aug. 15.—Commenced the voyage home from Rothesay, Isle of Bute, at 8.30 P.M., under double-reefed mainsail; midnight, anchored in Kilchattan Bay. Sailed afternoon of 16th, and anchored at 10 P.M. at Pladda Island, where we passed a rough and anxious night.

Aug. 17.—Got away at 7 A.M.; 10 A.M., passed the great Gannet Cliff of Ailsa Craig so close that we were becalmed with two reefs down; 9 P.M. off the South Rock, east coast of Ireland. 18th, 10 A.M. made the harbour of Kingstown,

Ireland, under three-reefed mainsail, blowing a gale from W.N.W. The vessel was in a terrible mess below, drenched with seawater, and everything, even the stove and the coal bunker in the forecastle, capsized from carrying on in the trough of the sea. At daylight a fine guardfish, 32 inches long, was found on deck. Distance 182 miles.

Aug. 21.—Sailed from Kingstown at 9 P.M. Winds were light, between S. and W., all down the Irish coast. 22nd, the lads had some porter in a stone bottle from Kingstown the previous day. After their dinner, and while I was below at luncheon, hearing a great fuss on deck, I called to know what was the matter; when George, holding a great earwig in his fingers, swollen to undue proportions by drowning in good liquor, and speaking as intelligently as his shudderings of aversion would permit, said, 'Look 'ere, sir! Look at this 'ere airywig I pulled out of my mouth! Faugh! I wouldn't drink another drop if there was a bucketful!'

Aug. 23.—5 P.M. wind W.S.W., strong, with rain. Opening the Atlantic round Carnsore Point, we got into heavy weather all at once; 8 P.M. took two reefs down.

During this time a tremendous gale was raging in the North Atlantic which, fortunately, extended to the British shores only in a modified form. Many of my readers will remember the story of the 'Great Eastern' in the trough of the sea, when one paddle-wheel was almost destroyed and the furniture in her saloons much damaged.

Aug. 25.—1 A.M. made out the lights of Trevose Head, Cornwall. All day turned to windward against a tremendous sea under two and three reefs; 8 P.M. hove-to about 6 miles N.W. of St. Ives, being afraid of the sea in the dark.

Aug. 26.—6 P.M. anchored off Penzance. Time from Kingstown nearly 5 days. Distance sailed, 350 miles.

Aug. 27.—The sails were partly hoisted to dry, which made the 'Sirius' sheer about at anchor. From some cause that could not be ascertained, but was supposed to be a defective shackle, the chain parted under water, while we were below at breakfast, and the vessel was driving on to the rocks opposite

64

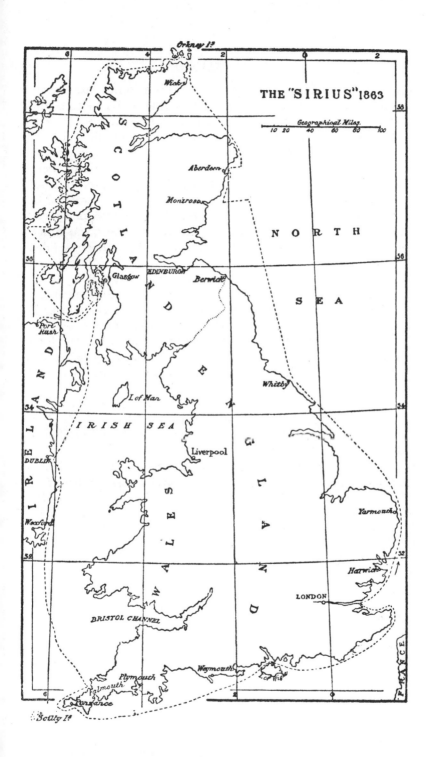

THE "SIRIUS" 1863

Geographical Miles.
10 20 40 60 80 100

NORTH

SEA

Orkney Is
Wick
SCOTLAND
Aberdeen
Montrose
Glasgow
EDINBURGH
Berwick
Port Rush
Whitby
IRELAND
I. of Man
IRISH SEA
Liverpool
DUBLIN
WALES
ENGLAND
Wexford
Yarmouth
Harwich
LONDON
BRISTOL CHANNEL
Plymouth
Falmouth
Penzance
Weymouth
I. of Wight
Scilly Is
FRANCE

the Penzance Coastguard Station, when some fishermen, passing in a boat, apprised us of our dangerous position, and warned us that there was not a moment to lose. Fortunately, when the jib was set, she cast her head the right way, and we escaped inside the Gear Rock. Never was there a narrower escape. Had not the fishermen most providentially been passing at that minute, it would have been too late, and our first intimation of danger would have been a great crash. The anchor and chain were not recovered, though experienced men went out on purpose to search for them. There was much ground-swell, and they were supposed to have been sanded over.

Aug. 30.—10 A.M. sailed from Penzance, wind S.E., fresh, and cloudy; 4 P.M., in company with several vessels near the Lizard, encountered a great storm from the eastward, in which our canvas was reduced from carrying the second topsail to close reefs. Schooners reduced from full sail to the forestaysail and close-reefed mainsail. After blowing almost a hurricane for two hours, the wind suddenly dropped and shifted to the southward.

Aug. 31.—2.30 A.M. Passed the Lizard Point with a strong wind from N.W., before which we ran until 9 A.M., Sept 1, when it fell calm near the Needles; 4 P.M. anchored at Cowes, Isle of Wight. Distance, 212 miles.

Sept. 10.—Left Cowes in full sail at 9.30 A.M. Off the North Foreland 9.30 A.M. of the 11th. Anchored at Greenhithe 1.30 P.M. of the 13th. Distance, 222 miles. Cruise, 2640 miles. Number of nights at sea, sailing or at anchor, twenty-eight.

' ORION '

'Orion,' 16½ tons, builder's measurement.
Built of teak, by G. Inman, of Lymington, 1865.
Length between perpendiculars, 38 feet; over all, 42 feet.
Breadth moulded, 10 feet 2 inches; extreme, 10 feet 5 inches.
Draught of water forward, 5 feet; aft, 7 feet.
Area of mainsail, 668 square feet; topsail, 294 square feet.
Weight of ballast, 11¾ tons.

Lengthened 6 feet by the stern 1873 and altered to yawl rig.
Measurement increased to 19½ tons.

		Geographical Miles sailed
1865.	Isle of Wight, Thames, Devon and Cornwall .	1,541
1866.	Thames and S. coast	1,323
1867.	Thames and S. coast	1,237
1868.	Scilly Islands	1,081
		5,182

	Geogr. Miles		Statute Miles
'Leo'	8,222	=	9,494
'Sirius'	11,693	=	13,503
'Orion'	5,182	=	5,984
Total	25,097	=	28,981

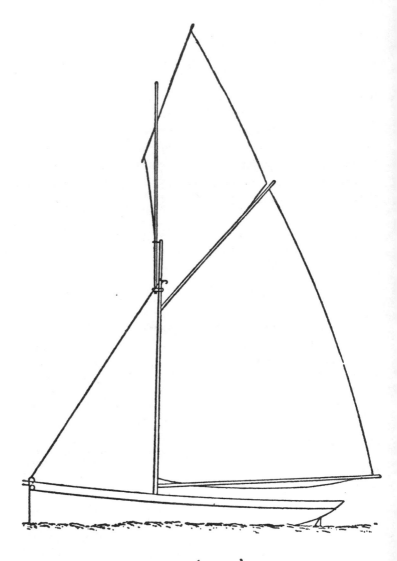

THE 'ORION'

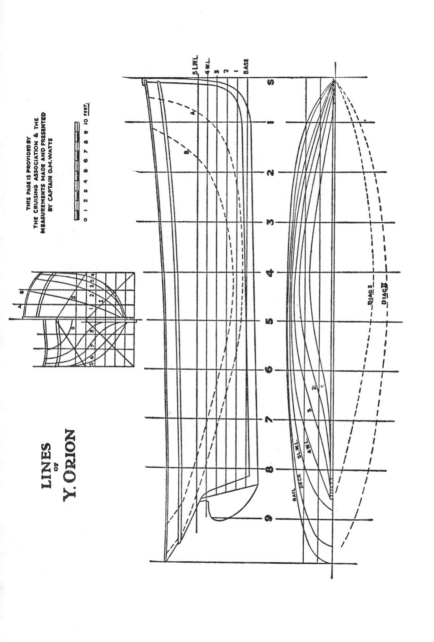

LINES
of
Y. ORION

THE 'ORION', 1868

THE 'Orion' was built for me in 1865 as a cutter, 16½ tons builder's measurement, and it is as a cutter I am now writing of her.

Aug. 6.—4.30 A.M., sailed from Greenhithe, Kent; wind S.W., light and cloudy; 11.45 A.M. hove to off Margate; took two reefs in mainsail; housed topmast; reefed bowsprit and shifted to smaller jib; 3 P.M. proceeded and beat into the Downs, anchoring there at 6.15 P.M. The wind, light at starting, gradually freshened, until it blew strong from the S.W. with rain; night, blew hard S.W. with much rain and a troublesome sea that prevented sleep.

Aug. 7.—Breakfasted at 6 A.M.; took third reef in mainsail, reefed foresail, and set third jib; 7 A.M. got under way and commenced beating to windward. The weather until noon was wet and miserable; afterwards the sun shone out pleasantly, the wind shifting to W.S.W., blowing heavily. 4.30 P.M. anchored in Dungeness Roads; glad to shelter from the heavy sea and drenching spray which in a hot sun incrusts one's face and everything on deck with salt.

Aug. 8.—Under way at 6 A.M. with one reef less in the sails; wind W., strong and fine, with considerable head sea; 6 P.M. hove to off Eastbourne to have dinner and a little quiet under the shelter of Beachy Head; 8 P.M. stood off to sea again for the night; 10 P.M. shook all reefs out; wind moderate, with less sea, and the moon shining brightly.

Aug. 9.—The wind gradually got lighter until 1.30 P.M., when it fell dead calm; after drifting with the tide through the Looe Channel, we set much canvas, in hope of making the Isle of Wight before dark; 9 P.M. 3 miles N.E. of the Nab Lightship; lightning in south and east; a light breeze came from the northward.

Aug. 10.—2.30 A.M. anchored in Cowes Harbour; wind fresh from the northward; bright moonlight.

70

Aug. 11.—Hauled up on a slip to get the keel-band repaired, and other small jobs done, which are most conveniently and expeditiously managed at the Isle of Wight.

Aug. 15.—Sailed from Cowes at 7.15 A.M., wind fresh from the south. Off Hampstead Ledge set jib-headed topsail; 8.50 A.M. passed through the North Channel, and put the vessel on a W.S.W. course; 11.30 A.M. altered course to W. by S.; rate by log, 7.875; 12.45 P.M. Portland Bill N. about 12 miles; course W.N.W., wind S.S.E., with heavy swell from W.; 9 P.M. anchored in Dartmouth Harbour; wind light, S.E.

All day had a short sea from the S. and S.E., with heavy head-swell from the W., the bowsprit plunging continually, till we were within 15 miles of Dartmouth. A most destructive storm was raging in France during the afternoon of this day; but though the sky looked stormy, we had only a few heavy spots of rain.

Aug. 20.—10.30 A.M. sailed from Dartmouth with a fresh N.W. wind; 11.30 A.M. wind died away and shortly fell dead calm; afternoon sailed up and down the coast with light airs from all quarters, and finally anchored off Torquay at 7 P.M.; wind N.W., a nice breeze.

Aug. 21.—Torquay Regatta; remained at anchor all day; in the forenoon took a carriage drive on shore to see the country. The day was partially cloudy, with little wind until the afternoon, when it blew a fresh breeze from W.S.W.; the night set in dark and rainy. Before turning in at 10.30 P.M. I noticed that the barometer had gone back $\frac{1}{10}$, to 29.75. This made me a little anxious, for we were so closely surrounded by yachts and a gunboat as to have no chance of getting out if the weather became bad, unless others went first and cleared the way; and we were as completely unprepared for anything serious as if we had been at anchor in harbour, instead of upon the open coast.

Aug. 22.—Awakened at 2 A.M. by the uneasy motion of the vessel, I immediately struck a match over the barometer, and, perceiving that its state was unsatisfactory, hastily dressed myself and called the men up to make snug, as a precaution.

Having secured the riding light to the runner-tackle to throw light on our work, we first stowed the boat, then housed topmast, and hove the bowsprit short in. Meanwhile the rain was pelting down, and the wind gradually backing to the S.E., throwing in a nasty sea. The mainsail in a very short time became so thick and heavy with the rain, that the labour of reeving the earings and taking the reefs down was very great indeed. At 4 A.M. it blew a heavy gale S.E.; barometer 29·5. 5 A.M. there was a terrible sea, all the yachts were pitching bows under, and most of them were beginning to drag home. I was glad to see three or four small yachts, that lay in our way, slip and run for the harbour, though it was only half-tide. Having unshackled our chain at 30 fathoms and buoyed it with a cork stool, we set the mainsail with four reefs down, reefed foresail and storm jib, and slipped at 5.30 A.M. We were the first who attempted voluntarily to beat out to sea. It certainly looked unpromising enough. Few persons would have thought it likely that a small vessel would work off shore in such a sea; yet after one short board in shore, we tacked and passed to windward of the whole fleet, which included four gunbrigs. The force of the wind being so great, the difficulty was not to make the yacht go, but to make her take it easy. Notwithstanding great caution in steering, she shipped one dreadful sea, that would have been disastrous if we had not seen it coming, and been prepared for it. We were soon followed by a cutter of 35 tons under a trysail, and a large schooner close reefed. The first to get away was a schooner of about 50 tons that dragged past us at anchor, and was going upon the rocks, when she managed to get canvas on, and slip just in time to save herself from destruction. It shocked me so much to see her, that after she drove past the gunboat astern I would not look at her again, and therefore did not see her escape. We felt most thankful to Providence that she was not ahead of us. Before we left there was a cutter coming down upon our vessel, frightening us out of our wits lest she should drag foul before we were ready. The scene at that time was awful, and it was very doubtful what would become of us, and of the greater number at anchor there. 7. A.M. the wind shifted suddenly to the S.W.; 9 A.M. the clouds broke away and the sun shone; wind W., almost a hurricane; barometer at the lowest point 29·23. At times the north and south shores of the Bay were partially obscured to us by the spoon-drift (thick clouds of spray) that swept along several feet above the surface of the sea. The wind being off shore, we sailed about and hove-to between Paignton and Broad Sand Bay, until 1 P.M., when, as there appeared to be little chance of the gale abating so as to enable us to recover the anchor and chain that day, we anchored with the kedge and 25 fathoms of bower chain, with 30 fathoms of stream chain shackled to it. 2 P.M. the barometer began to rise, notwithstanding the terrific squalls between W.S.W. and W.N.W., in which we dragged just enough to make it doubtful whether she would hold on or not. As night set in the weather became more moderate, though still very strong and squally from the westward.

Aug. 23.—Weighed the kedge at 7.30 A.M., and reached over to Torquay. Recovered the anchor and chain, and returned to Paignton. 2 P.M. weighed again and sailed round to Dartmouth under three-reefed mainsail, leaving four steamers and some other vessels at anchor off Brixham waiting for better weather. One good lesson I learnt—never again to be caught at anchor with a fleet of yachts upon an open coast on a regatta night, when half the fleet will certainly consist of ill-found vessels that anchor off only upon these occasions, with serious risk to themselves, and to others that have the misfortune to be near them. Fortunately, only one small yacht of 10 tons was lost; but if the wind had not shifted from the S.E., few, if any, of those that remained at anchor would have escaped. Elsewhere the losses were numerous that day.

Aug. 25.—Wind W.N.W. 5 P.M. sailed from Dartmouth, and reached down close-hauled into Start Bay, anchoring for the night off Haulsands.

Aug. 26.—Wind W.S.W., fresh and cloudy; 6 A.M. sailed from Start Bay, intending to put into Salcombe. Finding when a board had been made to the southward of the Start

Point that the 'Orion' would clear Bolt Head, it seemed such a pity to lose the opportunity of making a long reach down the coast, that we determined to continue the course. With prudent regard to economy we hove-to for an hour to prevent a wasteful expenditure of breakfast crockery, and then stood on for Fowey in Cornwall, arriving there at 3 P.M. in rough weather from the S.W. All night it blew hard from S.S.W., with rain.

Aug. 27.—Coming on the previous day saved a long and heavy beat to windward. The wind shifted towards morning to the W.N.W., and gave us another reach down the coast, of which we took advantage. Leaving Fowey Harbour at 2.30 P.M., we carried on whole mainsail down to the Lizard Point, anchoring for the night, at 7.30 P.M., off Perran Vose Cove. The wind being very strong, we rolled a great deal all night in the ground-swell from the Race.

Aug. 28.—Wind N.W., beautifully fine, with rising barometer. Rowed round to Howsell Bay, and, owing to the surf, landed on the sand with difficulty; sent the boat back, and walked round the splendid cliffs of the Lizard, returning on board in time for an early dinner. To do justice by description to the beauty of that coast, upon such a day, is beyond my power. 2.30 P.M. sailed for Penzance, with a nice breeze, which fell off considerably towards night. 10 P.M., having tacked north of St. Clement's Island, we passed inside the Low Lee and Carn Base Rocks, and came to anchor in Guavas Lake, off Penzance.

Aug. 29.—5.30 A.M. sailed from Penzance with a light breeze N.W. The appearance of the sky justified the expectation of a smart passage to Scilly with a northerly wind. And when, in answer to the hail of several fishing-luggers, we shouted our destination, and they all volunteered the same opinion, of course it seemed a certainty. One thing, however, is certain, and that is—that there is nothing certain at sea. Soon after passing Castle Trereen, we got into a troublesome westerly swell with a light head wind, which continued all the passage. Passing between the Lee Oar and the Runnel Stone, we tacked close to the bell buoy, which was lustily tolling out its most dismal warning. Its tolling is so eccentric, so irregular, that it would soon drive a musician mad. I know no sounds more unpleasant on a dark night, or more calculated to make one feel miserable, than the roar of the sea in a cavern, and the tolling of a bell buoy. These buoys, however, are of such immense service, that I should like to see them more generally used. 11.15 A.M., 1 mile West of Longships, set jib topsail; 4.30 P.M. Wolf-rock Lighthouse bearing E. by S. 7 miles. Tacked and stood towards the Islands; 10 P.M. tacked again close to the S.E. rocks of Scilly. The jib topsail was handed in at dusk, being too large and dangerous a sail to use in the dark. During the day it did good service, as we were turning the whole time against light and variable head winds, with a nasty swell that would seldom allow the heavier canvas to keep full. 11 P.M. I sent the hands below, and kept the 'Orion' standing off and on, through the night; wind W.N.W., a light breeze and cloudy. At times it was so dark and thick with rain that my only guide for tacking in shore—viz., St. Agnes Light— was totally hidden. There being no reflection of light from above, the sea under the stern was invisible, and by reason of its perfect clearness the phosphoric light, consequent upon our disturbance of the water, assumed the appearance of bright stars floating in atmosphere. The water was so intensely black, and its appearance so deceptive to the eye, that by a little stretch of imagination it would have seemed possible to descend into unfathomable depths, without meeting resistance. While sailing fast at night, the appearance under the stern is often most charming and enchanting. Upon this early morning it was enchanting, certainly, but not at all charming. At day-light we tacked into the Islands through St. Mary's Sound, and came to anchor in St. Mary's Pool at 7 A.M.

This anchorage is not to be recommended as either comfortable or very safe, but it is the most convenient for supplies, and the most central for excursions. Many days may be agreeably spent in boat excursions (weather permitting) to the different islands and rocks, especially to the Island of Tresco, where, in Mr. Smith's fine gardens, tropical trees and plants grow luxuriantly in the open air; also to the ruins of King Charles's Castle at the north end of the island, from which the view on a fine sunny day is perfectly charming. On one side is the restless north-west swell of the Atlantic, breaking magnificently upon the rocks; on the other are quiet waters enclosed within the picturesque islands and rocks, looking so blue and lovely, and withal so peaceful, that it is difficult to imagine them the scene of disaster and shipwreck. Some of the finest pilot cutters in England are owned at all the chief islands; and though they have ponderous moorings in the snuggest spots to be found, they are not always able to contend with the terrible sea thrown into the sounds and channels by westerly gales. Last winter a cutter parted from her moorings and was totally lost in St. Mary's Pool. A pilot told me that in the same gale he was on board a large Irish cutter, that parted both anchors in St. Mary's Road. They ran for Crow Sound, but he said no one on board had the slightest hope of being able to cross Crow Bar in such an awful sea. They succeeded, however, and saved the vessel by beaching her in the Sound. In 1861 the officer in command of the coastguard related to me a sad tale of five vessels stranding in St. Mary's Pool in a heavy gale, when many lives were lost. Their efforts to save the crews were seriously obstructed by blinding clouds of sand.

In June, 1861, on a cruise to Ireland, I visited Scilly and spent four days there. The weather being very foggy, I had more opportunity of observing the inhabitants of St. Mary's than other objects of interest. Their primitive appearance and habits at that time agreed perfectly with the account given of them by Dr. Borlase more than a hundred years ago. The greatest simplicity of manner and dress prevailed everywhere. Now all is changed, and chignons, crinolines, high-heeled boots, and children's necklaces, and earrings, must be reckoned among the most important articles of commerce. It was then difficult to get meat, or anything but stale Penzance bread and butter. Now plain provisions can be got there of as good quality as anywhere in the country. The cause of this sudden change is, that the sailing cutter which used to ply between Scilly and Penzance twice a week, with the mails, passengers, and cargo— making of course very unequal passages in point of time—was superseded in 1862 or 1863 by a beautiful little screw steamer, called the 'Little Western,' which makes three passages a week, each passage averaging about four hours, thus bringing Scilly near to Penzance, where London fashions are very fierce.

It may be confidently asserted that in one thing the Scillonians have made no advance since the days of the learned doctor before mentioned, viz., in the art of carriage-building. If, after my former visit, anyone had talked to me of carriages in these Islands, the largest of which is about $2\frac{1}{2}$ miles in length by $1\frac{1}{2}$ in breadth, I should have shown my ignorance by denying that there were any. But on that occasion I was there only on week-days. Now I was fortunate enough to be there on Sunday, and to see the leading families arrive at the church, in three or four heavily-laden vehicles of antique build, each drawn by one pony. I recognised them at once as old and familiar objects of earlier days, being of the exact form and appearance of the little pasteboard four-wheelers and phaetons that ingenious boys make at school, and paint artistically with gamboge and Indian ink. They are also very rusty with age, more stormbeaten than the pilot boats, and must be reckoned amongst the curiosities of the Islands.

For me there is only one walk at St. Mary's, and that is to the rocks at Peninnis Head. I have been there five or six times, and could visit them as many times more with equal pleasure and wonder. You will be told by the natives that they were arranged in such fantastic order by the Druids, by giants, and, in fact, by every kind of agency but the true one. You will observe, that if arranged by giants, they must have been giants indeed; compared with whom the giants we read of in Scripture were mere babies. A close inspection will satisfy anyone that the piling of these rocks is due to convulsions of Nature, and that the excessive moisture of the climate is the great giant that hollows out the Druids' basins, shapes the stones, and separates the blocks, by disintegration. When you visit Peninnis Head, to keep the cook in good temper, you had better order a late dinner; for time flies apace, and it is impossible, if the weather is clear and fine, to leave that elevated spot just when the sun is dipping into the sea, brilliant with coloured reflections, and studded with rocks and islands which look black amidst the brightness.

The Islands and rocks extend over a space of about 44 square miles, and have a population of about 2300. The inhabitants call themselves Scillonians, and to speak of them as Cornish is offensive. There are two fine lighthouses—one on St. Agnes Island, and the other on the Bishop Rock. The latter, which is a great triumph of engineering skill, is in such an exposed situation that in a storm a few years ago the bell was broken down by a sea from the height of 110 feet.

Sept. 5.—9.30 A.M. sailed from St. Mary's, and tacked out of the Islands through St. Mary's Sound, with a fresh breeze S.E., bound to Penzance. Turned to windward all day against a short chopping sea from S.E., with so heavy a swell from N.W. that ships in company were frequently hidden from view; 6.30 P.M. passed close to the Longships Rocks, upon which the N.W. swell was breaking high and with great violence; 7 P.M. wind fresh from E.S.E., handed topsail, and made short tacks in shore, in company with a considerable fleet of coasters that, like ourselves, were taking advantage of the inshore tide to work round the land before dark. 7.30 P.M. a strong weather tide was hurrying us along in too close proximity to the Runnel Stone, when we received timely warning from the alarm bell. A cutter following us at the distance of about a quarter of a mile, had to bear hard up and run to leeward for the same reason. It is the race of tide that makes this rock so formidable, and that would make operations for its removal almost, if not quite, impossible. 8 P.M. passed a brig and schooner in collision. The latter was sailing without lights, and was deservedly punished by losing her mainmast.

As we arrived in Mount's Bay too late to go into Penzance, and there was too much sea to bring up, we had to keep under way all night. The sky was cloudless, and as attractive to look

78

at as it well could be, especially after 2 A.M.—when Venus, rising over the Mount Castle, added her lustre to that of the moon, Jupiter, and Mars. At sunrise, September 6, the view was very charming, the glare of the sun being reflected not only from the windows of the town of Penzance, but from all the villas and villages for miles round. 6 A.M. went into harbour and moored alongside the East Quay, which, like the West Quay, is allowed by the Corporation to be in so offensive a state, encumbered with filth and coal-dust, that nothing short of real distress will drive me into the nasty harbour again. It would be just a living for a poor man to keep the quays clean, and have the coal-dust and *crottin de cheval* for remuneration.

Sept. 8.—After two days of calm, it came on to blow a gale from the E.N.E. The filth and coal-dust before mentioned, which should have been sold to defray the expense of the Corporation dinners, was not only most wastefully expended upon our deck and rigging, but penetrated into the cabins below, causing such annoyance and vexation as words could hardly describe. The nuisance was so unbearable, that it was considered advisable to escape into the open sea as soon as possible. Accordingly, at 10.30 A.M., having set the trysail and third jib, we reached out into the bay and anchored a good berth from St. Michael's Mount, to windward of a fleet of merchant vessels seeking shelter there. The next three or four hours were spent by the two hands in cleaning up and anathematising the Mayor and Corporation of Penzance. 6 P.M. landed on the Mount for a scramble, and returned on board at dusk, at which time the weather was moderate and the sea quiet. Shortly after 9 P.M. a troublesome swell set in from the Lizard. Its direction being at a right angle with the wind, we rolled heavily in the trough of the sea all night.

Sept. 9.—The rolling was so severe that at 6 A.M. we determined to seek a better anchorage. Work, however, was done with such difficulty, in consequence of the heavy sea, that it was 8 A.M. when we got under way with head sail only, and at 9 A.M. set trysail, to turn down to Mullion. The wind being light from the eastward, about forty vessels had left, and were working towards the Lizard under all sail; 10.30 A.M., the wind rising in gusts, they began to shorten sail; 11.30 A.M., blowing a heavy gale, handed our foresail and hove-to for breakfast off Looe Bar. All vessels in the Bay were beating up for the weather shore, between Port Leven and Mullion, under very short canvas; 1.30 A.M. anchored close to Mullion Island; from noon to 4 P.M. there was much spoondrift; 5.30 P.M. it was moderate enough to pull ashore in the boat. From the cliffs I counted sixty-four vessels at anchor, and was surprised to see how regularly they were arranged according to their ability to work off shore if the wind were to fly in. The 'Orion' was in the first line with three pilot cutters, then came sloops and yawls, and a brig-rigged steamship. Next, schooners and ketches, then brigs and barks; those in the first division were almost still on the water, the second were rolling perceptibly, the third decidedly uneasy, and the last, having no protection at all from Mullion Island, were rolling miserably. Night fine and starlight, with fresh wind off the land.

Sept. 10.—Blew hard off the land all day, with fine weather overhead. The only departure from the road was the steamship. On the other hand, the arrivals increased the fleet at anchor to over eighty sail. Spent a great part of the day in the boat, under a close-reefed sail, in visiting Mullion Island, where there are some pretty rock basins, lined with a pink sort of coral, and many varieties of seaweed and anemones. Also visited the beautiful sandy coves and caverns on the mainland, which are well worth seeing. At night hoisted the boat in and prepared to leave at short notice, as the barometer was going back.

Sept. 11.—The wind being moderate from E.S.E., with falling barometer, the fleet got under way and commenced working up Channel. We sailed from Mullion at 9 A.M. under very short canvas. Soon overtook the fleet, and arrived at Falmouth Harbour at 3.30 P.M., making a good but very rough passage. As the weather came on heavy again at night, and continued more or less so for several days, with the wind from S.E. to E.N.E., there was no peace at anchor off Falmouth. At times the wind was so violent that it was not advisable to land, on account of the difficulty of returning on board.

Sept. 14.—Wind E., strong and fine; under double-reefed mainsail, took a turn up the main harbour, then out into a very heavy sea, for a change. As all hands seemed soon to have had enough of it, we bore up and ran into Helford River. The wind being straight in, it was necessary to run up into the narrows to lie either in comfort or safety. In this river, if fine overhead, a considerable time may be spent most agreeably, either in the boat or on shore. To lovers of Nature it is beautiful; to lovers of tiles and brickbats it would be abominably dull.

Sept. 17.—The weather continued very violent. In the morning there was a severe thunderstorm with much wind and rain from S.E. and E.S.E. When the rain ceased, shortly after noon, we tacked out of the river against the young flood, under three-reefed mainsail, touching the ground once in stays, owing to a mistake of the leadsman. To have hung there would have been extremely mortifying, as the pilot, whose services had been declined, was watching us from the cliffs.

To windward of Falmouth the sea was so high that a reef had to be shaken out. From this cause, we made such slow progress, and the weather looked so threatening, that another reef was let out before going into the race off the Dodman Head, in which a great sea was shipped that knocked me to leeward, but did no harm. After this we bore up out of the Race, and passing inside the Guineas Rocks, could just lay the course to Fowey Harbour, which we were fortunate enough to make before dark. As it was much crowded with shipping, and the night set in dark and rainy, I should not have dared to enter an hour later, but must have close-reefed and kept the sea until daylight.

Sept. 22.—6 A.M. sailed from Fowey with a light breeze, N.E.; 5 P.M. anchored close to Drake Island, Plymouth, having been becalmed several hours outside the breakwater.

Sept. 24.—Second morning of calm and thick fog; 9.30 A.M.

fog cleared off, and sun shone out. Sailed from Plymouth under all sail; wind E., gradually shifting to southward. The day was remarkably fine, and the coast in the neighbourhood of the Start looked beautiful, but the sky was wild and unsettled, the scud flying fast from S.E. After rounding the Start Point, the wind shifted from S. to S.E., and freshened considerably. 8 P.M. anchored in Dartmouth. The wind soon increased to a gale, with much rain.

Sept. 25.—So much sea ran into the harbour that we shifted our anchorage from Warfleet to Kingswear, where there was less swell. Night fine; wind W.S.W.

Sept. 26.—Wind backed to the southward, and blew hard. Barometer fell to 29·325, but rose rapidly in the afternoon to 29·575, when the wind shifted to the S.W. Evening closed in dirty, with rain and lightning.

Sept. 27.—2 A.M. a great thunderstorm passed over, commencing with a terrific squall and deluge of rain. We had to turn out in the middle of it (a most unpleasant change from a warm bed), to carry out the kedge, fearing the 'Orion' would blow ashore. Up to 2 P.M. it blew hard, with much rain. After that hour, when the clouds broke and the sun shone, it blew a perfect hurricane, S.W., with great spoondrift. Barometer fell to 29·325, and rose again during the evening to 29·475. Wind W., fine and moonlight.

Sept. 28.—Wind back to the southward, looking dirty, with falling barometer. 1.30 P.M. blowing very hard, with a deluge of rain, and the barometer at the lowest point for several weeks 29·225. Again the wind shifted suddenly from S.E. to S.W., and the barometer rose $\frac{2}{10}$ during the afternoon.

But for the violent oscillations of the barometer nothing could look more promising for a smart run to the Isle of Wight.

A fine clear night, with half a gale West, was what I confidently expected, when at 5.30 P.M. we set the whole mainsail to beat out of that most difficult harbour. Though it blew so strong from S.W., we were becalmed alongside the rocks at Kettle Point, plunging the bowsprit under, in a heavy sea, certainly not the vessel's length from them, and fearing we should be carried on every moment. While in this predicament we perceived a boat, with three men in it, lying-to about two cables off. No doubt they had come down on chance, expecting to find us in trouble at that very spot. After ten minutes of great anxiety there came a light air, and the 'Orion' began to claw off. As soon as they observed that, though I considered we were still in great danger, they turned the boat's head, and rowed away. I have no doubt they knew that when we had got the wind again, we should keep it and get clear away. The wind came stronger and stronger, driving her bows into the head sea, with a succession of shocks that became more violent every instant. At last, a sufficient offing was gained to bear up and run past the Mewstone and rocks on the course for the night, which was E. by S., to pass well to the southward of Portland and the Shambles.

The barometer, after being stationary for an hour, persisted in rising again after nightfall, though the weather, when I went below to tea, at 8 P.M., looked horribly bad. The moon, seen through a greasy cloud, was sufficient warning by itself. At 8.30 Slade called out that he should be glad if I would go on deck, as it was becoming serious. I knew it by the roar and the motion, but wishing to make sure of a meal while it was possible, I delayed for another half-hour; by which time the barometer had discovered its mistake, and had taken a sudden turn downwards, and the gale had set in. Though it seemed a very hazardous proceeding to bring the vessel to the wind under such a press of sail, we were obliged to watch for an opportunity and do it, being too short-handed to reef before the wind. 9.45 P.M. bore up again on the course with three reefs down, then shifted third jib for storm, and stowed the former, wringing wet and stiff as pasteboard, on the cabin floor; 10 P.M. passed a bark lying-to which had previously passed us running while we were lying-to; 10.30 P.M. lowered throat and trussed mainsail. The wind shifting for a time to S.S.W., sent up a troublesome cross sea, that washed the deck pretty freely, extinguishing the binnacle lantern three times before the precaution was taken of protecting it with canvas.

At the same time the great sea was so threatening on the quarter that we had to run off dead before it every few minutes, and make an average by luffing to windward when it was safe to do so. The running to leeward became at length such a frequent necessity, that if persevered in, there was a chance of being embayed near Portland. Consequently, shortly after midnight, as it was very dark and thick with rain, and the gale was then very heavy, we watched for a chance and hove-to, with foresail to windward, not daring to run any longer.

The Portland Lights, bearing E. about 11 miles, were visible from the top of the sea. The play of the boom was so violent that the weather topping-lift parted immediately after coming to the wind. As the parting of the other would probably have caused great damage, it was necessary to take the mainsail off her without delay. We had been wishing it off her before, but were afraid to tackle a job of such difficulty until compelled to do it. Having lashed a cork fender to the lee rail, we got the boom down upon it inch by inch, and secured it with tackles and powerful lashings, then lowered and gathered in the sail. It was a long and heavy work for three hands in such a tremendous sea. When the mainsail was down the foresail was let draw, and she sailed herself to the southward with the helm lashed two points to leeward.

Notwithstanding the lee helm, which very frequently brought her up all shaking, I allowed two knots an hour gained to the southward. This was correct, as at 4 A.M. the Portland Lights bore N.E. At this time, being well to the southward of Portland, and anxious to go ahead and get out of it, we managed to set the trysail, reefed, and put her on the course again—which, as before, was very irregular, every sea requiring to be watched, as well as it was possible to do so in the dark.

Judging from the last sight of the Portland Lights that they would be in one about 6 A.M. distant 9 miles, I altered the course at that hour to east and re-set the log. 8 A.M. log marked 15 knots. The land from St. Alban's to the Durlston was visible, the latter bearing N.N.E. about 6 miles; altered course to E. by N. The sea was enormous—at times grand, and at times very terrible, looking as if it would break over the masthead. However, none came on board worth mentioning, except one small head, that didn't look where he was going, swamped me at the helm both inside and out, and broke down the canvas over the steerage. It was just a warning to rig the pump and to strengthen the steerage cover with battens underneath.

Being hungry, as it was neither safe to disturb the steerage cover nor possible to leave the helm, I was compelled to resort to a little reserve store of biscuits, which I had put in an inside breast-pocket to keep dry, but which were now soaked with salt water, and otherwise in a very unsatisfactory condition.

For hours I had been most uncomfortably nervous about the passage of the Needles Channel, which is a gradually shoaling bar of considerable extent connecting the Shingles Shoal and the Bridge Reef, and I thought about sailing round the Island to avoid the difficulty. This wretched feeling of anxiety died away considerably as the morning advanced, and I saw how safely we were borne on by some of the most alarming breakers. Several times in the deep water, huge seas broke in our wake, and came rushing on in a mountain of foam. To those unacquainted with the power of the vessel destruction would have seemed inevitable, but owing to her powerful quarters and short elliptical stern, she rose steadily and regularly, and the seas passed harmlessly under her, excepting the little head before mentioned, which was heaped up high and thin by collision with our own wave, and was driven on deck by the wind.

Shortly after 8 A.M. the sky was tolerably clear, and the wind less violent; but the clouds, thick with rain, were banking up heavily again in the S.W. For a while there seemed reason to hope we should outstrip them and make the Bar before they dispensed their favours, but they came on at such a rattling pace that we were overtaken in less than an hour, and the gale raged more furiously than ever, driving clouds of spoon-drift before it, and forcing us through the water at 9 knots, with only the little reefed trysail drawing.

The steering was so hard, that my left hand and arm were benumbed. I could use them as a log, feeling pressure at the shoulder, but could not feel the tiller. My mate was a first-class seaman, but his sight was not sharp enough to dodge the sea by night, nor to anticipate its course at any time; and the man who understands the vessel best, especially a small vessel, must be at the helm when a mistake or a little carelessness may cause all to be overwhelmed in a moment.

It was of such vital importance to cross in the best water that, as the dreaded time drew near, I would have given a good deal for a reassuring glimpse of the chart; but as it did not occur to me at the time to send a man into the forecastle to force the door of communication between the fore and after cabins, by which it might have been obtained, I had to trust to memory. I recollected passing close to the buoy two years before, and fortunately remembered the appearance of the Needles and Alum Bay sufficiently well to run through the Channel on that mark, viz., the N.W. side of the rocks and the long white cliff just coming into view out of a right line.

9 A.M. passed close to the Nun-buoy of the S.W. Shingles without seeing it. Though the man and the lad were keeping an anxious look-out, it was not sighted until we were past, and on the top of the next great sea beyond. It was not wanted, however, to show that we were in the Channel—the appearance of the sea proved that, it being the only spot free from dangerous breakers. While remarking this, we were picked up like a feather and carried over the inner edge of the Bar into deeper water by three or four enormous waves that towered up in walls of water just short of breaking. After this the sea lost its dangerous character.

The general scene, viewed from just inside the Bar, was awfully grand and imposing. On the Shingles the surf was tremendous; great seas closing in upon the knolls (shoal spots) came into collision with each other, and leaped high into the air in immense columns of spray. From the Needles to a quarter of a mile S.W., and thence across to Sun Corner, a space including all Scratchell Bay, was a confused mass of breakers, a cauldron of raging surf, from which arose a cloud of spray to the height of about 150 feet, shrouding the weather side and the upper part of the Needles Point and Rocks in a thick haze. Thence, assuming the form of a well-defined stratum of cloud, the spray travelled at a great rate up Alum Bay until it came to the coloured cliff, a mile distant, over which it curved gracefully on to the land above. Upon the bar itself, over which the ebb tide was just beginning to run, were about four prodigious rollers, through which there could have been little chance of passing in safety, had we unfortunately taken the course that is usual for any but the largest ships and run straight in for the Hurst Point Lighthouses. 9.35 A.M. hauled the log, which marked 28 knots, or 13 for 1 hr. 35 min. Allowing the same rate of sailing from 8 to 9 as for the previous two hours, leaves 5½ knots for the last 35 min.—equal to 9½ per hour—which was not surprising considering the hurricane it blew after 9 o'clock. 10 A.M. passed inside the Points, tide running hard out. Off Yarmouth there was a small fleet of vessels at anchor, including four steamers. One of them, the 'Duke of Cornwall,' Dublin paddle-steamer, was canted partly athwart the tide, and had a considerable list from the power of the wind. Passengers and crew were comfortably sheltering in the lee scuppers. The sea in the Solent was extremely rough and violent, but seemed like smooth water after our recent experience. We saw only one vessel under way between Hurst and Cowes—a pilot cutter beating down under reefed trysail. 12.30 P.M. arrived at Cowes, wet through, tired, and hungry, having had 13 hours at the helm, besides very heavy work when lying-to.

I am too great a novice to accept safety as a matter of course. The reaction upon my feelings after crossing the Bar was greater than I care to express, or desire to experience again if there be equal cause for it, however agreeable a successful result may be.

One feeling of unmixed satisfaction I had in the knowledge that my vessel was equal to such an occasion.

Oct. 2.—Wind E.N.E., fresh breeze and fine; 6 P.M. sailed from Cowes bound up Channel; 9.30 P.M., fine moonlight night, anchored near Selsea Bill.

Oct. 3.—Wind N.E., strong, and cloudy: 8.15 A.M. left the anchorage under trysail, foresail, and third jib, barometer falling; 9 A.M. passed the beacon in Looe Channel, pitching the bowsprit into a troublesome sea from the eastward, which continued all day; 10.30 A.M. the wind shifted suddenly to the eastward and blew a tremendous squall, which lasted so long that all the vessels in sight (six or seven brigs and schooners) bore up and ran for the Isle of Wight, expecting another gale. As I was particularly desirous to get home, I had the foresail reefed, storm jib set, and tacked to the northward, resolved not to give in so early in the day. This was fortunate, as at noon the wind backed to the N.E., and becoming more moderate, we shook reef out of foresail, and were able to lay the course again for Beachy Head. The land gradually faded from view, in torrents of rain, and the day was so piercing cold and miserable, the wind backing farther to the northward, that I cannot remember its like. 6.15 P.M. sighted Beachy Head Light abeam, barely visible through the haze, though supposed to be only a mile distant; 11 P.M. passed Dungeness.

Oct. 4.—1.30 A.M. off the South Foreland; wind W., very strong, weather showed signs of clearing. 4 A.M. off the North Foreland, very fine, but intensely cold. Off Margate the sun rose bright and clear, and the wind gradually died away, until it fell calm; noon, set the mainsail and a larger jib, under which sail we just managed to save our tide to Southend, where we anchored at 3 P.M.

Oct. 5.—Took on board an anchor and chain, which I lost in the Medway fifteen months previously, and sailed at 10 A.M. with a light wind easterly; 2.30 P.M. arrived at Greenhithe, and sailed into winter quarters in the Creek, thus ending a very heavy two months' cruise. Before night the sails were unbent and the vessel half stripped.

Distance sailed, out and home, 1080 n. miles = 1248 statute miles.

Number of nights at sea, 17; either sailing, or at anchor on the open coast.

VOYAGE OF THE 'ORION' R.T.Y.C., TO BANTRY, 1869

THE 'Orion,' although only 16½ tons builders' measurement, is so constructed that there is little difference between the builders' and the new measurement, *i.e.*, actual capacity. The truth of this is sufficiently indicated by the ballast and stores amounting to about 15 tons, which is equal to the dead weight carried by many yachts of 25 and 30 tons, whose new measurement is frequently equal to only half the nominal tonnage.

The cabins are so arranged that my visitors have the best and most convenient part of the vessel, being cut off from the forecastle by a space of 3 feet with double doors, and from the steerage by a cabin of 6½ feet with double doors, in which are my berth and very capacious lockers. The sail, warp, and running gear lockers are around and under the steerage. The tanks, two of 50 gallons, are also under the steerage, one on each side. In the forecastle, which is 14 feet long, are 2 galvanised iron bunks for the men, 2 coal bunkers, capable of carrying half a ton of coal, or its equivalent in coke, and very capacious stowage under the floor for chains, firewood, oils, paint, varnish, &c., of which there is generally a sufficient supply for the cruise.

The accommodation aft is about equal to the private berth of a P. and O. steamer, and forward I do not think the men are much worse off, excepting the inconvenience of the stove.

July 9, 1869.—Sailed from Greenhithe, Kent, with my usual crew of two hands, for the S.W. of Ireland, in company with the 'Eudora,' 20 tons, built for my friend Mr. Twycross, by Wanhill of Poole, in 1867. Although not a strictly arranged match, it was quite understood that there would be a struggle for the honour of getting first to Bantry, and that the men would be paid extra for their exertions. The wind being fresh from W.S.W., the start was made at 7.30 A.M., with topmasts housed. 1 P.M., passed the Nore, with small topsails and squaresails set, 'Eudora' leading. At 4.30 P.M. becalmed together off Margate. Handed squaresails. 'Orion,' being to windward when the breeze came from S.W., was first round the Foreland, but was passed off Broadstairs by the 'Eudora,' that had weather just suitable for her—viz., a nice working breeze and smooth water. While she was passing, an agreement was made to anchor in the Downs, and start fair again in the morning. 'Eudora,' being about three-quarters of a mile to windward, anchored in a 'rolling berth' off Deal Pier, and was followed by 'Orion' at 9 P.M.

July 10.—4.15 A.M., sailed from Deal, wind N.W., with second jib and small topsail set. 5.30 A.M., off Dover; wind fresh from N.N.W., water very smooth. The 'Eudora' reached about a mile ahead, but the wind falling off Folkestone brought the two vessels nearly together again. 'Eudora,' being first to get a light breeze, saved her tide round Dungeness, and went away with a free wind, leaving us muzzled by a head wind and strong flood tide, against which we had to contend for two hours, with every stitch of sail we could crowd on. At noon, rounded the Ness, and lay a course for Beachy Head. After breaking off and making the land at Fairlight, the wind southed again, and enabled us to lay the course down Channel.

It was not thought probable that we should see the 'Eudora' after the first day, as it was understood that our tactics would be different. Their determination was to keep the land aboard, and mine to do the reverse, unless the wind were off shore. There is a great difference of opinion on this point. I think my plan of avoiding the headlands on a long passage the best, for two reasons. The sea is longer and more regular in the deep water, and strong tides at the headlands when adverse tell more against than favourable tides tell in favour—the reason being this, that when in favour you are carried in an hour or two beyond its influence into the ordinary deep-sea tide, and when adverse you are stopped at or near the headland during the whole tide. There are exceptions, of course.

July 11.—1.30 A.M. Beachy Head N.N.W. 6 miles. Wind

light from S.E., course W. by N. 5 A.M., set squaresail. At
9 P.M. Portland lights in one, distant about ten miles.

July 12.—1.30 A.M. Portland lights still in one. Distance for
twenty-four hours 100 miles. With light winds between E. and
N.E., crossed the West Bay to within 10 miles of the Start
Point, when it fell dead calm. Afterwards, with light airs from
all quarters, managed to round the Start against tide at 10.30
P.M. Night dark, and threatening change of weather. Midnight,
off Salcombe; wind puffy off the land.

July 13.—2.30 A.M. handed topsail; wind N.N.E., fresh, with
rain. 4 A.M. Eddystone north 4 miles. 8.30 A.M. hove-to, took
two reefs down, and shifted jib to third. 11 A.M. passed the
Lizard Point close in. 2 P.M. hove-to under lee of the Land's
End, took third reef down, and reefed the foresail. 3 P.M.
Longships bearing E. 1½ miles, reset log, course N.W. by N.;
close-hauled, with heavy head sea. Midnight, all reefs out.
Log 43. Distance for twenty-four hours 130 miles.

July 14.—Wind light from N.N.E., with a troublesome swell;
set large topsail and jib topsail. Noon, Log 70 from Longships,
wind baffling and paltry from all quarters ahead. The only
event of the day was the refusal of the junior hand to go out on
the gaff in so much sea and reeve the topsail sheet, which,
having been carelessly bent by the mate, shook itself adrift
from the sail and unrove at the gaff end. It being a rule of
mine not to give an order I am not prepared to execute, I
said nothing, but went out and rove it myself. I found no fault
with the man for refusing, but remarked to the mate that he
had better jam his turns another time, and not cause such unnecessary trouble. Had I known that our antagonist had given
in, the mainsail might have been lowered, and the sheet rove
on deck.

July 15.—Same paltry weather, very hazy and hot. The sea,
blue all the previous day, was dark green in the early morning,
and again turned blue as we headed W.N.W. At 4.15 P.M. the
supposed bearing of Kinsale Head was N.W. six miles, which
was suspected to be wrong, when we fell in with a Cork pilot
cutter. The pilots bore down upon us, and, in answer to my

hail, gave the bearings of Kinsale Head N.E. by N. 16 miles, and Seven Heads North. When I roared out thanks for their kindness, they replied, 'That is what we came for, Sir,' which was evidently true, as they gave the bearings without a moment's hesitation. Would our North Sea men have done that? After contending so long with battling head winds, I am not ashamed to acknowledge being 15 miles S.W. ½ W. out of my reckoning, especially as I have lately read that H.M.S. 'Agincourt,' leading the fleet (under the command of Mr. Childers) to Lisbon, was 30 miles out of hers. My error, however, was quite on the right and cautious side. Shortly after parting from the pilot cutter the haze cleared away, and the land became visible.

July 16.—6.30 A.M. a light breeze sprang up from E.N.E., which gradually drew round with the sun to the southward, the day being intensely hot and hazy. At 2.40 P.M. passed Cape Clear. There was evidently some great work being carried on at the Fastnet Rock. I have since been informed that they have been engaged nearly three years filling up a gap which endangered the lighthouse. At 5.30 p.m., off the Mizen Head, narrowly escaped running against a sick shark, that was making floundering efforts to sink, but could not. Half the vessel's length westward would have carried her on to his broadside, and given us an alarming shock. After passing the Head, which is very wild and picturesque, the weather changed suddenly from hot sunshine to chilly S.E. wind and fog. Approaching Bantry I took as good a survey from the masthead before dark as the fog would allow. Cautiously tacking through the South Channel against tide, with the lead going all the time, we made the bar at 10.30 P.M., and an hour later let go the anchor, being afraid to put the helm up or down any more, lest we should run upon the mainland, or upon the rocky islets, which at daylight were found to be three-quarters of a mile and half a mile distant respectively. Anyone who has been on a mountainous coast in darkness and fog will understand this illusion. Heaving the lead in the Channel was an amusement to the men, as at every cast fish were seen by the phosphoric light darting away in all directions. The frequent shifts of wind during the voyage caused so much trouble day and night that two hours of unbroken sleep was a great luxury, and a thing to be talked about. Notwithstanding our fatigue (being awoke by a troublesome and untimely visit from the coastguard), heads were peering over the gunwale at 4 A.M. for a glimpse of the 'Eudora,' which, to our great surprise, was nowhere to be seen.

I have since learned that she twice anchored owing to adverse tides in the Channel; was next under the necessity of putting into Falmouth where much time was lost; and finally, the boy being seriously ill, was unfortunately compelled to put back at 7 P.M. of the 15th, when she was 35 miles N.N.W. of the Longships. As our position at 7 P.M. of that day was 135 miles N.W. by N. $\frac{1}{4}$ N. of the Longships, she had of course lost all chance, being 100 miles astern.

Our time from Greenhithe was 7 days 16 hours; under way from Deal, 6 days 19 hours. Distance sailed, 598 nautical miles. The supplies stood thus on arrival at Bantry: preserved provisions, untouched; fresh provisions, one day; water for three weeks; fuel for a month.

A VISIT TO THE BULL ROCK

THE weather having been moderate for a few days, we sailed from off the Blackwater in Kenmare river on the afternoon of August 18, and anchored for the night, at 8 P.M., in 13 fathoms, close to the cliffs east of Doon Point. This place is not marked as an anchorage on the chart, and is not a desirable berth, but it is better than drifting about all night in a calm. While the 'Orion,' with just steerage way, was heading in slowly for the anchorage, I rowed ahead in the boat, made the circuit of the little rocky bay, and then out straight to the spot where the anchor should be let go, with the Great Skellig touching Doon Point, and the moon over a certain hummock of the cliff. Without this precautionary examination and these impromptu bearings, I should not have dared to anchor sufficiently close in to be out of the Atlantic swell, which would have kept us awake all night with its ceaseless roll, and the consequent clatter and jarring of all articles on board not absolute fixtures.

Aug. 19.—Noon, sailed from Doon Point for the Dursey Head, off which lie two remarkable rocks exposed to the whole drift of the Atlantic, called the Cow and the Bull. The former, distant from the Head a mile and a half, is very fantastic in appearance. It is 203 feet high, has an arch on one side, and on the other a large gaping rent with a piece of rock jammed in, which seems to prevent the enormous slab from tumbling in

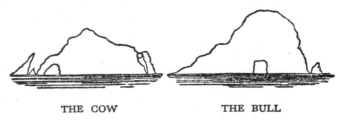

THE COW   THE BULL

upon the main rock. The latter, a mile farther seaward, is a very bold-looking rock 290 feet high, with a conspicuous tunnel through the centre.

Between the Head (which is rent into chasms, like most headlands on this coast, by the Atlantic storms) and the rocks are 35 fathoms water, with strong tides, and such a heavy sea that they are seldom approachable. Being much struck in 1861 with their very curious appearance, I resolved, if the opportunity presented itself during the cruise of 1869, to pay them a special visit, and if possible examine them from the boat. It was reported to me that boats could pass through the Bull, and even that a vessel might sail through; but I failed to meet any person who could speak upon better authority than hearsay.

The wind being light from S.S.W., with a swell from the west, it was late in the afternoon when we came up with the Cow, and got becalmed in the eddy tide so close to it that it was necessary to use the sweeps (long oars) to keep out of danger.

After clearing the Cow a quarter of a mile, I got into the

94

boat with one of the men, and returned to examine it; but being on the wrong side, and not having time to pull round to leeward, I was compelled to sheer off on account of the swell, which looked very formidable from the boat, and turn my attention to the Bull, which we approached with great caution on the lee side. The height of the swell was frequently measured during the day, and ascertained to vary from 5 feet to 7 feet, the length of the higher waves being about twice that of the lower ones.

Although a swell of this height is considered smooth water on the Irish coast, it certainly would not be so considered at Margate if launched against their pier on a fine day. Being a long ocean swell, it represents a large and heavy moving body of water, which travels with great rapidity, and rushes upon an obstruction with such sustained weight that, viewed from the sea, it rises to about twice its height in green water before breaking into foam. Harmless enough in the deep water, you are soon made to know that it is terribly powerful if you venture within its influence when it begins to feel bottom. When we were in the trough, after pulling one or two seas clear of the 'Orion,' she was out of our sight to the height of half the mainsail, and we were lost to their view altogether for long intervals, being in fact visible to them only when we both happened to be on the top of the sea at the same time. If I had not carefully measured the sea from the vessel, I should certainly have estimated the height considerably above 7 feet.

Opening the tunnel on the N.E. side, we lay-to for a while at a respectful distance, and took a careful survey of it to see if the swell showed any disposition to break, which would be a sure sign of rocks near the surface. As it looked all fair, we pulled in between the points of entrance (projecting rocks), upon which the sea broke with considerable violence, but left a space of dark water sufficiently wide for the boat to pass between the surf.

The interior, which is about 50 feet high from the surface of the water, 40 feet wide, and 500 feet through, is like a grand hall with an undulating floor. A sounding taken in the middle,

95

7¼ fathoms half tide, showed the height of the cavern, from the bottom to the roof, to be about 100 feet. The roof is horizontal, but rugged; the sides are perpendicular and very smooth, lined a few feet below high-water mark with little mussels, in such myriads that the rock looks as if it were covered with black velvet.

Fine as the entrance looked on the N.E. side, it was not to be compared for grandeur to that of the S.W., upon which the sun shone, lighting up the huge blocks, and giving it the appearance of an immense castle gateway, swarmed to the top with thousands of gannets (solan geese) and gulls. Besides those at rest, there were thousands on the wing, all talking at once.

The scene was altogether so lively and enchanting that I was delighted, and turned the boat's head with great reluctance to pass through the cavern again to the 'Orion,' which at that moment happened to be in a line with the centre of the arch, about half a mile off, looking, with the sun upon her, like a framed picture.

As the swell entered both ends at once, there was no 'run' to drive the boat backwards and forwards as in an ordinary cavern, but simply a vertical rise and fall of a few feet.

6.30 P.M. made for the land. 10 P.M. anchored in Garinish Bay, which in its safest and most protected part is so confined by a dangerous little reef, that I went ahead in the boat, and examined that side of the anchorage by rowing from Garinish Island to the reef, from the reef to the mainland at a right angle, and then diagonally to the spot where the anchor was to be let go. The night being moonlight and calm, I was able to do this, otherwise we must have anchored in a more exposed berth, or have kept the sea until daylight.

The great necessity for informing yourself correctly of the distances in these close anchorages, where it is only a question of a few boats' length between safety and danger, is that you may not be afraid to pay out sufficient chain to save the risk of dragging if it should come on to blow; also that you may know how to cast the vessel's head and work out in case of having to 'slip.'

For the information of anyone who wishes to know something of the general character of the south-west coast of Ireland, I may say that it is very wild and pretty, with many fine natural harbours. The scenery in some of them is magnificent, especially in Glengariff, Ardgroom, and Kilmaklloge—the former in Bantry Bay, the two latter in Kenmare River. Fish of all sorts is very plentiful, and can be bought for very little if you are too idle, or, as in my case, have not the time, to catch it.

The climate is mild, humid, and much subject to haze, particularly in wet weather, when the coast is so densely shrouded in mist that navigation is extremely dangerous. According to the book of sailing directions, all the harbours are easily distinguished by certain features of the landscape or conspicuous old towers and beacons; but to render the instructions complete there should be added 'weather permitting,' for as a rule in wet weather the leading marks are in the clouds.

To sail this coast with any comfort, the largest-scale Admiralty Charts are indispensable, as the rocks are numerous, and buoys and beacons very scarce.

On all the rocks in Kenmare river there is only one small beacon.

In choosing open anchorages on this coast in stormy weather from the south and west, it is important to bear in mind that the wind often veers suddenly to the northward, and blows frightfully.

I will close these remarks by saying that provisions are good and abundant at the chief towns, and the people generally so civil and obliging that it is pleasant to deal with them.

THE 'ORION,' R.T.Y.C.

To the Forth, Clyde, etc., 1871

July 20.—Spent the smaller hours of the morning in hauling out of dock, and at 4 A.M., with the usual complement of two hands, sailed from Greenhithe, Kent. 7.30, being in great confusion below, anchored off Southend during the flood tide, utilising the time in making snug for sea. 3 P.M., weighed anchor and sailed for the North; weather chilly and unseasonable.

July 22.—4 P.M., made Flamborough Head. 7.30, after passing through a short but smart thunderstorm, anchored for the night off Filey, Yorkshire; weather wet and cold.

July 23.—During the night and morning several picturesque-looking Dutch fishing-boats came into the bay, and anchored in such close order, that they were able to lash the boats together in tiers of four or six; I presume from motives of sociability only, as in my opinion such an arrangement was quite incompatible with comfort or safety. I wished to land at Filey; but as the thunderstorms continued at intervals, with strong puffs of wind, which might have chopped round to an easterly quarter at any moment, I considered it was unadvisable to remain any longer.

Noon.—Sailed from Filey under the trysail. Being desirous, in passing, of seeing all the towns that were not too much off the course, I stood in very close to Scarborough, and had a good view of it with glasses from the crosstrees. 6 P.M., calm, with adverse tide, anchored for the night in 10 fathoms off Haiburn Wick.

July 24.—4 A.M., under way, wind puffy from W. and N.W. 8.30, tacked close in to Whitby. A large fleet of luggers came down the harbour and stood off to sea on the herring-fishery, many of them being Cornish vessels.

July 25, Noon.—Strong and squally from N.W. After beating through the 'Inner Sound' of Farn Islands with the whole mainsail, and through the narrow and intricate channel leading into the harbour of Holy Island, Northumberland, we anchored off the village of Lindisfarne at 2.30 P.M. in sight of the beautiful old ruin of Lindisfarne Abbey. While sheering about on the evening of this day with a strong tide and fresh wind, the chain got foul of the keel-band, and we had to heel the yacht on the sand (27th) to clear it, and have the band repaired.

July 29.—Sailed at 6.30 A.M., wind so light that with all sail set we had great difficulty in getting to sea. 11 A.M., wind S.E., with rain. Set squaresail. 1.30 P.M., off St. Abb's Head, which, with the adjoining coast, I admired exceedingly. Wind E.S.E. fresh, with much rain. Observed quite a regiment of umbrellas on the hills, a large party having unfortunately chosen this day for a pleasure excursion. 7.15, not caring to run into a strange harbour after dark, anchored in Aberlady Bay, about 10 miles short of Granton, glad indeed to get below out of the drenching rain, and have a good 9 o'clock dinner.

July 30.—Calm. Dried sails at anchor.

July 31.—Calm, with light airs. Managed to drag along to Granton, arriving at 1 P.M., completing the outward voyage. Distance sailed, 425 nautical miles. It was a gentle passage, but very troublesome and very cold, the wind being seldom for two hours in the same direction, or of the same force.

From the Thames to the Forth, the only parts I admire as a whole are the coast of Yorkshire, the northern part of Northumberland, and the coast of Berwick. There are, no doubt, many interesting little spots in other counties that could not come under my observation. The greatest drawback to sailing on the east coast of England is, that it is cursed with unmanageable screw steamers, far beyond any other coast in the world. In strong and thick weather, which is much aggravated by their smoke, they are a constant source of uneasiness, especially during the night. Unless you are in a bay or far out at sea there is no rest to be had on account of them. Coasting north with light winds off shore from the time you make the coast of Durham until you leave the Forth for a wilder and less commercial country, the atmosphere is dark and heavy with the smoke of factories, mines, and steamers. Even during the night there are unceasing sounds from the shore of whistling, hammering, and steaming, and added to these during the day, bell-ringing and blasting. Only when it blows strong on shore with clear weather can it be pretended that there is anything approaching the romantic along all this coast, excepting parts of Northumberland, Berwick, and Haddington.

July 31 *to September* 2.—Stayed in the Firth of Forth, making Granton headquarters for letters, provisions, and excursions to Edinburgh. Granton is a good safe harbour, but spoilt for yachts by the traffic of the North British Railway, which ferries its great luggage-trains across the Forth day and night (Sundays excepted) by running them on board of large steam ferry-boats. In addition to the before-mentioned whistling, bell-ringing, and steaming, we have here the thunder of the laden trucks being run on or off the steamers by a rope and a stationary engine. Half an hour can be spent with pleasure, not unmixed with wonder, in observing the skilful management of this traffic.

The steamers are so engined that they can work their paddle-wheels in contrary directions, an arrangement that enables them to be placed end on to the landing-stage with great precision, when they disembark a train for the south, ship another for the north, and, turning round in their own length, are off with their ponderous freight in an incredibly short space of time, belching forth clouds of smoke and smuts that drive yachtsmen to despair or to sea who are particular about their canvas being soiled by dirty rigging and spars.

I used the harbour as little as possible, preferring sometimes to anchor outside, pull ashore for provisions and letters, and sail away again from the dirt and the noise to anchor off one of those beautiful parks with which the Forth abounds, and in which, by the courtesy and liberality of their owners, visitors, under certain proper restrictions, are free to ramble.

One of our excursions in calm weather was to Portobello,

the favourite watering-place of the Scotch capital, from which we were driven on the second day by the smoke of its factories and bad odours. There is no such pleasure town on the Forth, and I believe on all the east coast of Scotland, as will compare with even such inferior towns as Margate and Folkestone; all have their great ugly chimneys, and none consume their own smoke.

Aug. 10.—Anchored off Fidra Island and landed; afterwards ran with a light breeze to Canty Bay, near North Berwick, and anchored for the night in five fathoms. From here we rowed round the 'Bass Rock,' the great eastern home of the gannet, a wondrous sight certainly, but I think surpassed by 'Ailsa Craig,' in the Clyde, the great western home of these magnificent birds. We picked up one that had been wantonly shot by a fool in sport, and measured across the back and wings six feet. Every one who visits the Haddington coast should if possible see this great sight.

Aug. 11.—After breakfast rowed along the coast towards the South Carrs reef, landing in a bay under the ruins of Tantallon Castle, an old stronghold of the Douglas family. There is enough standing to show that it was of immense strength and importance. There are dungeons and dark staircases that might repay antiquarian research, but on account of the ruin being much resorted to by excursionists and picnic parties, you should borrow a pair of overshoes and a candle to make the inspection.

After luncheon sailed from this pretty coast—which is much exposed in rough weather—and essayed to reach Granton, being short of water; but owing to the calm weather did not reach there until 3 P.M. the following day (Saturday), when we went alongside the steamboat quay, took in water, &c., and sailed over to Donnibristle Park, on the Fife coast, anchoring there at 9.15 P.M., quite late enough to be under way in the Forth, which is dangerous at night on account of its numerous rocks and eccentric tides. There is not in the Forth a more charming piece of coast and country to lie off and land upon, weather permitting, than that which extends from St. David's

Point, the western boundary of Donnibristle, to Burntisland, a distance of five miles, which includes Aberdour and a beautifully-wooded hill sloping down to the sea, called the Hughes. This splendid wood with public walks in it is composed chiefly of the finest beech and sycamore trees. To describe all that is to be seen from an elevation of a few hundred feet, and enjoyed on a fine clear sunny day when there is wind enough to disperse the smoke of the towns, would require a book of many pages. Such days are rare. During our month's stay in the Forth, there were only about four so remarkably clear.

Besides the charming city of Edinburgh and the places already mentioned, we visited the beautiful parks of Donnibristle (Earl of Moray), Dalmeny (Earl of Rosebery), and Hopetoun (Earl of Hopetoun), the towns of Leith, Burntisland, and South Queensferry, the village of Aberdour, the islands Inchkeith, Inchcolm—upon which is the very interesting ruin of a monastery—and Inch Garvie, which has upon it the ruin of a state prison. Many other places of interest too numerous to mention were seen from the yacht or from the boat without landing.

Upon the morning of August 24—that fearful day when so many vessels were wrecked on the coasts of Norway and Sweden, and, amongst other disasters on our own side the North Sea, a steam-tug foundered with all hands off Tay Bar— we were anchored to leeward on the Fife coast, and hurried away from there immediately after breakfast on account of the threatening appearance of the weather and the barometer. We first tacked over to Granton, having enough wind for the whole mainsail, and anchoring outside the harbour, took in four or five days' provisions, letters, &c., and sailed again after a long shower at 3.15 P.M. in bright sunshine and fast-flying scud from S.S.W. with three reefs in mainsail, whole foresail, and third jib, intending to anchor off Hopetoun Park, then a weather shore about 8 miles up the Firth. After sailing pleasantly for three-quarters of an hour, the foresail had to be lowered for a heavy squall, with thunder and rain from W.S.W. This was followed by a gleam of hot sunshine, and an ominous lull in the wind; while a frightful-looking black cloud with grey foreground was advancing over the hills. 4.15 P.M., a fishing-boat running towards us under a lugsail faded from view in the coming deluge. In a minute or two more we were bending to the blast, so blinded with rain and spray that it was difficult to see the length of the vessel around. I had chosen my course, and tacked in anticipation so as to give the squall time to do its worst before it would be necessary to go about again. With foresail down and mainsail trussed, we were rushing along gunwale under towards the rocks, heaving the lead as if it were night. This awful fury, accompanied with heavy thunder, fortunately lasted only about five minutes, when it became light enough to show it was time to go about. In ten minutes more the storm was over, the thunder rumbling fainter every clap, and the sun shining hot as before; but the wind continued very strong and more westerly, with a fast-falling barometer, so that when abreast of Hopetoun, in a nasty chop of a sea, it was evident that a less exposed anchorage or a harbour must be found. The latter being decided upon, we put back for Granton with all speed, and none too soon; for, after another thunder-squall, the gale broke with great violence, driving clouds of spoondrift before it. Although there was so little canvas set as the third jib and three-reefed mainsail, the 'Orion' flew along with the wind on the quarter, gunwale down, as in the great squall, steering so wildly that she was hardly under command until I luffed her into the harbour, up which she travelled at such a speed that there was no opportunity for shortening sail until she was brought up head to wind with 30 fathoms of chain. As she dragged after the canvas was lowered, we paid out 15 fathoms more, and took up a small government mooring alongside a brig we had narrowly escaped fouling. Feeling secure in a good berth, we had dinner comfortably, and had reason to congratulate ourselves upon being all right as long as the gale lasted. This pleasant delusion was dispelled soon after dark by an excited official (not the gentlemanly harbour-master of Granton, nor his deputy, who was ill, but a longshore man temporarily appointed in the latter's place) ordering us in an uncivil tone to move out of the berth, which he knew was impossible, and make way for a large steamer, then at anchor lower down the harbour, adding that he had warned us of it when we brought up. Certainly we had seen on the quay an absurd man gesticulating frantically with his mouth open, but could not in such a hurricane hear a word he said; neither could his orders have been obeyed, had they been understood. Foreseeing great difficulty in moving the ship, we felt tolerably easy until they towed her to windward with a tug and carried a hawser athwart our bows, and another one under the stern, which threatened us with serious damage. Fortunately everybody was in such bad temper that the thing was bungled completely; the hawser athwart our bows parted, and the ship nearly got on the stonework. After that the captain refused to be moved any more, and our longshore man had to smother his rage and disappointment until the morning, when he succeeded in worrying us out of the berth, and giving a deal of labour and trouble for nothing.

Sailing gunwale under with three reefs down is not a pastime one would choose for pleasure. It only occurs under such circumstances as those described, viz., in a squall when there is want of sea room, or when too near shelter to sacrifice the time in further reducing canvas. An excursion-boat from Leith was five hours after time in steaming 15 miles to windward, landing her drenched and sea-sick passengers at midnight, for once satisfied they had had as much as they could reasonably demand for their money.

Wishing to leave the Forth and go to the Clyde, I determined to pass through the Forth and Clyde Canal, having been assured that it was quite practicable and pleasant. It was practicable, certainly, but not so pleasant that the saving of 300 or 400 miles of sea would induce me to do it again in a vessel so valuable and drawing so much water as the 'Orion'. Thanks to the kind attention of the collector at Grangemouth, who found us a good guide, and to extraordinarily good fortune, we got through without damage, and took a steam-tug immediately from Bowling on the Clyde to Gourock, to wash off the dirt in good sea-water, paint up afresh, and restore order on board.

Having doubled the distance from home by this passage of the canal, I will briefly refer to our stay in the estuaries of the Firth of Clyde, and then give an account of the sail from the Clyde to the Thames at a time when there were many disasters on our coasts.

Sept. 5.—Arrived in the Clyde. From the 6th to the 20th spent the time very agreeably in Gareloch, Loch Long, and the Kyles of Bute.

Sept. 19.—Shifted our anchorage from Loch Ridun, passed through the North Channel of Burntisland, Kyles of Bute, and anchored in 9 fathoms close to a fine burn, from which we took a hundred gallons of beautiful clear water for the voyage home by taking the boat alongside the rocks at high water, filling an india-rubber tank with a hose, and then pumping its contents into the iron tanks on board.

Sept. 20.—Sailed for Roseneath Bay, Gareloch, calling at Rothesay, Isle of Bute, for letters. Wind S.W., fresh and squally. The mountains and woods looked beautifully clear and fresh between the squalls, inviting one to stay another month, notwithstanding the lateness of the season, of which we were strongly reminded during the next three or four days by a boisterous and piercing east wind, which greatly interfered with the steamboat excursion traffic, and sent a large number of Clyde yachts to their winter quarters.

Monday the 25th being fixed upon for the departure, we lay off Helensburgh on the morning of that day, and completed stock of provisions. Situated at the entrance of Gareloch, and within an hour's journey by rail to Glasgow, it is a convenient town for supplies of all sorts, excepting ship chandlery and water, which can better be procured elsewhere. It has good anchorage, slack tides, and is out of the way of the great Clyde traffic.

Having hoisted in the boat we weighed anchor at 3 P.M., and, with the large topsail set, bore away to run down the

Clyde. Wind E., light and cloudy, barometer 29·875 falling. 5.30, wind E.S.E., fresh, handed topsail, fortunately in good order, as, judging by the appearance of the weather, there seemed little chance of its being wanted again for some time. Sailing east of the Cumbrae Islands, we cleared them at 7.10, and entered the broad water of the Firth. The sunset of this day was one of the most peculiar and gorgeous in my recollection, the prevailing colours, however, of green and yellow below the violet and red were a sure presage of bad weather.

Sept. 26.—2.30 A.M., passed Corsewall Point, the southern extremity of the Firth of Clyde, in the Irish North Channel. This point has a splendid revolving light of alternate white and red—a description of light in every way superior to those that plague mariners with their long eclipses, causing them often to be overlooked in a heavy sea and thick weather when their distance is considerable and position as regards the ship uncertain. The Mull of Galloway has a fine intermittent light, which is quite unobjectionable, being light 2½ minutes and eclipsed ½ minute. On the other hand, Beachy Head Light, one of the most important in the English Channel, is the worst and most troublesome of all with which I am acquainted, being illuminated only 15 seconds and eclipsed 1 minute 45 seconds. If its character were changed to intermittent by reversing the periods of light and dark, it would greatly increase its usefulness. In my opinion, no revolving light should suffer a long total eclipse, but should pale, or be alternated with red or green.

5.30 A.M.—Mull of Galloway E.S.E. about 6 miles. At this point we lost the protection of the land, and entered the Irish Sea with 50 miles of open water to windward. Of the first 90 miles, which had been got over very comfortably, the last 20 was a 'reach' along a weather shore, under a brilliant starlit sky with a roaring breeze. 6.15 A.M. hove to for an hour, housed topmast, took down two reefs in mainsail and shifted jib to third. 11.30, Calf of Man E.S.E. about 2 miles, wind E.S.E., very strong with rough sea, course S.S.W. While passing to leeward of the Isle of Man I had taken the precaution to lay in a good breakfast, and a wise provision it proved to be, for it was the last chance of sitting at table for three days. It is quite a pleasant change on a sea passage to have something fresh to look at. The Isle of Man, with its lofty hills and fantastic rocks on Calf Island, was new to us and therefore interesting, although only a small part was seen distinctly.

If the wind kept up two lights were expected to be visible during the night, but no more land for 250 miles. Keeping as close to windward along the coast of Wales as possible, sailing a proper stranger's course to the Land's End, no protection can be got from the land with easterly winds because there are three great promontories beset with strong tides, and outlying rocks that keep a vessel on an average 30 miles out at sea. A glance at the map will at once show this to be the case.

6.30 P.M.—South Stack light off Holyhead, E.S.E., about 5 miles. Weather looking extremely dirty, barometer 29·675, falling fast. Reefed the foresail, then hove the vessel to again, and took down third reef in mainsail. One man had to give in to the sea malady early in the day, much to his annoyance, although people say it is a good thing. From a variety of causes calculated to produce the effect, I had reason to apprehend, much to my annoyance, that he would be joined by good company before morning. No amount of motion on deck affects me, but battened down below with the charts and books, bending over the table, and clinging to it for support in a small vessel sailing 7 knots in the trough of a heavy sea, is a position that would severely try the arch-enemy himself, even without the additional discomfort of wet clothes, and privations of all sorts that poor mortals have to endure. To be certain of our exact position at all hours, in anticipation of the coming gale with its uncertainties, was a positive necessity that made the work below much harder than usual.

11 P.M.—Altered course to S.W. by S. Midnight, blowing heavily E.S.E., with high sea and thick rain. Rounded to again with foresail to windward, took down fourth reef in mainsail, and shifted jib to storm. Bardsey Island light was believed to have been seen on the beam before the rain com-

pletely obscured everything. Distance from Helensburgh, 202 knots; to the Land's End, 170.

For several hours the weather had been very violent, and the motion below so nearly unbearable, that no one would voluntarily subject himself to it who had not a determined and settled purpose in doing it. My settled purpose was, if possible, to get home while there was light to be got from the moon, which, whether clouded or not, relieved the wearisome night duty, and enabled one man to be below, provided there was no other work on hand but steering and keeping the look-out. This, in my estimation, is a good reason for sailing continuously and without regard to weather, especially in the fall of the year, when nights get longer by waiting.

Sept. 27.—12.30 A.M., reset log and altered course to S.W. by W. Towards 2 A.M. comfort became no longer a consideration. With Cardigan Bay well open, we were 40 miles to leeward of land. The rain descended in a perfect deluge, with a furious wind and terrific sea that washed the deck freely, but not dangerously. In half an hour more the sea assumed such a threatening aspect that it was unsafe to persevere, so we hove to, and immediately set about the laborious task of taking the mainsail off her.

In such a sea it is exhausting work for tired hands. First, the boom has to be secured to leeward with powerful lashings, that must be gradually tautened upon it while the topping-lifts are being eased, so as to prevent any play whatever. Then the sail, flapping violently, and stiff as millboard from saturation, has to be gathered in. When half done, a heavy sea pays her head off: in an instant the work is undone, and the canvas bellying like a balloon over the sea; fortunate, indeed, if sufficient hold of the leach can be retained to save it from being filled with water—an accident much to be dreaded. Long before the work is done one's face may feel the cold wet blast, but the body, heavily clothed and waterproofed, feels as if it were in the East Indies, and arms as if they belonged to somebody else. For five hours we were lying-to under the reefed foresail and storm jib, with her head N.E. by E., busily employed the whole time stowing the mainsail, repairing an accident to the bowsprit bitts (caused by a heavy sea striking the bowsprit and jib), and bending the trysail. 7.30 A.M.— Set the trysail, double-reefed and backed the foresail. 1.30 P.M., barometer still falling, and no prospect of change. Having to bear up for a vessel, I thought it better to put her on the course again and trust to her sea qualities to carry us through, rather than lie there any longer wasting time, as there was neither rest nor refreshment to be had in such a dreadful gale. About 4 P.M. a long cross swell was observed from the W. which caused me considerable anxiety lest the gale should shift to that quarter. 6 P.M., barometer lowest point 29·075. Wind N.E., very wet and cold. As night came on the wind gradually backed to the northward, unsteady and gusty, causing the trysail to gybe frequently. 11 P.M., barometer 29·225; altered course to S.S.W. The weather was miserably wet until early morning, when it became bright starlight; sea very heavy from N.N.E. with heavy cross swell W.

Sept. 28.—10 A.M., out reefs of trysail, and shifted jib to third. 1 P.M., set the mainsail single reefed, being anxious to make the Land's End before dark. Although the wind was fresh, we had to tackle the boom out on account of the heavy lee swell, which was a source of great annoyance. About 5 P.M. made out the land on weather bow. 6 P.M., barometer 29·725, rising still, but weather looking unsettled. Later, when the full moon rose, it looked so thoroughly dirty that it was certain another gale was at hand. The wind gradually veered to the southward, remained for half an hour, then backed to E.S.E., a nice breeze. Fortunately I was at the helm at midnight, and observed that the tide, running a race on the lee bow, had unexpectedly swept us close up to the Longships rocks, and into the company of a fore-and-aft schooner, that, with all sail set, could hardly stem the current with a 5½-knot breeze. We had made an excellent land-fall, which was a great satisfaction, for there is nothing but confusion and danger to be apprehended from a mistake on that coast.

Sept. 29.—For two hours we made a fine match of it, the

schooner being determined to prevent us from passing her to windward. This she was able to do, as we were troubled by a nasty little short head sea, that did not affect her at all. About 1.30 A.M., in a fine breeze, we passed successfully through her lee, but the wind failing she drew ahead again, put her helm up spitefully, and threatened us with collision. As this would not do, I bore well away, and then shot up in the wind to have another try to windward. This gave the schooner a good lead, much to the skipper's gratification. As the wind freshened and sea rose, she began to plunge too, which made such a sensible difference, that at 2.30, when the gale began in earnest, we came up with her hand over hand, and before the rain hid her from view, had the satisfaction of seeing her far down to leeward, heeling over with her nose well in the sea, shortening canvas. A gale with clear sky is tolerable, but when the whole atmosphere is dense with rain it is very much the reverse. That we had got round the Land's End in clear weather was a piece of good fortune for which there was reason to be thankful. 3 A.M., hove-to, took second and third reefs in mainsail and reefed foresail. Soaked down the neck and up the sleeves, painfully blinded with spray and rain, I cared for nothing but to make the weather shore, which lay 15 miles to windward. Apart from the drenching rain and the fatigue, I never remember a grander turn to windward. The sea was of that fitting length and height that brought out the 'Orion's' good qualities to perfection. Seething through it at her utmost power and speed, there was just room in the trough of the sea to recover herself nicely before rising to the succeeding wave, which she ascended gracefully without any shock, driving a continuous cloud of white spray to leeward. 7.30 A.M., off Portleven, intending to anchor, but bore up for Penzance, considering it too risky to anchor in a gale with a falling barometer. At the distance of a mile Penzance was quite invisible. 8.30 A.M., ran into harbour, and had the pleasure of an immediate wash and much-needed change of clothing, preparatory to a grand 11 o'clock breakfast. 9 P.M., turned in and slept eleven hours without waking, having had only two or three hours' sleep since 5 A.M. on Monday, 112 hours. Distance sailed, 415 nautical miles.

Sept. 30.—Wind N.W., fine; barometer 30. Dried clothes and sails, &c., in harbour. 3 P.M., barometer began to go back. 5 P.M., sailed from Penzance, wind W., cloudy, barometer 29·925. 6.45, passed the Lizard Point, course E. by S. 8 P.M., blowing strong S.W., with rain and rough sea.

Oct. 1.—12.15 A.M., Eddystone Light abeam about 6 miles. Hoping to see it out without reducing canvas, we carried on too long. 1 A.M., in the act of rounding-to in a gale, with torrents of rain and a heavy sea, the main sheet strop carried away, which allowed the boom to run off square, with only the standing part of the sheet upon it. Upon this no strain could be put for fear of parting it and losing the boom altogether, until we contrived to pass the fall round the boom, and swift it out to make three parts. By dint of much labour, standing at times up to the knees in water—the vessel meanwhile plunging and rolling dreadfully in the trough of the sea—we recovered the runaway, and immediately upon her coming to the wind set about repairing the damage. While turning out a locker below to find a piece of new rope for the strop, the perspiration ran down my face. By the time the main sheet was rove again and the sail ready for reefing, it blew so heavily that we took the mainsail off her, and put her before the sea under head sail only. 4 A.M., set the trysail, wind W.S.W. Moon and stars shining brilliantly between broken clouds and fast-flying scud. 5.30 A.M., passed the Start Point, wind N.W., strong and fine, barometer 29·45. After so great and sudden a fall, the barometer should have risen with wind N.W. and clear sky; as its tendency was still downwards, I felt so certain the lull was only temporary, that I luffed up for Torbay, and moored at Torquay at 8.30 A.M. in a miserably wet and uncomfortable condition. During the next twenty-four hours it blew hard from W. and N.W. in long and heavy squalls.

Oct. 3.—6 A.M., sailed from Torquay, wind N.W., light and fine, barometer 29·475. 7 A.M., set the balloon foresail to windward in place of squaresail. 6.45 P.M. passed Bill of Portland close in, wind N.W., fresh. This was the first fine day since leaving Scotland—in fact, from noon until midnight it was the very romance of sailing. Sun, moon, stars, sky, and sea, all were exceedingly beautiful, exciting admiration and frequent remark, especially during the gradual change from daylight to moonlight. 9 P.M., Durlston Head N.E. by E., course E.S.E., barometer 29·675.

Oct. 4.—1 A.M., off St. Catherine's, Isle of Wight, wind N.N.W., light and cloudy. 9 A.M., handed balloon foresail, wind heading. Position uncertain on account of the log being choked with weeds. No soundings 22 fathoms. Set second topsail and large jib. Later, the wind coming more aft, set balloon foresail to windward again. 11 P.M., becalmed off Beachy Head. Moon and stars very bright, clouds low down S. and W. with lightning.

Oct. 5.—3 A.M., Hastings, N.E. by E. Stiff squall from W., with heavy rain and thunder. 10 A.M., passed Dungeness against tide, wind W.S.W., fresh and remarkably fine. 1 P.M., South Foreland. 3, North Foreland. 6, anchored in the Gore Channel (near Margate). 9.30 P.M., got under way again and worked through the Horse and four fathoms Channel. Wind W.S.W., fresh and cloudy.

Oct. 6.—2 A.M., passed the Nore Light. 5.30, Gravesend against tide. 8.15 A.M., anchored off Greenhithe. Distance sailed from Helensburgh, 780 nautical miles = 900 statute miles.

Many persons ask the question, 'Do you call that pleasure?' I say, 'No,' as regards the long sea passages, which I treat quite as a matter of business, and get over as quickly as possible. I have observed that those who answer 'Yes' in books, and profess to have been intensely delighted with long sea passages in small boats, never go again. My cruises, when time permits, are on the wildest and most picturesque coasts of Great Britain and Ireland in pursuit of pleasure and health. As a rule I find both to perfection, and am willing to endure a little hardship to gain them.

The reasons for sailing so often in bad weather are that the

'Orion,' although small, is a vessel that can be relied upon in any emergency, and that it would seriously interfere with the most pleasurable part of the cruise to be wasting time in waiting for fair winds and smooth water.

Her buoyancy and exceeding liveliness in a heavy sea make her very uncomfortable below, and may cause a careless man to be lurched overboard, but where these qualities are wanting there is no safety for anybody on deck, even for the most careful.

I often complain of the carelessness of the men, and observe that those who can swim are absurdly reckless. Shifting jibs in a heavy sea is a work that requires skill and caution. The chain halyards swing heavily with the roll of the vessel and have a great tendency to lift a man off the deck who is careless in handling them.

However well a vessel is battened down, and however well you may be clothed in waterproofs, there is a deal of discomfort from wet and cold in gales. When the sea dashes with violence horizontally against the best made and best protected skylights and scuttles it will penetrate below, and when sprays representing many gallons in quantity strike you frequently and with great force, the water is sure to pass all your guards and find its way down the neck and up the sleeves. Moving about engaged in work, it is impossible to keep dry.

1875—'ORION' (19½ TONS)*

FROM THE THAMES TO WEST COAST OF SCOTLAND

July 7.—6 P.M., sailed from Greenhithe, bound to the west coast of Scotland, and anchored for the night in the Lower Hope; wind E., fresh.

July 8.—6 A.M., under way, and, with a reef in the mainsail, 'turned' (tacked) through Oaze Deeps and Queen's Channel; wind N.E., fresh; weather rainy and rough. 8.30 P.M., anchored off Sandgate; night calm and intensely black, with falling barometer.

July 9.—Early morning calm with dense fog; barometer 29·80. 10 A.M., still very thick, sailed from Sandgate under headsails and mizen; wind W.S.W., fresh, and threatening a gale. 11.15, set mainsail, and, at 12.45, the weather then looking unmistakably bad, anchored in Dungeness Road. During the afternoon it came on to blow so heavily, accompanied by torrents of rain, that several sailing vessels and three screw steamers sought shelter in the Road. Night rough and dark.

July 10.—3 A.M., barometer 29·45. 11 A.M., under way, with two reefs in mainsail, reefed foresail, reefed mizen, and third jib; wind W.N.W., very strong and fine; barometer 29·75. At noon the wind suddenly backed to W.S.W. and increased considerably in violence, but, as the sun shone brilliantly and the barometer continued to rise, it was impossible to regard the change as otherwise than temporary. The result, however, proved to be one of those exceptions that sometimes accompany a highly electrical condition of the atmosphere elsewhere, of which a barometer that is far from the centre of disturbance may, or may not, give warning; for, though the nucleus of the thunderstorm, which twelve hours later wrought great damage in Hampshire, did not actually appear within our horizon, there can be no doubt it was to the storm there gathering this

* [In 1873 'Orion' was lengthened 6 feet by the stern and altered to yawl rig.]

sudden change was due. The deck being swept by a short and hollow sea which occasioned a continuous torrent of foam over the windlass bitts, fore scuttle, and skylights, the 'Orion' was hove-to from 3 to 4 P.M. to enable the men to get their dinner. And later, as there was no deliberate intention on my part of turning down Channel in the teeth of a furious gale, at 8.30 we lowered and furled the mainsail, and hove-to for the night in the vicinity of Hastings, with one headsail aback, foresail and jib alternately; according as we wore her first on one tack and then on the other. With one headsail and the mizen full, it was impossible to prevent the vessel travelling less than three knots through the water without damaging the canvas and sheets by shaking in the wind; so, to keep her within the intended limits, clear of the line of Channel traffic, it was necessary to wear about every hour, which could be done by the helmsman alone, as the sails being hard-sheeted required no attention. It was now, when the sky became overcast and looked very wild, that the barometer, after attaining to 29·80, began to recede. Even had it not been contrary to tradition to 'put back,' owing to sacrifice of mileage and the demoralising effect on the crew, I should not have entertained the idea in this instance, when a slight shift of wind to the southward would have rendered anchorage in Dungeness Road, or in the Downs, less desirable than the present position.

July 11.—4 A.M., up to this hour all had gone well. The men were turned in below, and I was 'wearing ship,' as had already been done many times, when the mizen bumpkin snapped short off under the counter, and, flying inboard, attached to the violently flapping sail, drove me from the helm. The men being aroused by the commotion, help was speedily at hand, but no one could approach until the vessel broached herself to sufficiently to blow the wrecked gear over the lee quarter, when, as we had no means of repairing the damage, the mizen was unbent and sent below. Then both headsails were allowed to draw, and, with a gentle lee helm, we reached to windward as before. The men had not long retired to rest again when the foresheet horse was carried away. The foresail being reefed and saturated with spray, also having several turns of the sheet with the iron traveller attached, was very heavy, and threatened injury to anyone who ventured within its range, until, under pressure of the jib, we fell off sufficiently to enable it to be lowered over the lee bow, when it was gathered in and snugged to leeward. Then, tackles having been got up from below and bent on for sheets, it was hoisted again and the vessel brought to the wind.

As a cutter 38 feet between perpendiculars, the 'Orion' turned fairly well to windward under headsail alone; but, as a yawl, with an increased length of 6 feet 3 inches, and a head sea to contend with, under the third jib and reefed foresail, she would not lay nearer than 6 points. So, having two good seamen with me, it was decided to set the mainsail with three reefs in it, and try the chance of finding some degree of shelter at Beachy Head.

Neither they nor I will ever forget the twelve miles thrash to windward, with headsails sheeted like boards and the mainsheet slightly eased. It was terrible, but it was also exceedingly interesting and very grand.

The clouds—known as 'cirro-cumulus,' peculiar to a highly electrical condition of the atmosphere—were black as ink, but no rain fell; and the sea was lashed into fury, deluging us with such a constant stream of heavy spray, that it was only by presenting the crown of the sou'-wester to the wind and peering under the beam during the descent into the trough of the sea that it was possible to keep the latter on or to look to windward at all. At times the pressure was so severe that the entire lee side, bulwarks and stanchions, together 2 feet high, were buried out of sight, necessitating a lift into the wind, enough to shake the mainsail but not the headsails, until the fury of the exceptional gusts had passed. The men sat aft on the mizen beam, from which, in spite of the support afforded them by the mast and the shrouds, for want of foothold in some of the big 'scends,' one or other was sent floundering on the deck, to the great amusement of the one who held on. While, as helmsman, my seat was so insecure that, but for the rapid turns of the tiller rope, taken at the critical moment, I should have fared by far the worst of the three.

10 A.M., anchored in 5 fathoms of water off Eastbourne with 40 fathoms of chain, the shore marks, which were subjected to careful observation after the heaviest of the squalls (by which warning would be given if the anchor tended to come home) being the Royal Hotel on with the end of Eastbourne pier.

As the anchorage was protected to the extent of only two points by Beachy Head there was, of course, a heavy swell; but our position was so vast an improvement upon the previous few hours' experience that when the fire was lighted, breakfast under way, and the sea-stains, which no amount of precaution will entirely exclude from below, were removed, the greatest cheerfulness prevailed. To the reader it may seem a trivial remark that, after breakfast, the men turned to and made a pudding. But I observed its preparation with intense satisfaction, being well aware it was the last thing they would have thought of doing had they not been contented and happy.

The fact is, the triumphant advance from Hastings under the circumstances related, in the short space of three hours, had imparted such a degree of confidence in the capacity of the 'Orion' to overcome every difficulty likely to present itself during the cruise that any misgivings they might have entertained on this point were entirely dispelled. Whereas, had we run back, either on the previous afternoon or subsequently, they would have been in a state of anxiety whenever the clouds gathered threateningly on the horizon, and have expected a similar pusillanimous retreat.

Early in the night the wind veered to W.N.W., with a bright starlight sky. As it blew too hard to enable the vessel to swing to the tide, the effect of this change was to tail us off the land and into the trough of the swell, the rolling for a few hours being very severe.

July 12.—Wind W.N.W., strong and fine, barometer 30. 11 A.M., sailed from Eastbourne with two reefs out. Noon, all reefs out. Off Brighton the wind fell light, and so continued until the anchor was let go in Cowes Roads at 2.30 A.M. of 13th.

July 17.—Having repaired damages, set sail from Ratsey's moorings at noon, with one reef down; wind N.N.E., strong; weather rainy, and threatening a storm.

July 18.—2.45 A.M., passed Start Point. Later, spent many weary hours becalmed south of the Eddystone, weather gloomy and very hazy. During the greater part of this day destructive thunderstorms were raging in the Midland counties, inflicting a terrible amount of damage upon the farmers and the inhabitants of low-lying towns and villages.

July 19.—Wind fine and clear; views of the coast delightful. From the Manacles Reef to the Lizard worked the shore very close, under a large spread of canvas, wind S.W., a nice breeze. 7.30 P.M., delayed at the Lizard by adverse tide; handed jib-topsail, sea rather rough. Night fine, but cold.

July 20.—Wind W.S.W., fresh; sea short and troublesome. 1.15 A.M., bore up clear of the Runnel Stone and reached N.N.W. 2.15, Longships E.S.E., set log, and steered a N. by E. ½ E. course, to clear Carnsore Point, S.E. coast of Ireland. After breakfast set squaresail. Noon, took a meridian altitude, which agreed with the dead reckoning; but the low and cramped position one is compelled to assume, for personal safety, renders such an operation very difficult on board a small craft in violent motion, when contact can be got only while the vessel is out of the trough of the sea. Midnight, log 100, bright starlight, cold, with remarkably heavy dew. The course being a dead run before a troublesome swell, the boom-end dipped frequently, causing a violent jerk on its emergence, and much chafing of gear. The comparative lightness of the wind in proportion to the swell was the cause of this annoyance.

July 21.—Alternate calms and light airs all day. 10 A.M., handed squaresail and set jib topsail. 7 P.M., passed Carnsore Point. Night fine; wind N.W., light; barometer 30, falling.

July 22.—Clouds travelling from east and from west. 3 A.M., anchored in a calm; Arklow Lightship bearing about five miles

E. As morning advanced, the heavens became densely clouded to the north and west; long peals of thunder were audible in the distance, and occasionally large rain drops fell; but, for the most part, the sun shone brilliantly with scorching heat. We afterwards learnt that a storm of large area and of exceptional severity broke over Dublin and the Northern counties of Ireland at this time, of which we should have come in for a share had not our progress been arrested by the calm. Noon, barometer 29·85, falling; got under way with a light breeze S.E., but so shifty and uncertain that the third jib and small mizen were set as a precaution against surprise. 1 to 5 P.M., rain. 9.35, becalmed off Bray Head; weather cloudy and threatening.

July 23.—5.30 A.M., passed Rockabill, weather wet and cold; barometer 29·65. 10 A.M., set jib-headed topsail and square-sail, which did good service in a light breeze until 3 P.M., when, at the entrance of the Irish North Channel—of which the southern section, or first narrow, is 25 miles long and 18 miles wide—our energy was severely taxed by a sudden and rather angry shift of wind to the northward. Handed squaresail and topsail and housed topmast, as fast as the work could be done, and, after order was restored, made short tacks on the Irish coast until 8 P.M., when we took a reef down, and headed N.E. for the Scotch shore. Night boisterous and very rough.

July 24.—Having made a long board to windward off the Scotch coast, we cleared Corsewall Point (Wigtownshire) at 4.30 A.M., and, with the wind N.N.W., headed N.E. by N. for the Firth of Clyde. 7, passed to leeward of 'Ailsa Craig,' a circular-shaped island inhabited almost exclusively by the feathered tribe—among which the gannet is the most conspicuous—1097 feet high, and so precipitous up to 700 feet, that at a distance it looks like a gigantic corn-rick. 2.30 P.M., after a tedious passage of 7 days 3 hours from Cowes, let go the anchor off the little town of Helensburgh. Distance from Greenhithe, 700 nautical miles; distance actually sailed, 830.

For entertainment on a passage of the above description, where it is all work and no play, we are chiefly dependent upon glimpses of coast scenery, which, with rare exceptions, is never absolutely devoid of interest. However, the amount of relief from monotony to be derived from this source must be dependent upon the state of the weather; voyagers cannot avail themselves of the opportunities afforded them if, in addition to the 'general' charts on which the sailing is mostly conducted, they do not possess, or, if they possess, do not care to study, the 'detail' charts which will enable them to close with the land without the risk of becoming involved in perils of which the former, by reason of the smallness of their scale, cannot sufficiently warn them. Probably there is scarcely a sea-going yacht on which the detail charts could not be produced in cases of emergency; yet but a poor use is made of them if they are reserved only for such occasions.

It is a peculiar feature of Great Britain and Ireland that their eastern coasts are comparatively uninteresting, and that the farther we go westward the more interesting they become. Though the entire east coast of Ireland was worked pretty closely, the passage from the Isle of Wight, with the exception of the Lizard and the Land's End, was unusually devoid of interest, until the estuary of the Clyde was reached, when we had a grand day of clear atmosphere and bright sunshine, which brought the mountains of the Isle of Arran and the extensive ranges of mountains of Argyllshire into sharp prominence against the sky-line. So clear was it that, at a distance of 30 miles, the 'Cobbler at Rest' (described in Black's guide-book) could be easily distinguished, and 'Ailsa Craig,' which was sighted ahead at 4.30 A.M., and, at 2.30 P.M., though dwarfed by 'dip' and diminished by perspective to the size of a little rock, continued to be visible on the horizon astern at the distance of 43 miles.

July 28.—In consequence of a death in the family, I left the 'Orion' with two anchors down, off Helensburgh, and proceeded to London by train. It was then I had the opportunity of observing in the Midland counties the damage wrought by the thunderstorm of the 18th, to which reference has been made.

Aug. 2.—After a hateful night journey, returned on board.

Aug. 3.—Shifted anchorage to Greenock, and purchased an extra spirit compass, which was placed in a position on the companion where it could not possibly be affected by iron-work, and was henceforth used as a standard.

Aug. 4.—3 P.M., sailed for the Kyles of Bute; but, the wind failing, had to anchor in 18 fathoms, two miles short of our destination. Night beautifully fine but cold.

Aug. 5.—Shifted anchorage to the narrows, and took in water from a 'burn' (a small stream) which runs down a long hill through trees and underwood, and trickles bright and clear over the rocks into the sea. In this delightful spot—on the mainland side, and east of the narrows—a vessel of moderate draught, by laying a kedge inshore, can ride comfortably out of the current and the traffic of the Kyles. A fact pleasing to the men is that, in the season, nuts and blackberries abound. (Note.—There may be dwellings now which would render the water undesirable—but there were none then.)

Aug. 7.—Sailed from the Kyles of Bute at 11.30 A.M., wind S.E. round to N.E. in alternate puffs and calms, weather cloudy and threatening. 7 P.M., anchored in Campbeltown, Argyllshire, a very safe and commodious harbour.

Aug. 9.—10.45 A.M., sailed from Campbeltown with a reef down; wind N.E., fresh; barometer 29·875 f. 2 P.M., wind violent off the land, weather very black and threatening; hove-to off the Cantire, and took second and third reefs down, and commenced turning against a rough sea towards the Sound of Islay. 4.30, out two reefs. 7.30, in much rain and strong breeze passed the McArthur Head lighthouse, and at 8.30 anchored in Whitefarland Bay.

Aug. 10.—11.15 A.M., Wind S.S.E., fresh and fine; got under way with one reef down, and passed out of the Sound of Islay to the northward. 2 P.M., fell calm, and afterwards experienced light head winds. Evening set in wet and foggy, our position then being near the entrance of the Firth of Lorn. As the difficulties of navigation would increase farther on, and the 'Isles of the Sea' are steep-to on the north side and free from outlying dangers, at 9 P.M. we furled the mainsail and hove-to for the night under headsails and mizen, and, by tacking and wearing pretty frequently, contrived not to lose sight of them for any length of time until daylight and a partial clearance of the weather enabled us to proceed.

Aug. 11.—Morning wet; later, sunny and hazy, with light baffling winds from various quarters ahead. 8.45 P.M., anchored in Duart Bay, entrance to the South of Mull.

Aug. 12.—Wind W., very light. 7.30 A.M., sailed from Duart Bay. After breakfast set jib-headed topsail and squaresail; weather sunny and hot until 3 P.M., when the wind shifted to N.E., a smart sailing breeze, and it became cloudy and cold.

It may be thought the change to a foul wind was a disadvantage. But in waters with which I have had no previous acquaintance that are more or less bounded by mountains, provided there is not a strong current to stem, the change from a lazy run to an exhilarating turn to windward is almost always welcomed as an improvement (1) because in localities so especially liable to sudden squalls the vessel is more under command; (2) the interesting views ahead, which furnish so much enjoyment to a stranger, are not obstructed by the canvas; (3) that, where navigation is difficult, in a turn to windward more knowledge can be acquired than in a dozen passages when the wind is free. Such sudden changes of temperature as that above referred to are very frequent in the Scotch lochs. As a rule, if the wind sets fairly through a loch, it is mild; if calm and sunny, oppressively hot; but however warm it may have been previously, when the wind shifts and blows off the wet mountains it becomes exceedingly cold.

6.30 P.M., anchored at the head of Loch Linnhe, and after dinner, as we had not left the vessel for four days, landed and took a little exercise on shore.

Aug. 13.—Wind N., light and fine. 10.30 A.M., got under way, tacked through Corran Narrows into Loch Aber, and, the mountains being tolerably free from cloud, had an interesting sail of 7 miles up to the anchorage of Fort William at the foot of 'Ben Nevis,' the intended northern limit of the cruise. Distance from home, 912 nautical miles; distance sailed, 1050.

Aug. 14.—Opened cloudy and wet; but as after breakfast the weather showed signs of clearing, I landed, accompanied by one of my men, hurriedly engaged a guide, and at noon commenced the ascent of the mountain, which, though not particularly enamoured of that kind of toil, was the chief motive of my visit to the north.

Crossing the valley of the Nevis and the little roaring torrent of that name, the first 1500 feet is a steep ascent amidst rocks and verdure and wild flowers innumerable, in which hands as well as feet have to do their part. In my opinion this is by far the most pleasing piece of the performance, the panorama below being made up of the great sea lochs, pine woods, and green fields picturesquely intermingled, and, up to this height, not too distant to challenge the climber's frequent admiration. The next 500 feet is a gradual marshy slope without, as far as I remember, brush or underwood of any description, with a 'tarn' (or small lake) in the middle, or about half way, which the guides say is reputed to be unfathomable, but which, judging by the flat and marshy approaches on all sides, it would astonish me to find required even an ordinary hand line of 20 fathoms to reach bottom in the deepest part. From this point to the top it was an exhausting and mountainous climb of 2400 feet, chiefly on loose granite rubble, a step being taken forward of which, on average, half was lost by slipping backward.* From the summit, 4406 feet above sea level, the view is, of course, very extensive; but, as the surrounding mountains appear insignificant by reason of the observer's superior elevation, I should say, except at the time of sun-rising and sun-setting, not particularly interesting. After a good look round, the guide instructed us to lie down and crawl to the edge of the great precipice, 1700 feet deep, over which he extended his arm and let fall a big stone, which, after an interval of several seconds, produced a loud report, followed by echoes like 'file-firing' that were a long while dying away. While looking down

---

* Presumably the road constructed by the Government to the Observatory has rendered this part of the ascent much easier than at the time of which I am writing.

—the atmosphere then being cloudless and several patches of snow visible—a current of air, probably, only of a slightly higher temperature than the granite surface of the cliff, came in contact with it, and instantly a dense vapour, which formed under our eyes, ascended from below with such rapidity that a party of tourists who arrived only a few minutes later, and while we were watching this curious phenomenon, were enveloped in the cloud and saw nothing at all.

The descent through the cloud was cheerless and bitterly cold until the level of the 'tarn' was reached, when the surrounding objects again came into view and rendered the remainder of the excursion as agreeable as tired legs and an anxious longing for dinner would permit. The journey, which occupied 7 hours, was most successful; but being unaccustomed to a great climb, of which the upper half could only be compared to a steep sea beach, I remarked on my return, 'I would not make the ascent again next day for £50!'

Having an indiarubber boat on board the 'Orion,' and plenty of line, before leaving Fort William I offered to sound the 'tarn' if the guides would carry up the gear. But, as after a night's consideration it was evidently their opinion the 'tradition' should not be assailed, I thought it unadvisable to attempt it without the willing co-operation of those who might have been vexed if my surmise had proved true.

Weather permitting, I cannot imagine a mountain ascent in Scotland more interesting than that of 'Goat Fell' (2800 feet) in the Island of Arran; yet, precisely as it chanced to the tourists who followed me up 'Ben Nevis,' so it happened to me on the occasion of my visit in the 'Sirius' to that island in 1863. Thus, however promising the weather at starting, these instances of vexatious disappointments should warn those who ascend mountains for the sake of the view never to linger unnecessarily on the road.

Aug. 17.—Cleaned copper in harbour, and afterwards sailed over to Camus Bay, an exceedingly pretty anchorage well protected from violent winds and sea.

Aug. 18.—Wind W.S.W., a nice little breeze. 10.30 A.M.,

sailed from Camus Bay and turned down Loch Aber to Loch Leven. 1.30 P.M., arrived at the bar, which, as it was only one hour flood, was gently touched in crossing. Fortunately we carried a fair wind through the first and second narrows, and, later, came to an anchor off the entrance of Glencoe.

Aug. 19.—Landed at Invercoe and walked up the glen. Before dinner landed again, and, ascending a hill of 1700 feet alongside the anchorage, obtained a fine view of the loch and of the whole of Glencoe. On the top it was cold and bare of any vegetation except coarse grass; but up to 1000 feet, though always in a diminishing quantity, it was the most beautiful flowery hill I have ever seen.

Aug. 21.—After eighteen hours of strong wind and heavy rain the sun came out and showed waterfalls on the mountains in all directions. So numerous and formidable were many of these torrents that, when tacking near the shore, the sound of them could be distinctly heard. 11 A.M., got under way, and, against a fresh head wind, turned down to the Narrows, which, being only half a mile long and only a cable wide, with a rapid current, necessitated such smart handling to pass safely through them that it was a great relief when the wide and deep water of Loch Linnhe was regained. 1 P.M., fell flat calm, followed by light baffling airs till 3; then a nice breeze (W. by N.), with which we sailed against tide between Shuna Island and several known and visible rocks into the Lynn of Lorn, a wide channel between the island of Lismore and the mainland, and at 6.30 anchored in Ardentrive Bay, Kerrera Island, opposite the town of Oban. From early morning of the 22nd to 10 A.M. of the 24th it rained in torrents, almost without ceasing, and blew so strong that another anchor had to be let go to avoid tailing the shore.

Aug. 24.—11 A.M., shifted anchorage to Oban, replenished light stores, and then sailed to Port Mor, where we anchored at 1.30 P.M. immediately under the ruins of Dunolly Castle. The day being fine and clear, the visit to this picturesque ruin, situated in beautiful and well-kept grounds, was much enjoyed. 3 P.M., under way again, wind light, and about 4.30

anchored in Dunstaffnage Bay, thoroughly inspected the ruins of this fine old historical castle and its chapel, accompanied by the keeper, and returned on board in time for dinner, intending next morning to pass through 'Connell Sound' into Loch Etive.

Difficult as is the entrance to Loch Leven, the entrance to Loch Etive, except with a wind that enables mid channel to be kept, is much more so; it being almost impossible to pass through the 'Connell Falls' and the Upper Narrows under canvas alone unless circumstances allow that position to be carefully observed.

Loch Etive is an irregular shaped inlet 15 miles long, varying in width from one mile to a quarter of a mile, into which Loch Awe, of nearly the same length and draining about an equal extent of mountainous country, empties itself by the well-known turbulent river (or rapid) of the same name. Consequently, if the entrance to Loch Etive were half a mile wide, and clear of obstruction, the ebb stream could not be otherwise than abnormally violent. But, unfortunately for maritime explorers who depend upon wind for their motive power, the entrance is so contracted at the 'Connell Falls' that the slightest deviation from the central line of the current is almost certain to be attended with disastrous consequences, the channel, which has five fathoms in its deepest part, being but little more than a cable wide from shore to shore with a dangerous hummock of rock in the middle. The effect of the entrance being thus contracted by the headlands and obstructed by the rock is that the streams of flood and ebb cannot pass quickly enough to preserve a level of the waters on both side the falls; so that the only time, according to my idea, when the passage should be attempted by a stranger is during the brief period of change when the ebb current from within is checked by the rising flood outside, which occurs only once in twelve hours. Thus vessels leaving should pass out with the last of the loch ebb, and vessels entering should do so with the first of loch flood, the change taking place about the time of half flood outside, when the rocks of both the Lower and Upper Narrows are visible.

Manifestly, there are two other periods in the 24 hours when the passage can be made, viz., at slack water flood in the loch. But, without a strong fair wind that would ensure the clearance of all dangers in a very brief period of time, there are reasons why, as a stranger, I would rather not attempt it. At low water springs, the difference between the level of the loch and the channel outside is stated in the book to be 4 feet, and, I presume, at high water outside the difference is much the same the other way, the roar of the raging waters at the time the inequality is greatest being audible at a considerable distance.

The above remarks are not intended to influence the judgment of others, but to illustrate the considerations that influenced me as to the most fitting time of entering and leaving, it being my custom, when there is a choice, to navigate difficult channels with which I have had no previous acquaintance on a rising tide, when a mistake may possibly be rectified; and not on a falling one, when every minute of delay tends but to seal the fate of the vessel, and, perhaps, compromise the safety of all on board.

In the middle of dinner it struck me that the circumstances were more favourable at that moment than they might be in the morning; so, as there were still three hours of daylight, and the navigation was of too novel and engrossing a nature to conduce to a healthful night's rest, I decided to get under way forthwith and make the passage without an instant of unnecessary delay. As on the occasion of leaving the rock-bound basin at the head of Loch Scavig, I. of Skye (referred to in the log of the 'Sirius,' 1863), the resolution being taken, I could not have swallowed another mouthful of solid food for any consideration whatever. In every respect the decision was most opportune. With a light fair wind and the first of the loch flood, the Falls and the Upper Narrows were successfully passed, and a safe distance from the latter gained before the wind failed and darkness set in, though neither so completely but that we were able to drag into Stonefield Bay and secure a comfortable anchorage for the night. Afterwards it became so dark that it appeared as if the mountains were aboard and jammed us in on every side, an unromantic illusion quite common in anchorages near lofty land, when it seems to those who are unaccustomed to such positions as if the vessel could not swing the length of her chain without getting ashore.

Aug. 25.—Much rain and strong wind S.W. 11 A.M., got under way with two reefs down, took a turn up and down the widest part of the loch, and at 1 P.M. anchored in Aird's Bay, off Bunawe. During the next two days our amusements consisted of walks on the picturesque banks of the River Awe, an experimental row up the river until overpowered by the current, and a carriage drive through the Brander Pass to Loch Awe. Weather fine.

Aug. 28.—Shifted our berth to Ardchattan Bay. On the passage down anchored temporarily near a bright mountain stream and filled up water.

Aug. 30.—After a night of heavy rain and strong wind the weather became sufficiently fine to enable the passage out to be attempted. The wind was even worse than 'shy,' and would require an occasional tack to be made; but, having seen the dangerous parts on the way up, and decided it was possible to observe the mid-channel rule by shooting them while the vessel was in stays, I did not consider it altogether a disadvantage. And so it proved. For, having passed the Upper Narrows into Connell Sound too early on the ebb, the sound of rushing water at the Falls became audible on deck, and it was deemed necessary to put the yacht round and head up stream until from the masthead I observed the turmoil had considerably abated, when her head was again turned to the outlet. Timing the weather board so as to keep full to the last moment, and with an oar out on each bow to correct any tendency to swerve, the Falls were speedily cleared, the sensation on board being not unlike the 'scend' of a long swell; and, in a commotion like a mill-stream, we were carried half a mile farther without an effort until Dunstaffnage Road was reached, when the canvas again filled to a fresh westerly wind which enabled us to beat out to sea. To the northward there was a heavy bank of clouds from which low growls of thunder were heard at intervals during the afternoon; but, though a great storm was raging over the extreme north of Scotland, the only inconvenience we experienced was a drenching rain, in which Oban was made about 4.30 P.M., and the anchor let go in 13 fathoms north of the pier.

As before stated, the ascent of Ben Nevis was the chief object of the cruise; but visits to Glencoe and to the River Awe were also principal items in the programme arranged in my mind and well studied before leaving Greenhithe; so that a feeling of disappointment would have remained with me to this day if, from whatever cause, there had been a failure in either of these performances. Four or five days having been spent to advantage at each of the above interesting spots, I may say curiosity was satisfied; and in reference to the last of the three that, short of absolute necessity, which can never arise, nothing would induce me to repeat the experience. An old Highlander, repairing a boat at Bunawe, said he 'had never seen a yacht like that up there before,' which, for sufficient reasons, I thought not at all improbable. Though at times, in these enclosed lochs, the sun shone bright and clear, affording grand views of the mountains, for the most part the wet and cold were almost intolerable.

Sept. 1.—9.30 A.M., sailed from Oban with very little wind, and the water so smooth and glassy that the reflections of the high rocky banks of Kerrera Sound, which in many parts are crowned with trees, were extremely beautiful. After a long and troublesome calm, a fresh breeze sprang up from the southward against which we turned down between Sheep and Seil Islands to the entrance of Scarba Sound. Though occasionally hampered by rain and thick weather hiding the rocks and landmarks on which a stranger to this coast has constantly to rely for the confirmation of his position, up to this point the navigation had not been difficult. But commencing at the northern entrance of Scarba Sound—which is formed by the Islands of Lunga and Scarba to the west, and Luing to the east—down to the southern extremity of the Island of Jura, a distance of about 20 miles, the navigation is so complicated by rocks and furious currents that we must go to the Pentland Firth and the Orkneys to find its parallel. Fortunately the weather was clear when this part was reached, and the awkward passage into the Sound, which is marked by a lighthouse on Pladda Island, was successfully accomplished; when, thinking enough had been done for the day, and that it would be pleasant to dine in peace, we brought up in a little roadstead it would not be my pleasure to visit again except under necessity, close to the Island of Lunga, where, with 40 fathoms of chain, we rode throughout the night, just inside a tide race of foaming water into which, if the 'Orion' had swung outwards, a biscuit might have been thrown. After dinner, landed on the island for a stroll, and looked down from a height of 150 feet on the current raging in the narrow channel which divides this island from Scarba; but the scene was neither entertaining at the moment nor a pleasant subject of contemplation for anyone who, if under way, might possibly be forced through it in a calm.

Sept. 2.—Wind S., strong and showery. 10.30 A.M., sailed from Lunga, under reefed mainsail, reefed mizen, whole foresail, and third jib. Tacked down Scarba Sound and met with no difficulty until, having passed between the Islands of Corr-Easar and Risan-tu, and weathered the latter island to its southern extremity, we made our tenth tack (shown by the charts, on which all the tracks of this part of the cruise are sketched) to pass through a channel called the 'Dorus Morr,' which separates the Island of Garraeasar from Craignish Point, and is notorious for the rapidity of its current. Had we been a few minutes earlier, or even able to gain twice our length ahead, the passage would have been cleared; but with the flood gaining strength every minute and pressing us close upon the outermost rocky prominence of Craignish, I accepted the defeat, put the helm down, spun round like a top, and, in little more time than it takes to write it, we were ejected from the channel. Had there been no wind to give steerage way, our inevitable destination would have been the 'Gulf of Corre-brechan,' between Jura and Scarba, with its horrid whirlpool and tumbling sea, towards which the flood stream of the 'Dorus

Morr' directly sets, and against which the 'Book of Sailing Directions' especially warns strangers, advising them not to waste time in fruitless efforts to escape, but to 'batten down' and, if possible, follow the instructions. But, the wind being strong and the 'Orion' well under command, we were enabled to reach closehauled down the lee side of Garraeasar and its nest of islets and rocks, and, after another failure very similar to the above, during which time several miles of water, in a short racy sea, were covered, succeeded in weathering them with not a vessel's length to spare. Thence, except that for a time the weather was inconveniently thick with rain, it was easy sailing to Loch Crinan, where we let go the anchor at 2.30 P.M., took a long and pleasant walk on shore, arranged for a passage through the canal next day, and returned on board to enjoy a good dinner and a quiet night, for which, after recent experiences, we were well prepared.

Sept. 3.—The weather being boisterous, and Mrs. McMullen feeling indisposed for another rough turn round the Mull of Cantire like that which was experienced on the outward passage, we passed through the Crinan Canal, fortunately with no worse damage than a sheet of copper rucked, paint rubbed, and warps chafed, though several times I felt the mast was endangered by the over-nice calculation of those whose duty it is to open the bridges, and by the speed with which the driver of the horse insisted on towing into the locks, of which, I believe, there are thirteen; so that, notwithstanding the prettiness of the country through which this nine-mile canal is cut, I felt heartily glad when Loch Gilphead was reached and the anchor down again in open sea.

By this course we were introduced to the lower part of Loch Fyne, the largest and finest sea loch in Scotland, and, with a feeling of relief that is experienced on regaining homely quarters, had returned to the easy navigation of the Clyde estuary, which, if measured from the southern extremity of Arran to the heads of its numerous lochs, affords a splendid cruising ground for yachtsmen of about 400 square miles amidst beautiful mountain scenery, that, in respect of easy tides, clear deep sea water, and comparative freedom from dangerous obstructions, is unrivalled in the British Islands.

Sept. 4.—10 A.M., sailed from Loch Gilphead under moderate canvas; wind W. and W.S.W., strong and puffy. The course was a close-hauled reach of $9\frac{1}{2}$ miles against tide to East Loch Tarbert, and a broad reach of 15 miles across tide to Garroch Head, which was passed at 1.10 P.M. While crossing Inchmarnoch Water, with a moderate beam sea, the log registered 9 knots for one hour = 10·3 statute miles, or 15 feet per second, which rate we have on various occasions attained before, being compelled to shorten sail, but not, so far as observed, been able to exceed. No doubt higher rates may be obtained by yachts ballasted with lead outside and of a greater proportionate length to beam; but to persevere with this speed when sailing in the trough of a heavy sea in a craft of so low a seaboard as that of a yacht of 20 tons, would risk the loss of everything movable on deck, and be attended with serious danger to the crew. Though sailing a craft than which, in my belief, there is not, on a $41\frac{1}{2}$-feet keel and 44 feet between perpendiculars, a more powerful sea boat in existence, I have frequently, when reaching 7 and 8 knots in the trough of the sea, found it necessary to leave the course for a minute or two, and either meet a breaking sea almost end on, or bear away and bring the sea almost aft—according to which was best calculated to meet the circumstance of the moment. The latter alternative is quickest in operation, but the advisability of its adoption, besides the question of sea-room, depends upon whether the vessel is full-bodied, or has a long snaky run and a greatly extended counter; also, whether the threatening 'curler' is before or abaft the beam—as, with the exception of the main swell, it is an error to suppose the sea runs in strictly parallel lines; and lastly, it depends on the amount of canvas carried and the manner the sails are trimmed. When 'running' hard in bad weather at sea, my custom is to carry moderate head sail, well sheeted, so as to be able to come to wind, either to avoid an obstruction or to 'heave to,' at the shortest possible notice. That, while carrying on day and night in all weathers, I never got into collision, had a man overboard, or lost a bow-sprit, may not unreasonably be attributed to this precaution.

Resuming after this digression—4.20 P.M., in a gradually failing wind, anchored off Helensburgh and sent ashore for letters and needful supplies, and then proceeded to the pretty little bay of 'Roseneath,' a sylvan and retired anchorage less than two miles distant, having a little church of its own, and, among other objects of interest, the most gigantic fir trees in the kingdom. Separated by a lofty hill from the smoke and the noisy din of the Clyde industries, it is difficult to realise that they are not a great many miles away.

Sept. 6.—3.30 P.M., sailed from Roseneath with a pleasant breeze S.S.W., and, at 6.30, anchored within the entrance of Loch Goil, where a green sward extends from the steep and rocky foot of 'Cheese Hill' (2500 feet) to the water's edge. Starting from the greensward, the ascent of a few hundred feet up a rocky little watercourse, whose direction is marked by a wide fringe of hazels, briars, ferns, and wild flowers, varied by the mountain ash in full berry, together with the view of the dark mountains around, and the silvery sea loch, on which our trim little barque was quietly riding, below, was most delightful. I know of no scramble that gave more pleasure than this well-remembered climb, which probably few, except the natives, would ever think of visiting.

During our stay, which extended to the 9th, we rowed to the interesting ruins of Carrick Castle, and to regain the yacht, with a hard wind in our teeth, had to skirt the opposite side of the loch, where the shore line is so precipitous as to be almost inaccessible. Also took the opportunity of an exceptionally fine day to re-varnish the bulwarks, &c., on deck, and repaint the vessel outside. One evening, for curiosity, the signal gun was fired, and echoes awakened that seemed as if they would never entirely die away. Though, instead of 2 feet, a distance of 200 yards from the gun would have been a great improvement, the effect was very grand. About the same time, when the heavens were otherwise densely clouded, the marvellous effect produced by oblique rays of sunshine upon a mountain peak saturated with moisture was observed for a few seconds, which, though often faithfully represented on canvas, is difficult of belief unless actually witnessed.

Sept. 9.—10.30 A.M., sailed from Loch Goil; wind W., fresh, and very fine. Landed on west shore of Loch Long and procured some fine specimens of ferns. Afterwards sailed to the Kyles of Bute, and, from my favourite 'burn' took water aboard—about 35 gallons each trip—until our sea stock was completed.

Sept. 10.—3 P.M., under way; weather very fine. 7, got hopelessly becalmed and had to anchor in deep water outside of Gourock, in such close proximity to the main road and the omnibus traffic that the clatter of hoofs on the kerb-stones was like that of an 'unreformed' London street. 11th, Proceeded to Roseneath. 13th, Convoyed Mrs. McMullen to the train at Glasgow, *en route* for Brighton, and, on my return, completed our stores for the voyage home.

Sept. 14.—10 A.M., sailed from Helensburgh, under mainsail and foresail, second jib, second topsail, and small mizen; wind variable between S. and E., barometer 30·40; weather fine. 2 P.M., cleared the Cumbrae Islands by the inner passage. After alternate puffs and calms, the wind came steadily from the eastward until 4, when, in force and direction, it again became undecided and occasioned much disappointment. 6.25, sunset very beautiful, streaks of yellow, green, and blue predominating; weather warm and hazy. Night fine and moonlight, but looking like change; barometer 30·35 f.

Sept. 15.—2 A.M., becalmed near the Laggan Beacon in the North Channel, tide adverse, and drifting us nearer to the rocks than was desirable. 5.30, wind S.E. by E., fresh; course S. by W. from Port Patrick. Set log. 7.15, Mull of Galloway E.S.E.; wind S.E., strong, sea short. 12.15 P.M., passed the Calf of Man, the average rate for 6¾ hours being a little over 7 knots. Reset log, and altered course to S.W. ½ S., when, having emerged from the shelter of the Isle of Man, the sea became rough, and the rate, at times, improved to 9. Night set in hazy and cloudy. 9.45 P.M., when sailing under great pressure, the sister-hooks of the upper main halyard block gave way and let the throat down with a run, fortunately without bursting the parral line. Having a spare block of the same character below, the damage was repaired in about half an hour—the topsail having been clewed up and the vessel kept on her course the while. Midnight, handed topsail; barometer 30·30 f.

Sept. 16.—12.45 A.M., Arklow North Light-vessel bearing N.W. about 8 miles, and log 91 from Calf of Man, altered course to S.W. by S. ½ S., weather fine and clear. 7 A.M., took a reef in mainsail and housed topmast. 10.45, Small's Lighthouse E.S.E. 6 miles, log 168; showing a loss of 23 miles on the direct steamer's course of 145—due to the intentional deviation towards the coast of Ireland, sheering on the sea, and, latterly, to long contention with an adverse tide. (My reason for not steering a more weatherly course was to avoid the risk of being lurched in a calm and thick weather in the vicinity of the South Stack and the Smalls, where tides run hard and the coast is encumbered with outlying rocks. Never having been bound to a Welsh harbour, it is a custom I have always observed when entering or leaving the Irish Sea.) 3 P.M., wind to S.E., with rain; shifted jib to third, expecting bad weather. 4, rain ceased and wind backed to E.S.E., light. 11 P.M., log 233, barometer 30 f., night fine.

Sept. 17.—At sunrise, sighted Cape Cornwall properly open of the course. 8.30 A.M., passed the Longships, distance about 2 miles, wind E.S.E., strong and squally, sea high. Breakfasted under difficulties. 10, tacked round the Wolf Rock, and had an opportunity, that seldom happens by chance, of closely observing the noble proportions of its lighthouse. On the western side it is green with vegetation to the height of 40 or 50 feet above the sea, showing the excessive degree of violence it has to encounter from that quarter. With an adverse tide, progress up Channel was so slow that the reef was shaken out of the mainsail, second jib substituted for third, and the topmast got on end. 5.30 P.M., passed the Lizard, having made a board to windward before entering the Race. 8, set second topsail, and regretted it immediately. 10, hove-to off the Manacles, about 5 miles south of Falmouth, with foresail down, jib aback, and mainsail trussed, during a severe thunderstorm and strong wind from the southward; the darkness between the brilliant flashes of lightning being so intense, and the rain so heavy and blinding, that it appeared impossible to see beyond the length of the vessel around. Midnight, handed topsail, set foresail, and resumed the course.

Sept. 18.—Though thunderstorms continued at intervals till daylight, they were of so moderate a character compared with the first that I was able to keep watch alone. 4 A.M., log 19 from Manacles, wind variable between E.S.E. and E., clouds flying fast from the southward. 9.45, tacked at Pencarra Head and stood off S.S.E. 1 P.M., set second topsail, sea short and troublesome. 3.15, tacked to N.E. by E., and 7.30, to S.S.E., Plymouth Breakwater Light bearing N.N.W. 4 miles. Handed topsail; night dark and rainy, barometer 29·95. Midnight, becalmed about 5 miles S.W. by S. of Start Point, followed by light airs from S. and W., with heavy rain.

However favoured the first 400 miles, our progress from the Wolf, on account of the variable and unsatisfactory nature of the weather, was tedious in the extreme. Since if, as in racing, our canvas had been accommodated to the strength of the wind, we should have been occupied shifting wet sails almost every hour of the day and night, which, with so limited a crew, if practicable, would not have been reasonable.

The reason why 'midnight' is more frequently referred to than any other time is not only that, even with the smallest crew, the change of watch is absolutely regular at that period— there being no duties below to interfere with it—but that, being also the period of greatest darkness, it is the most anxious hour for observations of the weather and the vessel's position of the twenty-four. The details may seem tedious to minds not nautically imbued; but without them those who have knowledge of the geography of our coast and a desire to do so could not in fancy accompany us on a cruise of this nature, which certainly has its drawbacks to be encountered as well as pleasures to be enjoyed when undertaken, as in my case, with but limited time.

Sept. 19.—4 A.M., storm clouds and rain; wind, what little there was, all round the compass. 7, fresh breeze S.S.E. 9, very light, S., with much rain. 10.30, rain ceased, set second topsail. 3 P.M., set jib topsail and made good way. 5.30, wind light and aft; handed jib topsail, wet and heavy with dew, though the sun was shining. 7.30, Portland Bill N.N.E. Night fine and moonlight, with remarkably heavy dew; lightning N. and S. Midnight, becalmed.

THE 'ORION,' 1877

THOSE of my readers who are not sailors may be looking for a further description of the 'Orion.' I will endeavour to give this roughly, so as to avoid confusing them with too many figures.

She was built for me by Mr. Inman, of Lymington, in 1865, and rigged as a cutter; was lengthened 6 feet by the stern in 1873, and rigged as a yawl. The alteration made her 19½ tons builders' measurement. The keel is of elm; frame, oak; skin, teak; fittings, above and below, mahogany; keelson, iron; fastenings, copper and Muntz's metal. Ballast, including weight of keelson, 11½ tons. Carries 160 gallons of water, in two tanks; ½ a ton of coals, or its equivalent in coke, in two bunkers; and general stores sufficient for three months, stowed under the forecastle floor and in lockers out of sight; three anchors, together 2½ cwt.; two chains, 11½ cwt.; warps, &c. Her length over all is 48 feet, breadth 10 feet 2 inches, and, when on dry land, stands 10½ feet high from the ground to the rail. Afloat she draws 7 feet aft, and 5 feet 6 inches forward.

The mast is a red spar 40½ feet long and 9½ inches diameter, divided thus—housing 6½, deck to hounds 27½, masthead 6½ feet.

The topmast is 27½ feet; gaff 22 feet; boom 29 feet, with a diameter of 7 inches; bowsprit 25 feet, with a diameter of 7½ inches—8½ feet inboard and 16½ out.

The main truck is 55 feet from the deck, and the mizen truck 25 feet.

The weights are: mast and topmast 8½ cwt., and the wire rigging to support them 2½ cwt.; mizenmast rigging and spars 2 cwt.; bowsprit 3 cwt.; mainboom 2¾ cwt.; gaff and mainsail 2½ cwt.; the third jib, carried on this passage home, a few pounds over ½ cwt.; foresail a little under ½ cwt.; storm mizen over ¼ cwt.; running rigging, including chain jib halyards, 3 cwt., of which half would come on deck, sailing.

Adding all together—ballast, chains, sails, water, fuel, and stores, there are 15 tons below; and masts, bowsprit, spars, rigging, mainsail, boat, &c., about 1 ton 7 cwt. above deck.

These weights, if not absolutely correct, are nearly so. The greater part I have weighed, including the ballast, mainboom, topmast, and many other spars. Anchors are marked, and chains calculated from a table. The canvas carried when coming home weighed over 3 cwt.

With a view to economy, my custom is to keep everything in the best order possible. The vessel is covered with a canvas awning during the winter, to protect the varnished mahogany from the weather. Including prime cost, the expense of the awning is about £3 per annum; otherwise, the annual expense of scraping and dressing—I may also add, *ruining* the oak and mahogany—would be about £10. The masts must be scraped, but all other spars are rubbed down with sharp sand and canvas, and finished with powdered pumice-stone and canvas. The bolts of canvas, of which the sails are made, are 'Burnettized' before making up. Although this process does not entirely preserve them from mildew in extreme cases of neglect, it does so to a very considerable extent, and is undoubtedly a great saving. Excepting the large foresail, squaresail, and jib topsail, the sails are all of double canvas, Nos. 2, 3, 4, and 6. The advantages are—that they hold more wind, stand any amount of sheeting and tackling, without losing their original shape, and are altogether more economical. My wire rigging is twelve years old. The shrouds are parcelled, canvassed and blacked. All this, if expensive at first, is real economy.

In the days when Vauxhall and Pimlico were in the country there used to be a sailing club at Battersea, whither our yachtsmen were wont to resort as they do to Gravesend. The latter town, at that time, was reached by stage coach or by the old sailing hoy. I seem to have a faint recollection of a fleet of small yachts assembled near Battersea Bridge, either before or after a race, about the year 1835.

Before I had anything to do with boats, which was not until 1850, my father used occasionally to talk of his yachting ex-

periences in a 10-ton boat. The favourite yarn, without intending anything disrespectful to the adventurers of the day,
was about a cruise from Battersea to Gravesend, in which they
ran great risks from sky and sea. He told us how that the man
in charge—in modern language, the captain—shouted down
to the little cabin, 'On deck, gentlemen! On deck! Down all
sail! There's a squall coming!' If he had lived longer I should
have been greatly interested in extracting further particulars
about the amateurs of the time; that is if he had been willing
to give them, which is not quite certain, considering that the
yarn could only have been wanted for the purpose of institu-
ting a comparison unfavourable to himself and his con-
temporaries. Some old Cornish fishermen will not allow that
there is any improvement in boats, or in the art of handling
them. They say 'it never blows now as it did in their younger
days.' I once had with me an old North Sea fisherman who
declared that lightships and buoys were no improvement, and
backed his argument with the assertion that 'wrecks were
much more numerous now than in his younger days—he
didn't care about increased traffic.'

My father would not believe in the safety of a model yacht
of less than 3 tons; but shortly before his death, after watching
me one day from the beach at Dover, he allowed me to give
him a sail in the 'Leo.' He was not very comfortable, however,
and did not think her such a fine ship as I did! Had he lived
two years longer and received a letter from the 'Leo' at
Penzance, stating that I had been to the Land's End, and was
about to start on my return to Greenwich, it seems that,
judged by the light of former experience, words would have
failed to express his astonishment.

In my turn I was cut out by the 'Metallic Lifeboat Company
of New York,' who, a few years later, found men willing, in
advertising their patent, to risk starvation by crossing the
Atlantic, and exhibiting the 'Red, White, and Blue' at the
Crystal Palace.

I have never sailed in one of these lifeboats, which, according
to all accounts, possess the rare advantage of being able to

turn over in a heavy sea without foundering, and, for a change, give the crew a ride on the bottom, until by accident or design they come right side up again, and allow the men to get inside and have something to eat.

My 'Leo' was a heavily ballasted pretty little model yacht of 4 feet draught, that would have gone down like a stone if overpowered in a squall, or mismanaged in a heavy sea, nor would the advantage of getting inside again have entered into the calculation if one had been only lucky enough to have succeeded in getting out.

My opinion has often been asked about these lifeboats crossing the Atlantic. The one referred to above had an advertisement of the builders on the bow, and was, one may reasonably suppose, either lent or given to the adventurers to make what they could out of it—by exhibition. After her return from the Paris Exhibition she lay astern of the 'Orion' in Greenhithe Creek, until she was taken back to America on a ship's deck. I have always understood that, financially, she was a failure, chiefly owing to her being exhibited as a full rigged ship, with royals and studdingsails set, which was manifestly too preposterous even for the credulity of the shallowest landlubber. Others have crossed in emulation of that feat, but all apparently with a view to make dollars by exhibition, which is so repugnant to British taste that they have left our shores no better freighted than they came. That the boat will not sink is great ground of confidence; but, after the first success, they who adventure on a similar voyage expose themselves to hardships, and the chance of terrible privations, for no useful purpose. I intend no disparagement to American enterprise when I state my belief that thousands from our side would be willing to perform the same feat provided they had a better object in view than any we have as yet seen.

There have been some plucky exhibitions of single-handed sailing by gentlemen whose inexperience as seamen has led them into very erroneous estimates on many points connected with the sea. One great objection to published statements, founded on such estimates, is that, if read seriously by our rising generation of amateur sailors, they would be discouraged from making any attempt at sea whatever. Everyone must be struck with the inconsistency of gentlemen relating dangers enough, if true, to keep everybody else away, and yet declaring over and over again that 'they enjoyed it immensely.' I have never complained of a heavy sea. On the other hand, I have never praised it for anything but its grandeur, which, in a measure, it was compulsory to behold, whether agreeable or otherwise.

No doubt there is a natural disposition in men, writing their own experience of hardships, to indulge in a degree of licence they are unwilling to own, and of which in many instances they are quite unaware. Whether or not this liberty is taken by myself or others, should, where personal experience is wanting, be judged by every reader according to the rules of common sense.

I have sometimes, in conversation, spoken of waves passing into the 'majestic stage'—a term I clearly understand, and feel, when viewing it, although difficult of explanation. In the ocean, or in the Channel, during westerly gales of many days' duration, the wind will perhaps back and veer several times a few points between S.W. and N.W., accompanied by corresponding movements of the barometer. The result will be a long and high westerly swell, very grand in appearance, with, on the top of it, a short sea from the quarter in which the wind is then blowing. I object to the term 'ground swell,' unless caused by an obstruction to the current at the sea bottom sending waves to the surface, as at Portland, the Lizard, and the Land's End, &c. In deep water it is this comparatively short sea on the top of the main swell that breaks, and floods a vessel's deck, sometimes doing considerable damage, because, breaking at a great elevation, it acquires increased momentum from the height of its fall, and because a large ship, being already in regular motion from the main swell, is not prepared to rise a second or third time to the 'cross sea' on the top of it. A small vessel does that, and the motion, when close-hauled or reaching, is horrible. The short sea goes down soon after the

142

wind has fallen, but the swell remains for several days, although gradually subsiding.

There is a great deal of misapprehension about the speed of small yachts. Few of them carry patent logs, hence they always sail faster than those who do. Under double-reefed mainsail, with the peak eased down, and the squaresail, I have registered 19 knots in two hours—equal to 11 statute miles per hour—running before a heavy sea in the Channel, and then have had to hand the squaresail in anticipation of a squall that did not fail to keep its promise.

A vessel only 44½ feet long must have a powerful midship section to run at that speed with safety, and must carry more canvas than it would be possible to come to the wind with. The disposition to sheer violently on the top of a high sea is very marked, and more difficult to counteract with the helm than when sailing easy; at that speed she seems to hang on the crest of a breaking sea, instead of allowing it to pass her quickly; at that moment you feel the pressure taken off the tiller, and she is whirled along until the break of the sea is past the rudder. The consequences of an accidental gybe and a broach-to would be so serious that I am careful not to risk the tiller in the hands of a man who is not well acquainted with the peculiarities of the vessel. All vessels have peculiarities that are learnt only by practice, so that a man who understands them knows beforehand what they will do. His judgment is formed by the run of the sea—whether it tends to one quarter more than the other—or whether it will break before coming up with the vessel. If a heavy sea always ran in nice parallel lines it would be very little trouble, but it does not, and every wave that looks threatening must be watched, and the helm altered to bring it dead aft. I should not like to run a small racing yacht before such a sea as this excepting under easy canvas. One cannot help feeling at the time what a dangerous sail a flying squaresail—laced to the yard—is to broach to with when blowing hard—or to be caught aback with by a sudden shift of wind in a squall. A vessel running out from Cherbourg under such a sail at 1 A.M., 24th July, would have experienced this. The shift of wind was instantaneous from S. to N.W.—a greater change than I have ever observed before. From W. to N.W., and from W.N.W. to N., in a squall, is so common in westerly gales, that when clouds bank up heavily in a northerly quarter it should be expected.

The highest rate I have logged 'reaching' is 9 knots, with the jib-headed topsail set; but rates quite as high have been attained under three-reefed mainsail, when not exposed to a heavy sea. Between the Needles Point and St. Catherine's, blowing hard from S.W., with a heavy sea, I have logged 8 knots under double-reefed mainsail, reefed foresail, third jib, and storm mizen—notwithstanding we were much delayed by luffing, or bearing away, according to circumstances, for dangerous seas. For sea forward of the beam I always luff—abaft the beam, always bear away, when not too close to land.

It is a great pace to travel in a heavy sea, with a vessel so low in the water as a good yacht of 20 tons must be. Necessarily battened down when 'reaching' in the trough of a high sea, the motion of a 20-ton vessel—while attending to the charts, or trying to get some food, in the close atmosphere below—is dreadful. I have known a man who had been at sea 50 years come on deck with a piece of biscuit in his hand, declaring he would have been sick if he had stayed below another minute. I myself have several times had to forego meals for the same reason. But this quick motion, which is characteristic of powerful small vessels, is their safety; for it is manifest that unless they quickly recover their 'scend,' and rise high over the sea, they must take a large quantity of water on board.

Some large ships are said to sail fast on a wind in moderate weather, but I have never met with one yet that had improved her position upon us after several hours' parting. Blowing hard enough for *us* to require three reefs down, they are good ships if they can do better than 'hold their own.' We never make less than three knots dead to windward, often more, which depends not so much on the height of the sea as on its character. Where no protection can be got from the land, in heavy weather it is safer and more comfortable to keep the deepest water. In fine weather we practically sail within 4½ points of the wind; blowing hard, with a heavy sea, my custom is to ease the mainsheet a little and sail 5 points.

Three and four knots per hour dead to windward sounds small; but I am writing of actual practice in heavy weather, when, with the exception of larger yachts, nothing seems able to come near us; 70 to 80 miles a day against a strong wind is not pleasant sailing, but it is worth doing if you want to make progress. To make this good—the rate through the water being 6 and 7 knots—requires careful steering. Those who have never seen a heavy sea, talk and think lightly of it, but it sometimes happens that the finest 'fore and afters' are compelled to heave-to, for fear of drowning the hands.

The word 'gale' amongst yachtsmen is quite a relative term. It would be a gale for a 10-ton modern racing yacht, when a wholesome cruiser of that tonnage would not think much of it. I think it may be considered a yachtsman's gale at sea when two or three reefs are an absolute necessity, and when nothing but smart fore and aft vessels attempt to turn to windward.

I was once requested to remark upon the anchorages in the Channel. The reason why so few are recommended in the Sailing Directions is because the instructions are for ships and coasters—vessels that are not able to beat off shore, blowing hard. Every yacht going to sea should be provided with the general chart for long distances, and with all the detail charts of half-inch scale and upwards for working along shore. It is advisable to read all that the books have to say against an anchorage, and then disregard the warnings if you think proper. For instance, the anchorage off Selsea village, called the Park, is not recommended, but it is an excellent road for yachts, and a great favourite of mine with the wind between S.W. and North. Having proper charts, it is easy to judge— by the outline of the coast, the soundings, and the nature of the bottom—whether it is advisable to anchor or not. Coasting vessels are rarely provided with this information, but yachts should never be without it.

Yachts anchoring for the night, or for longer, off such places as Freshwater, in the Isle of Wight, Beare Road, Lizard Point, Etretat, &c., should—unless the weather be very fine, with a good barometer—take a reef or two in the mainsail, have a moderate-sized jib on the bowsprit, always have a buoy ready to mark the chain in case of having to slip, and never delay a moment longer than necessary when the wind comes fresh off the sea. The distance from low water mark should not be less than a third of a mile; and if a thunder storm were brewing in any quarter of the compass it would be according to my taste to 'clear out quickly.'

THE SAIL FROM GREENHITHE TO CHERBOURG

Being unwell, and feeling the necessity for a sea change, I left Greenhithe, Kent, on July 13, 1877, in the 'Orion,' with ten days' provision on board, intending to sail down the north coast of France as far as Cherbourg, also to anchor occasionally on the coast before reaching there, if the scenery tempted me to effect a landing, and if weather permitted. Such places as Yport and Etretat, for instance, are far more attractive to me than the large and fashionable towns. Their beautiful cliffs, retired aspect, and houses covered with flowering creepers, please me excessively.

Nothing, in my opinion, is more invigorating and delightful, or better calculated to make one forgetful of little ills, than landing at a picturesque spot for a few hours' scramble on cliffs and rocks, or taking a cruise in the boat—under sail or otherwise—amongst the caverns and peculiarities of a pretty coast, returning to dine and sleep on the open sea, free to stay or free to leave, without harbour smells and restrictions, or annoyances of any sort.

The worst to be apprehended in a general way, with good seamen on board, is having to leave in haste during the night, with the loss of an anchor and a few fathoms of chain, which depends upon whether you are able to leave in good time, before the sea becomes too heavy to heave up the anchor. In this case the chain is unshackled and buoyed ready for slipping, the sails are set, and when she sheers the right way the chain is slipped.

Such was to have been the first part of the cruise from which I expected much benefit. After a stay at Cherbourg we were to sail to Dartmouth, and take Mrs. McMullen on board for a month's pleasure among the Devonshire harbours; then, according to custom, I should return home with the men alone —bearing always in mind that I came out for sea air and plenty of work, and should make best use of the opportunity.

My crew consisted of two men from a neighbouring town, whose surnames I purposely omit, for the sake of their families, and because I have no desire to be personally vindictive. They are representatives of a class to be found not only at sea— where they are very dangerous as look-out men—but in every other occupation on shore.

Henry, who had been to many parts of the world, and had sailed in other yachts before, was with me last year as mate and seaman, and applied for the berth again. He knew my hard sailing habits, having thrashed up Channel with two reefs down, against an E.S.E. wind, between 1st and 3rd October, making the passage from the Isle of Wight to Greenhithe in 44¼ hours. I mention the time—and also the fact that there was no fire lighted for 36 hours—to show that it could not have been otherwise than extremely violent. When there was any talk of a rough sea, he made such frequent and boastful reference to this turn to windward, that one would have supposed he liked it far better than I did, and that he was prepared to encounter any quantity of it.

George, cook and seaman, was recommended to me by Henry, in whom I had great confidence. Being a stranger, I warned him of the hard sailing, spoke of being days under way without going into port, and mentioned the heat of the forecastle when there was much firing. I habitually take this precaution before providing the clothes—in order to save myself the annoyance of a man 'throwing up' before the cruise is at an end. He professed himself thoroughly satisfied with these

147

arrangements, and resolved to go the cruise. Both men had, I believe, respectable homes, and both sent money there—instead of to the public-house. During the preliminary preparations I heard neither bad language nor quarrelling; all was so pleasant under the influence of ten hours' sleep, home alternate nights, unlimited tobacco smoke, no foul winds, and no salt water, that at home I expressed regret that we were not bound for Scotland—a trip which necessitates much continuous sailing, day and night. They talked freely of the cruise to Cherbourg—whither they had never been before—as if it were an anticipated pleasure.

July 13.—Under these hopeful circumstances we sailed from Greenhithe at 4 P.M., with a fresh wind from S.W., and reached down to Birchington, near Margate, anchoring in the Gore Channel at 9.30 P.M. In Gravesend Reach a conversation ensued as to the merits of a sea life, both men agreeing that it was hateful, and that they had rather be farmers, or almost anything than sailors. I remarked that if they had been brought up to any other employment they would probably have been quite as dissatisfied, and have thought a sea life the very thing to suit them. I could not help thinking that the expression of these sentiments would have been better timed a month earlier.

July 14.—Blowing strong off the land—consequently right through the Downs. Remained at anchor, doing odd jobs; and walked to Birchington in the afternoon to get the burner of the riding-light repaired. As we were to be away from the English coast for two or three weeks, the men asked me to advance them £2 each to send to their wives. My confidence and respect for them were such that I assented with pleasure, although they were in advance already; but the effect of putting myself pecuniarily under their lee was most mischievous, and showed itself in a few hours. They began to reckon their value to me according to the kindness I showed them, taxing my forbearance, and putting the price higher every day. If I dismissed them, or if they discharged themselves, they would not only plunge me into great vexation, but be absolute gainers. I never was in such a position before, and, being unwell, felt less disposed to contend with it. Intentionally avoiding violent and irritating language, I several times brought them to a sense of duty, and we got on charmingly until the wind or the sea gave new offence.

July 15.—4 A.M., barometer at lowest; 10 A.M., wind S.W., very strong and fine, barometer rising fast. In the expectation that the wind would fly into N.W., I thought it prudent to heave up and make for the Downs. 11.30 A.M., got under way, with two reefs down, and had rather a heavy beat against wind and tide to the Little Downs, anchoring there at 7.30 P.M. The men, at my suggestion, had their dinner before rounding the North Foreland, so that inwardly at least they were well prepared for a smart sail, which did me so much good that I enjoyed my dinner more than for several previous weeks.

July 16.—The men were on the grumble from turning to windward the previous day. When called at 5.30 A.M. they grumbled furiously that they were kept sailing all day and had to turn out early, getting no proper rest, although they had to acknowledge having turned in at 10 P.M., making 7½ hours in bed. Turning out myself at five, and observing that the weather looked bad, I had called them at that hour with the intention of getting the anchor at slack water, as I felt certain there would be a trouble about it when the tide came to windward. To satisfy their childish complaint, and being in doubt whether they would work properly, I allowed them to lie an hour longer, and then had breakfast before loosing the canvas.

8.30 A.M.—Commenced to heave in, and soon experienced a difficulty: sheering violently on the weather tide, the chain worked into a joint of the iron keel-band, almost tearing it off to the forefoot, and there got jammed. Blowing hard astern, with a rough sea, the situation was most awkward. After many fruitless attempts to clear it, it struck me that we might rouse it out with a tackle leading aft to the channel, paying out suddenly from the hawsepipe; this proving successful, we got away at 10.30, and made for Dover to have the damage repaired—turning to windward again with two reefs down. Off the South Foreland we escaped several heavy seas by luffing into them, but at last met one that would not be denied; the cabin skylight being unfastened, it was a damper below as well as on deck. 2.30 P.M., arrived at Dover, and went straight into the Granville Dock.

July 18 *and* 19.—By arrangement with the harbour-master and the shipwrights went on the hard (the slip being engaged), and heeled over to have the keel-band repaired, taking advantage of the grounding to clean the copper. Then there was more grumbling on the part of George, who wanted to do as little as possible.

Each evening we returned into the floating basin, and both men went ashore for two or three hours.

July 20.—Called the men at 6 A.M. Had to shift berth by order of harbour-master, then to get ready for leaving the dock at 7.30. When I told George to help get the jib out, he said he wanted to light the fire and clean out the forecastle. Being peremptorily ordered to come, he made an exhibition of himself, and showed he was master of other than polite language. I called him aft, and asked him point blank if he would elect to go ashore, or if he would remain and promise to conduct himself better. Freely and instantly promising as desired, I accepted his substitute for an apology, in the hope that it would not occur again, as I was anxious to get on to the French coast without further delay. At 8.30 cleared the harbour with the wind about W.N.W., puffy but fine. 1 P.M. off Dungeness— under whole mainsail, foresail, second jib, and second mizen— the wind backed to west, and came on to blow rather fresh, knocking up a little short sea that made the vessel a trifle uncomfortable at the men's dinner-time, and sent some smart little sprays over; whereupon great and loud grumbling began again. Henry came aft and took a seat on the mizen beam, saying—'it was very hard they could not get their dinner in peace, but must have it spoilt with sea water.' The chain-pipe —for which a proper cover is provided—being uncovered, through their own negligence, a little water ran down on the table, as it was certain to do; also the fore scuttle was left wide open. Absurdly neglecting to take any steps to protect themselves, they came aft to complain that no other yacht went thrashing to windward like that, and, if they had much of it, they should leave at Dartmouth.

I was so angry at this crowning absurdity and childish nonsense, that, after thinking it over for a quarter of an hour, I put about and stood up Channel, undecided, until the last moment, whether to run back home and lay up at once, or call at Dover for fresh hands, or anchor in Dungeness Road for the night and think it over. Deciding upon the latter course as the most reasonable, I brought up there at 3.30, weather extremely fine, but rather fresh. While running back I told them that 22 years ago I had to put back off Hastings, in the 'Leo' of less than 3 tons, but that I had not done so since under any circumstances whatever. Disgusted with their trumpery and unseamanlike complaints, I had done so *now*, because it was useless to proceed with men who objected to turning to windward, as it was not likely we should be able to command fair winds and smooth water wherever we went. Running back with a whole mainsail in fine sunny weather was so contemptible that it was enough to make one sick with shame and vexation. Then both wanted to disclaim having anything to do with the running back.

Steering hard with the mainsheet 'pinned in' on purpose to delay arrival at Dungeness Point—which was to be *Decision Point* with me, either for home or the anchorage—the interesting discussion was cut short by a spray over the weather quarter which soused us all, and made *me* laugh, the others going forward in high dudgeon, as if they had been ladies dressed for a party, afraid of their curls coming down.

Dungeness Road, with westerly winds, is a delightful, and, to me, an invigorating anchorage. Under other circumstances I should have enjoyed it much; but only just recovering health, depressed and overpowered with vexation, I felt that it would be a relief to be at home. When the anchor was down, both men were so civil and attentive—with the prospect of smooth water and ten hours' sleep—that you would have thought they had passed a day of severe trial, and had got through it with great credit. Night fine and moonlight. About 100 vessels in the roads, chiefly small traders.

July 21.—The first thing after breakfast I called upon each man, separately, to state whether he desired to leave the vessel, or intended to complete the cruise; and, if the latter, would promise not to repeat these detestable and absurd complaints. Feeling ashamed to abandon her for such trumpery causes, they both instantly elected to remain, promised faithfully to give up silly grumblings, to behave civilly and well, to follow me wherever I led, and take the rough and the smooth together, like men. As nothing could appear more satisfactory than such a return to common sense, I lost the miserable gloom and disgust that had come over me at the prospect of having to return and find other men, which probably I should have done, considering the purpose for which I came out. Not having sufficient confidence in them to test their new promises immediately with an adverse wind, we remained at anchor, finding such employment as is always to be found on board a vessel.

July 22.—The fleet left early in the morning. Being Sunday, my intention had been to remain at anchor. But the wind southing, with a falling barometer and an appearance of thunder in the S.E., I decided to get under way at 10.30 A.M.

The Channel was so full of vessels turning to windward, many of them large ships, that, with the prospect of a storm and southerly wind, I determined to take advantage of the wind again veering to W.S.W. to make a long board to the southward and get out of the rut. 6.45 P.M., 24 miles S.S.W. of Dungeness, the wind backed to the southward and looked very stormy, then fell calm. 8.30, wind S.S.W., light, re-set the patent log, and stood to the westward. The high land of Fairleigh was remarkably distinct against a streak of bright sky under the dark clouds.

July 23.—1 A.M., heading W. by N. ½ N., close hauled, Beachy Head light bore N.W. by N. 21 miles. 6.30, Beachy Head N. by E. 15 miles, took a fresh departure. 1 P.M., barometer falling rather fast. 3 P.M., in a rain squall, the wind shifted to west, then fell calm, and again backed to the southward.

My two poor men having had only six hours each below during the night, were in such a languid and sleepy state, that as the sea was a little rough I let them off the washing down. After breakfast one turned in for three hours, and after dinner the other ditto; besides that, I saw comparatively little of them, for directly I took the helm they were away down forward with some excuse or other, and immediately there was a smell of pipe.

They were always complaining about the heat of the forecastle, with little reason, one would suppose, since they were continually lolling about down there smoking, in harbour and at sea. The fact is, they were enervated by excessive smoking. Smoking when they turned out in the morning, smoking at work, and at every spare interval throughout the day until bedtime, rendered them sleepy and idle in the extreme. This is my explanation and *excuse* for their silly conduct.

Earlier in the day a conversation about fear had taken place, which rather interested me. After we returned home last season, a curious yarn was circulated—to the effect that I was very much frightened coming up Channel. I could not learn how it arose, nor whence it came, since this man Henry denied it then; but in this conversation he said, 'Now, you was very much frightened the night we turned through that Channel, sir, wasn't you?' 'Well,' I said, 'frightened is not the word I should use, since I was not obliged to be there, and could have avoided it altogether if it had pleased me to do so. If you mean that I was extremely anxious about the successful navigation of so dangerous a place, with my own property and three lives at stake, you are right.' Turning to George, I said, 'Would you like to sail through such a channel at night with any man who was not very anxious?' He replied, 'No, sir; that I wouldn't.'

At 8 P.M. it rained hard, and looked so very dirty, that we hove-to and took two reefs down. The sail was wet, and Henry's share of the first reef was taken so carelessly, that if the third and fourth reefs had been required, the points would not have met. As he was unwilling to alter them and disposed to be insolent, I took in the slack myself. At 8.45, made a good landfall, the light of Cape Barfleur, distant 20 miles, appearing on the weather bow. The lighthouse stands on a low point, and is a magnificent building, higher than the Monument of London. As I had not slept at all on the passage, I requested that both men would keep the deck, and relieve me from unnecessary fatigue, until we came up with the dangerous and rocky coast of Barfleur, where the difficulties of making Cherbourg at night or in thick weather begin. Notwithstanding this request, Henry went below and turned in at 9 o'clock, which compelled me to be up, as it was not safe for only one man to be on deck in bad weather, and in the track of the Havre navigation. About 10 P.M. the Barfleur light was lost for an hour in thick rain, which caused me some anxiety, as the tides are strong and peculiar, setting hard through the rocks, which extend a long way from the coast. My attention ought to have been directed entirely to the charts and the lights, and the men should have steered the course and kept the look-out. At midnight, abreast of the Cape, I called Henry on deck, when George went below and stayed there. Shortly after Henry took the helm, I asked him (from below) if Cape Levi light was broad on the bow. He answered, 'that he should not call it on the bow at all, but on the beam, and Barfleur light on the quarter,' which was untrue and misleading. Had I taken his word for it, and told him to luff a point or two, instead of looking up to see for myself, we should have been in dreadful peril. Of course, further words ensued, of anything but a pleasant nature.

July 24.—1 A.M., I was below with the charts when the wind shifted suddenly from South to N.W. in a heavy squall, putting us on a lee shore with a nasty chopping sea; the lights were all lost in heavy rain, and there was no one on deck to let go a halyard or tend a sheet. Fortunately, we were able to carry on until I put her about, and thus escaped an awkward situation. Heaving-to for daylight—which need not have been done with two good men—we drifted so far out that it was 5 o'clock before we were able to get inside Cherbourg break-water, after shaking out the reefs to beat against tide and wind, the latter having fallen to light and backed to the S.W. As it would take an hour to beat up to the anchorage off the town, and both men were on deck doing nothing, I told them to wash down, intending to let them stay below after breakfast, and not have it to do then—an excellent arrangement, that would have suited men in their senses; but it did not suit them. So they first proceeded to light their pipes, and then languidly to the work, coming aft with the pipes in their mouths, carrying on a grumbling conversation at me and the vessel, loud enough for me to hear. I took no notice of them beyond sharply pointing out the places they missed, as I had just resolved to publish their complaints, and thought it better to 'give them plenty of rope'—a mode of proceeding under difficulties that has since become 'parliamentary.' Their promises were proved to be so worthless, that I could no longer feel the slightest respect for them. The kindly feeling that had hitherto sub-sisted—and prompted me to expostulate with them at the time, and point out how absurdly they were behaving—had quite departed; if I may be excused for saying so, hanging them mentally had taken its place. 6 A.M., anchored off the town of Cherbourg.

This ended the first part of the cruise, which, in severity, would bear no comparison to what some of their townsmen had borne cheerfully, and without a murmur, in my hearing. We were at no time under shorter canvas than two reefs, and never had half the sea encountered on many previous occasions.

July 25.—Called the men at the usual hour. I cannot sup-press a feeling of contempt for seamen who require to be called after nine hours in bed. I remonstrated frequently—that turning in two hours later than they did, it was ridiculous that I should have to call them, or else have the work behind-hand for the day. If late, through my oversleeping, they knocked off in the middle of washing down to go to breakfast; then, after a leisure pipe, proceeded to finish the work. The clock in the forecastle was only valued for negative purposes, viz., to show how early it was in the morning, or how late it was for meals and for bedtime.

Our spare spars, weighing about 2 cwt., are rested on spar-cleats, and lashed to the stanchions. They should be shifted about twice a week. Upon this particular morning, instead of putting them down quietly, it was being done with such unnecessary clatter over my head, that it was like rifle firing in the cabin. Being in good humour with each other—which was not always the case—it was, 'Mind your toes, mate,' 'Mind your fingers,' but not a thought for my comfort beneath. I bore it for some time—I cannot say patiently—and then called out, angrily, to stop it. Little did they think that my employment in bed was summing them up in the log-book, which, during an experience of 27 years, I had never felt called upon to do before. Let us leave this wearisome subject for a while and turn our attention to something more agreeable.

Cherbourg, the great arsenal and dockyard of the north of France, is not very far from the Channel Islands. A glance at the chart, and a page or two of the book of directions, will convince anyone that it is a difficult and dangerous coast to make in a calm, or with a strong fair wind, when the landmarks are hidden in rain and mist. To the eastward are the races and rocks around Barfleur and Levi; to the westward is the race of Alderney—both equally unpleasant, as a surprise, when you do not want them.

The town of Cherbourg is situated at the head of a bay, in which, at one time, it was dangerous to be caught at anchor with onshore winds. In 1853 the breakwater, two nautical miles in length, was completed by order of the late Emperor, after being in progress 70 years. Its eastern end extends to within a quarter of a mile of the reefs of 'Ile Pelée,' which protect the bay from any great sea on that side. The western side is more open, having no such convenient reef to approach; but, inasmuch as this arm overlaps 'Fort du Homet,' the appearance from the road, where yachts and small merchant vessels anchor, is that of being landlocked. With westerly winds a considerable swell is thrown into the bay through this opening, which however inconvenient to some persons, is not dangerous to any. There is a capital harbour and floating basin, entered between two fine stone jetties, for those who prefer the dust and bustle of a town, with smooth water, to a fine healthy sea anchorage with the inconvenience of a little motion. For many reasons my preference is decidedly for the latter. You can get under way for a cruise, or sail about in the boat; and what a jolly place for a sail!—about five square miles of protected water, with something to interest you all round. In my opinion, its freedom from squalls places it far above any English port for pleasure sailing.

Well, but what about provisions in bad weather? Close reef the boat's sail, and have a little more fun and adventure in getting them. Instead of becoming weary of the town, as I should do if imprisoned in the basin, I take a pleasure in the daily visit. The people in the shops and at the stalls in the market are all so civil and obliging, that it is quite agreeable and amusing to be forced to attend to the catering yourself. When you have had enough French, and have tired yourself a little, it is another real pleasure to return to the vessel and pure sea air again.

The distance from the quay straight out to the breakwater is over two miles—from the quay to our anchorage only half a mile. At this distance, in fine weather, you see the military inspections going on, and hear the band tolerably well. There seem to be military movements of some sort every day, and always with band ahead, to make the profession as attractive and popular as possible. Then there is bugling and drumming at intervals, from daylight till bedtime, which, thanks to the distance, sounds very well at the anchorage. At night the lights look lively and pretty, the red harbour lights adding something to the picture. On a warm summer night, when the moon appears over the wooded hills, or the stars are shining, it is difficult to persuade oneself to turn in.

Near the quay there is an old church, with a very deep-toned bell, which is tolled every night at 10 o'clock. I cannot express how the sound of this bell charms me. One night at anchor there, a few years ago, I was watching the approach of a heavy thunderstorm from the eastward, when the clock struck ten, followed, after a short interval, by the tolling of the great bell. The whole scene, while it lasted, was delightfully impressive and solemn; but all minds are not affected in the same manner.

The breakwater is a grand work. There are, on the land side, four convenient harbours in it, for disembarking ammunition, stores, and men at the forts; two are in the centre and one at each end. From whatever direction a storm came suddenly, a boat could not easily be blown away. You see very little rowing. Boats from the men-of-war and the various government works are passing and repassing all day, always under sail, if wind enough. There are capital pleasure boats for hire, carrying a jib and three working lug sails, which they apparently manage with great skill. The docks and quays, as works of civil engineering, are so perfect in detail as to challenge frequent admiration; but some of the most useful features of them—beautiful flights of granite steps, for instance, and ornamental corners—are marred by the disgusting habits of the common people. In the magnificent docks at Havre there are several landing steps in every basin, and not one of them is safe to descend in the dark to reach the boat—with a lantern in one hand, the other, that should be free to save yourself in case of a slip, is required to guard your lungs from contamination. This nuisance, aggravated by the heat of the sun and the dust blowing off the quays, annoyed me so much when once detained there several days with a sprained leg, that I wished never to go into a French floating basin again. It is not so much the fault of the people, as of the dock or other authorities, who fail to provide proper accommodation for decency and cleanliness. I think the great French nation should see to this, and not allow their public works to be defiled in this manner.

If you wish to visit the dockyard a note from our Consul secures every civility and attention. I must say that I have everywhere found the French officials most agreeable and obliging.

The town will bear no comparison with Havre; but it is improving, and there are some very fair streets in it, where everything can be purchased at reasonable prices. The baths and reading room are at the Casino; the sea bathing is excellent, and on clean sand.

I will close these desultory remarks on Cherbourg by advising small yachts, anchored anywhere near the harbour's mouth, to have a kedge out. The current has no strength, but the ebb from the harbour joining at a right angle that of the bay, causes a gyratory motion that is likely to lead to a foul anchor.

This time I had no passport, and was not asked for any. In 1872 I anchored and landed four times on the coast—at Etretat, Trouville, Querqueville, and Urville. At the first three no one asked any questions, but at the last place, which is about half-way between Cherbourg and Cape de la Hague, we were stopped on the beach by the military coastguard, who insisted upon our returning to the yacht for the passport, which had been forgotten—or walking in their company to the guard-house three miles off. Although a stiffish pull we fetched the passport, upon which the men, who were only common soldiers, apologised for the trouble they had given me, and said, 'go where you like, sir.' It was just after the reign of the Commune, and they could not understand a gentleman taking his pleasure on the 'sad sea wave'—they would have said 'horrid sea wave'—and then landing where there was no town, just to walk about a pretty country of which they thought nothing. 'No yacht ever anchored there before; how could they know that what I said was true unless they saw the passport?' There was the vessel rolling in the offing enough to make them sick to look at it. I invited the chief spokesman to go off and see for himself, which he not only declined verbally, but looked— 'not if I know it.'

After a delightful country walk, and scramble over huge rocks that had many large basins lined with a sort of pink coral and seaweed, I went on board and returned to Cherbourg. We had left Cherbourg first thing after breakfast, with two reefs down, wind S.W.; reached along the coast to Ormanville; then bore up and returned as far as Urville—anchoring there because the church and the country looked so picturesque, and the chart showed it was practicable. This is an example of what I call a day's healthful, unalloyed pleasure, which could not have been enjoyed with my late idle and grumbling crew. There would have been complaint at getting up early—at going out with two reefs down—at anchoring off Urville—and finally at not being ready to turn in at 9 o'clock. Let us make haste to hear their last complaints, for happily we are getting near the end of their unmanly nonsense, and shall never hear any more.

July 27.—Under the soothing influence of much sleep—and no sailing—they had been so amiable that I expected on the morrow another request for advance money. Preferring that the request should not be made, I let them know, incidentally and quietly, that their broken promises and bad conduct at sea were fresh on my memory. My motive for doing this was to defer angry explanations until I could think of some way out of the unpleasant position, which, without interfering materially with the enjoyment of the visit to France, annoyed me considerably when it was the subject of contemplation.

The rail and stern gratings, which are made of ash and American elm, require to be sanded occasionally to keep them white. First, I told Henry in the boat that they were weather stained and would have to be sanded in the morning. As George would have to help, I repeated the same to him, just to prepare him likewise for a trifling task of which I ought not to have had occasion to speak. Next morning, while cleaning down, there was loud grumbling about the heavy work. One silly remark, amongst others that were indirectly addressed to me in the cabin, was, that 'she ought to be under a glass case in the park.' At breakfast time Henry came aft to the companion and said that, as I was dissatisfied with his work, and 'he was sure he always did his very best,' he should give me a week's notice to leave at Dartmouth. I said, 'Very well.' As a rule when people make this assertion, it is a sign that their 'very best' has often been questioned!

In the course of the afternoon it was necessary to refer to the subject again, as Henry had told me that he felt much hurt at my telling George that the rail and stern gratings were 'beastly dirty.' Upon being taxed with the exaggeration—that had been so common a thing from the beginning—George had to modify the statement in Henry's presence, and stood convicted of falsehood and wilfully making mischief; this made him so angry that *he* said he should leave at Dartmouth too. Then Henry observed that the explanation made all the difference; which remark it suited me not to hear, as they were a good pair, and their notices having been given and accepted, helped to solve a difficulty that had perplexed me much during the day, viz., how best to get rid of them without being subject to an exorbitant demand for dismissal in a foreign port. I had in fact just returned from making inquiries about a steamer to carry them away.

July 28, *Saturday.*—Up to the morning of this day I had been in a state of wretched uncertainty what to do. It vexed me exceedingly that they should go home and report that I cruelly overworked them—kept them sailing all day, and allowed no proper rest at night. The reverse was the fact; the difficulty was to prove it against the statements of two idle men, reckless of the truth. At last, thoroughly aroused by their grumbling and insolent remarks about the rail and gratings, which conclusively proved that there was no hope of amendment, I made up my mind that as I could not trust them alone with the helm in a dangerous place after their previous misconduct, they should go neither to Dartmouth nor home with me; and upon further consideration, I determined to prove how unmanly and contemptible were their complaints by taking sole charge, and, if possible, working back single-handed the way we came out. A feeling of gratification and relief came over me at having hit upon a punishment, neither harsh nor revengeful, but that was ignominious

161

and contemptuous for men unjustly whining about over-work.

That this was the 'right way' of dealing with these men—as representatives of a class—and of proving, beyond a doubt, the frivolity of their complaints, I shall establish by extracts from a much-applauded speech by Mr. G. Potter, 'a trusted trades union leader,' at a masons' strike meeting held at the Cannon Street Hotel, 5th October, 1877.

Mr. G. Potter said, 'that they should not object to the masters, provided they fought fairly.'——'If they would take their jackets off and do the work themselves they would have no objection.'

On Sunday morning after breakfast I found them evidently suffering from a suppressed sense of injury. It was not until the next day I learnt, at least according to their statement, that none of the men belonging to other yachts were turned out to wash down on Sunday morning. If true, it cannot be regarded as a praiseworthy remission of duty, out of regard for the sanctity of the day, unless extended to the cook and stewards, who have harder and more disagreeable work at anchor than all the rest of the crew put together. At all events, it was a new and happy discovery in favour of another hour in bed, and was seized upon accordingly. Not that they cared a bit for the sanctity of the day, for, by their own statement and my own observation, I found that their custom, at home, was to spend the day in listless idleness—and on board also, unless I could induce them to act differently. Those who are most loud in their objections to Sunday 'duty' are, generally, those who least regard it as a day of religious observance.

When this matter of washing down was mentioned, I replied —that I cared nothing at all for what they did or did not do on other yachts—that it had always been a rule of *mine* to have a clean vessel on Sunday, before flying colours, and that it always would be.

As regards sailing on Sunday. If under way—making a passage—it is a matter of course. If in port, I prefer not to leave. But if we are at anchor in an open roadstead, the rules of common sense must be observed on *that* day as on any other. Pitching bows under, on Sunday, in a state of anxiety about the anchor holding, I can answer for it by experience, is anything but a day of rest. If the men were conscientiously engaged in devotional exercises I should be sorry to disturb them. But if the choice lay between danger, discomfort, and idleness on the one hand—and safety combined with fair and legitimately imposed duties on the other—I should unhesitatingly choose the latter.

Monday, July 30, opened with a fine treat. They quarrelled violently over the work on deck—each accusing the other of shirking. I thought to myself, 'Go it, my lads, you are on the right tack at last.' The day being fine, I ordered a coat of black paint—to make her more 'fit for the glass case in the park.' On shore it was frightfully hot; the people were asleep in the shops and beside the stalls in the markets; streets were deserted; the gutters 'quite French,' and business almost at a standstill. Before the painting began, I went ashore to make arrangements in furtherance of my plans—amongst other things, ascertained the expense to London, and that the steamer would sail next night at 10 o'clock.

In the evening, after dinner, I went forward on deck to enlighten the men as to the 'bag and baggage' policy. It sounds harsh, it is perhaps historical, 'but really,' it is only an intimation, that you may pack up your traps and go if you like.

I began by informing them that the idea of the cruise to Dartmouth had been abandoned soon after our arrival at Cherbourg, in consequence of their disgraceful conduct—and continued, 'I remember, the first day out, you said that you hated the sea. Your notices prove that you desire to join your families as soon as possible. Now, there is a chance of your doing so by a steamer sailing from here to-morrow, and you had better avail yourselves of it.' Of course they were surprised, and a fuss ensued about being dismissed at a foreign port. I said, 'Very well, you may please yourselves. You owe me a week's service from to-day. The proposed cruise is abandoned through your misconduct. If you refuse my terms, whatever the weather is—if we have four reefs down—I intend to go to sea to-morrow, and have a cruise for my own pleasure to the Land's End. You can serve your time and be landed at an English port, or go by steamer to Southampton. I will leave you to make your choice.'

Not many minutes elapsed before they came to tell me that they would agree to leave by the steamer.

Having heard that I had been out of bed before, just the number of days coincident with the length of their notice, they shrewdly suspected that what had happened before might happen again, and let them in for a harder week's work than would agree with their constitution. Then a money difficulty arose, which, after some unpleasantness, was settled to my satisfaction. Later on, one came aft to the companion to inform me that they were both completely satisfied, and agreed to have a special cleaning up next day, put the forecastle in nice order, and do everything I desired.

July 31.—I felt unwell, and attributed it partly to the heat of the weather, and the smell of the back streets of the town on the previous day. Everybody knows that in all French towns the poor inhabitants of the upper floors pour their waste water down pipes into the street gutters. Before it is 'wasted' all the good properties of water are exhausted, so that our analysts would have to reverse the order of their investigation, and ascertain the percentage of 'pure water' the sample contained. I tried sulphuric acid, laudanum, and granular magnesia—all in turn. The former is my favourite medicine, and, I believe, perfectly safe; but, without advice, I thought it best to have a turn at champagne, which, after all, proved the best physic for a very busy day.

I had new wicks, saturated in spirits of turpentine, put into the lanterns, and a fresh supply of oil into the feeders; had topmast housed; extra tackles prepared—one 30 feet long, with spare trysail sheet blocks for taking the mainsheet in along the deck—others for various purposes, such as hauling the foresheet to windward and getting the jibsheet aft; strops of different-sized ropes to suit every requirement; short white ropes with an eye in one end, to break the canvas in, &c. The making of all these things may have occasioned some surprise, and probably led to the conclusion that sailors of less stamina than Englishmen would take their berths. It was not likely they would have the faintest suspicion of the truth, for it is characteristic of men of this stamp, to think that if they are taken away there will not be a man left. However, I was very careful not to drop a hint on the subject, for several reasons, two of them being: 1. The possibility of failure in getting the vessel under way at all, and the knowledge that a false report might get abroad and be a source of anxiety to my friends. 2. The fear of that would have added to the worry of a delay on the passage, and perhaps have induced me to act against judgment, in the desire to hasten on. The letters, securing five or six days' liberty, left me untrammelled. I was determined to go ahead, but free to 'ease her,' 'stop her,' or 'go astern.' It was a position that almost ensured success and speedy execution. Talking beforehand is—to those who are ashamed to fail —like burning the traditional boats that should accompany one on every difficult expedition; it leads to precipitancy, and is likely to be the cause of failure.

I had no complaint against them the next day. Everything was honestly done, as per arrangement. After an earlier dinner than usual, for me, they put their bags into the boat, and we started for the shore. Upon their thanking me again for the fair treatment they had received, I said, 'I am glad to hear you acknowledge it; there is no vindictive feeling on my part, but our acquaintance must end here, as I cannot consent to know you if we meet again.' The rest of the distance was rowed in silence.

They remained in the boat while I went to pay a visit in the town and to post the letters, and on my return clambered up the iron ladder to the quay—with a mutual 'good evening'—crossing a boat belonging to the English yacht 'Dachshund' (20 tons) in so doing.

Having disposed of the men, and thus brought the account

up to the night of Tuesday, the 31st, I will return for a few minutes to the business that took me ashore on Monday, before any communication was made to the men, which will at least establish the fact that there was no undue haste, but that everything was carried out with deliberation.

As a matter of common prudence, I had thought proper to state the case and confide my intentions to some gentleman. I would have done so on Sunday—having drawn up a statement for the purpose—but there was no one known to me on board the yachts at anchor, of whom to attempt to make a confidant. At last I thought of a gentleman on shore who, though unknown to me, was in every way the most fit and proper person, and I made an appointment for Monday. I met with every discouragement, as may be supposed, and if dissuasive argument and kind offers of assistance could have availed, he would have succeeded in reversing my decision; but like a true gentleman he abstained from pressing me unduly, dropped the subject, and behaved in a manner that I shall ever remember with pleasure and gratitude. On seeing me next day, shortly before the men left, 'he hoped I had altered my mind'—a remark that elicited no response, although the men were already in harbour, and the subject was not referred to again. It was understood that he and his nice little children would favour me with a visit the following day—if there to have the pleasure of receiving them—which it relieved me to think showed that he doubted my resolution. In my own mind the visit was certain not to come off, if there was wind enough to sail, for it was known to me that the excitement consequent upon such an undertaking was telling upon me adversely, and would not permit an hour's unnecessary delay without adding to the risk of failure.

Thinking of contingencies and how to meet them, I had scarcely slept the previous night. Bed, under the circumstances, was injurious, and I felt it so. More is presented to the mind in half an hour, lying down, than can reasonably be expected to occur in a month, and generally in a less intelligible shape than when up and doing. I have experienced this a hundred times before, but never with such intensity, as I never had so many things to engage my attention at once.

Although secret, it was yet such a fixed purpose that no one of good judgment would have attempted to interfere with me further, nor, if he had only partially known the preparations disclosed to my readers, would he have thought it necessary. I believed that everything was duly considered; notwithstanding, if by accident or otherwise the same line of action were again forced upon me, improvements in 'labour saving' might be made.

My complete and intimate knowledge of the quality, strength, and weight of everything belonging to hull and rigging of the 7-ton lugger, which had been built for me, with a view to single-handed sailing—and of the 'Orion'—supplied me with the means of estimating difficulties to be overcome that nobody else could possibly possess. *Three* is a good multiplier for weight of anchor, chain, and mainsail; for time in getting under way, bringing up, or reefing; but nothing like sufficient for cubic space, spars, spread and weight of canvas, or for ballast. It is true that the nominal, or builder's tonnage—which refers only to length and breadth on deck—of the lugger is more than one-third that of the 'Orion,' but the actual capacity is not more than a fourth, if so much. This comparison makes it clear that without largely increased mechanical aid, or several extra hands, it would be impossible to get the 'Orion' under way. She had that aid to a greater extent than artificers and riggers thought necessary at the time she was built; it has been increased in some respects since; and the result of experiments, tried at home, showed that there would be great advantage in increasing it again beyond all known proportions, without in the slightest degree interfering with the appearance of the vessel.

It may be taken as proved that, at all times, I did fully a third share of working the vessel when the men were there. If I had not done so as a habit, it would have been inconceivably ridiculous to think of undertaking it single-handed. With the exception of heaving up the anchor, setting up the

167

bobstay, hoisting and furling the mainsail, or taking a reef down, I had probably done most things occasionally, and thought little or nothing about it. The five things specially mentioned were always done by all hands working together—and if by two, then I was not the one left out, unless the helm and mainsheet required tending. Yet they complained that the work was too heavy, and, pointing to a yacht of 15 tons, said, 'Why, even that little thing has two men and a boy, and their gear is not more than half the weight of ours.' I may remark that it seems absurd to have said that of a vessel of 15 tons, but as regards the rigging, it was true. My chief object in undertaking the task was to prove to past, present, and future what one determined will can accomplish, and show what *unmanly* seamen they must be who cannot do, without complaining, I will not say a third, but half the work that I could—whose weight was not, as somewhere suggested in print, anything like 14 stone, but 8 st. 10 lb., while theirs was over 10 stone, and over 12 stone, respectively.

I trust this book will be read by some who are interested in labour afloat and ashore; and that something approximating to an estimate of what may reasonably be expected of a man—without complaint of overwork—will be deduced from it. If not, one motive for undertaking the work has failed, the more so as—in furtherance of this object—it was carried to an extent not at first contemplated.

Some will say, 'This is all very well; you did the work you liked best; but what about the cleaning and general drudgery, in which you took no part with the men?' The book must answer that, and I trust will not fail in convincing those whose knowledge renders persuasion unnecessary. My desire was to test, by personal experience, the genuineness of the men's complaints about overwork. Simply taking the place of one man would have been of no practical use whatever, since, if I had done three parts of the work, it would, from the novelty or unlikelihood of the proceeding, have remained an open question, even in some 'generous minds,' whether a fair share had been done by me at all. For the criticism of those who cannot class themselves under this head I care nothing.

July 31.—At sea the 'Orion's' boat is carried, bottom up, on one side the deck. One gunwale rests on the booby hatch, clear of the skylights, and the other on the deck, with her side against the bulwarks. Lashed in this position she closes one side of the deck for traffic—an inconvenience little felt, with the other side quite free. Weighing about 2 cwt., it requires two men, and great care, to turn her over in such a confined space without damaging herself or the skylights.

As the men in the 'Dachshund's' boat would shortly be going off to the yacht, I asked them to step aboard and help me, which they promised to do. From a remark made by one of them, and which I suppose he repeated to the owner of the yacht, it is clear my men had been unwise enough to brag that they had left me in the lurch. I was a martyr, it is true—but of several days' older date.

At 7.30 I arrived alongside the 'Orion,' hooked on the davit tackles, jumped aboard, and hoisted up the boat at once, a bit at a time, first one end and then the other; when I had changed shore-going suit for old light working clothes, I lashed everything in the boat belonging to her, cast off runner tackle and ridge rope, and swung her in board. As the men had not come, I was in the act of preparing a plan for turning her over with the runner tackle and topsail halyards, when a boat came alongside with three gentlemen who had kindly come instead of the men. My boat was settled in her place when one of them said, 'Surely you are not going to take this vessel to sea by yourself?' I answered, 'Please excuse me from making any reply; I wish to be silent on the subject, since it is impossible to say what will be done. I appeal to you as gentlemen to abstain from making any remarks which might give rise to reports based on no solid foundation, and be a source of anxiety to my friends.' This they readily promised, and with a mutual 'Good-night,' departed to their own vessel.

My davits are guyed, and connected by small chain, dividing in the middle; each one is made up separately for stowage, chains and tackle are frapped with the tackle fall, stowed abaft the mizenmast under the stern gratings, and lashed to the mainhorse timbers; they are awkward shaped half-hundredweights that damage everything they touch, unless carefully handled. Having set up runner and ridge rope, oiled all iron work, greased all leather work—going round with oil bottle and grease can—I had a general look round on deck, and then went below, where there was plenty to do. After an intensely hot day the night was very cloudy and close, barometer slightly receding, and every appearance of a storm; heavy clouds had been seen in the west, and distant thunder heard during the afternoon, but fortunately for me it held off, and remained calm.

I have said that it was advisable to try the effect of astringents during the day, but dared not persevere with any one of them, without advice, lest by any chance harm and delay should result. It is said that 'a thing determined, is half done'; there is no doubt about it, although this rule, like all others, is subject to exceptions. That it was not so in my case was due, as far as my limited powers are concerned—do not smile prematurely—to the great care I took of myself. Sufficient brandy was burnt to fill an ordinary flask; two pint bottles of good champagne, to be taken in small doses, were placed in readiness, and a patent tap screwed into one of them for immediate use; and shortly after getting to heavy work, being exposed to the night air, necessarily in a state of semi-nudity, I went below and put a nine-inch band of flannel three times round the loins; this was a great success, and relieved me of a legitimate source of anxiety. It may be well to explain that burning brandy for a minute or so modifies its injurious properties, and renders it softer and more palatable to invalids and those who dislike it. *My medicine*, however, was outside the breakwater, and out there I was determined to find it, if the work could be accomplished with half the success that attends the *finale* of modern romances. In those, however, the habitations are generally scenes of merriment before the happy conclusion. I cannot say how delightful—to me—mine is when all goes right, but now, with a dead calm outside, and tremendous work ahead, there was a strange and almost oppressive silence below, that, with open doors exposing the tenantless and dark forecastle to partial view, made itself felt. There was no ripple against the vessel's bows, no sigh of wind in the rigging, but heavy· gloom overhead, and corresponding dulness below. I burned the brandy in an Ætna, set on the table, and standing on a dish for safety. After heating it externally with methylated spirit, the match was applied, and instantly there arose a startling flame of blue, tipped with yellow, 6 to 8 inches wide, and 12 to 15 inches high, which threw a weird light fore and aft, such as you sometimes see upon the stage. The effect was so extraordinary—combined with the exceeding stillness of the night—that, if one of our grave philosophers, who explain everything, and believe nothing, had been with me and seen one of Pepper's ghosts descending the fore ladder, the probability is that investigation would have been postponed, and that the after ladder would have been a scene of undignified contention.

Everything movable in the forecastle—table, cans, buckets, cooking utensils, and crockery—had to be lashed or jammed up ready for sea; dead lights in the bow screwed up; stove funnel unshipped and the flange covered on deck. It is as great a pleasure and comfort to see everything in its place when the vessel is plunging in a heavy sea, as the *discomfort* is great in having them tossing and tumbling about, adding confusion and a dirty mess to that which is perhaps already sufficiently trying. I have found crockery, glass, and even the clock, uninjured, in places so seemingly impossible, that I have ceased to be surprised at anything occurring in the races open to the Atlantic.

I drank a large quantity of liquid, chiefly warm cocoa; once tried a pint mug of Liebig, but found it so nauseous that the dose was not repeated; several times mixed a teaspoonful of granular magnesia in water to assuage raging thirst, and at intervals a wine glass of champagne, or a little brandy weakened with water; it seems an odd mixture, and my readers may laugh, but there is a limit to quantity when you come to pints, and a limit is imposed by quality when stimulants are in question. So I just took what I fancied or felt most to require, occasionally eating a little biscuit. By degrees I settled things in my own cabins and pantry, put everything forward—in the way of clothes, eatables, &c.—that was likely to be wanted, and everything back out of sight that would not be wanted, so as to have neither thought, trouble, nor delay, in procuring anything required. The same with all ropes, tackles, and strops.

Attention to these matters ran away with hours of time; and if all my movements had been registered by a pedometer, and my steps up and down the eight rounds of the ladder counted, it would not surprise me to find that I had taken a good constitutional, and might have looked over London from the golden gallery of St. Paul's. The necessity of economising strength was not overlooked, but trying to think of a dozen things at once would have wasted time and led to confusion. Between 7.30 P.M. of the 31st and 9 o'clock next morning I had eleven hours' work to get outside the breakwater. If asked to give a strict account of my time, it would not be possible, but one or two suggestions will go far to make it clear. Many things require to be held; you have to go and fix them, return to your own work, and then back to release them again. There is plenty of that in handling the mainsail. All ropes, after temporary use, were coiled down in their places.

It may seem tedious to my readers to take them back again for a few hours, but it will be excused when they remember that I was carrying on more than one work at a time (or something very like it), and must for convenience relate each separately.

After the forecastle was settled, and the meal called tea disposed of, I went on deck at 9.30, took the covers off the mainsail, rolled them up, and stowed them away. Let no one be surprised to hear that, notwithstanding my hands were in first-rate working order, I considered it essential to put on a pair of calf-skin gloves. The laughable sight they presented in the morning quite justified their use, and proved conclusively that it would have been impossible to get through the work without them. After uncovering the sail, main and peak halyards were hooked on, and hand tautened; peak tyer and all stops cast off—the last being the bunt tyer, which let fall a hundredweight and a half of canvas to the deck and against my legs. It would most likely knock anyone down who was unprepared for it; to me it was a sufficient reminder of the labour required to pick it up again.

My intention was to take the first reef down completely, the second partially. To do that I left the boom in the crutch, to have it in a line with the mizenmast; hoisted the peak a few feet, overhauled the whole of the sail to lighten the foot as much as possible; put a strop on the mizenmast—standing on the boom to fix it; hooked a tackle into it, and into the cringle of the second reef, and bowsed it aft; jammed the fall, while I lightened up the foot of the sail, and bowsed aft again until it was as taut as a bar; rove the first earing—previously soaping it well; settled it satisfactorily in its place by hand, and then set up hard with the reef tackle; lashed the earing to the boom with about a dozen racking turns of small manilla line—which I have never known to give out, but have often found as troublesome to take off as to put on; and then proceeded to tie the reef up. All this is hand-cutting work. Including the slab reef, there is canvas more than a yard deep and 28 feet long to be partly gathered up and partly rolled, if you wish to be neat. When there is no one to help, you must hold it on the boom with one leg, or sit upon it, while tying the reef points. Stout canvas is very obstinate. Directly the full muscular power of the hands is relaxed to bring the points together, it slacks out and must be done again. Sometimes I hold one point with the teeth, but that depends upon the position. It seems simple enough; so it is, if you don't mind seeing the canvas hanging in festoons between the points and don't care whether you will be able to take the other reefs or not. But I do care; moreover, in language too mild to express my real sentiments, I dislike a *sloven*; and if an hour more had been required to take a perfect reef, another hour it should have had. A slovenly

173

reef, a slovenly furl, and a dirty mast look disgraceful in a yacht of any pretensions; and I always think, when the mast wants scraping very badly, that the master wants scraping, too. I had the riding light to work by, and shifted it, as required, from one part of the rigging to another.

My favourite bell on the quay, which begins tolling at the rate of about 10 strokes a minute, sounded very melancholy until the clapper got into full swing. I said to myself, 'Please go ahead, I don't like it!'

The first earing being secured, I shifted the reef tackle to the second, and repeated the process, hauling out third cringle to the mizen, and lashing the second earing to the boom, like the first. The reef, however, was not tied up, so I had only one reef down for sailing; but, without appreciably reducing the area of the canvas, in regard to labour, I was half-way on with the second. After reeving the third earing, and knotting it, I added two turns of small rope to the gaff strops to strengthen them against possible weakness, and turned my attention to the boom, which is a fine useful spar, but a terrible bad shipmate in a breeze.

The ordinary rolling tackles were cast off and stowed away; the trysail sheet tackle, which, next to the mainsheet, is the most powerful on board, was securely lashed to the main-horse timber on the starboard side, and the upper block—which has large sister-hooks—hooked into a fourstrand manilla strop on the boom end. The weight of the sail being off the boom, I topped it with the burton, about two feet higher than usual. Having satisfied myself, by inspection, that it was right, I set the other topping-lift to the same standard, belayed and clinched both falls, intending they should each bear only half the strain, and not be slacked up again until the end of the passage. Each topping-lift being capable of doing the whole work, I 'set up against them' with the mainsheet and trysail tackle, which formed a triangle under the boom-end, and secured the boom as in a vice. By coming to the wind, the same could be done any time during the passage, for reefing or taking the sail off, without any danger whatever to myself.

The importance of having the boom thus under control cannot be over estimated.

With the prospect of sailing so soon, it appeared, at first sight, an act of folly to go through the labour of furling the sail again. But if the storm that threatened all night, and made it so dark, had come on and saturated the canvas, it is doubtful whether, owing to the greatly increased weight, I could have succeeded in setting it at all; so furled it was, at an expense of energy difficult to estimate, except in this way—that I would rather set the mainsail twice than furl it once.

It has already been said that much of the work in the main and after cabins was done by degrees; in fact, it was reserved to fill up the intervals between such heavy and exhausting labour as I have been describing, and which could not possibly be carried on continuously. Sheltered below from the direct influence of the night air, which felt chilly to my bare head and scantily-clothed body, moderate occupation gradually cooled and rested me far more safely and effectually than sitting or lying down for a few minutes; the latter would have necessitated extra clothing—dangerous to throw off again—have induced sleep, and indisposed me to proceed.

All my working sails are of double canvas, Nos. 2, 3, and 4, and are roped accordingly. The advantages are—that they hold more wind, wear better, and never lose their original shape. If they require more setting at first, they also require less attention afterwards. To set the small mizen properly requires all the force you can exert with a whip-and-tye purchase. As the leathered iron traveller jams under the fall of the halyard, and prevents the block getting too high, you may set up until you are satisfied; my limit—alone or with assistance—is, when no more can be got. The same rule, easy to be remembered, but difficult to make others carry out, applies to everything on board that requires force. When the tack is purchased down there is a luff like a bar, and well stretched halyards, that, if dry when set up, give no more trouble for a day or two. The lacing, of soft manilla, is rove 'in and out' while hoisting. As the head of this sail is 19 feet from the deck, and I have no fancy for climbing without footholds, my plan is to stand on the main boom, reach the upper turns with a boathook, and finish off the lower ones by hand. At first the taut lacing makes the luff a little irregular, but, when the sail is sheeted and the breeze is fresh, it falls nicely into place, and looks well.

This was my next job, which began by taking the sail from the locker, and ended by its being furled on the mast and stopped with canvas tyers. Then the jib claimed my attention; it had to be put on deck from the cabin, and dragged forward in the bag. Getting a jib out without help is long and hard work by daylight—worse in the dark, when the upper part of the chain halyards cannot be seen. When the foresail also was ready, it and the jib were stopped up together in the lower cover of the former, with a long canvas tyer, and the outer part of the jib was stopped along the bowsprit.

The luff of this jib is 30 feet. When set on a reefed bowsprit the sheet just clears the forestay. If, on the passage, the outhaul stretched or rendered a few inches, it would require a general re-setting. To avoid work that might be very inconvenient, I set it on the full bowsprit about two or three feet short of the end, which allowed a margin for slacking that could be corrected in a minute by the jib purchase; I also took the precaution to mouse the hook of the traveller, to guard against the possibility of the tack shaking free if anything went wrong.

The bowsprit—a 7½ inch 3 cwt. spar, 16½ feet outboard— I had no reason to fear, whatever the weather; so the work on that and the jib, like that on the boom and the mizen, I regarded as permanent, excepting that the jib might have to be let in a foot or two, if the third reef were taken in the mainsail. The last job I should desire to face, when alone in a heavy sea, would be shifting jibs with chain halyards; so there was no intention of doing it, excepting in an extreme case that was not likely to occur; to show how unlikely, it may be mentioned that I never shift third, for storm, jib until the fourth reef is taken in the mainsail. That has occurred only about four or five times in twelve years. We have carried this jib in such heavy gales, turning to windward with three reefs down, that

176

I have known a square foot of the tabled clew to be blown away piecemeal during an afternoon—going to the 'Sultan review,' in 1867; have had the foresheet horse carried away with a reefed foresail, and the mizen bumpkin carried away with a reefed mizen—going to Scotland in 1875; and the bowsprit sprung, returning from Scotland in the same year; for which reason the present spar is about a hundredweight heavier than the last. The jib is large for heavy weather, but when sheeted dead flat, with a tackle, if necessary, it has the inestimable advantage of enabling us to luff for heavy puffs, and lift the mainsail, or throw her head up for a dangerous sea, with the certainty of paying off again without losing headway. In the 'Orion,' the third, as against the storm, jib, is good for two knots an hour more through the water. Besides increased area, it counteracts the strong tendency to weather helm, generally exhibited in vessels of great gripe, and has the advantages before mentioned.

Aug. 1.—1.30 A.M., the jib and foresail being secured, I went below, as the wind was too light to make it worth while doing more work on deck for the present. Sailing from Cherbourg in a very light breeze, with the prospect of being becalmed, was more to be feared than any strength of wind. In just such a breeze on a former occasion, we steered to the northward under twice the spread of canvas I was going to carry now, and drifted down to within half a mile of Alderney breakwater, narrowly escaping being carried through the Race, or, worse, through the Swinge. Had I gone out in such a paltry breeze now, and found myself drifting helplessly—perhaps first towards the rocks off Barfleur, and then down to Alderney—the question might pertinently have been asked—in fact, I should probably have asked it myself—'Now, you was very frightened, sir, wasn't you?' and should have had no difficulty about answering in the affirmative! If determined not to shift the jib for a smaller one, I was equally determined not to carry an inch more canvas than was already prepared; no duration of calm would have induced me to shake the reef out of the mainsail.

Either the success of the work, or the care I had taken of myself, had done me good, for certain it is that at 2 o'clock I felt hungry, and sat down to a supper of cold mutton, lettuce, bread and butter, and Bass's ale. The lettuce and the ale, after the gallon of liquids that had gone before, might reasonably have been excluded from the banquet, but, as both had the advantage of being cold and wet, they were wonderfully palatable.

When the table was cleared, I laid down on the sofa with a greatcoat over me—just to think for a few minutes—when I was startled by a gun from one of the forts. To my astonishment it was broad daylight, and the time 4.30. It was still very cloudy, but there was a breeze from W.N.W. After a wash to freshen up, I went on deck for the final effort.

There were 22 fathoms of chain out. The first operation was to heave in 12 fathoms. One end of the handle ships on the windlass, the other into an eyebolt on the gunwale. This handle, worked round and round, gives quick delivery; but it is hard work. On the opposite end of the barrel of the windlass an American patent is fitted; this, working fore and aft with a long straight lever, delivers slowly, but is less laborious. I used first one and then the other, according as the vessel sheered, and made it lighter or heavier. But it was nearly all heavy, and explained itself soon enough by bringing the anchor—a Porter's patent—to the surface, crown first, at 7 fathoms, trailing the other 15 fathoms along the bottom. I said to myself, 'Oh! here's a pretty mess.' By some means, difficult to explain, a half hitch was taken on the tumbler at the back of the palm, and the weight of chain beyond kept it fast. I got a luff tackle on the forestay, and hooked the crown of the anchor, but it was too much for me without a second tackle, which I was hastening to procure.

Driving first in the direction of a schooner at anchor, and when clear of that—in consequence of the wind northing—towards the shoal water, the situation was most trying. Fortunately, at this moment, I spied a fishing boat turning to windward, and hailed it, in the belief that my chain had been

178

fouled by another vessel's gear, of which the men would be glad to take possession, and release me. They came under the bow as soon as possible after lowering sail, rested the anchor on the bow of their large boat, and cleared it in a minute. Having seen nothing of the previous performance, and thinking that I was only temporarily on deck on consequence of the anchor dragging, they generously declined to act upon my polite suggestion, 'that, having had trouble enough already, they had better reeve this (the cat-fall), and leave the rest to me,' and proceeded with equal politeness to lay the anchor out again, to my secret mortification. However, smiling pleasantly, I quietly cribbed 3 or 4 fathoms of chain while they were engaged doing it.

When they came alongside for their money, which was fortunately ready and waiting, I started a conversation about the weather and the fish they had caught—judiciously chosen subjects, which transferred the interest from my deck to the clouds, and to the bottom of their own boat, and enabled us all to talk at once, with desirable confusion. My motive was to stave off inquiry, or expression of surprise at finding me with gloves on, working at so heavy a job, while the crew were supposed to be asleep below.

It did not suit me to let them know that I was alone on board. They had been so obliging in laying out the anchor, that they might have disregarded my remonstrance against giving themselves the trouble of invading my deck, and, in an honest and good-natured way, have caused me much annoyance. Considering that their smacks, of my tonnage, would have had about six hands, the whole truth would have been too much for them, but the fact of my being alone, in such a smart and solid-looking craft, could not have failed to become the talk of the wine shops, and of the foreign fleet of various nationalities at anchor. If the knowledge spread, there was palpably so much to tempt cupidity, that I should have been too suspicious of my neighbours to have cared to turn in at night. If it be suggested that it would have been easy to lock and barricade myself below, in a state of preparation for unwelcome visitors,

I say, 'that's true enough,' but if it came to a question of locking and barricading, I would rather be locked out, for steamers are not discriminating as to those who want to be run into and those who don't. From Englishmen there could have been no concealment: but Frenchmen, being occasionally misled as to our manners and customs, might, if the matter were afterwards discussed, have arrived at the conclusion that I was engaged in an act of charity and benevolence, such as my lazy crew at that early hour of the morning would have highly appreciated. For every reason it was better to run no risk of being talked about, since it remained to be proved whether I could get under way at all. Even then something might have occurred to bring me back to the road again. In this cautious spirit, I knocked off work, and went below until they had sailed too far away to be likely to return; then 'turned to' afresh, and hove short.

The bobstay is used to stay the outer end of the bowsprit down, and prevent it from curving upwards when the strain of the jib is upon it. There is a tackle between the chain on the stem and the bowsprit end, consisting of two iron blocks, one single and one double, through which the fall leads in-board on a level with the deck. When sufficient strain is put upon this fall the bowsprit is curved downwards, which is the position it should maintain. When the men are present we always put a luff tackle on the fall, and apply our united strength to get it sufficiently down. Occasionally it might be a good subject for a picture, for, just when everything is at its grandest tension, the strop gives way, or, if carelessly put on, slips on the wet rope, and down we go all of a heap. As I could make little impression on it single-handed, I made up for the absence of men by putting another luff tackle on to the fall of the second, which gave me the power to do it handsomely. It required 24 feet of the last tackle fall to steeve the bowsprit down 10 inches. Having belayed that, I set the mizen, which has a boom of 13 feet—unstopped the jib and foresail—rove fore-sheet—cast off all mainsail tyers, excepting the bunt—ran up my colours, fore and aft—hove the anchor a short stay peak—lashed the helm a-starboard, for sternway, to cast to the northward—broke anchor out of ground and hove up, foul of the bobstay; I had, therefore, to go out over the bow, and stand on the bobstay shackle to reeve the cat-fall through the ring of the anchor. As she was driving to leeward, I secured it temporarily to the weather bowsprit shroud, until the jib was set and sheeted. Aft, and righted the helm; forward, and catted the anchor; set the foresail and sheeted it.

I had spectators at the distance of about a cable. A schooner's crew had been assembled for an hour, trying what to make of it, instead of washing down—supposing they ever did such a thing!

With the wind from N. by E. I was approaching the reefs of Ile Pelée, to leeward of the eastern entrance, and had to fish the anchor—that is to get the fluke on the gunwale. In a most awkward position, with arms extended 15 or 18 inches from the body it was an overpowering lift. The foresail halyards were in use—to get the topsail halyards there was no time, as the mainsail wanted setting badly. It is needless to say that I was more than comfortably warm from previous exertion, but made another effort, that succeeded at the expense of the fine fresh paint on the bulwark, secured it temporarily, cast off the bunt tyer, walked aft with fall of peak halyard, and steered the peak well up between the topping-lifts, then hoisted away, throat and peak alternately, taking care to let neither get much in advance of the other, springing up from the top of the halyard bitts, which gave me a 6-foot haul at a time. When the mainsail was high enough to get sufficient way on for staying, I cast off the trysail tackle from the boom, filled on her and went about, as close to the rocks of Pelée as I cared to be. Filled the jib, and left the foresail sheet to windward, to allow time, on the weather board, to finish my work. When the mainsail was as high as my weight would carry it, I belayed the main halyards to the bitts with great care, and, in language technical, if inelegant, hoisted the throat into its place by 'swigging,' which gives great power when done with both hands, but is dangerous if the gear is bad or carelessly belayed, purchased the peak, let draw the foresail, and went aft to the helm. Put about again for the passage east of the break-water, having previously made a bight in the tiller-rope to slip over the tiller, short of hard down, without stopping to take turns. That allowed me time, in stays, to purchase the jib, and sheet it, before being quite full on the other tack—aft, to right the tiller—forward, to lash the anchor securely before bowing into the open sea, now close at hand—let draw the foresail and passed the breakwater at 8.45 P.M., just four hours after commencing work in the morning, which, added to the seven hours before supper, made up the eleven hours' work previously mentioned.

My intention, if the wind were foul or scant, was to work the French half of the Channel for 130 miles—if free, to sail 100 miles E. ½ N., when Beachy Head should bear N.N.W. 24 miles; then act according to circumstances. The prime object in view was to avoid the much-frequented tracks during the dark hours. I do not know the proportion, but my belief, perhaps an erroneous one, is, that for one vessel larger than a fishing smack on the French side of mid-channel there are fifteen or twenty on the other.

The appearance overhead was just that of a storm having expended itself elsewhere. The clouds were dividing into heavy masses from N.N.W., the lower scud and the wind from N. by E., fresh enough for the reefed sail, and so cold to me that, when clear of the outer rock of Pelée, it was necessary to clothe accordingly, and take a little strong, much needed refreshment.

Looking up a point to windward of the course, she steered herself well, while, being made hungry by the brandy and biscuit, I now attempted a real breakfast, before getting into the Race off Cape Levi. Wanting time to boil water for cocoa, I thought, 'Why not do a little French, and call it second breakfast?' So I lodged on the edge of a sofa, clear of the move-ments of the swing table, rushing up the ladder every two minutes to see if all were going right, and down again for another mouthful of stale bread, butter, and potted meat (dreadful rubbish), topping up with a tumbler of claret. The latter was grateful to my parched throat, but, besides adding to a mixture already 'well mixed'—my name is 'Bull'—it causes me to make grimaces, and does not agree with any part of me. During my school days in Paris I had such a reputation for resisting everything French that an excellent old friend, who died in consequence of the hardships of the siege of 1871, used always to speak of me as that 'John Bull' Dick.

The main and mizen sheets were moderately easy. The head sails, sheeted hard and flat as boards, were intended to remain so throughout the passage. In the event of being compelled to come to the wind for a vessel in the way, or for any urgent cause, it would have been impossible for me to spend a long time forward sheeting the head sails with tackles, to the neglect of the helm and mainsheet, to say nothing of the probability of another complaint of 'overwork' less frivolous than the last, and a notice to myself to 'leave' at Dover! In a hard breeze, close-hauled, two men cannot handle the sheet of this jib or the foresail without shaking in the wind, and sometimes cannot do it by hand then.

Before breakfast everything had settled down into fair working order. The halyards were all coiled and toggled to keep them in their places, the sun, shining out gloriously at times, made the coast and the dark green sea look charming, and I could not help calling the attention of the man at the helm to the fact. It has somewhere been suggested in print, that where such strict discipline were observed, the man at the helm was not likely to have been spoken to. But as gentlemen in Parliament and elsewhere seem to derive much satisfaction and amusement from hearing themselves, it would be exceptionally harsh and tyrannical to forbid a man making a speech or singing a song when there is no one else to do it.

Was there cause for being merry? Ample! When, during the previous three days, the uncertainties of the future were much in my thoughts, my chief comfort—and encouragement to proceed—was derived from consideration of the hardest trials and difficulties in my experience. The last, and most alarming, was being forced in half a gale of wind through an old wreck on a sandbank several miles from land, from which, after four hours' detention, and anxiety enough to turn one's hair white, we escaped without injury, and beat to windward under three-reefed mainsail. I have often been impatient and confused over work that was trifling compared to that of the previous night, which went forward with order and regularity from the commencement, without a hitch or an unpleasantness of any sort. In a sense of supreme satisfaction—perhaps exultation—at seeing the canvas well set, everything in its place, the beautiful surroundings, the extraordinary independence—in fact, everything successful beyond almost a presumptuous expectation—I had better reason to be contented than can ever be known to anyone else, and found no difficulty whatever in being 'as jolly as possible under the circumstances.'

Was I tired? No!—vexation and disappointment make one weary. Everything went right. Supplied with water, provisions, and fuel for a month; in a beautiful little well-found ship of undoubted capacity and power, of which not only every timber and plank, but every spar, sail, and rope were known to me, there ought to have been, and there was, a degree of confidence and contentment that went a long way to neutralize fatigue.

With a seven-knot breeze for my moderate canvas, there was plenty of sea through the races, which are marked by lines of broken water, at intervals, for several miles out of Cherbourg, and are caused by strong tidal currents running over irregular depths. After a few warnings which it would have been imprudent to neglect, I put on my waterproofs in time to save a terrible drencher off Cape Levi, that came tumbling in forward and over the boat like a cataract, filled the deck, and would have washed me from the tiller if I had not seen it coming and taken two or three extra turns of the tiller rope, and held on tight. Fortunately, there was no one to cry about it and 'give notice to leave,' so it was soon forgotten in more congenial excitements when my neck and shirtsleeves began to dry up again; a sea like that always finds its way to those weak places in the 'armour.'

11 A.M., Barfleur S.S.W. Ile Pelée S. by W. 15 miles; set

patent log. At 1 P.M. lost sight of land, wind N.N.W., fresh and cloudy, with a good sea on the quarter. I passed a fishing boat out of Cherbourg, a schooner off Barfleur, and saw one of the great Havre steamships homeward bound from America. Besides these, throughout the day, I only noticed two or three small vessels crossing my course. I had the horizon mostly to myself, and was literally 'Monarch.' After the great exertion of the previous night the ruling of my own little kingdom seemed but a light and easy matter, in the absence of 'obstructives' and of a 'foreign complication.' Of the first I had rid myself; of the second I hoped to steer clear—especially during the night.

One difficulty, under otherwise favourable circumstances, was the question of meals. I continued to support myself, at intervals, with brandy, champagne, granular magnesia, or claret—the last two to quench extreme thirst—and biscuit, or bread and butter with a little meat, but never took anything until compelled by necessity, nor for a single moment thought of smoking. To have prepared a regular meal I must have hove-to, lighted a fire, and, amongst other things, warmed bread in the oven. Strange to say, I cannot bear stale bread, especially French. At sea, with a crew, I always have enough bread warmed up and made like new at breakfast time to last the day.

A vessel sailing free, with a strong breeze varying ever so little in force from one minute to another, and affected by the varying forms and heights of waves, cannot be made to steer herself even moderately straight for more than a few minutes, often not for one. On a wind it is quite different. The helm and the canvas can be so trimmed, that, with occasional attention, and at some sacrifice of speed, she will sail herself for hours. While shortening my distance 6 or 7 miles every hour, I could not consent to the sacrifice of 18 or 20 miles for the sake of a meal that, in all probability, would have made me sleepy, and if the wind failed, of which there is always a chance, might well have been a cause of regret next day. From a nautical point of view, it would have been an unpardonable error for which I could never have forgiven myself, if misfortune had overtaken me in consequence.

Having everything to do, of course the helm was frequently lashed and left. On these occasions, owing to the freshness of the wind, she sheered so much to windward during my two or three minutes' absence, that I allowed half a point for it, and considered the true course E. by N., which proved a good correction. It seemed that sheering to windward, like everything else, required an exception to prove the rule, and she gave me an awkward instance of it when I was below, before dark. Whether the helm was too hard up, or whether she yawed on a sea, which was equally likely, there was a terrible noise on deck, and a sudden heel to port, which told its own tale. I was at the helm in a moment, and carefully gybed her back again; then went to see about damages. The outer end of the mizen boom was forward of the mast, and pointing to the leach of the mainsail, so I topped it up, and left the sail flapping violently while I went forward to the weather runner, which was at liberty, and dashing about with one of the runner plates attached, threatening destruction to the glass in the main skylight. As only one runner plate was carried away, I set up the standing part to an eyebolt in the deck, and went aft again. Perceiving that the leathered selvagee strop of the mizen sheet was gone from the boom, I let go the outhaul, gathered the sail in as well as I could, and stopped it to the mast with a canvas tyer; then went below, for rope—to make a new strop—a marlinespike, and tools to unship the mizen boom. When the strop was made, fitted into its place, and the block seized in, I had to go out on the weather outrigger shroud to reeve the sheet through the iron block, which done, the boom was shipped and sail trimmed again just before it became too dark to see.

The next thing was to boil water with spirit and make some cocoa. Then I got up the binnacle light, and sat steering awhile to cool down. Even an unpleasant diversion, like that just related, had its use in relieving monotony and preventing stagnation. Not that there was much fear of it; for when I began to cool, my feet and ankles, that had been sopping wet all day, became so miserably cold from the fresh soaking that, however healthy salt water may be, I was obliged to go below, change socks, and put on high waterproof boots—for the night.

Someone says—'There you are; no sooner settled down to the helm than off again.' Just so; and if, without experience, I were reading of somebody else, I should say, as probably my readers have said—'What could there be to do when once fairly under way, and not a single object in sight?' Well, there were a hundred things, of which this is a sample. Moreover, it should be remembered, that even the nearest things at hand —the main and mizen sheets—required the helm to be lashed and left; everything else necessitated a walk at least as far as once the length of the room in which the reader is sitting, and often a descent to the cabin in addition.

To economise the dirty work of lamp trimming, I put off getting up the side lights until warned by seeing a steamer's lights to leeward. The lamps had been fresh trimmed on Monday, but they were in such a nasty oily mess, that I had first to clean them with cotton waste to make them fit for handling. After the gybe, I was particular about leaving the helm for more than very short intervals. It didn't suit me to be brought-to, shaking in the wind—I couldn't afford another gybe, and didn't want to run into anything, so what with the helm and the lookout, it took me a long while to get the lights up.

From the first the reef down had been a great comfort to me, and now more than ever. The weather was very cloudy, and wind strong, with a great deal of motion. Each lantern was a separate job, and necessitated a careful crouching walk forward along the lee scuppers, holding on by the ridge rope, with the sea washing up over the ankles. As after this my hands had to be washed below, I took the precaution to wear gloves when handling them again. Then there was the log to haul in, every two hours, to see it was not choked with weed— a very common occurrence in the Channel—and the mileage to be taken at the binnacle light; this, more often than not, pours a little stream down one's sleeve. The lanterns to be frequently inspected, and twice taken below, one at a time, to remove the char, and keep them burning with proper brilliancy; the binnacle light ditto. Waterproofs twice peeled off—below, of course—to put on extra clothing towards morning, the chart to be attended to and marked, and entries to be made on the slate, besides that ever-recurring matter of refreshment. If all this were not enough to check a disposition to sleep there was cold water enough flying about—chiefly rebounding from the boat on deck—to keep one quite up to the mark; I fancy the man at the helm occasionally heard some rather ill-tempered remarks about this.

The steamer before referred to was the only vessel seen throughout the night. At midnight I made Beachy Head light, bearing N. by E. 20 miles, which tallied well with the course marked; but the log, which indicated $83\frac{1}{2}$—with 15 to add for distance sailed before it was set off Barfleur—was 10 miles in excess of the actual distance from Cherbourg, and showed how considerable was the loss of time and direct mileage by sheering off the course when necessarily absent from the helm.*

Aug. 2.—Altered course to N.E. by E. At daybreak, saw the hills of Fairleigh, and at 5.45 passed Dungeness against tide, weather looking bad, and blowing extremely cold off the Romney marshes. Several vessels were in company bound up Channel, of which I kept clear by steering more to the northward. Outside my ordinary shirt and flannels I had a thick serge shirt, two coats, and a stout waterproof, besides a large woollen comforter; inside the indiarubber knee boots, a pair of high woollen stockings over woollen socks, two pairs of trousers, and a waterproof covering over the legs. With all this on, I felt the cold extremely.

9.45 A.M., off Shakespeare Cliff; I threw off the heavy clothing and prepared for work. Backed the foresail, rounded-

* The loss from this cause amounted to about 15 miles on the whole course, or, in other words, increased the distance sailed between Cherbourg and Dover, which should have been 150 miles, to 165. In computing time and distance on the next page, the extra 15 miles are not taken into consideration.

to, hauled aft main and mizen sheets, triced up bobstay with a watch tackle, cleared the halyards for letting go, uncovered chain-pipe, cast off chain stopper below, and got the anchor ready. Bore up again for Dover, and lowered the foresail. This reads as if it were done in five minutes, but it was hard work, and occupied me a long while. Thus prepared, I stood in for the anchorage, and brought up off the town at 11 o'clock, 27 hours from the time of heaving up off Cherbourg.

The first 130 miles from Cherbourg breakwater was done in 20 hours; the last 18 miles, to Shakespeare Cliff, in 5 hours against tide. It was a fine passage with a reefed mainsail, and head sheets flat aft. The proper canvas would have been whole mainsail, large mizen, jib-headed topsail, foresail and second jib, had there been men to tend the sheets and hand the sails in case of need; but that would have been 'carrying on!'

Undecided whether to go into harbour or not, I set to work and stowed all the canvas. As there was a nasty roll in the Bay, I began by securing the boom with the trysail tackle and main-sheet, and then lowered the mainsail. Stopped the jib on the bowsprit with canvas tyers, and the head of it in with the fore-sail. Furled the mizen on the mast, stopped it with canvas tyers, and frapped the boom in with the topping-lift, to keep it quiet, and then turned my attention to the heaviest and most difficult job of all, which occupied me nearly an hour. When, after one or two failures, all the mainsail was rolled up and supported on my shoulder, it took about five minutes— weighted and smothered as I was—to pass the rope round a circumference of 6 or 7 feet, from one hand to the other, to break the canvas in with. Once that was on fairly, and tautened round the bunt of the sail, the rest was a matter of detail. I put all the canvas tyers on next, to keep the sail up to the gaff, and then tautened and improved them over and over again, using a spare tyer for the purpose, until it was furled to my satisfaction.

It may be fairly inferred from this that I was not in the distressed condition one might expect. If more reefs and shift of jibs had been required, it is reasonable to suppose I could have done all that was necessary, hard as it would have been. About 1 o'clock two gentlemen, having just received the letter despatched from Cherbourg, came off from the Royal Cinque Ports Yacht Club, and advised me to go into harbour, kindly adding, that when the tide was high enough they would return and lend me a hand. Breakfast had been badly wanted for a long while. 'But work first and pleasure afterwards!' There would have been neither in perfection with the prospect of two hours' exhausting labour to follow. Now, after a good wash and change of clothes, I should be able to sit down comfortably and enjoy it. Having carefully cleaned out the stove, there was no difficulty about the fire, although it was my first attempt. While washing, dressing, and tidying up below, the water was boiling and bread baking, and at 2 o'clock —30 hours overdue—I sat down to a capital breakfast of broiled ham, hot bread, and splendid coffee, with Swiss milk. No Lord Mayor's banquet was equal to that!

When my friends returned at 3 o'clock they found me little disposed to work, which I suspected would be the case, and was the main reason for persevering in doing the work first; and also the reason for ordering the men to wash down going into Cherbourg, when they were idling on deck, doing nothing. If I had been in their place, it is what I should have chosen to do for my own comfort and convenience, without wanting to be told.

Under headsails and mizen we turned into the mouth of the harbour, and there, meeting a strong head wind, had to down canvas and warp up between the jetties, across the harbour, and into the basin. What detestable, hard, and dirty work it is. The warps have to be slacked down into the mud to let harbour tugs and all sorts of troublesome things pass over them; then they come aboard and through your hands in a disgusting state, not fit for men in decent clothes to handle. I felt quite ashamed that two gentlemen should have such disagreeable labour on my account. However, it was all over at last, and I got into a snug berth alongside a nice little schooner belonging to Mr. Kirby, the Rear Commodore of the club, who kindly offered me every assistance in his power. The captain and the men being equally willing and obliging, I spent as pleasant a time as it was possible for me to do in a close harbour.

Many persons, who are not sailors, supposed that I came over in a calm, because, at the end of a paragraph in the newspapers announcing my arrival at Dover, it said—'Weather calm and wet.' That was simply the usual weather report of the day on which the paragraph appeared—the day after my arrival. In calm weather, on the Scotch coast, I was, on one occasion, two whole days and nights sailing 40 miles; and upon another, five days and nights from the Thames to the Isle of Wight. These are instances of the most weary and vexatious work in my experience.

In consequence of the 'Orion' being reported from Cherbourg, the Custom-house officers came on board as soon as she was moored and asked—'Have you anything on board liable to duty?'

'Nothing. My custom has always been to have a sufficient supply of everything from London—duty paid; never to take anything out of bond; and never to purchase stores of any sort in a foreign port.'

'But you cannot answer for the crew?'—'Yes, I can.'

'How can you possibly do that, sir?'—'Because I can, and do.'

'Haven't you got any crew?'—'No.'

'What have you done with them?'—'Unshipped them at Cherbourg because the work was too heavy.'

'Have you sailed this vessel over, all alone?'—'Yes.'

'But they may have left something behind?'—'Nothing worth a halfpenny between the two, I'll guarantee; but there is the vessel open to you from end to end; I shall be happy to submit everything to examination.'

'That will do, sir.'—'Good afternoon.'

The men of Mr. Kirby's yacht put on the sail covers for me, washed and coiled down the warps, &c.

After a rather late dinner, I turned in at 9 o'clock and slept soundly.

Aug. 3.—Turned out at 6 a.m. A lad came to light the fire but did not understand the stove. So, somewhat in the same spirit as the author of 'the Casual' undertook his self-imposed disagreeable duty, I determined to undertake the whole of the work myself and find out by experience what men had to complain of.

Such moderate employment as keeping the vessel in order was probably advantageous after the late exertion, especially as I had resolved not to take fresh men, but to sail the 'Orion' home to Greenhithe, alone.—No doubt it would have been regarded in certain quarters as a confession of weakness—where none existed—to have hesitated about the other 70 miles, after doing the 150! Excepting that my hands were sore—notwithstanding the gloves—and muscles rather stiff, I felt no ill effects whatever.

Aug. 4.—Came on deck at 5 a.m. with buckets, scrubbing brushes, mop, and washleather, wearing a serge shirt, canvas trousers, no shoes and stockings—and bare arms; in fact with nothing on to spoil, but rather in good condition for going overboard, I set to work with the determination to carry it out properly. I felt a little bashful, with so many eyes upon me when the men turned out on board the yachts and ships in the dock, but soon overcame that feeling.

I began on the white elm rail forward, and worked round forward again—100 ft. of an average surface of 6 in.; then skylights, booby hatch, cockpit, deck, bulwarks, &c. The white elm scrubbing is equal to a plank 50 ft. long, 1 foot wide; deck 350 ft.; mahogany and oak 200 ft. The last must be dried with the washleather to preserve the varnish in good order, which necessitates going over it again, and brings the total up to 800 superficial feet of work, besides so much of the black paint outside as can be reached from the deck, which is equal to 200 or 300 feet more. Then there are scores of buckets of water to be drawn over the side, which is reckoned so much work in itself that, when two men are working together, one draws water and the other scrubs. The ropes are suspended out of the way, and afterwards coiled down in their places.

The whole occupied me 3½ hours. Two men generally spend 1½ to 2 hours over it, according as they are diligent or lazy. With the exception of washing down the 7-ton lugger I had never undertaken anything of the kind before, so, reasonably expected from the reports I had heard, from men taking a rest in the middle—which is absurdly common—and from the fact of my arms being quite unaccustomed to it, that if got through at all, I should be 'invalided' for the rest of the day. This was such utter nonsense that after breakfast I could have started again, without any inconvenience whatever. With a pipe in my mouth it would have taken half as long again, or, what is more likely still, never have been done properly at all.

The fire being lighted I cleaned out and tidied the forecastle; washed, dressed, and sat down comfortably to breakfast in the cabin at 9.30. By 11 o'clock everything was washed up and stowed away, forecastle and cabins in good order to receive visitors, and altogether it was so thoroughly jolly and pleasant that I felt the profoundest contempt for men who, having only half of it to do, could make a fuss over such a trifle. If anyone should be disposed to doubt the thoroughness and completeness of my work, they cannot fail to perceive, upon due consideration, that this was mere pastime compared to the labour of the previous days.

With the exception of luncheon there was nothing more to be done, for, by the courtesy of the Dover Club, yacht owners in harbour belonging to the Royal Cinque Ports Club are honorary members and are able to dine there—which I did with great satisfaction to myself every evening.

Aug. 6—was the day of Dover town regatta. Nearly all yachts went out of harbour between 5 and 7 a.m. Small ones to sail in the regatta; the others to sea.

I had been on deck since 5.30, hauling here and slacking there, expecting the harbour men would be allowed, as on other occasions, to help me into the outer harbour. But, almost at the last moment, this help was denied me by the deputy Harbourmaster. Objecting to be suffocated with heat in there another day, I begged so hard to be put 'just outside the gates'—a thing beggars never do—that, overcome by the novelty of the request, he at last assented. Ordinarily Mr. Deputy is most pleasant and obliging, but worried before breakfast by several large yachts struggling and fighting to get to sea all at once, in a calm, exhausted his patience, and as *they* were too big to be talked to, he visited his cooled coffee and chilled bacon upon me, a poor defenceless creature who could not, without assistance, move from the buoy he was moored to. Spectators must have suspected me of being 'wicked,' as in the outer harbour there was 'no peace'—from being ordered ahead, and ordered astern. The exigencies of the service no doubt demanded this, but it was most unpleasant to me all the same; at last, in desperation, I struck a bargain with some men in a boat to tow me to the anchorage in the Bay—about a third of a mile off the Clubhouse—where I let go the anchor at 11 o'clock, quite glad to be once more independent, like 'Mark Tapley' of glorious memory.

The first use I made of my liberty was to cast off superfluous clothing, put on canvas trousers, and proceed to wash off the harbour stains, above and below—which occupied me 4 hours, under a burning sun. The scrubbing was warm work indeed, but heaving about gallons of cold pure sea water, and putting things into nice order again, was pleasant enough.

By 4 o'clock I had a good appetite for dinner; after which, wrote a letter to Greenhithe asking for assistance, if by chance the 'Orion' should be there next day and appear to be in want of it. As my own boat remained turned over and stowed as at Cherbourg, I landed in a shore boat, for a few minutes, to post the letter, and then returned on board; shifted clothes as on the former occasion, put on the 'magic' roll of flannel to protect my stomach and loins from chill, and commenced the arduous work of getting under way.

The jib was run out on the bowsprit, and the mizen bent, in the dock; so there was that less to do now. There being little wind, I set all the canvas excepting the foresail, and set up the bobstay before heaving the anchor right up at 8.30 p.m. The process being the same as before, it is unnecessary to go into details, but the exhaustion was less, as I was in first-rate condition—well rested, well fed, and without a shade of misgiving as to the successful termination of the little voyage home.

The motive for getting under way, with night coming on—which at first sight seems rash, but was not—may as well be explained here. It would be high water at Greenhithe at 11.30 a.m. next day, and, of course, not again until nearly midnight. If good fortune attended me, the more open sea part would be sailed in the dark; the difficult and intricate south channels, in the early morning; the troublesome sailing and steam traffic of the Thames, encountered in the forenoon. But sailing from Dover in the morning, there would have been an 'absolute necessity' for letting go the anchor on the passage, furling the sails, and hoisting them again. The necessary labour consequent upon stopping a tide during the night, instead of giving rest would have worn me out; so it was not to be thought of, if it could possibly be avoided.

The wind was light from the eastward, weather hazy and partially cloudy. I stood out of the Bay immediately, and hove-to for half an hour, with the foresail to windward—in the eastern going tide—to get the side-lights up, and coil down the halyards. When all was ready, I 'let draw' the foresail and made a board to the southward and eastward, far enough to clear the South Foreland, with a good berth, on the other tack; and worked the Gulf Stream, to avoid the shipping at anchor in the Downs.

From the South Foreland Dover looked quite gay with its semi-circle of lights and the regatta fireworks—presenting a homely and cheerful sight, compared with the dull aspect out at sea.

The electric lights of the South Foreland are powerful enough to illuminate low filmy clouds within a mile radius—as if the moon were behind them. They are interesting, and appear, when observed attentively at the distance of two or three miles, to vary in strength and colour every minute. It is not a good thing, however, for the helmsman, or the lookout, to amuse himself watching these pretty lights on a dark night, when there is likely to be anything in the way, for they are dazzling almost to blindness.

10.30 p.m., Dover out of sight; Deal and Ramsgate visible as pretty illuminations at the distance of 4 and 10 miles respectively. After an hour's calm, in which I felt thankful not to be drifting amongst the ships in the Downs, a light breeze sprang up from S.W. In the vicinity of the Gull lightship a steam tug towing a ship passed me to the westward, after keeping me a long while in suspense, followed by two steamers in succession, that, to my great relief, took a course different from the ship, and passed to the eastward of the lightship. I felt grateful to the Corporation of the Trinity House for thus leading them away, and publicly thanked them on the spot. The screw steamer, when carelessly handled, is a dreadful engine of destruction, and long ago earned the name of 'Silent Deaths' bestowed upon them by the North Sea fishermen—a name sufficiently expressive not to require further explanation, and, unfortunately, not always undeserved. Captains of steamers, when ashore, are, like other folk, sometimes flattered to their face and ill spoken of behind their back. At sea it is not so. Our manners are better. We never speak so well of them as when their back is turned.

The effect of a long and hard day's work, and good victualling instead of short commons, was to make me sleepy, especially as the sailing was dull and slow. Sitting at the helm, on a stool without any support for the back, is a safe enough position under the circumstances to fall asleep in, for the instant that forgetfulness steals over you the chance of keeping your seat is about the same as that of an egg standing on end. I do not like to say what happened to me, lest you should laugh at my expense, but caution others that, if overpowered with sleep at the helm, they will find the deck much in the way of their head and shoulders. I saw and knew everything, far and near, steered the course, and tended the lamps most carefully, but was not so wide awake as required by the Rule of the Road at Sea.

The experience of a few days before was in marked contrast

to this. From the moment the French gun aroused me from my two hours' nap on the Wednesday morning at Cherbourg, until Thursday night at Dover, I had not even an attack of drowsiness, attributable partly to the briskness of the weather, but more, I believe, to the fact of being considerably underfed. Moreover, as related elsewhere, I had been up and busily employed since 6 A.M. the previous day (Tuesday), not even attempting to lie down, or being desirous to do so, with this one exception, for 63 hours. But of this dreary night I was thoroughly tired, and devoutly wished for morning, particularly as the weather became exceedingly gloomy, and threatened a storm.

At daybreak, near the North Foreland, I put on waterproofs and sou'wester for a smart shower, which also brought a welcome southerly breeze with it. 5 A.M., hauled aft sheets at the Foreland, and lay up along the north coast of Kent. The smell off the wet harvest fields was most refreshing and delightful. The rain passing off, I took advantage of the favourable change to boil water for cocoa and get breakfast, between Margate and Herne Bay; but it was an unsatisfactory performance without heaving-to, for which there was no time, unless all hope of making Greenhithe at high water were abandoned. The chance was a very poor one up to 8.30, when the wind shifted a couple of points to S.S.W., and came strong out of Whitstable Bay, improving the pace from 3 to 8 knots; at the same time the clouds dispersed and the sun shone out pleasantly.

A nice-looking ketch, with every stitch of canvas set, passed the North Foreland two miles ahead of me. When the breeze freshened she was about half a mile ahead; at the Nore—9.30 —a quarter of a mile. Two or three times in Sea Reach I was near enough to read 'Lively of Exeter,' but could not pass her, because, every half hour as we advanced up the Reach, the sheets wanted hauling aft a little, which caused me to drop astern, as I had to leave the helm and shake up to do it. The skipper of the ketch was at the helm, 'doing his very best' to prevent me passing, and evidently enjoyed the fun as much as I did. At the top of Sea Reach I had to haul aft all sheets, using a tackle for the jib, which cost me much time, and gave 'Lively' a lead of half a mile—but somewhat to leeward. The first time we met, in the Lower Hope, sailing to windward, she was a quarter of a mile astern, which shows that reaching under a press of sail with a vessel like that is one thing and sailing to windward another; I had to go about four times, and on each occasion made a bight in the tiller-rope to slip over the tiller, short of hard down, which allowed time to work the head sails and run aft again in time to prevent her breaking off more than two or three points. There is a moment in stays when the jib sheet may be got by hand; I succeeded perfectly each time, and twice in Clement's Reach; but should not have cared to go on working like that all day.

The country on each side was so bright and clear that the sail up Gravesend Reach at the top of high water was charming. 'Lively' had scarcely got into the Reach when I passed Gravesend at noon.

At Broadness, opposite Grays, the tide was making down. After running before the wind in Northfleet Hope the mainsheet had to be hauled aft for going to windward in Clement's Reach. There was so much sheet to get in that she 'filled' and 'paid off' before it could be completed, and although I fought hard to retain my grasp, it was no use; the sheet went out, and all my breath with it.

By experiments since tried, I can pull horizontally, or lift, 210 lb. My ordinary working strain is 120 lb.; with one hand, 60 lb. When the mainsheet overpowers me, the pressure exceeds a ton.

At 12.30 I was off Greenhithe, in a difficulty about taking the canvas off, and holding my way against tide, without the risk of falling athwart one of the numerous craft at anchor. As before stated, a letter had been posted at Dover to ask for assistance from the training ship 'Arethusa' in case of this occurring, but, as between Cherbourg and Dover, I was again before the post, the letter not being delivered until three hours later. So I 'did my very best'—bother the stupid words, they are that man Henry's—and fetched up between the 'Arethusa' and the shore, with the canvas half down, in confusion, hailing lustily for assistance to the moorings, which was promptly and kindly rendered as soon as my position was observed.

There is no opportunity for saying 'perseverance was rewarded at last'—which implies triumph over discouraging vexations and unexpected difficulties, for, with the exception of the foul anchor at Cherbourg, I am thankful to say that I did not experience any.

I lost between 2 lb. and 3 lb. in weight during these few days, and recovered it, with interest, in the next few weeks.

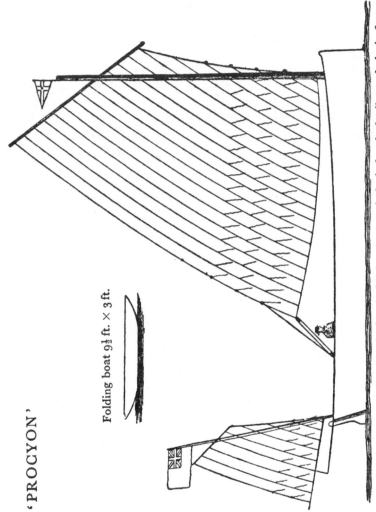

'PROCYON'

Folding boat 9½ ft. × 3 ft.

Scale ⅛ in. to foot.   Yard 13 ft., head of sail 12 ft.   13 cloths in head of sail, 19 cloths in foot.

'PROCYON'

Pine dinghey 7 ft. × 3 ft. 3 in. to replace folding boat

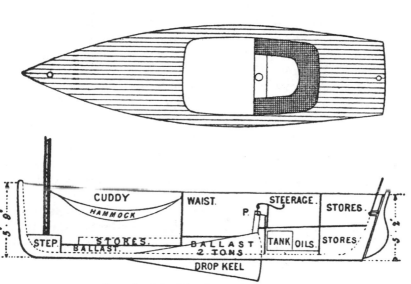

Length 28 ft. 6 in., breadth 7 ft. 9 in.

EXPERIMENTAL CRUISE IN THE 'PROCYON', 1878

As partly referred to already, in 1873 I sailed this boat single-handed from Greenhithe to the Isle of Wight and Lymington. Upon that occasion I was so destitute of the numerous comforts necessary to render such an arduous undertaking even tolerable that, after a rest of three days at Dover, I beat down Channel against a head wind and rough sea, without seeking shelter in any other port. I was forty hours under way at one time, and then, after a few hours' rest off Selsea Bill, finished up with five hours of double-reefed mainsail and three of single; for no other reason than that the living was so unsatisfactory, I desired to 'knock it off' as quickly as possible.

I have never recommended single-handed sailing, and will not abuse my new-claimed privilege by doing so now. All I propose is to give a description of the boat and a simple account of the sailing, including preparations for rendering myself independent of all extraneous aid for a month; an independence I intended resolutely to maintain for that period, even against 'sea-prowlers' in search of a job, who, before now, have been known to force their unbidden services where they were neither desired nor needed—a species of piracy in philanthropic guise upon which an exorbitant claim may be founded, that finds no favour with seamen of any class, and is never practised by the respectable 'long-shore' men of the coast. If assistance were required I should not hesitate to welcome it, as I have done on previous occasions; but my acquaintance with the boat would be slight if I were not able to judge of its necessity for myself. These remarks arise out of a discussion that was forced upon me by a man belonging to a disappointed lugger's crew, who came out of his way to taunt me in Dover Harbour with having regretted, when it was too late, that I had not accepted their services, and agreed to give them a *trifle* to pilot me into Ramsgate. If he could have heard the congratulations

202

of the bystanders upon my having avoided their interference, and the hostile remarks that were made after he left, he and his co-philanthropists would be less ready in future to air grievances based upon mere assumption.

As I had only a month to spare, and it would take nearly that time to prepare the 'Orion' for sea, I resolved to have another sea trial of the 'Procyon.' Borrowing from the former vessel anything I thought likely to contribute to my safety and convenience, I surrounded myself with every comfort that could be rendered available in the limited space afforded by a 7-ton boat.

When all was on board and stowed away, the congestion of lockers, and general block up below, was so nearly complete that the precise whereabouts of many little useful articles belonging to the domestic department became doubtful. However, my memory being sufficiently good to know they were there, it frequently happened that I contentedly submitted to be deprived of them for the time being, knowing that, whenever it suited me to take the trouble, they could be obtained. If this seems rather 'Irish,' it is human nature. Anyway, I was satisfied; and there was no one else to complain.

The 'Procyon' was built for me in 1867, and lengthened 5 feet by the stern in 1870, by Messrs. Holloway, of Whitstable. The sails are by Messrs. Lapthorn, of Gosport. The entire expense was £217, and I have always done them the justice to admit that the substantial nature of the work was commensurate with the cost, and supported their high local reputation for honest and finished workmanship. Her length is 28½ feet, extreme breadth 7¾ feet, and average depth inside 5 feet. Draught, aft 3 feet, forward 2 feet. Her height as she stands on the ground with a 6-inch keel is 5 feet 10 inches forward and 5 feet 2 inches aft. The extra height forward, which answers its purpose completely, is to counteract the effect of placing the mast so near the stem. The height of the 'cuddy' is 4 feet from the floor to the deck beams, and its length is 12 feet. On each side there is a low bench fitted up as a locker, which might be rendered available for sleeping bunks; but I prefer to swing a hammock between the mast and the mainbeam.

The space under the after deck, which is 5 feet long, is protected from the weather by a bulkhead and doors. Fitted up with capacious shelves and leeboards, the stowage here is considerable; even the space under the floor and down to the deadwood being utilised for articles not liable to injury by water.

She has what is technically called a 'centre-board,' but which, on account of its moderate dimensions, I prefer to call an auxiliary keel, since its drop below the main keel is but from nothing forward to 18 inches aft, or an average drop of 9 inches for its length of 10 feet. It is of ¾ sheet iron, and weighs 2 cwt. The advantage I claim for this form of drop-keel is, that it is so powerfully held by the main keel (6 inches deep) that there is but little chance of its being twisted or damaged by accidental contact with the ground. Rocks or sand simply force it up; but if, when sailing fast, you have the misfortune to encounter a bank of stiff clay, there is a chance of being held until the tide rises; in the meanwhile, if there is any motion, it acts as an awkward lever to strain the garboard seams, as would any other which did not bend or break off. The keel case being under the waist platform, and considerably below the waterline, is, of course, entirely closed and caulked, excepting the shaft for the lifting chain which ascends through the main thwart. Into this shaft the pump discharges its rusty water, instead of on to the deck or over the side. On each side of the keel-case—which we have hitherto thought sufficiently protected from the strain—the iron ballast, amounting to two tons, is stowed; so that all these awkward things are out of sight excepting the shaft and the pump. Truly, she is a jolly boat, and a model of strength; but recent experience has shown the necessity of protecting this part a little more, for which a plan has been submitted, and approved by the builders. To obviate the unpleasant sound occasioned by the pitching and rolling of a clincher-built boat, several of the 'lands' above and below the waterline are filled in, so that she is as silent at sea as if she were carvel-built.

The height of the mainmast, which is stepped only 18 inches from the stem, is 21 feet above the gunwale; its diameter is 6 inches (or circumference, on deck 19 inches, at the sheave in masthead 14 inches), and weight, including ironwork and gear, 1¾ cwt. The mizenmast, in height, 13 feet above the gunwale, is stepped just within the transom; thus there is a clear drift of 26 feet between the masts.

Persons viewing her suppose that the mast being so far forward must tend to pay her head off when reaching or closehauled; but, the mainsail sheeting 21 feet abaft, the effect is so much the reverse that she carries a strong weather helm reaching, and if left to herself in a breeze, closehauled, invariably tends to wind, whether the mizen is set or not.

The mainsail—of No. 5 double, 2 feet canvas split—is a working lug, with an upper tack-tackle hooked into an extra cringle above the third reef for peaking the sail, and a lower tack-tackle at the foot of the mast for trimming it. When the lower tack is triced up the sail works clear overhead, enabling one to work forward on deck with safety. The length of the yard is 13 feet, the head of the sail 12 feet, and the foot 18½ feet.

When a reef is to be taken down, or sail temporarily shortened for a squall, I hook the reef-tackle into the fourth cringle of the after leach, lower away main halyards sufficiently, take in the slack of the upper tack-tackle until it is nearly two blocks, peak the yard again by 'setting up' halyards, and then bowse the sheet aft with the reef-tackle. When this is done, half the sail remains properly set, and the boat is under command during the process of reefing, or until the squall has expended its violence. If a reef is to be taken, the lower tack-tackle and mainsheet have to be transferred to the cringles above and the sister-hooks moused, the two hoops on the mast shifted a cringle higher, the tack and sheet rolled up and secured with short pieces of small manilla rope having an eye spliced in one end, eighteen reef points tied, fall of mainsheet belayed— leaving plenty of slack, so as not to interfere with hoisting the sail, reef-tackle cast off, and upper tack-tackle overhauled. Then hoist away mainsail, taking care to keep your head out

THE 'PROCYON'

of the way of the upper mainsheet-block when the sail flaps in the wind, peak with upper tack-tackle until the sail is girt from the tack to the peak, bowse down lower tack, throw her up into the wind and get the sheet aft. If the sail is not then as flat as it might be, I put a strap on the fall of the main halyards (which leads aft to the waist through a block at the foot of the mast), hook in a luff-tackle, shake up in the wind and bowse away until no more can be got, belay the slack of main halyards and remove the strap and tackle. With a strong crew— as in match sailing—the lower tack would be set up and the mainsheet hauled aft before hoisting; but single-handed the sail must be free of all impediment, to enable it to be hoisted at all. When dry the weight of this sail with yard is 92 lb. The stormsail differs from the mainsail only in size, being 6 feet on the head and $13\frac{1}{2}$ feet on the foot. The hoist is the same, and its weight with yard $\frac{1}{4}$ cwt. It is necessary to state these particulars to account for the time expended in making or taking in sail, and to account for one's hands getting into such bad condition after every two or three days' rough encounter with the elements.

The riding gear consists of 30 fathoms $\frac{5}{16}$ chain, a bass rope of 40 fathoms, and another of 25, besides sundry pieces of manilla, to supply deficiencies and for mooring ropes. There are three anchors, 38 lb., 28 lb., and 20 lb., and a grapnel.

Amongst articles in the inventory, some of which belong to the 'Orion,' are the following: McDonald's patent folding boat; a 30-gallon boat tank, of india-rubber, stowed beneath the after platform, and worked out with a zinc hand-pump; filter in basket-work; a two-gallon water-can; cabin table with flaps, containing cellaret; folding table, to fit up in the waist of a boat in harbour; an American chair with arms; a camp stool and two cork stools, the latter serviceable as extra seats, or to buoy dropped moorings; a hammock, horsehair bed, feather pillow, and blankets; portable closet; canvas awning, 13 feet by 8, which, besides largely increasing the accommodation, secures comfort and privacy in harbour; zinc safe in basket-work, 2 feet by 1, kept under main thwart in the waist; a 7 lb.

hand-lead and 10-fathom line, a 3 lb. ditto and 3-fathom line; Walker's patent log and 25-fathom line; two binnacles, with spirit compasses and lanterns; two riding lights, one a patent triangular, with extra coloured slides; a cabin lantern and a candle-lamp; an eight-day clock, lashed up firm, and protected from damp by a waterproof covering; a fair assortment of carpenter's tools, including axe, crowbar, and saw; various sizes of galvanised iron shackles, hooks, and thimbles; brass thimbles, screws, copper nails, &c.; spare canvas for parcellings; oils, lamp-feeders, scissors, oakum, and cotton waste; a petroleum stove, the 'Acme,' in which alterations to adapt it to boat service were carefully carried out to suit my views by Messrs. Deane & Co., of London Bridge. I divided the large flat reservoir into three compartments fore and aft, or in the direction of the wick, which is a 4-inch. Communicating with each other only by an opening of $\frac{1}{8}$ of an inch at the other end, I considered that, if the boat were heeling over and plunging about, the centre compartment containing the wick would never be empty while there was any appreciable quantity of oil to consume. The burner was soldered in, the indicator closed in the same manner, and the feeder protected from leakage by a washer. As I only required the oven for baking stale bread, I had the bottom part closed against any possible smoke from the flame. With these alterations it answered admirably, and frequently rendered the situation tolerable, even to cheerfulness, when it would otherwise, from the excessive rains and extreme violence of the elements, have been almost unbearable.

Determined to be independent of the shore for long intervals, if I chose, and to have only light marketing to do occasionally, I laid in a sufficient supply of Bass's pale ale and of claret to last for a month, a small quantity of whisky, and a bottle of brandy for medicinal purposes, which I softened by burning before starting; potatoes for a month, a ham for broiling, some kippered salmon, followed up when gone by Scotch herrings in tins to alternate with the ham for breakfast, a locker full of preserved meats of various kinds, Swiss milk, cocoa, tea, and an ample supply of the best coffee I could buy in London, cake, biscuits, jams, sweetmeats, and tobacco.

What with my wardrobe contained in three sail bags, and a portmanteau, and the hundred etceteras, such as coffee-pot, teapot, crockery, glass, knives and forks, &c., &c., all of which had a proper place assigned them, without which half the articles enumerated would have been useless; topping all up with about 2 cwt. of new rope, spare tackles, straps, &c., sorted and secured with yarns to the timbers along the sides of the cabin, where they could be instantly selected as desired; he must have been a man less easily satisfied than I am who could have viewed the significant confusion reigning in the domestic department at starting otherwise than as evidence that he was well found, even though champagne and pâté de foie gras were not included in the list of necessaries.

Aug. 7.—The captain of the training ship 'Arethusa' having obligingly consented to allow my tank to be supplied with filtered water from that vessel, I was towed out of the creek and alongside by one of her boats. The wind being too light to sail, and the confusion on board very great, as it always is until a place has been found for everything, I hauled off when the tank was filled, and let go the anchor for the night.

Aug. 8.—I felt so extremely unwell, and had made so little progress in reducing the confusion to anything like order, that up to the very moment of sailing I was undecided whether to proceed or to return into the creek. So strong was this feeling, really due to such a condition of ill-health that I almost loathed food, that at 4.30 P.M. when I got under way I warned my ship-keeper in the creek to expect my return in two or three days. The wind was light from south-west, with a cloudy and thundery appearance. Being much occupied in various ways, and there being nothing in the way at the time, I suffered the boat to be drifted into the lower bight of Gravesend Reach, when suddenly the wind shifted for a moment to the northward, and then fell flat calm. Observing the buoy off Cliff Creek, and a schooner at anchor just beyond, I became slightly alarmed; but perceiving that the buoy was well open of the schooner, and that her masts were likewise well open of each other, it seemed impossible I should drift in upon them. This, however, being the case, I bounded forward and let go the anchor, unfortunately not in time to bring her up, and she fell athwart-hawse the schooner, with her jibboom in my main-sail about 15 feet from the deck. The canvas being stout, and the sheet not flat aft, the elastic resistance it offered gradually checked her way, and allowed her to fall more gently than she would otherwise have done upon the schooner's port bow; when she heeled so alarmingly, from the rush of tide, that the master considerately hove me a rope by which to escape if she foundered. My first impression was that the mast would come down, and I stooped below the coamings to avoid being smothered by the canvas or entangled in the ropes. Seeing that the gear stood the strain, I went aft and let the mainsheet run out and partially unreeve, which cleared the mainsail from the jibboom end and righted her a little. By this time the Coast-guard officer and four men from the station at Cliff Creek, with the promptness and kindly readiness to assist which everywhere characterizes the service, arrived upon the scene. Jammed on the schooner's port bow with my mast on the starboard side of her bowsprit, the only hope of escape lay in passing round to her starboard side. While the schooner paid out chain, which momentarily eased the pressure, our united efforts were directed to forging the lugger half her length ahead. This caused her to hang on the schooner's stem, slightly abaft the midships, her head being prevented from swinging down by her own chain, which now became taut as a bar on the port bow, and held her athwart stream, until the mizen, being first violently swayed to loosen the wedges, was unstepped and laid upon the deck. Paying out my chain, while the men bore her off bodily, she passed fairly on to the schooner's starboard bow; and then, keeping her head to with a rope while they bore the stern off with spars, she swung round and brought up gently alongside with no harm done. The anchor was so deeply imbedded that it required the strength of all hands and a hard sheer to break it out of the ground, which done, she was sheered into a berth below the schooner and the anchor let go for the night.

When the mizen was stepped and the mainsail furled, and it was ascertained that she was not making any water, compliments suitable to the occasion were exchanged. The master of the schooner behaved admirably, and—rare but most agreeable experience—wanted to return part of what I thought was due to him. At my request they then left me to wash down and restore order. When that was done I got some tea, put up the riding light before the mast, and turned in at midnight to think about it. Before starting, and when sailing down, I felt that if she were sunk, or given away to anyone who could handle her properly and would keep her in good order, it would be no great matter; but now the feeling was entirely changed. Had she been less powerfully built or less well found than she was—it was not on board there I should have 'turned in' that night.

Aug. 9.—A gloomy and dirty morning, with a fresh wind from the nor'ard, a lively ripple, and a drizzly rain. After a cold sluice, which on board ship has often to do duty for sleep, I hastened to get under way, notwithstanding that, being quite undecided where to go, I was far more disposed to lie there and do nothing. But during the ebb tide a strong north wind renders the riding off Cliff Creek very undesirable in a boat of light draught with a single anchor and a dinghey astern. Not simply on account of the motion, to which a sailor ought not to object, but because the boat, being light and buoyant, would run over her anchor, take violent sheers from side to side, and pass half the time in the trough of the sea, with the chain grinding and sweeping the keel from forward aft, or from aft forward, ending in a violent jerk and a moment's peace; only to begin the same round over again, to which it would be absurd if a sailor did not object, especially in close proximity to other vessels and a lee shore.

It was 5 A.M. when I commenced operations by taking down the riding light. From the trouble it gave, owing to the quick motion of the boat requiring me to hold on with one arm, and the narrow escape the lantern had of being dashed to pieces against the mast, I resolved not to hoist it in the same position again. 6 A.M. under way with the whole mainsail set to a roaring breeze and heading down the river. Having come out for health I had decided by the time the sail was nicely trimmed that it was advisable to go in search of it, and that there was no more likely place to find it than in the neighbourhood of the South Foreland. So I conquered the miserable state of indecision that had plagued me for two whole days, and being averse to half measures, was bound to Dover.

At the start it was chilly and uncomfortable; but as the morning advanced the wind gradually backed to the north-west, the rain ceased, and the sun gleamed occasionally through the broken clouds.

The preparation of meals when a vessel is on a wind and sea moderate is far easier than when running free. Presupposing a moderate degree of attention, if the sails are properly trimmed, a vessel should be able to sail herself close-hauled during a temporary absence from the helm; but running free, according to my experience, the helm cannot be left a minute without sheering off the course, and either broaching-to or threatening a gybe.

Although quite unable to enjoy food of any description, I took the opportunity of the course being almost clear of vessels, between the Nore and Herne Bay, to light the stove and get some breakfast. Running dead before the wind it was a most troublesome and unsatisfactory performance, especially as in obedience to a rule, indispensable to comfort, cleanliness, and economy—a rule no more admitting of exceptions than the laws of the Medes and Persians—everything had to be washed up and stowed away again in its place. This seems too easy to be dignified with the name of 'work.' But if there were no need to watch the vessel and be constantly correcting the course, greasy utensils, when there is a scarcity of boiling water, are very troublesome to deal with; and to clean out properly a French coffee-pot in four parts is a work of art for an un-practised hand. That such employment is at all times exceed-

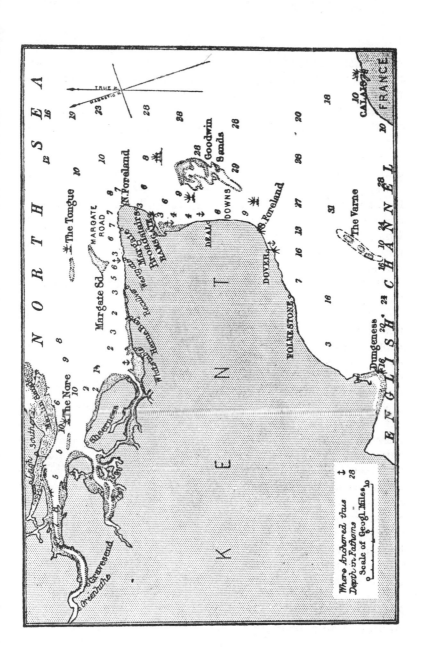

ingly distasteful, should be a sufficient reason for making a rule on the subject, and observing it strictly, whatever the hour and the personal inconvenience. For if things are not washed up when used, it is not deferring the cleaning to a more convenient time, but paving the way for habitually using them dirty. If objection be taken to such work as ungentlemanly, no one will dispute that neglect of cleanliness and order, begotten of idleness and silly pride, is infinitely more so. The coffee-pot and cooking utensils were put away clean on a shelf forward of the mast, and kept noiseless by a piece of spare canvas jammed between them. Inside the cabin bulkhead I had put up a long strip of leather, nailed firmly at both ends and divided with nails at intervals, in which to insert the knives, forks, spoons, and lamp scissors, so that they could neither stray nor jingle with the motion, and were always at hand.

The domestic work was fortunately over when the wind freshened so much that the boat staggered under the sail, and kept me a close prisoner at the helm. The course, now straight for the North Foreland from Herne Bay, brought the wind and sea on the quarter, and made the steering so active and fatiguing that I had to 'purchase' the lee tiller-rope, by passing it round a cleat on the main thwart, and pull on the bight of it.

I have an iron tiller about 7 feet long, but prefer to use a yoke of my own design. It is constructed of iron, with arms 3 feet long. At the end of each arm is a brass-sheaved iron block fitted with a horizontal joint and a limited swivel, which allows the block to accommodate itself to the angle required, without the possibility of twisting the standing and running parts of the rope together. It is a powerful purchase, and the ropes are long enough to lead to any part of the vessel, excepting quite forward. On the wind, or running dead before it, the steering is easy; but reaching fast with the sea on the quarter or abeam, the helmsman has plenty to do.

11.15 A.M., passed the Reculvers, against tide; and 1 P.M. Margate Pier, which seemed deserted; as at that hour the swells had all gone home to dinner.

Rounding the Foreland before the sea, the patent folding boat—which is no 'swell' to look at—seemed desirous to follow their example and desert me. Sheering on the sea, it jerked the headfast so violently, that I feared it might break adrift and compel me to put the lugger on the wind to pick it up again; which, under so heavy a press of canvas, I was ill prepared to do.

It may be asked how I came to be towing a folding boat on such a rough day, instead of having her doubled up and snugly stowed on board. The fact is, I had her strengthened to such an extent to fit her for my rough work that she weighed over 90 lb. instead of 50, and was so stiff in working that I was not disposed to expend the strength required to take her up, fold, and berth her on board. Moreover, being so heavy and cumbersome for one hand to deal with, she marked everything with which she came in contact with her paint and greasy hinges. Standard cwts. and even $\frac{1}{2}$ cwts., with their compact form and convenient rings for lifting, are not playthings; but they are so in comparison with similar weights represented by awkward-shaped parcels several feet in length, and having no handles whatever—particularly so when the motion of the vessel is great, and it is difficult to move or to stand without holding on.

I never pass the North Foreland on a sunny day without admiring it extremely, not for its boldness and grandeur, for, in comparison with the South Foreland, Beachy Head, and the towering chalk cliffs of the Isle of Wight, it has neither, but for its numerous miniature bays and sandy coves, formed by the pretty indentations of the white cliffs, and its wealth of agriculture, trees, and windmills exposed to the view down to the cliff-edge by the gentle and unbroken elevation of the land behind—the charming little nook of Kingsgate and the lighthouses forming a centre-piece of the whole. Passing this picturesque little spot with a fine breeze off the land and a moderate swell, which, owing to the projecting reefs of the Foreland, had ceased to be troublesome, was really delightful, and could only have been more so if I had been able to enjoy a good luncheon and the orthodox pipe, which, unless there is something wrong in the sanitary department, seldom fails to accompany a much appreciated meal at sea.

4.15 P.M., off Deal Pier. Band playing—boys fishing—boats sailing—paterfamilias, and the whole tribe, out for a row—the beach alive with ramblers in search of 'precious stones' and other treasures cast up by the sea—a scene of peaceful enjoyment which never ceases to interest those who are able to stand close enough in shore to observe it. The wind having backed to the westward, came off in puffs alternated with flat calms—a sure sign of its decline for the day.

I expected to make Dover about seven o'clock, but at the South Foreland encountered the full strength of the tide; at the same time the wind was light and nearly ahead. Here I came up with a few laden colliers, with one of which I had a little friendly chat in passing, and could not avoid noticing how much more handy and seaworthy they appeared with the Plimsoll load-line than in the recklessly heavy trim of years gone by. They were, however, quickly left far behind, when, to cheat the tide as much as possible, I made short tacks; several times standing in to comparatively shallow water under the towering cliffs, which, while there is the faintest glimmer of twilight, never cease echoing the plaintive, simply energetic, or else angry cries of invisible sea birds—whether relating in inflated language the story of their first venture on the watery region below, 'curtain lecturing,' or engaged in perpetual disputes as to the possession of 'coigns of vantage,' I never can make out.

As there was no prospect of reaching Dover before dark, and the boat was not heeling much, I seized the opportunity to have a sort of luncheon-dinner at the helm, of cold roast lamb, bread, lettuce, and a small bottle of 'Bass,' carefully transferring the plates, &c., to the weather side the last moment before going about. Abreast of the 'Castle Cliff,' a galley under sail to windward bore down upon me, to ask if I wanted assistance into harbour. Upon my civilly declining them several times—for all their class are very pressing—they left me with 'No

216

offence, I hope,' a species of parting salutation I observe never proceeds from nice men; so that I was glad I had kept my own counsel, and had not supplied them with another excuse for importunity—the danger of bringing up for the night at sea.

With the anchor ready for letting go, the main tack triced up, and the halyards clear, I stood close in to the beach, where I supposed the club-house to be; then ran off a proper distance, heaving the lead, and at 9 P.M. let go the anchor, having been fifteen hours under way.

Although it was a beautiful starlight night, and the bay with its numerous town-lights looked very homely and peaceful, I took two reefs in the mainsail before furling it, had some tea, and a general clear up, and then turned into my hammock for a much-needed night's rest.

Aug. 10, *Sunday.*—After church time, landed for letters. 3 P.M., weighed anchor and went into harbour, just in time to furl and cover the sails, get dinner, and attend evening service. My hands were so sore from a cut finger and abrasions, that it was advisable to allow them time to heal. Even in harbour there is very little time for idling; as, in attending entirely upon oneself, and keeping such order as should infallibly distinguish private property, there is always plenty of employment. Besides, I was engaged in correspondence which left barely time to scan the newspapers, and, for all the service they were, the box of books with which I had provided myself might have been left at home.

Dover is undoubtedly the best rendezvous for yachts between the Thames and the Isle of Wight—especially for those whose owners have the good fortune to belong to the Royal Cinque Ports Yacht Club, which occupies a central position on the shore of the bay, and commands a better view from its windows than any club in the kingdom. Dover is, however, rising so rapidly in commercial importance, and its docks are becoming so crowded, that it will be a great boon to yachtsmen and to the overworked officials of the port when the bay is enclosed (like Portland), and the former are enabled to ride in safety at anchor outside. Even then, some will avail themselves of the inner recesses of the port to escape the swell, which, in bad weather, no breakwaters will entirely exclude.

Aug. 14.—Very little wind, and a burning sun, which, in harbour, was so oppressive and relaxing that I went out and anchored in the bay. The wind being so light that the lugger would ride to the weight of the chain rather than to the anchor, I took the precaution to lay a kedge inshore and put a good strain upon it—a precaution which should never be neglected when there is a prospect of lying exposed to the sea for any length of time. The object of this is to prevent the vessel swinging over and fouling the bower anchor, upon which her safety depends.

Determined not to abandon my position for a trifle, I paid out all the chain, and rode to a patent cable buffer, belonging to the 'Orion,' which, being too powerful to afford sufficient play for such a light riding gear, I modified, by hooking one end of a stout tackle into a strap at the foot of the mast, the other end into the shackle of the buffer placed 10 feet abaft the mast, and rode to the fall of the tackle, keeping all rope inboard and enough of the chain to 'bitt' securely abaft all. The effect of this arrangement was to allow the chain an elasticity of *four inches*, if the strain were sufficient to compress the buffer *one inch*; and if the fall of the tackle parted—which was scarcely possible—the chain was still perfectly secured. By experiments tried at home, in which the same tackle was used, it required a strain of 8 cwt. to compress the buffer 3 inches—a strain which a 7-ton boat could throw upon it only under extreme circumstances.

The motive for riding to a buffer (or compressor) is obvious to experienced seamen, but to others an explanation may possibly be serviceable. Leaving out the question of tidal currents, which, with few exceptions, aggravate the difficulties of hard riding, my remarks must be supposed to apply to roadsteads little subject to their direct influence.

A vessel, wind-rode in moderate weather, and having a proper scope of chain—which, on account of its weight, assumes the form of a curve—rides with a greater or less proportion of it on the ground, according to the strength of wind—in which case the strain upon the anchor is horizontal, or in the direction most favourable to its resistance. Thus, while the wind is not sufficiently strong to force the vessel to the greatest possible distance from her anchor, she rides easily; since the curvature of the chain acts as a spring which gives to the sea when the vessel rises upon it, and brings her back on the 'scend' when the sea passes aft.

In a gale, when the vessel is forced to the greatest possible distance from her anchor, the strain, being in a direct line from the hawsepipe to the anchor, is diagonal, and tends to lift the stock off the ground—a position which, in smooth water and a steady strain, may be consistent with comfort and safety, but in a heavy sea is not consistent with either. Supposing the anchor to hold firm and the chain to be at its greatest tension when the vessel is in the hollow of a sea, the water being deepened by the height of the succeeding wave, it is clear she must spring forward a proportionate number of feet to allow the wave to pass under her. The strain being suddenly relaxed when the sea passes aft, the 'scend' slacks the chain, and—by force of wind—she immediately begins to gather way astern. With this tendency already in operation, the next sea, if a severe one and a breaker, would force her considerably beyond the range of her chain but for the resistance of the anchor, which brings her up with a sudden jerk, called a 'snub,' that is heard and felt in every part of the vessel, and which may be attended with any of the following serious consequences:— She may ship the sea; carry away the pawls, and surge all the chain if, from neglect, not 'weather bitted'; capsize the windlass; start the anchor; or snap the chain. To the first and two last of these accidents, the best built and best found ships and yachts are liable. The second and third result from defective construction, previous strain, or age. From observation, I should think the proportion of yachts—especially among the smaller ones—that could ride to their windlass and bitts in a heavy breeze on the land, is very small indeed; but even with the best and most powerful, there is serious cause for anxiety when the vessel snubs with a full scope of chain. In the absence of a cable buffer—which from experience of a gale in Torbay I am convinced no sea-going yacht, or ship, should ever be without—ropes may be bent to the chain forward of the wind-lass, and secured to the mast; provided the turns on the chain are taken in such form as to be easily cast off or cut away clean, in case it becomes necessary to 'slip' and get to sea—a con-tingency for which every precaution should be made, whether there is a determination to hold on or not. Other and neater dispositions might be made in *anticipation* of bad weather, but none can be so simple or effective as the buffer.

The burning heat of the day was followed by a sea fog as dense as it has ever been my lot to witness. From eight o'clock in the evening until eleven o'clock next day not a vestige of the town, or any other object, was visible from my anchorage. That I had ample opportunity of estimating the merits of every species of sound signal incidental to a fog on the 'great high-way of nations,' and could not plead sleep as an excuse for neglecting the riding light, can be gathered from the following. Ships' bells and fog horns, and steamers' whistles, in every key, according to size and power of steam employed in producing the blast, were going all night long. A deep-toned bell at the Admiralty Pier uttered a solemn warning at intervals of $7\frac{1}{2}$ minutes—its funereal tone most forcibly reminding one of the uncertainty of life. Every two minutes the South Sand Head lightship contributed to the babel of sounds the guttural screech of its fog horn—a detestable sound, calculated to warn the careless of the existence of an 'evil place beyond.' For some hours during the night a gun was fired from the inner pier-head at intervals of ten minutes, to direct an overdue mail boat, if she should chance to be within hearing. Lastly, the wind was so light that the chain hung 'up and down,' and a teasing little swell from the southward caused it to strike against the stem of the boat with every roll. Although a most unpleasant night, I consoled myself with the thought that 'it might have been worse'; for, if I might have been in harbour, the chance was equally great I should have been drifting helplessly at sea, and the compromise was much in my favour.

Aug. 15.—Dense fog, alternated with intervals of brilliant sunshine after midday. Landed on the beach in the dinghey, called at the club for letters, and did a little marketing. Night set in fine. Wind S.W., light. Barometer falling.

Aug. 16, A.M., wind S.W., with rain. After luncheon the wind shifted to the westward, and the sun shone pleasantly enough to induce me to land on the beach, which I did pretty fairly, in spite of the swell then beginning to be troublesome. But in putting off again an hour later, my frail boat shipped so much water that it was difficult to make headway against wind and sea. Unfortunately I had omitted to take a baler. Being a flat-bottomed boat, the water lurched heavily from side to side, and it was only by counteracting with my weight the tendency to capsize that she was kept afloat. That I was glad to be on board the lugger again need hardly be said.

The barometer should have improved with the change of wind; but it did not, and the sea rising with an ominously freshening wind created a doubt in my mind as to the advisability of lying there during the night. After an uncomfortable dinner in the open air—taken there partly because I was not sufficiently well to enjoy a meal in the cabin when the motion was so severe, and partly for the purpose of observation —notwithstanding the sky was beautiful and the evening most enjoyable, I buoyed the moorings with a cork stool, slipped them, and with as much wind as I could look at under a double-reefed mainsail, saved daylight into harbour. About 11 P.M. the wind backed to the south-west, and a heavy gale set in, accompanied with torrents of rain.

Aug. 17 (*Sunday*).—Blew hard from W.S.W., with a tremendous sea in the offing. The sight of the day was to watch the sea roll in by the Lord Warden Hotel and in the bay. If overnight any doubt had remained on my mind as to the necessity of abandoning the anchorage, it must have been dispelled instantly when, at low water, I counted only four big seas between my cork buoy and the breaker on shore—a position I could not have maintained during the preceding low water when the wind was S.W., although the depth was 2 fathoms and the draught of the lugger only 3 feet. Had I listened to advice, I should have been anchored even still nearer to the shore.

As I had been seen riding there two days, and was known only to have gone into harbour, I left the moorings without any doubt of their safety from depredators. But my confidence waned when told, by men well acquainted with their proclivities, that the sea-prowlers—who, by-the-bye, are nearly related to the 'black doll' gibbeted in the back streets—would probably take them up if they got the chance, send them in to the 'receiver of wreck,' and claim a reward. Determined to resist any such attempt at extortion, which, whether successful or not, must have occasioned me intense annoyance, I took steps to prevent it, or, at least, to ensure a disappointment if it were attempted.

On our coasts, with proper allowance of space for getting under way, the draught of large ships prevents them being anchored inadvertently within the line of breakers. But small vessels are often anchored in dangerous positions through attention being directed solely to their limited draught of water, instead of the far more important consideration of the possible line of breakers—which depends entirely upon the shelving of the ground outside. For instance, vessels of like build varying from 5 to 100 tons, and in draught from 3 to 10 feet, might ride a gale with equal safety in 4 fathoms, low water, provided shoal soundings extended to a sufficient distance outside, to moderate the sea rolling in from the deep water beyond. Whereas, the circumstances being in other respects similar, if the soundings increased rapidly outside, their position would become extremely perilous towards the period of low water; and not the largest, but the smallest and least powerful would be the first to succumb to the violence of the sea—the question of a few feet difference in draught not being a matter of consideration in this case.

It is said to have been ascertained that a wave breaks when

the depth of water in the trough is equal to the height from the trough to the crest; its character then undergoing an alteration from a wave of oscillation to a wave of transference. Thus in a calm after wind, a boat (or any floating substance), in respect of horizontal motion, will remain stationary outside the breaker unless a higher wave involves it in its break, when it is hurried towards the shore with a violence and rapidity that no anchors or exertions of oarsmen can withstand. This may be true in regard to a wave from deep water meeting a rapidly shelving bank; but I am certain that where the bank shelves very gradually, the change, in a modified degree, begins to take place earlier, or as soon as the base of the wave is retarded by contact with the ground. Otherwise, in a moderate sea, divers would not, from this cause, be obstructed in their work in depths of 5 fathoms and upwards, as we know to be the case.

I once had an example of this when seeking a landing in Mount's Bay, on the coast of Cornwall. Attracted by the beauty and quiet aspect of the shore at a distance, and wanting the experience I acquired an hour later, we ran down to the Loo Sands in the 'Sirius,' 11 tons, and 6 feet draught, with a nice topsail breeze on the quarter, and a swell that was not at all inconveniently felt on board. Not until it was ascertained that we were in 5-fathom water on the sea next the breaker, and, from that comparatively near position, were able to observe the immense distance the latter travelled up the steep sand, did we become aware of the formidable nature of the swell, and the impossibility of landing there. As the sea was long, and, in my estimation, not more than 5 feet high, there was no danger in approaching thus near with the wind free enough to luff out at discretion. From this impracticable spot we made for the Pra Sands, about two miles to the northward. Under the lee of a considerable rocky projection, called Black Point, the sea appeared so calm that, determined not to be disappointed of a ramble on shore, the mate was left in charge to 'stand on and off' while three of us went away in the dinghey. She was a nice little boat, 10 feet by 3 feet 6 inches, with a flat floor and full quarters, to which good qualities we eventually owed our safety. Quite under lee of the Point an attempt to land in a gully between the rocks was made, which so nearly proved disastrous that we backed out in haste, and after pulling two or three minutes lay on our oars abreast of the sand at a distance certainly of not less than half a cable (or 100 yards), intending only to look about a little, and then return to the vessel. While lying in this position broadside on, I saw a sea coming which, although there was not a speck of white upon it, had such an evident appearance of mischief, that I shouted to the bow oar, 'Get her head round quickly!' which was only just accomplished, when we felt ourselves travelling stern first at a prodigious rate towards the shore. Although still in comparatively deep water, with a 'dry boat,' I felt so certain resistance would be worse than useless that I directed all my attention to keeping her end on with gentle way ahead. Pulling gently with one hand, and, to ensure keeping our seats, clutching the gunwale with the other, we awaited the inevitable onset with no agreeable sensations. Presently she again reared on end, and in a perfect cataract of foam, which bounded over head and ears and half filled the boat, we were again in rapid motion, stern first, towards the shore. The moment she stranded, which was on the recoil and about half-way between the 'break' and its 'mark' on the sand, we got out and formed a group, holding firmly to each other's arms and to the boat. When the rush came we moved forward with it, at every step shoaling the water, so that it never reached above our legs; the water-logged boat serving as an anchor to steady us against the recoil. Before the next wave came the boat had been canted, to clear her of water; and by its aid we beached her high and dry. Everything movable—such as sculls, head and stern sheets, rudder, &c.—which had washed out while moving up the sand, was picked up close by; and beyond the latter being broken when she reared on end the second time, there was no harm done; which shows how necessary it is that seats should be kept in a time of danger. Later, I engaged two men to help us off between a lull in the heavier seas, which was not accomplished without difficulty and shipping much water. Never was a wholesome and beamy vessel more thoroughly appreciated than when, after a long pull to windward, we stepped on board the 'Sirius' again that day.

The round-topped wave outside the breaker on the Loo Sands clearly was a wave of oscillation. The character of the two which stranded us on the more gradual incline of the Pra Sands needs no remark, excepting that the depth from the trough to the ground of the first was certainly twice, if not thrice, as deep as from the trough to the crest; otherwise, it must have curled and swamped us, as did the second.

Where shallowness of the sea offers no obstructions, the recognised proportion between the height and length of waves is 1 to 10—which proportion holds good during the period of formation, and while the force of wind continues; but with a failing wind waves decrease in height without contracting in length; thus the depth at which the disturbance of a wave is felt by a diver, or its base is retarded by contact with the ground, depends *not* upon its height from trough to cast, but upon its volume. Viewed at a right angle, I believe that *absence of perspective* (as there would be in blades of corn growing on a hill) throws part of the length of a wave into its apparent height, and causes it to appear, at least, twice as high as it really is—an illusion instantly dispelled by a parallel view, or in the direction of the trough. The highest sea recorded by Sir Jas. C. Ross is 36 feet, and by Lieutenant Maury, U.S.N., 32 feet, with a velocity of 26 miles. The greatest length ascertained by Sir Geo. Grey, on a voyage home from Australia, by paying out a line astern, was 338 feet and its velocity 28 miles; which very nearly accords with similar observations made by others near the Cape of Good Hope. On an average, under way—or if a ship were stationary, which practically amounts to the same thing—she would encounter three or four such waves per minute. To imagine how severe this must be, let anyone sitting quietly at dinner on shore fancy the floor of the room undulating to this fearful extent, or even a fourth part of it, and he will perceive how unnecessary is exaggeration of the reality. When blowing hard, an angry sea 7 to 10 feet high is very formidable to a small vessel, as those who take a run to Margate or across the Channel in steamers fifty times the size of the 'Procyon' cannot but be aware. Those who think lightly of a sea only 5 feet high should observe it in moderate weather, when there is no cause for apprehension, from a small boat to leeward of Salcombe Bar. And those who doubt a sea 7 to 10 feet high being formidable, should see it, as a swell 200 feet long, strike the outer rocks of Scilly, or run upon the Longships; yet it is not a tenth part so formidable to encounter under way in deep water in this form, as in that of an angry sea whose length is but from 70 to 100 feet, or in tidal currents off the headlands, where it is often considerably shorter.

Aug. 18.—Went out for a cruise with two reefs down, and afterwards returned into harbour, as there was too much sea for taking in the moorings.

Aug. 19.—Morning fine and sunny. Had the hose from the quay, and filled up water. 1 P.M., in a light W.S.W. breeze and a drizzly rain, I sailed out to the moorings and took them in. After luncheon, weighed both anchors and shifted my berth into deeper water. Intending to leave Dover in the morning, I stowed the kedge anchor away, and rode to the bower only, with 14 fathoms of chain fast to the cable buffer. Where bound to, it was impossible to say; as the weather was so thoroughly out of gear that the chances were many against any plan resolved upon overnight being practicable in the morning. The barometer was steady at 29·9, and yet the fitful drizzle of midday, that looked as if at any moment it might yield to the sun's power, changed into a continuous rain and thick haze as the afternoon advanced.

The reader may perhaps imagine that the hours passed slowly. If so, he can have no idea of the time consumed in all this anchor work; in washing down thoroughly with pure sea water—indispensable to comfort after a few days in harbour; in double-reefing the mainsail and furling the sails; in seeing everything clear and in its place—that it might be possible to make sail in the dark; in attending to the lanterns, stove, stores, and general cabin work; and finally in preparing a hot dinner. Long before the latter was disposed of, the night had set in dark and threatening, with a teasing swell, which, about the bed-time of folks on shore, caused me some anxiety. With every roll of the lugger there was a noise like the blow of a mallet, which might have rejoiced the heart of any spiritualist, but was a great annoyance to me. Having ascertained that the chain was not in fault this time, I diligently set to work to account for it. After a tedious search on deck and in the lockers fore and aft, I leaned over the table in the cabin and threw the rays of the lantern on the heel of the mast and into the eyes of the vessel. To my surprise, I noticed that the mast step was loose, and, *apparently*, the timbers and planking of the starboard bow in movement. Observing about three-eighths of an inch play between the step and the timbers, I arrived at the conclusion that the fastenings of the step had been injured when she was athwart the schooner off Cliff Creek, and that the leverage of the mast, in 'carrying on' and in rolling at anchor since, had forced the fastenings of the bow to that extent. Afraid to drive wedges, for fear of increasing the mischief, I essayed to stop the noise—caused by the friction of wet hard wood—by cutting away a piece of oak step with a chisel and mallet; but the position was so awkward for such tough work, that I succeeded only in rendering myself uncomfortably warm. Unable to satisfy myself that there was no cause for apprehension—which could be ascertained only by going aground—I returned to examine it over and over again, and hardly like to say what I anticipated if she rolled excessively. As the night was too dark to move except under compulsion, and I had no confidence in the dinghey astern, no alternative presented itself to my mind but to fill the indiarubber boat, exercise patience until the morning, and in the meantime draw upon Mark Tapley's infallible means of consolation as largely as circumstances would permit.

For needful rest of limbs I turned into the hammock 'all standing,' to think what had best be done. My first idea was to go into harbour as soon as possible; but when I considered the great advantage of submitting her for examination to those who built her and were acquainted with the fastenings I decided to go to Whitstable.

Aug. 20.—During the best of the eastern tide in the offing there is a strong eddy at the anchorage, which swings a vessel in the contrary direction, or with her stern towards the pier. This was the position at 2 P.M., when, the wind having freshened from W.S.W., the sea several times hit under the quarters and descended on board in a heavy shower of spray. The motion being so violent as to swing me against the storm-sail, the latter required to be temporarily lowered out of its berth, to allow the hammock the fullest possible play; as upon these occasions it takes entire charge of the cuddy, with myself —barring any special cause for apprehension—snugly stowed in the interior. Confessedly *not* snug, I turned out, partly to ensure the riding light was doing its duty, but chiefly for the purpose of taking a general survey of the situation. There was, however, nothing to be seen except lights dimmed with haze, complete darkness out at sea, and a heavy pall of black over-head, indicative of an impending change. As the hammock counteracts the effects of a severe rolling—which is trouble-some, when to struggle against being dislodged from a seat is the only occupation on hand—I took refuge in it again, and must own, devoutedly wished for daylight. Whether dozing or not, I cannot say; but shortly after four o'clock I became aware that she was wind-rode and very lively. The wind whistling in the halyards, and a confirmatory glance at the barometer, convinced me that the anchor must be secured without delay, or it would have to be abandoned along with 15 fathoms of chain. Raining in torrents, with the higher part of Dover in the clouds and the South Foreland cliffs shrouded in impenetrable haze, the outlook was not cheerful when, clothed in water-proofs, and in the following order, I set about a task which the value of an anchor and chain would not induce me to repeat at a similar expense of energy and risk of amputating fingers in handling the chain. I mean that 'practice makes perfect'; and, looking back, I am conscious that the appliances at my disposal were not used as advantageously as they might have been, or would be if the same task had to be undertaken again. People wonder I have not a winch, but such a one as is carried in small yachts would have been torn out of the deck the first severe 'snub' which the rope tackles resisted—though more than once I stepped aside, in expectation of a catastrophe.

Having stowed away the hammock and the riding light, I set the mizen, and prepared the mainsail for hoisting; hove in the chain to 7 fathoms with tackles, hoisted the mainsail, peaked with upper tack, and hauled aft sheet, leaving the lower tack free; cast to sideboard, and when about on the other tack, with a hard port helm, sailed the anchor out of the ground, righted helm, and shook up in the wind. Standing ready in the waist, I hauled in the chain until the anchor was under foot, and then, kneeling down forward, and watching an opportunity, got it aboard without punishing the bow with the flukes, trimmed the sail, and bore away for the Foreland at 5 A.M. The wind was S.S.W., as strong as she would bear without a further reduction of canvas, and when I saw how she heeled to it, and sped along in the trough of the sea, I exclaimed—for I do indulge in exclamations occasionally— 'Thank God I took two reefs down overnight!' The waist was cumbered with gear. Interlaced with the chain, tackles and halyards, hard and kinked with the wet, were lurched to leeward by the sea in such a mass of confusion that, minding the helm as best I could, the work of disentangling and stowing them away occupied me a long while. Notwithstanding I had taken a little burnt brandy and biscuit at intervals, by the time the Foreland was rounded, and Deal in sight, I felt there was a terrible void within, and for the first time since leaving Greenhithe began to anticipate the pleasure of a substantial breakfast, which the adverse tide and long distance to be run before she could be hove-to were certain to postpone to a very late hour. I passed Ramsgate at 8.30, looking cheerless and miserable in the drenching rain, and at 10.30 rounded the North Foreland, when the tide became favourable. According to common sense, and the laws which govern prudent mariners,

I should have remained at the helm and have thought only of saving the flood tide to Whitstable; but if to unbend sometimes is allowable, there was abundant excuse in this instance. So, without loss of time, after luffing out of the rough sea into the comparatively smooth water of Margate Roads, the yard was lowered as for reefing, the upper tack-tackle bowsed down to two blocks, and the mainsheet hauled flat aft from the fourth cringle with the reef tackle, which completed the operation and was equivalent to putting her temporarily under four reefs. As with this canvas she will neither break off nor put herself about without the assistance of the helm, it is a practical example of the plan, previously explained, for 'heaving-to' in bad weather. When this was done, and the lugger was standing up for the roads with no more demand upon my services than occasional supervision and correction, I threw off waterproofs, and I fear indulged in an unseemly exhibition of hilarity.

At first she laid 'well up,' or along the coast, affording me a good opportunity for a wash and for the earlier preliminaries of breakfast, such as baking the bread and boiling the water; but though I successfully prepared, and eventually did ample justice to, an unexceptionable meal of ham fried in butter, warm bread, and excellent coffee with Swiss milk, its peaceable enjoyment was marred by a furious and untimely shift of wind to W.S.W., which caused her to break off, compelled my attendance at the helm on account of vessels at anchor in the roads, knocked up a turbulent little sea, which drenched me with spray, and threatened the crockery and untasted breakfast with annihilation. When, in spite of her plunging and heeling, these little inconveniences were overcome, and utensils were washed up and stowed away, there was a bit of a scramble to get the third reef taken down, and the sail trimmed in time to go about on the south edge of Margate sand. Fortunately the rain entirely ceased at noon—a change I was quite able to appreciate after twenty-four hours' experience of it.

Encountering the ebb tide at Herne Bay, I shook out a reef to beat along shore, an interesting, but rather tedious, kind of sailing, in which the light 3-fathom hand-lead was particularly useful. Shortly afterwards the mainsheet carried away—an accident I viewed with perfect equanimity, since, though it cost me some trouble to repair, there was abundant cause for congratulation that it occurred at so convenient a time and place. Continuing the 'short boards,' I saved water over 'the Street,' the chief outlying danger of Whitstable, and at 4 P.M. anchored outside the fleet of smacks off the town.

Famous as Whitstable is for its oysters, and in that sense interesting, between the hours of sunset and sunrise it is the most miserable and depressing anchorage I know. To be utterly alone at sea is cheerful compared to lying at anchor in proximity to a fleet of deserted smacks, which, as the tide falls, take the ground and heel over, with their masts pointing to every quarter of the compass, like 'headstones' in an ancient or neglected graveyard. So complete is the desertion that if there is life on board any of them, which I doubt, it can be only of that minute kind which knows no distinction of persons after the cabin lamp is extinguished for the night.

Determined to save the night post if possible, I stepped into the dinghey after dinner, rowed as far as the falling tide would permit, and then essayed a quarter of a mile of mud flat to gain the beach. Like the Pilgrim's 'Slough,' there is firm ground if you know where to find it, but, for want of 'direction,' I found there was not only a chance of leaving my sea-boots behind, but, from the feel of it in the dark, a possibility of getting bemired up to the neck. As this was a 'branch of navigation' to which my attention had not before been directed, and with which I cared not to make a 'deeper' acquaintance, I prudently acknowledged a defeat, got back to the vessel with difficulty, had tea, and turned in.

Aug. 21.—Although not sensible of extraordinary fatigue over night, in the morning my hands were very painful, and every muscle in my body as sore as a boy's salient parts after his first attempt at skating. Excepting several days' cessation from work, there is no remedy so efficacious as renewed exertion; so, somewhat against the grain, I turned out in reasonable time to wash down, and soon forgot all but the hands, which, unless cuts and abrasions are carefully shielded, only go from bad to worse. These little complaints were not new, but, as might be expected, were intensified by the heavy work of the previous day. The weather was not warm, yet from 9 A.M. it was a day of incessant thunder, chiefly remarkable for the variety and grandeur of the clouds. After breakfast I sailed in close to the builder's yard, and at high water berthed alongside some piles on the beach to have the lugger examined. The noise complained of was discovered to be caused by the mast step having shrunk from the support it originally had from the timbers, which, when she heeled under the schooner's bow with the pressure of her jibboom in the mainsail, threw the entire leverage of the mast upon the bolt connecting the step with the keel and broke it. The bow fastenings fortunately proving intact, the damage to the step was temporarily repaired without lifting the mast. Altogether it was a very satisfactory visit, since, if nothing had required attention, it was worth while to be armed against suspicions, which, having once arisen after such an accident, would have been intensified with every return of bad weather. As after several hours' thunder and a great storm later in the afternoon it was not improbable the wind would veer to the north and send in a surf, I had a sufficient number of hands in attendance to guard against accident in hauling off the beach at high water.

Aug. 22.—2 A.M., wind S.W., fine overhead, but an unsettled appearance to windward. Hauled off, and, with a native on board to pilot through the fleet of smacks in the dark, ran out under sail, and took up a berth outside, and below all. When the sail was furled the pilot left me, and I turned into the hammock at 3.30 for a short rest. Notwithstanding there was abundance of cheerful sunshine and very little rain, the appearance of the weather at dawn did not belie itself in respect of wind. Long before I was washed and dressed, the cabin cleaned, and other household duties attended to, a gale set in from S.W., and knocked up a turbulent sea, which, from the necessity of steadying myself and securing everything it was desirable to keep right side up, hampered me greatly in the work. In the preparation and management of breakfast I found even more ingenuity required to preserve capsizable articles from destruction and waste than if blowing hard under way, when their safety is ensured by simply placing them to leeward. Whereas sheering about at anchor in a rough sea, with no longer warning than is represented by the swing of a pendulum, the contents of the coffee-pot and the frying-pan are apt to mingle with fugitive crockery—fortunate, indeed, for the proprietor if they meet in a place so little inconvenient to himself as on the floor. If my friends and others who doubt that hard work is really beneficial had been able to see me, wedged securely in a corner by the cuddy doors, enjoying breakfast that morning, they must have been converted into enthusiastic advocates of a theory it was the avowed intention of this cruise to put severely to the test. If I attempted a precise description of the motion of a boat like the 'Procyon' at anchor in a rough sea, it would read like gross exaggeration, since nothing short of witnessing it will convey an adequate impression of its violence. When she sheered into the trough of the sea people watching from the shore wondered the mast stayed in her, and I thought if it had a mind to go this was certainly a fair opportunity.

About 11 A.M. the oyster fleet returned under three-reefed mainsails and spitfire jibs before there was sufficient water for several of them to beat up to their moorings. It blew so hard that the near approach of some of them caused me anxiety, lest by any accident they should miss stays, and drift down upon the 'Procyon.' As until now there had been no time to scrub down, I devoted three hours to it, and when in my estimation she was comfortably clean, had luncheon, which, notwithstanding there was an abundance of so-called 'delicacies' in tins, consisted more often than not of a cold chop or a piece of rump-steak, purposely cooked in excess of the requirements of the previous evening's dinner. With appetite rendered keen by exertion and pure sea air I thoroughly enjoyed this simple fare, provided it was supplemented with unlimited fresh butter and the regulation allowance of 'Bass,' about which there happened to be a disappointment upon this occasion, owing to the supply in the cellaret having been suffered to run short. To obtain it I must have removed a number of things aft, crept into a place like a dog-kennel, and have remained there a long while repairing stowage—an unpleasant job, which even confidence in immunity from sea-sickness did not tempt me to undertake in the midst of so violent a commotion. Requiring nothing more at Whitstable, and indisposed to be tossed about in like manner during the night, I determined to get under way and seek a smoother anchorage.

The process, resorted to in Dover Bay, of heaving ahead with tackles until the chain was sufficiently short to sail the anchor out of the ground, was repeated with success; notwithstanding, the work was extremely hard, and she 'snubbed' severely.

The difficulty of getting under way when blowing hard is not due to the weight of anchor and chain, though, of course, their weight is an important addition. The difficulty consists in forging ahead against wind and sea a dead weight of about 5 tons, which, but for being held by the anchor, would tend from 3 to 5 knots an hour in the contrary direction. In the absence of wind pressure, or a tidal current equivalent to it in force, the work of weighing anchor is about equal to hoisting the mainsail. 'Snubbing' is peculiar to the unyielding nature of chain, and is inevitable when riding short in a sea way. It may, however, occur, in a modified degree, when riding short with rope.

When at last the anchor was stowed and the sails trimmed, I had a trouble with the dinghey, which, being half-filled with water shipped during the day, would not tow until it was got rid of by hauling her on to the lee gunwale with her head upwards, and when emptied launching her again suddenly stern first. Everything being now in order, I put about at 5 P.M., and bore away to the eastward under double-reefed mainsail, with the wind on the quarter, glad enough of the rest afforded by a pleasant run of two hours to Westgate, near Margate, where the anchor was let go for the night in tolerably smooth water at the distance of about a third of a mile from the shore.

With the furling of the sails the hard work of the day was brought to a close, and there was nothing to do but attend to the domestic comforts, which consisted chiefly of preparing and then peaceably enjoying a good hot dinner.

Though the numerous lights of Margate make a pretty illumination in the distance, and there is a light visible here and there in the windows of cottages on shore, it is a lonely anchorage, exposed to the North Sea—intolerably dull for anyone whose time is not too completely and agreeably occupied to care for it. That, however, not being my case, I noticed with admiration the gradual transformation from a mellow-tinted sunset to a beautiful starlight night, and did not for a moment regret there was not a sound to be heard but the soughing of wind on the masts and the ripple of the sea on shore.

Some of my readers, judging only by their own feelings, may wonder how it is possible to carry on, and even find pleasure in, such ceaseless work as this. From my point of view, the following irresistible inducements are a sufficient explanation:—

1. Though, manifestly, it cannot under all circumstances of wind and weather be agreeable, it has a favourable effect upon my health, which lightens hardships and renders almost any amount of work tolerable. 2. An insatiable pleasure in the art of sailing, which, especially in strong weather, offers such an endless variety of problems for solution that there is always something fresh to engage the attention, as well as experience to be acquired. 3. A lively interest in natural objects and phenomena, observed to greatest advantage on the sea, which, even in the roughest weather, afford continuous entertainment to those who are not indifferent to their contemplation. Lastly, respecting single-handed work at sea. In the sensation of entire independence, resulting from justifiable self-reliance, there is an indescribable charm, such as I imagine could be experienced only in a superior degree by a man able, at his will, to accomplish aerial flights in any direction—an art which

some have rashly essayed, but which there is no probability will ever triumph over the art of sailing to windward at sea.

That those who care for none of these things should voluntarily expose themselves to the chances and discomforts of the sea is, perhaps, even more incomprehensible to me than to anyone else. If—apart from racing and fishing—all who went to sea sympathised with what I consider the legitimate objects of amateur sailing, it would be impossible they should find amusement in wantonly killing and maiming the harmless and beautiful sea birds; much less that, for most inadequate motives, they should think of capturing them with baited hooks, and, even worse still, entangling them in hooks trailed over the stern—methods indicative of callousness to the infliction of torture, which I regret to see instigated by example in a very popular book.

In reference to the apparent helplessness of my position, imprisoned in the cuddy and asleep in the hammock at night, the question has more than once been put to me—If when anchored in lonely places on the coast I had any fear of being surprised by intruders? The fact of being there is a proof that I regard such an accident as highly improbable. At the same time, I occasionally find it conducive to sound and healthy slumber to know that I am not dependent upon the forbearance of any man, if such a foolish thing were by chance to be attempted.

The cause of my work being ceaseless was the exceptionally bad state of the weather, which, after long continuance, I expected at every rise of the barometer would take a favourable turn. Paradoxical as it may appear, the same cause operated in a compensatory direction, by rendering the general work less irksome than under other circumstances it might have been, since it occasioned so much hard labour in the 'marine department' that the ordinary routine, by comparison, became only light and easy employment. How it happened the 'Procyon' was exposed to such an unusual amount of rough weather was this: Unable to forget the month was *August*, and that fine weather was long overdue, also having an intense dislike to harbour work and tidal restrictions, immediately the barometer rose I took up a position from which to make a favourable start for any place which, at the time, might seem desirable; but circumstances beyond my control thwarted me in a manner never before experienced. If, judged by the event, some of the positions I took up seem to have been rather risky, it was always in expectation of the favourable change indicated by the barometer proving reasonably permanent.

Favourable as was the weather for a good sleep, after a heavy nine o'clock dinner early bed was out of the question—even if a thorough clear up, a few pipes, tea, and a little reading before turning in were not according to my notions of comfort indispensable.

Aug. 23.—When I turned in my impression was that the lugger would remain wind-rode, but shortly after falling into a sound sleep I was apprised of her having swung to windward by the dinghey 'charging' into the stern and bumping alongside. I anathematised her considerably, but finding that ineffectual to abate the annoyance, turned out, and took her on board. Unable to collapse her on the after deck, and unwilling to waste more time in considering how to dispose of her, I lashed her there, and returned to the hammock at 2 A.M. The morning was superbly fine when I went below, but the next view at 7 o'clock disclosed a leaden sky and drizzly rain. The first business after breakfast was to dispose of the folding boat, which, as the barometer was again receding, and the weather seemed hopelessly bad, I determined not to tow astern any more. With a spare spar laid across the coamings of the open part of the lugger for a roller, and a guy rope from the masthead to her bow, I passed her on to the fore deck, where there was room to work, and there folded her, by a method which is certainly ingenious, into the following dimensions— 10 feet 6 by 15 inches by 6 inches. In this form I lashed her to the gunwale on the port side forward, where she least obstructed my movements, though her weight was less desirable there than anywhere else.

The next day being Sunday, and fresh provisions running short, it was desirable to make a harbour. At first I had visions of Dover, but as the wind freshened and backed to the southward with torrents of rain, my pretensions abated, and I resolved to be satisfied with Ramsgate. 11 A.M.—Well housed in waterproofs, I got under way with two reefs down, and, thinking there was no need to hurry over so moderate a distance, ran to leeward, and trimmed sails and helm for sailing herself closehauled, while I took advantage of the copious downpour of soft water to remove the shore stains, contracted at Whitstable, from the lower part of the mainsail. An hour later I passed Margate—which looked anything but the resort of pleasure it is said to be; and in half an hour more, on my very best behaviour at the helm—for the clouds looked terribly black and angry—emerged from the protection of the North Foreland, and stood on closehauled towards the North Goodwin. A mile or two out, I was so completely overpowered with sea and wind that it appeared as if taking the third reef down would not be a sufficient relief; so, being hungry and indisposed to the exhausting labour of shifting sails with protection so near, I put back, and at 1.30 brought up off Margate with No. 2 anchor and a bass rope.

I was too near the harbour to escape being pestered with offers of assistance, though, lying quietly in smooth water with the burgee and ensign flying in their proper places, and otherwise in perfect order, there was not the least probability that any could be required. Expecting the wind would shift to the northward and send in a rough sea, I wished not to remain anywhere on that coast during Sunday—certainly had no intention to risk getting my boat knocked about among a crowd of smacks in Margate Harbour; so that the situation was becoming vexatiously perplexing, when, fortunately, the wind shifted to the south-west, and moderated sufficiently to enable me to proceed.

3 P.M.—Weighed anchor, and bore away for the Foreland, where I encountered a foul wind and an adverse tide. To have 'weathered' satisfactorily, a reef should have been taken out

of the mainsail; but the wind continued gusty, and the work had been too hard lately for me to run the risk of having to take it in again; so I made up for deficiency of canvas by shorter boards—in other words, 'cutting it exceedingly fine'—which I was enabled to do by a diligent use of the lead every time of standing in towards the cliffs. Notwithstanding this sort of sailing was unlikely to be pursued by a novice, off Broadstairs I was hailed from a pilot boat, which had been in company for some time, with offers to take me into their harbour. As usual with men who consider their services indispensable to the most trifling undertaking, they would not be satisfied with a plain answer—as courteous as can be given in a strong wind—but seemingly annoyed that I did not instantly strike colours and capitulate, wanted to know if 'I intended to remain out all night?' to which the laconic reply was, 'Can't say!' The spokesman then insolently added, 'It's my belief you don't know where you're going.' It was my belief that I did, and also that Broadstairs was not quite beyond my capacity if it had been desirable to run in there—but I made no reply. Exposed to the full force of the tide during the last mile, it was 8 P.M. and almost dark when I gained Ramsgate, and luffed up into the 'west gully.'

Without in the least intending to depreciate others, I must say that the immediate and obliging assistance of the harbour authorities is worthy of remark. Declining to enter the basin, at my own suggestion I was towed into a berth between the luggers lying at moorings near the lighthouse; where the only drawback to comfort—partially remedied during the night by hauling off with a 'breast-rope' on the other side—was rolling, and striking violently against my neighbours' fenders.

When the sails were furled and ropes coiled, I put out the dinghey to go to market. The night was so extremely dark that in rowing round the east gully at low water to the clock-house, caution was needed to avoid capsizing or damaging my frail bark amid the numerous boats, buoys, and warps. Though unable to impart light, the water when agitated by the sculls was intensely luminous; not with the sparkling phosphorescence

239

of the ocean, but the solid-looking, creamy phosphorescence of decomposed vegetable and animal matter, peculiar to harbours and the mouths of rivers under certain conditions of the atmosphere, and of stillness during the period of low water. If there had been any doubt about the shops being open at that late hour, it was quickly dispelled by the blaze of gaslight and dense crowd in the streets, which presented the appearance of a fair. Having called at the Harbour Office, according to instructions received from the pier men, and made several purchases, I groped my way down the slimy foreshore below the shingle to the boat, and was right glad to escape to the quiet of my little home and a healthier atmosphere, which, however objectionable in the town generally, is abominably vitiated in the neighbourhood of the entrance gates on the quay, especially during the excursion season.

It was fortunate I partook of a substantial luncheon off Margate, seeing that it was past ten o'clock, and dinner had yet to be prepared. For one who never turns day into night, I admit it seems unreasonable to turn night into day; but sleep was so secondary to the business in hand that not an item of the routine described on a previous page was omitted because of the lateness of the hour. On the contrary, I was in a condition to enjoy it even more keenly. To have dined earlier off pre-served 'haricot mutton' or 'stewed rump-steak,' both very good in their way, might have seemed more reasonable; but they are not to my taste when, with a little trouble and delay, it is possible to procure fresh meat.

Aug. 24 (*Sunday*).—At last the wind had veered to the north-ward, and, judging from the fine appearance of the morning, promised a welcome relief to the anxieties of the farmer. But the change was of short duration; for at 3 P.M. the wind was back to its old quarter, and, though a beautiful day, the signs of another gale were unmistakable. To me it was the most discordant and wearisome day of the cruise. A number of fishing smacks belonging to other ports—not that, for a moment, I imagine the latter circumstance made any difference —had come in and located themselves in my immediate vicinity; so that having no one in whose charge to leave the lugger, I was compelled to remain on board. The majority of the crews were young men and boys, who could not have been strangers to the modern School Boards, yet their vocabulary was so restricted as to furnish but one offensive adjective to qualify—not the nouns only, but, far grosser absurdity—every 'part of speech'; and one 'supplementary' noun, still more offensive, which they seemed to think applicable to everything animate and inanimate under the sun. That these lads are not, as some suppose, on account of evil example at home, genuine objects of sympathy in this matter is clear; for when the same young men, attracted by the strange appearance of my folding boat, came to talk with me, their remarks and conversation were sensible and perfectly free from offence, proving that the uncivilized language they use habitually among themselves arises not from ignorance, in the sense of not knowing better, but from the less excusable ignorance of considering it *'manly.'* If to the liberal education imparted by the School Boards were added a just appreciation of the value of these objectionable words, and the examination for honours extended to where, when, and how they may be intelligently applied, not only would the interests of education be advanced, but the improvement wrought by the School Boards would be more satisfactorily demonstrated than it is at present.

Aug. 25.—Blew hard from S.W., barometer 29·75. Heartily tired of the monotony of a prison life in harbour, and the stupid occupation of fending off my neighbour—with whom, in spite of all precautions, wind and sea brought me occasionally into violent contact—at 3 P.M. I stowed the dinghey as before, took three reefs in the mainsail, and resolved to seek a more agreeable anchorage at sea. With a change of wind to W.S.W. the barometer had slightly risen, and the clouds dispersed, giving promise of a fine night, and, from the anchorage contemplated, an advantageous start for Dover in the morning, if the weather became fair, as I had reason to expect. Supplemented by the surface current, due to the strong up-Channel wind, the tide, setting like a sluice to the north-east, allowed me but a narrow margin to clear the east pier-head; which, however, was passed in good style without shipping any sea. My intention was to make a short board to the southward, and then, on the other tack, endeavour to weather Ramsgate, and get into the comparatively slack water of Pegwell Bay. But the sea was hollow and confused—as at such times it always is in that part—and I had to stand on a long while before the opportunity to 'stay' so small a craft under short canvas presented itself. It vexed, though it did not much surprise me, that the three-reefed mainsail, setting so low to the mast, was overmatched by the high chopping sea and strong lee current; so that, on this and the next two or three boards, instead of weathering, she lost ground as far as the Old Cudd Channel buoys. In the sense of continuing 'under way,' the question, 'If I intended to remain out all night?' might have seemed pertinent at this juncture, for the hours were speeding, when I ventured to shake out a reef and, by making short tacks in shore, immediately began to improve my position. Having succeeded in weathering Ramsgate at dusk, I continued beating to windward until 9 P.M., when, by way of experiment, I brought up with the 28 lb. anchor and 30 fathoms of bass rope —keeping the bower anchor and chain in reserve, but ready for use if required—on Sandwich Flats, about two miles from Ramsgate, and a mile from the nearest beach.

If, at first, disappointment attended the failure to overcome the adverse influences of wind and tide and sea combined, it was due to forgetfulness of the impossibility of driving by pressure of canvas, as we do vessels of more power and greater draught, a boat not wholly decked through a sea I soon discovered had no 'foot' to it. But when more reasonable tactics ensured success, equanimity returned, and I enjoyed a breeze which, if it conferred no more enduring benefit, at least laid a good foundation for dinner.

While the canvas was being stowed, the potatoes were 'steaming,' a method I prefer to 'boiling,' because they require less attention and, when off the fire, keep in good condition until the meat is ready. If, in reference to the question of 'frying-pan' *versus* 'gridiron,' the former is objected to, I can assure anyone who, temporarily, may have to be his own cook, that it depends upon himself rather than upon the implement, provided a clean enamelled pan is used, and a few minutes of undivided attention are bestowed upon the business in hand.

The motion was of course considerable, but, being free from the 'jars' of various sorts encountered in harbour, did not appreciably interfere with my comfort. The night was superbly starlight, and owing to the clearness of the atmosphere the view of Ramsgate from the anchorage exceedingly pretty, the windows of the houses, I suppose on account of the latter being crowded with visitors, presenting a blaze of light in addition to the numerous gas-lamps of the town, the whole being relieved from sameness by the powerful red light of the harbour and the green 'leading lights' on the cliff. For a time this charming picture was enhanced by a display of coloured rockets, thrown up from Broadstairs, appearing in a line with and immediately above it. If, at any time, the pursuit of pleasure is unattended with vanity and vexation, it is in the quiet enjoyment of a fine sunset followed by a brilliant star-light night at sea. In comparison with the idle monotony, and in some respects hateful experience, of the past two days, the contrast was so delightful that only absolute necessity could have induced me to return.

Although most particular in calculating the number of feet before letting go the anchor, about 11 P.M. I unexpectedly received warning in the trough of the sea that no allowance had been made for the longer ebb, and consequent depression of tide, due to the strong south-west wind. It being past low water by the tide-table, I had little fear she would actually strand, though the 'run' of the sea, now setting almost at a right angle to the wind, forced the lugger to windward of the line of her anchor. The flood soon made, and relieved me from apprehension, but it was a great oversight, and showed that an off-shore wind must not be entirely relied upon for keeping a craft to leeward of her anchor when the sea begins to feel the ground. Barometer 29·85.

Aug. 26.—Turned out in good time to consider the prospects of the day, which took no long time to 'sum up.' Wind, fresh from south-west—barometer, dull—sun, shining—scud flying fast in advance of a heavy bank of grey cloud in the Channel, from which at intervals issued long, low growls of thunder. As Dover was apparently out of the question, and Ramsgate entirely against inclination, the alternative lay between 'seeing it out' on the spot, or beating a retreat of twelve miles to Margate Roads. Constitutionally averse to retrograde movements, I chose the former, and forthwith proceeded to shift my berth into deeper water. As yet the wind was not so strong but that it was possible to weigh anchor by hand; whereas, had the chain been out, the longer process of 'tackling' must have been resorted to. Having brought up again with the same anchor and 35 fathoms of rope, I turned my attention from the threatening clouds above to the more immediately interesting subject of breakfast below, where the kettle was already spouting a cheery jet of steam athwart the cabin.

If I seem to have given too much prominence to the item of meals, it is because I regard their healthy enjoyment as the mainspring of work which otherwise could not have been carried on beyond a very limited time. Thus, in gauging the physical or mental condition of a crew, meals are an unfailing index to the state of the social barometer, discovering the existence of 'waves of depression,' whether caused by anxiety, debility, or discontent.

Enlivened by a gleam of sunshine occasionally, the day was not entirely bad, though the wind was so extremely violent as to cause the lugger to ride to leeward with a great strain on the anchor, when in ordinary weather the tide would have forced her to ride to windward. In addition to a turbulent short sea off the land, on the port bow I had the big 'Channel sea' rolling partly athwart wind into Pegwell Bay, the two together creating a compound motion that threw the recollection of the Whitstable anchorage into the shade. Routine work and about two hours' carpentering below furnished plenty of occupation until four o'clock, when the wind once more veered to the westward with a rising barometer, according to its now almost established daily custom. As fresh supplies were again running short, and marketing cannot be done on Sandwich flats for love or money, in the hope—if not firm faith —that the clouds had drained themselves dry and the wind blown itself out at last, I determined upon another advance towards Dover, and at 5 P.M. set the mainsail double reefed for a reach down against tide to Deal. I had 35 fathoms of rope out, and not the least chance of getting any of it in by hand as in the morning; so I cast to windward with the sails hard sheeted, and when about on the other tack sailed straight for the anchor, my only difficulty this time being that of overhauling the rope fast enough. The instant it tautened in my hand I 'took a turn' and lifted the anchor out of the ground. This was my first experience of rope *versus* chain, which, instead of exhausting me to speechlessness, enabled me to laugh approvingly the while at its charming simplicity and complete success. I used to think rope was used by smacks only in the absence of chain, but now, for temporarily anchoring small craft at sea, am convinced of its superiority, and shall adopt it in future.

Under a brilliant sky, I had a delightful little sail, 'gunwale down,' that in the absence of sea-sickness must have approved itself to the most fastidious taste; and that even an 'unhappy sufferer' would have regarded as a welcome change who had passed the previous twelve hours on board. The position I chose was in four fathoms low water, abreast of Upper Deal, and about three-quarters of a mile from the pier. The sea was toning down when I brought up with the same riding gear as before, and, having started my preparations for dinner—which, fortunately in point of time, promised to be on the table at a less fashionable hour than usual—proceeded to make snug for the night. A boat had been alongside with a proposal to take me ashore for the trifling sum of six shillings, which, considering the wind was off shore—and excepting a moderate swell on the beach was only like landing at Gravesend—I said would make the few things I required rather expensive. Upon their requesting me to name the sum I was willing to give, my reply was 'Nothing.' 'Then it's no use to wait?' 'Not the slightest.' 'Good night.'

What a superb night it was! One might almost have been excused for supposing it would never rain again—yet the stars were over bright! Excepting for the long easy pitch and roll, I seemed to have come home after the rude buffeting of the day, and to be the centre of an illumination got up for my especial gratification. On the starboard hand were the lights of the town—on the port hand, the lights of between two and three hundred sail at anchor—and astern, the concentrated, but rather faint illumination of Ramsgate, looking not unlike Vauxhall Gardens in the time of their prosperity. I enjoyed the scene thoroughly, deeply, and little cared to think how quickly it could change.

Aug. 27.—I had only just turned out after an unusually refreshing sleep—such as follows a gale and dispersion of clouds, but, with me, never precedes it if the clouds are gathering towards night—when one of my visitors of the previous evening came alongside, and immediately agreed to land me and put me on board again for two shillings. Of course! considering he would have rowed a whole family about for an hour for that money, or even have contended with another boat in a race of a mile out and a mile home to pick up an old box for firewood not worth sixpence. Besides, I could have landed myself for nothing had I chosen to have done so.

Having posted letters and purchased a few necessaries, I returned on board to breakfast, right glad to have attended to business first, since it had rained already, and was looking exceedingly dirty in the south-west, with an unmistakably dull barometer.

The wind soon made itself heard in strong gusts from the direction of Lower Deal, and, while attending to my duties below, I felt the lugger rising higher and plunging deeper every minute as the sea came rolling up in constantly increasing volume from the South Foreland. Had not a miserable rain accompanied the sea, I should have found entertainment in watching its effect upon my neighbours; but rain and spray combined were too drenching for me to leave the cabin except on business.

After breakfast I was hailed from a large lugger standing off under stormsails to know 'If I would give them a trifle to take me into Ramsgate?' to which I replied, 'I would rather give you a trifle to keep me out.' The last words that reached me were, 'We'll come alongside,' which, though not attempted to be put into execution, I accepted as a warning not to bandy words that, on one side, it might possibly be convenient to misconstrue. My custom is to fly a club burgee, whatever the weather; but to fly an ensign in a gale is extravagant and unusual, unless there is a special motive. I had such a motive now, and ran mine up to its proper place—the mizenmast head; the purpose being to intimate plainly that assistance was not needed, and would be declined. As to my knowledge nothing passed within hailing distance during the next twenty-four hours, I presume its signification was understood; though it is doubtful if, after twelve o'clock, any but a very powerful crew or a steamer could have come, if they would.

The wind increased in force, and gradually southed until it set straight through the Downs with a tremendous sea, which would not have occasioned me much inconvenience—though occasionally the lugger seemed to leap almost out of water with its violence—if the wind had not caught her in that position, first on one bow and then on the other, and caused her to range considerably. The effect of ranging with so large a scope was to expose her broadside more or less to the sea, and cause her to lurch heavily until she regained her position astream of the anchor. To correct this, I set the mizen and hoisted a small jib as a trysail—sheet upwards and aback against the mast to prevent it being blown to pieces—cast to the westward, and when the sheer had forged her sufficiently ahead, let go a second anchor and hauled down the jib. Paying out 20 fathoms of rope, she fell into her former position and remained tolerably steady for a time with an equal strain upon both anchors. The ropes were 'parcelled' to protect them from chafing in the 'gammon-iron,' which answered admirably as a 'hawse-pipe'; and to prevent the strain being thrown directly upon the short nip of the belaying cleats, a turn was first taken round the mast.

After a substantial luncheon and a pipe, I looked up at 3.30 P.M. to see if there were any prospect of the usual afternoon clearance, and discovered that she had dragged the two anchors in line. As the heavier one, with 40 fathoms of rope, now fairly backed the smaller one, with 20 fathoms, I had no reason to be dissatisfied; for the question was no longer one of personal comfort below, but of holding ground against the wind, which by this time was terrific.

The fleet had increased in number by vessels running in under very short canvas from the Channel; but, to my knowledge, none passed to the southward. Nor is it likely any ordinary vessel did so, since I heard afterwards of a steamer due at Boulogne from the Thames at nine o'clock that night which failed to reach there until twelve hours later; and of a cutter-rigged smack which failed to weather the North Foreland.

Observing that the barometer continued to decline, and that there was no indication of a break in the clouds, it became necessary to make the preparations for the coming night, during which, if the wind backed to the south-east without moderating, the anchors would probably have to be slipped, and the sea encountered under way. Moreover, it was certain she could not carry the mainsail, even close-reefed, and that the work of preparation would be far too long and heavy to be undertaken excepting in daylight—especially as the deck was slippery and unprotected with bulwarks.

First, the mainsail had to be unbent from the mast; then, to enable it to be covered and stowed in the berth I contemplated, between the waist coaming and the gunwale, it had to be opened out on the deck, and, notwithstanding its wet and harsh condition, be furled almost as snugly as if it were dry. This, on account of the high sea running, the most trying task of the day, required time and perseverance; but it was accomplished at last to my satisfaction, and the sail lashed securely to the gunwale on the starboard side, where its weight counterbalanced the dinghey and spars on the opposite side. This heavy gear would have been stowed on the lower platform, had not my comfort below and complete freedom from any sort of obstruction been far more important than the trifling disadvantage of a moderate deck load.

To avoid spending more time on deck forward than was absolutely necessary, the stormsail, being dry and in every way easier to handle than the mainsail, was opened out below and reefed there; then lifted forward and bent to the mast. When the tackles were overhauled and seen to be clear for hoisting almost beyond the possibility of a hitch, and the sheet bent on, I furled the sail and partially covered it—so that there would be nothing to do but uncover, cast off stops, and hoist away. The precaution of covering may seem superfluous, since rain and spray wetted it considerably before the cover could be put on; but if the canvas and tackles had been permitted to harden by saturation the difficulty of hoisting would have been increased, and the latter, probably, have kinked and jammed at a critical moment. The ensign, in a 'reasonably' tattered condition, had been hauled down at sunset, and shortly afterwards the riding light got up—which, in spite of the violence of the elements, I contrived to keep burning with steady brilliance throughout the night by partially closing the ventilator with thin canvas.

Beyond an occasional glance towards the landmarks, to see that the anchors were holding firm, for several hours my attention was so exclusively directed to my own affairs, that if the whole fleet had vanished I should have been unconscious of the fact. It would be absurd to pretend that such work, in itself, was agreeable; yet the pleasure of knowing it was done, and that everything was in a reasonable state of efficiency and preparation to meet a more adverse change, if it should come, was immense. As with the most highly favoured mortals on shore comfort is only comparative, it cannot be difficult to understand how thoroughly jolly it was below when the stove was lighted, wringing wet garments exchanged for dry, and a savoury rump-steak and potatoes under way for dinner. Besides the powerful beam thrown across the cabin from the stove—I had an oil lamp with reflector at the after end of the cabin, and a candle lamp forward—for the more gloomy it is on deck the more desirable is cheerfulness below. Outside the cabin, the larger riding light belonging to the 'Orion,' and specially chosen for duty upon this occasion, shed a strong light over the vessel; its rays, as I sat by the open cuddy doors, seeming to be absorbed immediately beyond the gunwale and the mizenmast in a wall of impenetrable darkness.

Though I have passed many a suspicious-looking night at anchor upon various parts of the coast of Great Britain and Ireland, the situation struck me as novel when at 10.30, in a condition of wistful expectancy, I was tending the sputtering and odoriferous steak, compelled, for the credit of my occupation, to follow attentively and even anticipate the violent plunges and lurches of the vessel—listening, the while, to the roar of the wind and the dashing of rain and spray against the after bulkhead; and, at times, watching almost with curiosity the sudden depression of the stern followed by as sudden a rise above my head, according to the position she occupied on the passing wave. In such circumstances it sounds strange that there should be anything short of actual discomfort in sitting down to dinner at a late hour of the night by the open doors of the cuddy; but, excepting the motion, there was none whatever, as the thermometer was fairly high, and the wind too strong from ahead to allow any rain to fall within several feet of the entrance to the cabin. I was very curious to see the barometer—which, from an early hour of the day up to the last time of seeing it, had moved steadily downward—but restrained my curiosity for the present; considering that if the fall was checked nothing would be gained by ascertaining it, whereas if a serious further decline had taken place, knowledge of it might interfere with the dinner, which, with a pint of Bass, plumcake for pudding, and a pipe for dessert, was in every respect a most successful performance.

Excepting as an experiment, there is nothing to be said in favour of risking a gale at anchor; but if for any reason it may seem desirable to do so rather than get under way, the advantage of being wind-rode is great and undeniable. With modifications as to time, the tide, of course, flowed and ebbed as usual; but at no time during the four days it fell under my observation did I perceive any surface current to windward. Throughout this particular day all the vessels I saw were swung to the northward with taut cables; and on the following day, when the wind was more off shore, only a few were partially canted athwart stream. From Monday evening until Thursday afternoon the 'Procyon' never once swung to the southward; had she done so, and commenced running ahead of her anchor, the position would have been untenable, and I should have considered it 'notice to quit.'

At midnight the barometer showed a slight improvement, and the rain partially ceased; but there was no change to excuse a relaxation of vigilance, for it was extremely dark, and it was not improbable that a lugger of the coast might at any moment run up inside the fleet, unsuspicious of anything lying closer in. As a boat of 7 tons plunging in a heavy sea with a taut strain on her anchors will not bear a shock, however slight, I paid more than ordinary attention to the riding light, which, though burning well and calculated to last till long after sunrise, I carefully retrimmed at 2 A.M. The wind having gradually veered a couple of points to south-west, and thereby relieved me of any anxiety as to its direction during the remainder of the dark hours, I ventured to turn in; but kept a lantern burning below, and myself in readiness for the deck at short notice. Barometer 29·65.

Aug. 28.—Barometer 29·6, wind S.W. by W., blowing hard, very much rain. It was difficult to believe in its continuance—seeing it was supposed to be summer—but when the morning duties were got through, and the weather, excepting that there was less sea at the anchorage, showed no sign of improvement, I began to feel perplexed as to the next move; for tossing there began to be irksome, and I was determined to have nothing to do with the beach, unless I could land myself, which was out of the question. Two or three large smacks passed down under very short canvas, otherwise business on the water was almost suspended. Had it been fine overhead, there would have been an amusing scene of boats passing under canvas between the ships and the shore; but the gloom and the soaking rain offered no compensation for the risk of another black night at anchor, and perhaps a shift of wind to the opposite quarter of the compass; so I decided to shake the reef out of the stormsail, and endeavour to beat round the Foreland to Dover.

After a substantial luncheon, having seen that everything movable fore and aft was securely lashed, the canvas prepared, and the mizen set, I took advantage of the short lulls between the puffs to get the kedge anchor aboard, and then, with the stormsail set, sailed the other out of the ground with very little trouble. These and all other manœuvres strictly belonging to the 'marine department' (getting under way on a tideless lee shore without sternway, for instance), carried out with precision, are among the most interesting problems of sea-sailing.

The first half-hour, while standing down closehauled and heading rather off, was spent in stowing anchors and coiling ropes, of which the largest required to be hove overboard and towed before it would coil into its berth. 2 P.M.—I made a board to windward off Lower Deal, and later another abreast of Kingsdown, to make final preparations for the next two hours' work, which would assuredly try the lugger's powers to the utmost. Having seen that the lower tack was home to the last inch possible, I clapped a tackle on the fall of the halyards, shook up in the wind, and gave the yard an extra bowse up until the sail stood like a board. The gear need be good to stand such treatment; but an ill-standing sail to windward—especially when, without stopping her way, a craft requires to be temporarily relieved from overpowering pressure by judicious 'lifting'—is an abomination, and not unlikely to lead to a vessel becoming unmanageable; since it is impossible to luff for a breaking sea without violently flapping the canvas, and paying off broadside to the sea the moment headway is lost.

With colours flying and everything done I could think of, I hoped she would not disappoint me, as on the occasion of leaving Ramsgate; albeit, the fault after all was mine for not giving her the stormsail, which though in area only equal to the close-reefed mainsail, is far more powerful in heavy weather, owing to its 7 feet greater hoist rendering it impossible to be becalmed to any appreciable extent by the sea. (From the deck the hoist is 18 feet, and the peak of the sail above the water-line 24 feet.)

The tide was past two-thirds ebb, when it should have been visibly setting to the southward; but, with the exception of one here and there partially canted, vessels remained swung to the northward. Protected by the cliffs of the South Foreland, from which the wind came down in violent gusts, off Kingsdown the sea was moderate; though passengers unaccustomed to it, had there been any, might have been of a different opinion. But with every cable's advance to the southward, the lugger began to leap higher and plunge deeper, until, exposed to the full drift of the Channel, she needed her best powers and all the assistance I could give to enable her to surmount the towering sea, which but for occasionally throwing her head into the wind and cleaving the breaking crest 'end on,' would have overwhelmed her in a moment. Having no one else to speak to—though it is uncertain if that would have made any difference—I encouraged her as one does a horse, and, not for the first time, found she understood me well.

After thirty hours' rain, a meteorologist with no more pressing subject to engage his attention might, from the heavier downpour, clearer definition, and more threatening aspect of the clouds—appearances which indicate a break up into squalls—have predicted at least a temporary cessation before sunset. This actually occurred, but not in time to benefit me. On the contrary, I had the six hours' rain required to make up the day and a half condensed into two, which searched my damaged waterproofs to such an extent that I welcomed, rather than otherwise, a drenching stream of salt spray from the weather bow to mix with it, and make it more healthy.

Keeping a vigilant watch on the sea, and not for an instant unmindful of the irreparable mischief that could be wrought on an undecked craft by a miscalculation or inadvertence, I stood on until the easternmost cliffs were four miles astern; when I put about, and—with a trifling lee helm—hove-to awhile, to get rid of the water, that in spite of every precaution it had been impossible wholly to exclude. This done, there was another reach of five miles to Dover, which was accomplished in good time, notwithstanding the canvas was kept constantly 'lifting' to free the lee gunwale; and the numerous delays occasioned by luffing—even to the extent of heaving-to—to meet the lofty curlers, which gave her such terrific lurches that everything possible to unship or break away did so, and it was necessary to hold on tight to save being shot out to leeward. The effect of this unavoidable 'lifting' and luffing was to bring the Admiralty Pier so far under the lee, that the lugger could have weathered it with a wide berth had her destination been beyond. Fortunately it was not—as will presently appear; and at 4.30 P.M. she bounded off the last big sea into the comparatively smooth water of the bay. As, in so violent a wind, the attempt to beat into harbour at low water would probably have been attended with some vexatious incident to mar the day's success, I sailed about for an hour in the bay without easing the sheets, which had been undisturbed since the sails were trimmed off Kingsdown—and took the opportunity, when she was running before the wind and tolerably upright, to pump her out. 5.30 P.M.—Went into harbour, and moored alongside a Channel steamer.

Shortly after my arrival in the bay a large pilot lugger I had observed beating to windward under double-reefed foresail and mizen came in and brought up—to which vessel, without doubt, a man previously referred to belonged. His business on board the steamer to which the 'Procyon' was made fast was to convince me of the mistake I had made the previous day in declining to give them a 'trifle' to take me into Ramsgate. A bystander suggested that a Dealman's trifle might possibly have been 'five-and-twenty pounds,' if, under the circumstances, any of them had been once admitted on board— which, judging from his offensive manner, I thought highly probable. Considering that Ramsgate was precisely where I had left it so recently, the acceptance of their offer would have been absurd. At the same time, without practice, no one would be likely to steer a strange boat safely with a yoke in a heavy sea, so that, as any service they contemplated rendering which could entitle them to a high reward must have been attended with danger to themselves, it is difficult to see how in any sense it could have been beneficial to me.

Although, to my regret, the result of this day's work was to bring the cruise abruptly to an end, in point of time and distance against adverse influences—regard being had to the small size and weight of the boat—it was one of the most successful and interesting experiments I remember. The distance, 9 nautical miles for a steamer following the coast, and 13 for a boat under canvas sailing up to four and a half points with the wind S.W. by W., was accomplished in two and three-quarter hours, including the coiling of ropes and the numerous little stoppages related. Under a whole mainsail, with moderate weather and an average tide, the difference in time could not have been great.

Knowing it was impossible to pump dry under canvas in a sea-way, I pumped her again in harbour; but what with dinner, stowing canvas, docking, &c., the quantity of water failed to attract notice. Having, with the exception of an hour at Ramsgate and an hour at Deal, been on board for a week, I sought a little change on shore, chiefly at the club; and on my return at 11 P.M., more out of curiosity than as a measure of prudence, again tried the pump. Finding the water flow freely, it occurred to me to count the strokes, which, to my astonishment, ran up to nearly 1500 before she was free. A handier little pump was never put into a boat, but its power is insufficient for an emergency—especially in the event of shipping a heavy sea—and will be increased. It can be worked deeper and lower with the same result; but to keep the barrel full and a steady flow through the nozzle (or inch discharge pipe), the easiest work is 90 strokes of the brake a minute, which, by experiment since tried, is found to deliver $4\frac{1}{2}$ gallons in that time. Thus the quantity leaked in five hours was 75 gallons (equal to a dead weight of $6\frac{1}{2}$ cwt.), which required 17 minutes' work to pump out. These particulars are mentioned in view of an incident which occurred later.

This was not a very serious quantity, but as it proved mischief had been done somewhere, I raised the cabin floor with a chisel, removed the ballast forward, and having ascertained there was no fault there, concluded—rightly, as it turned out—that in the heavy lurches to leeward on the passage the ballast had damaged the fastenings of the keel case. Happily the case was so supported by standards and transverse bearers that it could not break away; at the same time, it would have been the height of imprudence to risk any more sailing to windward, or anchorage off the coast at night, until it was repaired.

The account of the last seven days shows the exceptional character of the weather that prevailed every day but one. In the daytime of Sunday the 24th, or on any night excepting the 27th, the passage from Whitstable to Dover could have been done with ease; but I had no motive for sailing on Sunday or during the night, and was content to take my chance during reasonable hours of the day. Though a week of dreadful rains, hard winds, and little sunshine, it was anything but dull, excepting in harbour. On the contrary, there was such abundant employment of a congenial nature that the clock was always 'too fast,' and the number of hours spent in hammock far below a landsman's requirements. Amongst the stores laid in and preserved in tins were cake, jams, French chocolate and bonbons, which would have seen the light the first week only to be thrown overboard, but latterly had come to be highly prized. The fact is if, from causes explained, I failed to visit the parts of the coast contemplated at starting, the chief object of the cruise was attained, viz., a condition of health for which nothing was too hard, to which nothing came amiss. Barometer 29·675,.showed but a slight improvement since the morning. All night and throughout the following day it blew hard from the westward, with squalls and heavy rain at intervals.

Aug. 30.—Wind W.S.W., very fine, with a rising barometer. Greatly inconvenienced by soreness of the hands and muscles, the former of which I endeavoured to cure with spirits of turpentine. I purposed resting at Dover until Monday, but considered that the opportunity of moderate weather to reach the builders at Whitstable should not be neglected. The fair weather for which everybody had been looking so long had really set in at last, not quite too late for me, because to the damaged keel case a quiet passage was a necessity. In brilliant sunshine and the clearest atmosphere imaginable, the coast looked so charming that the day would have been one of great enjoyment, had not regret at being compelled to leave it been aggravated by a series of vexations more or less serious, of which failure to get any breakfast was not the least.

The determination to leave was taken suddenly, when there was barely time to get provisions from the town, and pass into the outer harbour before the dock gates were closed. My intention was to hang on to a buoy, have breakfast, and put everything in order before sailing. But in an evil moment the old adage came into my mind that 'time and tide wait for no man,' and I resolved to do all this under way, forgetful of the swell in the Channel from the bad weather of the previous day. Running dead before the wind with a moderate breeze and the whole mainsail, after clearing the harbour the helm could not be left a moment without the swell causing the lugger to take a violent sheer. The bay was scarcely crossed when, during a short absence, she gybed and capsized the petroleum stove, that in the hurry of leaving I had forgotten to secure, making an offensive mess on the floor of the cabin, which was troublesome to clean and annoyed me considerably. The 'Procyon' has a spar 21 feet long, to be used as a bowsprit in light weather at sea, as a ridgepole for the awning in harbour, or to boom out the mainsail when running before the wind. For the latter purpose it is handy enough in smooth water, but with no one to steady the helm or the mainsheet while the lashing was put on, it cost me a quarter of an hour's hard work to get it rigged out upon this occasion.

The wind was puffy and too light for the impatience of a hungry man; so that it was one o'clock, or three hours after the start, when, with the wind still aft and fresh, I ran suddenly and most strangely across a strongly defined line on the sea into a flat calm off the North Foreland. Immediately this occurred I unshipped the boom, sheeted the sails, and had a good luncheon at the helm. In about half an hour a fresh breeze sprang up again from the south-west as curiously partial as any I remember to have witnessed. Instantly it reached me I made a short tack to windward of the 'Longnose Ledge'; and when about again, lay closehauled along the coast, 'gunwale down,' in the direction of Margate; leaving vessels, not more than half a mile to leeward, with the wind blowing from the cliffs directly towards them, hopelessly becalmed until they were 'hull down' in the distance.

To hold the breeze I had to keep to the chalk ledges so close aboard that the heel of the drop-keel (18 inches below the main keel) occasionally touched the longer projections. This in smooth water was perfectly harmless, its action being simply that of a 'tell-tale' to warn me a few fathoms farther off. It was fine fun and most successful while there was a hard bottom to deal with, but off the Reculvers, near the period of low water, and fully three-quarters of a mile from the shore, I had the misfortune to cut into an outlying bank of stiff clay, which held the drop-keel firmly and defied every effort with tackles and levers to force it up. Under the circumstances there was nothing better to do than exercise patience, light the stove, and prepare dinner. If it be true that 'it is ill working on an empty stomach,' it was indeed fortunate I thus utilized the time; for while some fine mutton chops and potatoes were being disposed of, though she made no 'list,' such work as I had never seen before, and never want to see again, was being cut out for me.

When a boat is aground and the breeze fresh there is a peculiar 'slopping' sound caused by the ripple striking her in the 'run' or under the 'bilge.' Such a sound had been audible for some time, and though it grew louder and seemed nearer, as it would do supposing the tide to be falling, I attached no importance to it. The first course was got over, and the second of cherry jam, &c., was about to commence, when I was startled out of propriety by the water coming through the cabin floor at my feet.

All alone, with the prospect of so much trouble ahead, if the greatest delicacies of the season had been spread before me I could not have swallowed another mouthful without suffocating. The first thing was to take up a trap in the waist platform, notice the height of water on the ballast, and see if I could gain upon it by pumping. Finding this practicable I returned to the cabin, hastily washed up and stowed away the dinner things, and then settled down to work. The tide was not falling, but flowing against her starboard side, and apparently when she did move, forcing her upon a shoaler spot of the bank. This was the sorest point of all, and occasioned the bank and my own incautiousness for getting there to be so soundly rated that I lighted a pipe with no other object than to preserve peace and quietness—in other words, to check the flow of useless anathemas.

The shaft of the keel case into which the pump discharges is 9 inches above the waterline. This is the precise measure of the further depth to which the boat could possibly be immersed without the water overflowing there and foundering her. As 2½ tons of ballast and stores immersed her 3 feet, it can scarcely be wrong to assume that an increase of less than a ton and a half would bring the water to the top of the shaft, and render the pump useless, while the gunwale would still be 15 inches above the waterline. That the shaft was not constructed higher was my fault, since when I considered it high enough for safety, undoubtedly too much regard was paid to neatness of appearance. Hitherto it has proved more than equal to every requirement; but from recent experience, acquired during the last days of this cruise, it is easy to imagine a case in which a few inches more height might be desirable, and I have ordered the addition to be made.

It was 6.15 when, having hauled down the ensign, I took my station at the pump, and seven o'clock when she came off the bank and allowed the keel to be partially hauled up. The extent of the damage being unknown to me I resolved, if the pump sucked before reaching Herne Bay, to endeavour to get her home, discharge the stores, and return to Whitstable, if not, to make the builders' yard at the latter place as soon as possible.

That the labour would be severe was certain; so to reduce the chances of a breakdown to a minimum, I worked systematically from the commencement two hundred strokes right and left hand alternately, sometimes 'forehanded,' sometimes 'backhanded,' at the same time steering the lugger close hauled in the direction of Warden Point, Isle of Sheppey. Fortunately unable to see the amount of work before me, I laboured assiduously in expectation after the first hour that every minute would be the last. Already, under the conditions before stated, enough to founder her had been thrown out, and Herne Bay was not reached. After the latter town was passed, desiring not to attract attention and invite questions, I had a rest of two or three minutes while a boat was passing in the opposite direction, once knocked off to light a pipe, and once to procure a mug of tea. With these exceptions, amounting in all to about ten minutes, the regular discharge of 4½ gallons per minute was steadily maintained to the end.

The night was beautifully fine and moonlight, with a pleasant breeze that just enabled me to lay up for Whitstable Point. At nine o'clock, three hours from the discovery of the leak, the pump sucked, and shortly afterwards, the tide not having risen sufficiently to enable me to round the Point inside the 'Street' Shoal, she took the ground. The drop-keel being now up and the main keel protected with a half-inch iron band three inches wide, it was immaterial how often she grounded, provided the water were smooth. The motive for taking this course was to avoid running to leeward round the 'Street,' and having to beat up the 'Swale,' which would have been useless in every way; since, while there was insufficient water at the Point, there was none at the builders' yard, and the occasional pauses of three or four minutes released me from the helm. During one of them, attracted by the conspicuous whiteness of the sails in the moonlight and the sharp 'click' of the pump, a man pulled off in a boat, who, but for a job in which he was engaged, would have accompanied me through the fleet of deserted smacks, a species of pilotage that, with their long projecting bowsprits and a foul wind, I rather feared. However, there was no alternative; so, after a couple of boards to windward I sailed into the midst of them, and luffing for some and bearing up for others, got through all clear and anchored off the yard at 9 P.M.

First the sails were made up and coated, and then, to enable her to stand upright on the hard ground when the tide fell, the legs—oaken supports 5 feet long, bolted to the sides and kept in position with guys—were put on. This, with her jumping about, was a long and heavy job without help to steady them while the bolts were being driven. When, except pumping at intervals, there was nothing more to do, I lighted the stove, and though at first inclined to go in for invalid fare, altered my mind, and at 1 A.M. entirely made good the missing breakfast of the previous morning, coffee, fried ham, pipe and all. By 3.30, by which time the leak had declined to 400 strokes an hour, she settled on the ground and allowed me to turn in.

As, with a view to its improvement, I considered it worth while to ascertain the capacity of the pump, the nozzle was forced out of the head of the keel case when she was beached in the morning, and with the assistance of others it was tested several times by a proved measure and a watch. From this data it appears that the quantity of water thrown out before the pump sucked the previous night was 675 gallons = 2 tons 18 cwt., and during the following six hours before grounding

150 gallons = 13 cwt., amounting in all to a dead weight of 3½ tons. For sufficient reasons it was desirable to postpone the beaching until next day, but the sea was rough, and it was not safe to delay a tide.

Thus ended an accidentally contracted cruise of rather more than three weeks, out of which not more than twelve nights were spent in harbour, that, in an equal space of time, for continued violence of the elements and hard work, has not been exceeded in my experience. If I may be permitted to allude to another adventure that undoubtedly seems more severe, it should be remembered that the time extended only to a week; that I had a powerful winch and suitable appliances for the work; that there was more space, and the weather less violent. Besides, aware how serious it would be to get ashore or to meet with an accident of any description, I scrupulously kept to deep water, and being in a powerful decked vessel with no centreboard complications, had no abominable pumping to do.

'ORION'

FROM THE THAMES TO THE WOLF ROCK
WITH AN AMATEUR CREW, 1882

NOT caring to fit out the 'Orion' (19 tons) to do precisely as I had done so many times before, I sounded two young friends, Horace Detmar and William Todd, owners of little sailing craft and used to roughing it, to ascertain if they were willing to accompany me on a short cruise down Channel as sailors before the mast, without any professional assistance whatever. As they jumped at the proposal and entirely approved my plans, I forthwith set to work and fitted out the 'Orion,' with the assistance of my ship-keeper (a superannuated coastguard) and two boys from the training-ship 'Arethusa.' Beyond this, for heavy lifts, hauling out of dock, &c., I had extra help from the same source, as my friends were not able to join until we were prepared for sea.

Although, in accordance with our verbal agreement 'that there should be no talking beforehand,' my intentions were not avowed until the volunteer crew turned up, which left me free to go forward or to retreat if from any sufficient cause it was desired, having undertaken the work I determined to persevere with it to the end, and succeeded in having everything prepared for their reception at the time appointed.

It was understood that all close harbours, such as Ramsgate, Dover, and the like, would be avoided as much as possible during the five or six weeks allotted to the cruise, and that stoppages for needful rest and recreation would be passed at such anchorages as are used by pilot cutters now, and were used by the revenue cutters of former days.

Water and fuel, and all but perishable stores sufficient for the entire cruise, were taken on board at Greenhithe. Thus, with an ample supply of tinned meats and bread, hard and soft, there was no fear of falling short of wholesome food if compelled to keep off the land longer than there was reason to anticipate.

July 7.—We sailed from Greenhithe, Kent, with a strong wind from the southward, and were compelled to anchor in the Lower Hope, in consequence of a plate-glass side light in the booby hatch being accidentally smashed off Gravesend. As the means of repairing such accidents have always been included in the 'Orion's' stores, we turned glaziers for the nonce, and, after coming to an anchor for the night, repaired the damage.

July 8.—Under way at 7 A.M. with one reef down, wind S.W., and ran to the North Foreland; and after a smart turn to windward, anchored off Deal at 3 P.M. Weather dull; barometer, 29·65.

July 9, *Sunday.*—Spent a pleasant day at anchor. Weather strong and squally, with rather much swell.

July 10.—Wind hard and squally from S.W., and very cold. Had a heavy beat to windward round the South Foreland to Dover, during which the jib outhaul was carried away, necessitating a run before the sea for repairs; also a heavy sea was shipped, which, consequent upon the terrific lurch, caused some damage to the crockery and glass below. Being anxious to receive and post letters at Dover, we anchored in the bay for the night, and rode to a large scope of chain and the 'cable buffer.' Weather cloudy and strong; sea very rough; barometer 29·5.

July 11.—Turned down to Dymchurch (Dungeness Road), and again anchored for the night with a large scope of chain and the cable buffer. Weather rainy and strong with much swell.

July 12.—Got under way late in the day; but, the wind failing and flying round to all parts of the compass, with the appearance of a storm, anchored again in a good berth off Lydd. Weather dark and cloudy, with a cross swell from S.W. and from east.

July 13.—Wind W.S.W., fresh and fine, but with falling barometer. Five miles south of Dungeness, carried away inner iron block of starboard bowsprit shroud. Repaired from stores and proceeded.

July 14.—After a rough and wet night, turning to windward on the south coast, we desired to anchor in Selsea Road (about four miles south of Bognor), in the hope of being able to procure a good breakfast; but, the wind being violent and the sea too heavy, thrashed on to Ryde, I. of W., and anchored there at 2 P.M. We remained inside the island for six days, chiefly in Lymington river, being hand-sore and tired from handling so much wet canvas and ropes that were rendered harsh and untractable by frequent saturation.

July 20.—Having a suspicion that our anchor had dragged foul of a large vessel's moorings, I determined to satisfy myself on the point before breakfast. And a grand addition to the usual morning's work it proved! Everyone who is acquainted with this species of work knows what it means when with every 'Heave Ho!—Heave!' just five or six inches of the chain can be got, diminishing towards the last to three, two, one. But for the assistance of an 'American crank' in addition to the ordinary means of working the winch, it would have been impossible, without help, to have hove the anchor to the surface at all. In view of this contingency, I was much amused the previous day by having a demand made upon me for 'mooring accommodation.' My reply was that, 'It would be time enough to pay when it was proved there was anything to be thankful for.'

The habitual blocking with permanent moorings of every available spot in this little river is a great nuisance to strangers seeking shelter there in blowing weather; the ground being so soft that the anchor is almost certain to drag foul before the vessel can be securely moored.

Sailed from Lymington river at 11.30 A.M., bound to Cherbourg (Normandy); wind W.S.W., strong and fine. On a strong flood tide we stood over towards Yarmouth, passing through a fleet of weather-bound vessels; and, being desirous to give my young friends a good view of that picturesque little town, I stood on close-hauled too near the shore before putting the 'Orion' about, and, when actually in stays, took the soft mud just above the pier. With the assistance of three men from a schooner at anchor close by, and my own kedge and hawser, we got off in less than an hour, and proceeded to beat down against a head sea to the Needles. We cleared the Needles at 2.30 P.M., and headed S.S.W. for Cherbourg, with the patent log overboard.

I suppose there is not a yachtsman or a sailor of experience living who can perceive that this grounding was only a little annoyance, which those who close shave the land in inland waters for their amusement are liable to every day, and think of no more account than intentionally taking the ground for the many purposes that small craft habitually do. Yet, for some reason difficult to fathom, seeing that the vessel is under 20 tons register, is exclusively my own private property, and was uninsured, I have received a request to attend at the office of Receiver of Wrecks, and fill up a form which would be applicable to the stranding of the steamship 'Mosel' at the Lizard Point. While engaged in hauling off, a boat from Yarmouth, with three men in her, came alongside and wanted to board. That I peremptorily forbade, for reasons that everyone will understand. Then the coastguard boat, with an officer in charge, arrived, and the latter I cordially received, being in reality no stranger. But when he exhibited a portentous scroll with much printing on it, which I was too busy to examine, and wanted me to fill in a mass of particulars, such as would be applicable to the above-mentioned stranding at the Lizard, I told him that he could see exactly how the matter stood, and that, as the yacht was mine and uninsured, I must decline to sign anything I did not understand; in fact, that it was absurd, and that taking notice of such silly little mishaps, of daily occurrence, would destroy all confidence in the correctness of the official returns. Had I been insured the case would have been different; but even then, as the utmost I had to complain of was the chafing of a manilla hawser, it would have been ridiculous. I have been insured only four times, and never made a claim—once on a voyage to Ireland, twice on voyages to

Scotland, and last year, chiefly in consequence of the enormous increase of steam traffic, on a general cruise in the Channel. I offered to insure upon this cruise also, and for the same reason, but, owing to my announced determination to sail with an amateur crew, was refused. Thus the premium was saved, and I became responsible only to myself.

July 21, 5 A.M.—When by account twenty miles from the Normandy coast, we noticed a strong scent from the hayfields. Wind S.W., light and fine. 8.30, Barfleur and Cape Levi lighthouses were respectively 11 miles distant by cross bearings, when the wind fell calm, and we were drifted eastward to the meridian of the former. During the afternoon, with a strong breeze from the S.W., which severely tried the bowsprit, we beat into Cherbourg by the eastern entrance, and, having anchored off the town at 5.30 P.M., hastened to furl the canvas before a heavy downpour set in for the night.

July 25.—Went on a slipway in the outer harbour and cleaned the copper. For this job I hired men by agreement, who so scamped the work that the following morning we completed it ourselves, and at high water returned to our previous anchorage in the roads.

July 28.—Wind S.W., light and fine. With a large spread of canvas we sailed for the Cornish coast, and for a long while had just cause to apprehend being drifted into the Race of Alderney, or the Swinge, for which the pretty scenery the calm clear atmosphere enabled us to enjoy offered very inadequate compensation. But, a fresh breeze springing up, with a long swell from the S.W., we got clear away, and at 2 P.M., by cross bearings of the western point of Alderney and the Casquets, were thirty-two miles W.N.W. of Cherbourg. Until 10.30 the night was superb and moonlight, when a dense sea fog came on, which, with a short interval about midnight, continued until 2.30 P.M. of the following day. The fog was so wetting, that halyards, tacks, and sheets had to be eased during the night.

July 29, 6.30 P.M.—The wind having headed us off the course, with a strong adverse tide, we bore up for the Start

Point, and anchored north of the lighthouse at 8 P.M. The sails being heavy with moisture, and having been hard set up for turning to windward, took us an hour and a half to stow—I mean to furl in a manner that anyone might see and criticise. From the severity of the purchasing, the bolt-ropes of the jib and topsail 'crackled' like burning firewood while being forced into the bags—a sure indication that more than ordinary energy would be required to get the 'bunt tyer' on the mainsail when its turn arrived, and that those who had no long finger-nails to turn back would be a step in advance of those who had. If asked how many hands a yacht of a given tonnage should carry, I should reply by another question—what is the weight and quality of her canvas? For it is in reefing, handing, and furling canvas of high quality, more than in anchor work, that deficiency of manual power becomes conspicuous. The canvas of an 18-ton schooner, beside which I was once lying in Dover harbour, when on a single-handed cruise in the 'Procyon' 7-ton lugger, was quite flimsy compared to the lugger's mainsail of No. 5 double; while the latter, which has often punished my hands, is light in comparison with the lower sails of the 'Orion,' whose mainsail and foresail are of No. 2, and working jibs of No. 3 double—a substance of canvas that for my work has important advantages, which I would not sacrifice to any other consideration whatever. The details are necessary to account for the time and labour expended in their manipulation, often hinted at in my cruises without being clearly explained. Night calm and moonlight.

July 30 (*Sunday*).—Had a glorious day at anchor. Dried sails, and landed at the lighthouse for a stroll. Wind W., fresh and fine. Night extremely grand.

July 31.—Under way 7.30 with a light air E., and hove-to with foresail to windward. During breakfast drove round the Start Point at a safe distance. 9.30, wind W., a nice breeze; set large topsail and commenced turning to windward. Views of the coast charming, and unsurpassable in Great Britain. Eight miles west of the Start spoke a torpedo boat, with seven hands, under canvas for Brazil, which, by master's request, I reported at Falmouth. Although the sun was shining, when the wind freshened, the air, as on previous days, became so exceedingly chilly as to require thick clothing. 3.45 P.M. passed south of the Eddystone to view the new lighthouse. Sea choppy. 8 P.M., tacked off Looe, Cornwall; wind N.W. by W., fresh. During the night passed close to several fishing boats, some without lights, their position being announced to us by the sea gulls that were uttering their cries incessantly around them.

Aug. 1.—2 A.M., weather thick and rainy. Hove to in Veryan Bay, south of the Dodman Head, to get supper and wait for daylight to enter Falmouth. 6 A.M., anchored off the town; morning fine and sunny after the rain. Noon, landed for provisions, and at 2.30 sailed again, with a strong wind, W.N.W., for the Lizard, where, before anchoring at 7 P.M. in Perran Vose Cove, we became enveloped in a dense fog, which caused some vessels to put back, while others, the wind being violent and with a fast rising sea, shortened canvas and hove-to. The night, however, became fine, and from our anchorage, where there was a tolerable swell, we could view with perfect equanimity the 'outward-bounders' taking a 'header' into the Race.

Aug. 2.—Wind W.N.W., strong and fine. Housed topmast, and with one reef earing down, but reef not tied up, made sail for the Land's End. 10.45 A.M., dived into the Race, heading S.W. by W. The sea was most troublesome for an hour, burying the bowsprit and invading the deck frequently, so that a fine barque in full sail seemed to give us the 'go by' completely. Tacked about noon, and then stood N. by W. in a bigger sea, but of so much better quality that it let our bowsprit alone, when we turned the tables so completely upon our late antagonist that her identity was lost amidst a fleet to leeward. It was fine sailing, the weather at that time being beautifully clear, though cold enough for October. 3 P.M., passed to windward of the Runnel Stone Buoy—carrying a bell with numerous clappers, which strike without reference to time or harmony—the rock itself being occasionally visible in the trough of the sea. The Longships and the land beyond were also very plain when we tacked and stood off for the Wolf Rock lighthouse, round which we sailed, but at a respectful distance, on account of the race of tide and heavy sea. The voices of its occupants, who appeared in the gallery and at the windows, first on one side and then on the other, and with whom we exchanged frequent salutations, were drowned by the noise of the elements. To windward of the lighthouse we pitched into some tide rollers, that would have played sad havoc with the head-gear had it not been very powerful. In the first of these tremendous 'scends,' one of the weather runner-plates was carried away, and there was evidence afterwards that everything that could move throughout the vessel was more or less displaced. 4.30 P.M., waved adieu, and commenced to run back to the Lizard, against tide, and dead before wind and sea—the most objectionable point of sailing in a fore-and-aft rigged vessel. 6 P.M., the sky became overcast, and, in spite of a high barometer, the weather set in so wet and miserably cold that at 8.45 we were exceedingly glad to bring up at the anchorage we had left in the morning. Exceptionally tired and hungry, the terrible job we had with the saturated canvas and hard wet ropes, happily followed by a good dinner of hot loin of mutton and potatoes at 11 P.M., are incidents that never pass entirely out of recollection. Upon an occasion like this the general clear-up is undoubtedly rather trying; but in open anchorage, where there is no certainty that at any hour you will not be called upon hastily to make sail and stand out to sea, whatever work below might by lazy people be left to the morrow, on deck order must be thorough and complete. Anchorage at sea night after night, especially upon an iron bound coast, is fraught with nothing but danger where these conditions are not recognised and strictly observed. The Lizard coast is very interesting and enjoyable in fine weather; but in clouds and darkness, when there is reason to be anxious, its beauty vanishes in a moment.

Aug. 3.—Dried sails, &c. Crew landed for a ramble to Kynance Cove and other interesting spots, while I found abundant occupation on board. Wind N.N.E., a moderate breeze. Night fine and clear, with a gentle swell from the eastward.

Aug. 4.—Wind fresh from N.N.E. After the usual wash down, in which all hands participated, and which was only once omitted owing to the rough sea rendering it impracticable, we sailed at 8.30, and shortly afterwards hove to with foresail to windward, heading slowly on the course while we were getting breakfast and attending to such various duties below as, if attended to in the order of daily custom, would have deferred the time of sailing for two hours, and have lost us eight miles. But for the low temperature, the day was most delightful. All the headlands and bays of this much-indented coast were clearly distinguishable in the distance, and the sea, in colour a compromise between a dark sapphire and a dark emerald, was sparkling and clear as crystal. 4.30 P.M., passed north of the Eddystone in a strong breeze, the foam in our wake looking as white as fresh-fallen snow. 8.15, after a magnificent sunset, which charmed us with its effects upon the rugged shore, the wind having almost died away, we luffed up into Lanacombe Bay, near the Start Point, and anchored for the night in seven fathoms of low water; a spot which, if possible, was more charming than any anchorage that preceded it. Night moonlight, starlight, calm and clear, with an agreeable scent of cornfields off the land. Anyone unaccustomed to anchorages in the immediate vicinity of high land can hardly fail to be alarmed at its apparent nearness after dark, when the sense of perspective, by which distance is estimated in daylight, no longer exists. Thus, the darker the night, the more complete is the illusion of the cliffs and the hills behind them being merged into one lofty perpendicular, which overshadows the vessel by its black reflection in the sea, advancing almost to her side, and seems to leave not a fathom of space to swing, much less to get under way, without finding oneself ashore. Readers may not understand our enthusiasm in regard to these day-and-night views that so constantly engage our attention and challenge our admiration. They will perhaps think we might notice a view and dismiss it; but it is in reality our chiefest and almost sole recreation on deck in fine weather, without which a voluntary cruise at sea would seem far too tame as an amusement to compensate for the actual labour, expense, and constant watchfulness it entails. Followed as a pastime, it is not unlike the pleasure human nature has invariably found in successfully gathering roses off thorns; for, however amiable the sea may appear to us in its quiet moments, or, even better, when contemplating its grandeur from the fireside at home, it is a mighty power and a rough playmate; and even steam, the yachtsman's craze of the day, will never render it anything else.

Aug. 5.—Sailed from Lanacombe Bay at 8.30 with a nice breeze, N.N.W., and when round the Start Point hauled the foresail to windward, and allowed the 'Orion' to sail herself to Dartmouth, where we anchored in the Range, and rowed up to the town in the boat for letters and provisions. Later returned to the Start, and anchored about a mile north of the lighthouse, in five fathoms low water. The weather looking cloudy and threatening, we rode with a large scope and the cable buffer. At night the sky cleared and became magnificently fine. Generally the boat is turned in at night ready for sea; but occasionally, as in this instance, when determined to ride if possible, a strop is passed round her, and, with one of the luff tackles, kept handy for various uses, the strain is relieved from the davits and thrown upon the standing part of the runner. My davits are abaft the main rigging, for greater convenience in handling the boat, which is never carried in the davits under way.

Aug. 6 (*Sunday*).—The first really hot summer day of the cruise. From morning till night, afloat and ashore, it was a day of unalloyed enjoyment; such as, in my opinion, concurred in by my mates, would be impossible in harbour. The bouquet, that is never absent from my table at sea, though unfortunately ranking with perishable stores, was replenished with a grand collection of wild flowers, in which ferns, honeysuckle, and ox-eye daisies were most conspicuous.

Aug. 7.—Sailed at 8.30; wind light, weather fine and warm. 3 P.M., four miles E.S.E. of Torquay, under large canvas, lay a course for Portland; wind S.W., veering gradually to N.W. 6.30 P.M., hove-to for an hour, with both headsails aback and mainsheet pinned in, to keep her from travelling off the course, and to preserve the gravy for its proper use during dinner. Night fine; moonlight in early morning.

Aug. 8.—3 A.M., Portland Bill N.E. by N.; tacked in a shifting head wind, and later weathered the Shambles Lightship. 6.30 A.M., hove-to off Lulworth, Dorset, for a comfortable breakfast, and then beat up to St. Alban's head. 6 P.M., anchored in Alum Bay, I. of W.; wind S.W., fresh and fine. While lying here we observed the unfortunate steamship 'Mosel,' which stranded next day at the Lizard.

Aug. 9.—Under way at 10.30; wind E., fresh and fine. Passed out at the Needles and beat up outside the island, standing inshore when there was any place of special interest to observe, such as Blackgang, St. Catherine's, and Ventnor. 6 P.M., made the Looe Channel, when the tide turned. 8 P.M., wind W.N.W., light; anchored off Selsea in four fathoms low water.

Aug. 10.—Wind E.N.E., a moderate breeze and miserably cold. 6 A.M., under way. 8 A.M., hove to off Bognor. 6 P.M., anchored for the night off Brighton, and landed to post letters and procure supplies.

Aug. 11.—Wind E.N.E. veering to S.E., fresh and fine. 6.45 A.M., got under way, and, chiefly in regard to the pleasant agricultural and homely views on shore, had a magnificent turn to windward past Newhaven and Seaford, and round the grand cliffs of Beachy Head against tide. There we encountered a true easterly wind in every sense, accompanied by a short sea, averaging twenty-one to the minute, which greatly impeded our progress. (On the Cornish and Irish coasts I have met seas averaging five and even four to the minute, which may properly be described as a 'long sea.') 3.45 P.M., tacked off Eastbourne, and, after rounding the Royal Sovereign shoals, stood in towards Hastings, where the sea was too rough to anchor as desired; so we continued under way, and at 9 P.M. hove to off Fairleigh, with the foresail to windward, which allowed one hand to turn in comfortably below. Night fine and starlight, a heavy dew, and very cold.

Aug. 12.—Wind E., fresh and fine. 8.30, passed Dungeness. 1 P.M., anchored off Dover, and landed for letters. 5.30, the weather looking too stormy for Dover Roads, we sailed again, and beat against tide round the lofty cliffs of the South Foreland, intending to anchor for the night off Upper Deal. We had partaken of an excellent hot dinner below in turn, between 8.30 and 10 P.M., when the wind suddenly left us hopelessly becalmed and drifting at the southern entrance of the Gull Stream. At this time the horizon was black all round, with frequent flashes of lightning and thunder rumbling in the distance. Being very anxious about a group of bright lights, one of them the three triangular lights of a Trinity wreck steamer, I ordered the anchor to be cleared, and that especial attention should be directed to the chain below, to guard against any hitch if an emergency should arise. This precaution was fortunate, for, notwithstanding a light air sprang up, which held out a promise of escape, it soon became evident that the spring tide, which runs with great violence in that part of the Downs, was sweeping us rapidly into danger. Apart from this alarming complication, if an anchorage in Dover Bay were deemed unadvisable on account of the threatening appearance of the weather, certainly this was a case of 'out of the frying-pan into the fire.' At 10.30 P.M., when the sound of a rush of tide upon some obstruction was plainly audible, and evidently very near, we let go the anchor, 'all standing,' and did not attempt to check her until the 30-fathoms shackle passed out of the hawse-pipe, and then paid out 10 more for extra security. Though close to the lights, the horizon was so dark that, even with the binoculars, we could not distinguish a vestige of anything beside, so had to wait for daylight to ascertain how the case really stood. While stowing the canvas, several steamers bore down upon us with their three lights, and then suddenly sheered away for the Gull Lightship. When our mate

274

descended from aloft, after unlacing the topsail, he remarked that the light immediately astern of us had an unusual appearance, and that he could not help thinking it must be on the mast of a sunken ship. As we were riding easily, with a good scope of chain, and it was useless to sit up speculating upon these matters, we turned in at 1.30 A.M., and soon forgot all about it.

Aug. 13 (*Sunday*).—At five o'clock, feeling more anxious about the weather than anything else, I turned out, and saw, as surmised, that our near neighbour was the mast of a large ship, with five wire shrouds on a side, and ratlings entire, which accounted for the great rush of water we heard overnight: that the Trinity steamer was about two cables east of the wreck, and that three Whitstable smacks, with diving gear on board, were also in attendance. An ominous swell from the south, with a squall rising in that quarter, and thunder rumbling in the south-west, warned me that no time should be lost in extricating ourselves from so awkward a position. Though the 'Orion' was swung down, or away from the wreck, at this hour, we were still within the influence of its eddy; so that while the chain was being hove-in she swung towards it again and again, until she became wind-rode with a strong breeze from the southward, and had the sunken ship under her lee. This was our position, when, the headsails and mizen having been previously prepared for hoisting and the anchor hove short, the latter was broken out of the ground by a violent gust of wind, which also cast the yacht's head to the eastward, and threatened to drift her broadside on to the wreck. Transferring my assistance where most needed, we worked hard to get the anchor in sight before it was likely to foul any obstruction, and at the same time hoisted the jib, under which she forged ahead and out of the most alarming predicament, save one, that has come under my experience. The crucial point had not yet arrived, but the brunt of the work, which had been exceptionally severe, was over, when four men from one of the smacks pulled alongside, to suggest that we were already foul of wreckage, and to offer assistance. But they returned without many words being wasted on either side; and, as the wind was just then threatening a gale, in ten minutes more they were fully employed in looking after their own affairs. Under headsails and mizen, we ran against tide to the North Foreland, during the greatest violence of the wind outstripping the smacks, which were in full retreat to Ramsgate; and about noon, having anchored in the Gore Channel, near Reculvers, where the wind was off the land, had a quiet and pleasant time for the remainder of the day.

Aug. 14.—With all plain sail, including the jib-headed top-sail, sailed from the Gore Channel at 6.30 A.M., and arrived at Greenhithe 12.30. Wind S.W., a moderate breeze to strong. The 'Orion' was docked same tide—the first night in harbour since quitting Cherbourg on July 28th—and by the evening of the 16th she was stripped.

To save misapprehension on two or three points, perhaps you will allow me to make a few observations more. That I did not distrust the spirited qualities of my friends is proved by the fact that when insurance on current terms for first-class yachts was only in one quarter declined on their account, I assumed the risk without further inquiry, or in the slightest degree modifying my plans. Besides the vessel and gear, which alone would have been covered by the insurance, there were among my personal effects many things I should have been much grieved to lose, including a very powerful microscope with lenses by well-known names. Thus the expenses, of course, and the entire risk, together with every responsibility for success or failure, were mine. But if everything had been theirs, they could not have shown more consideration for their own than they did for mine, nor have worked more assiduously and anxiously to guard against failure. That the experiment succeeded beyond my highest expectations was due to the fact that my crew proved to be as manly as they were gentlemanly; and that, in spite of the hard work, they, as well as I, can look back with nothing but pleasant recollections to the adventure, is due to their appreciation of the magnificent scenery that our coast presents to those who know where to find it; also that between the intervals of nearly constant employment at anchor the time was chiefly spent in little excursions to the shore, where weeds, birds, rocks, and caverns, &c., abounded. Upon one rock we visited in the boat the birds were so tame that they suffered us to lie quietly alongside and remark their peculiarities—even a ludicrous little farce, amounting to a bloodless quarrel, being enacted in our presence. Our sketchers and caricaturists would have been delighted with this.

Surprise has been expressed by those who know nothing of the labour required to keep a yacht in a complete state of efficiency and cleanliness that we found no time to read the newspapers. I will explain this by a practical illustration, instancing the cruise of the previous year, which happened to be nearly over the same course. The two seamen employed on that occasion, who were good average specimens and of good repute in their town, complained to my ship-keeper that they were 'driven like slaves'. Well, here are the statistics for last year, and for this; to which I will only add that of my cruise round Great Britain in 1863, though upwards of twenty others, not less instructive, could be furnished if required.

The cruise complained of lasted seventy-two days, and the nautical mileage was 830, or an average of 11·5 *per diem*. The nights at sea under way were four, nights anchored at sea twelve, and nights in harbour fifty-six.

Upon this occasion (1882) with my two young amateurs, who were light weights of the respective ages of 20 and 23, the cruise lasted thirty-eight days, and the nautical mileage was 1050, or an average of 27·8. The nights at sea under way were five, nights anchored at sea nineteen, and nights in harbour fourteen.

In 1863 the cruise lasted ninety-eight days, and the nautical mileage was 2640, or an average of 26·9. The nights at sea under way and at anchor were twenty-eight, and nights in harbour seventy, of which thirty were passed in the more or less exposed anchorages of the Firth of Clyde.

If I gave more assistance to the amateurs than to the professionals, not only should the difference between trained and untrained hands be taken into consideration, but that more was accomplished in half the time. All the same, there never was an occasion that could have given rise to the absurd complaint, when the men were tired and I was not, or when their hours were long and mine were not longer, having, in addition to my share of the active seamanship, to conduct a difficult navigation which I have never ventured to leave to chance. Moreover, if I were not habituated to take my full share of the heavy work, how, by any possibility, could I upon a certain occasion have managed it alone? The difference lies simply in the estimate of work done by a volunteer and by a paid hand.

In domestic matters, except the cooking—in which it is a recognised axiom that difference of opinion spoils the broth—each one managed for himself, as if he were at sea alone.

On this cruise, which may not inappropriately be described as 'fun in earnest,' I had an advantage in the society of educated men instead, as not unfrequently met with in my experience, of men who could neither read nor write, and who, as a rule, I have found infinitely more impracticable than those who can. In saying this, I am not unmindful that there is no rule without exceptions—and perhaps distinguished exceptions too!

THE 'ORION', ON THE JUBILEE COURSE, 1887

ROUND GREAT BRITAIN AND IRELAND

AT the general meeting of the Royal Thames Yacht Club, held at their Club house, Albemarle-street, on Friday, March 11th, 1887, the Jubilee Yacht Race, round Great Britain and Ireland, was announced; the speaker saying, in words quoted from the *Field* report, 'It would bring together rigs of all nations. It would also improve the build of yachts in that very wholesome direction—seaworthiness, comfort, and economy. Moreover, it would tend to develop the important qualities of seamanship and cool endurance in the sailors,' &c.; every word of which, when read in the report, I thought most sensible.

H.R.H. the Prince of Wales, who presided on the occasion, expressed his unqualified sympathy with the proposal and its objects, and, among other remarks which were greeted with cheers, said, 'It will, I am sure, ever remain in the annals of the club, and of the yachting world generally, as a most interesting memento and memorial of the Jubilee of the Queen.' I quote the above only to show the excellent spirit of loyalty in which the project was conceived, and, however it might afterwards have come to be looked upon by others, the effect it had upon me.

Though owner of a craft far too small for a thought of contending in the race to be entertained for a moment, I read the proposal and the terms in which it was expressed with unqualified satisfaction.

Having on various occasions cruised on the Irish and Scotch coasts, and once made the circuit of Great Britain, it had long been a subject of regret with me that I had never made a complete circuit of both islands.

The course being essentially one of sentiment—viz., to sail round Her Majesty's home dominions, and, because of the difficulties of navigation and the length of time required, only on that account reasonable, it seemed to me so undesirable that the yachts should be started from Southend and finish at Dover, several miles short of completing the circuit, that I ventured to suggest if they were to finish the race at Dover, they should be started from the same point.

In the brief summary and distance column which appears at the end of the following account, though the variations in the areas of canvas carried are given in the form of a maximum and minimum for every day, the figures very inadequately represent the vast number of changes which our endeavour by day and night to carry the utmost the vessel would bear actually necessitated. Regarding plain lower canvas as the average standard of a vessel's sail power, the 'Orion's' is 1200 square feet. On this voyage the smallest area was 1030, and that only for a few hours; whereas on former cruises much satisfactory work has been performed with areas ranging downwards to 700 (four reefs), and, exceptionally, down to figures very considerably below that quantity.

Where used, the terms first and second topsail, mean large topsail and jib-header; mizens the same.

My crew consisted of Mr. Horace Detmar, who sailed with me to the Wolf Rock in 1882 (as mate, masthead and bowsprit end man) and two able seamen, Thomas Pettman and William Mackley, both of Gravesend, who had qualified for the sea in sailing colliers and yachts, and were engaged, after the 'Orion' had been inspected at my request, on the special understanding that they might be required to keep the sea for a month without entering port. Beyond that no information was vouchsafed, nor, in deference to the opinion I had expressed at our first interview, that 'talking beforehand by owners of small craft leads to failure,' was any question asked.

Being four in number, we were, of course, divided into two watches, according to sea usage, with one paid hand in each watch. There was, however, much work, such as setting and handing canvas by day as well as by night, or gybing when the squaresail was set, that, to be carried out properly without delaying the vessel on her course, required a third hand on deck, in which case, unless at the time of changing the watch, the extra hand was always supplied from aft.

Our hours, regularly observed throughout the voyage, were —6 A.M., all hands on deck to wash down; 8, men's breakfast; 8.30, cabin breakfast; 1 P.M., men's dinner; 2.30, cabin dinner; 5, men's tea; 6.30, cabin tea; midnight, supper and grog. Being accustomed to dine late, at first it was difficult to fall in with this arrangement; but the comfort of the men, on which the success of the voyage so greatly depended, was a sufficient reason for adopting it. Besides the large stove, which was always lighted in the morning, and, if required, kept in till three, there was a petroleum stove—the reservoir of which I had specially adapted to sea use—as capable of boiling, stewing, and steaming as the other, without giving off the inconvenient heat inseparable from the use of coke. After breakfast (subject to work on deck, which always had the preference in point of time) an hour was spent in clearing up below. Among other things demanding attention, the water hose was passed forward, dinner and other meals arranged for, and the required stores—together with any others, such as biscuits, cocoa, tea, butter, &c., of which a moderate stock was kept in the forecastle—handed out.

I have said we were divided into two watches for the purposes of navigation; but, constant as were the duties of the deck, it is evident there must have been a large amount of work below which on larger vessels is performed by men specially appointed, but that, in our case, had to be dovetailed in with the former.

June 8.—6 P.M., with distinguishing flag, white with blue star, at the main, and Royal Cinque Ports colours at the mizen, sailed from Greenhithe 8.30; anchored for the night off Yantlet.

June 9.—5 A.M., under way; wind W.S.W. and W.N.W., and carried a nice breeze down to Dover. 7 P.M., anchored in the bay, landed, and laid in stock of fresh meat. Night fine.

June 10.—Noon, sailed from Dover for the north, under plain lower sail and second topsail; wind E., weather fine overhead, but rough and cold; almost fetched the Kentish Knock, when the wind failed. 11.30 P.M., anchored with kedge, after drifting astern for three hours. Grand moonlight and starlight night.

June 11.—5 A.M., resumed course N.E., with a light air W.S.W., which gradually improved to an eight-knot breeze. 7.50 A.M., passed Kentish Knock Lightship, first topsail and squaresail set. 4 P.M., handed squaresail and set foresail; wind to W.N.W. for half an hour, and then fell calm. 8 P.M., anchored during flood tide off Yarmouth; barometer fell two-tenths during the day; weather cloudy, and threatening a thunderstorm.

June 12.—4 A.M., under way; wind W., cloudy and cold. 2 P.M., took a fresh departure off Cromer; course N. by W. 5.30 P.M., passed Dudgeon Lightship; during the day, which was generally fine, the wind varied frequently between W. and N.W., sometimes fresh, but mostly very light or calm. Between noon and midnight the jib-topsail, which is a large cotton sail, was twice handed, to save the topmast from going over the side.

June 13.—The wind gradually freshened to an eight-knot breeze, and then became so strong that at 6.30 A.M. the topsail was handed. 7 A.M., off Flamborough Head, weather fine and clear, views of the coast exceedingly interesting. 8.30 A.M., fell almost calm for an hour, with a sloppy sea; set second topsail, but shortly had to hand it again. 2.30 P.M., off Whitby, wind shifted to N.W. and increased. 5 P.M., sea short and hollow, twenty-three to the minute. Being some miles to leeward of the course, we tacked to the westward, took a reef down, and, when about again inshore, shifted large mizen for small. 7 P.M., wind backed to W.N.W., and allowed us to lay the course. 11 to 12 P.M., between Sunderland and Shields, passed through a fleet of 'drifters,' and by good luck, combined with so much judgment in luffing and bearing away as one is able to exercise under such difficult circumstances, succeeded in avoiding their nets. To fall in with these boats on a dark night is a strange and weird scene. Each boat carries an open fire of coals, which, being blown into a flame by the strong wind, illumines the faces and hands of its occupants, who may be seen gesticulating violently and heard shouting something you are fortunately unable to hear, the object being to drive you over somebody else's nets in preference to their own.

June 14.—3 A.M., the wind, which had shown signs of failing since midnight, gradually veered to N.N.E. and fell calm, and with it the thermometer, which, if I may judge by the amount of clothing that failed to protect me from the piercing cold, must have declined to near freezing point. 8 A.M., a light breeze, S.S.W.; barometer 30·25; weather looking doubtful. 9.30 A.M., set first topsail and square sail. 1 to 3 P.M., gentle rain; passed the Farn Islands, and laid a course N. by E. ½ E., 110 miles, for Buchan Ness. 8 P.M., handed topsail, fearing the topmast would be carried away; also eased down peak of mainsail, fearing a gybe. 10 P.M., the wind having moderated, set second topsail. Night fine, but cloudy and rough.

June 15.—Morning fair, but intensely cold until 5.30, when the sun came out warm. Wind light, with a nasty troublesome swell. After breakfast, shifted second topsail for first, and set squaresail; weather cloudy and cold, wind from all quarters, lasting but a few moments, and causing continuous work. 8 P.M., calm continued, with much cloud and every appearance of a thunderstorm; then light airs, shifting frequently between S.S.E. and W.N.W., which enabled us to make Kinnaird Head at midnight.

June 16.—A hot sun all day, with light and chilly winds from south and west—the pretty sure precursor of a fog. 7 P.M., passed Noss Head, and later, during which interval a grampus was seen, got becalmed off Freswick Bay, in water too deep to anchor, even if anchorage in such a spot had been desirable. 10 P.M., commenced drifting slowly towards Duncansby Head, and at 11, much against inclination, entered the Pentland Firth with the sea like a mirror, and a light air from N.E., ascertained by striking a lucifer match. If an exhaustive study of directions by the best authorities, and the most approved charts, combined with a previous experience, could impart confidence on such an occasion as this, presumably I had less cause for anxiety than the majority who pass through without a pilot. At the same time, the dangers to be guarded against are so numerous, and so strongly emphasised in the 'Sailing Directions,' that it is impossible for anyone who had studied them to drift helplessly through the Pentland Firth in a too easy frame of mind. With the north-easterly draught of air, we managed to pass between the islands of Stroma and Swona, one-third over from the former; the movements of the black clouds we had observed the last two or three days, travelling from the westward, being explained to us by a long and momentarily increasing swell from the Atlantic. At first the currents swirling to the surface between the islands were marked and well defined; but gradually they became lost in a confused swell, which, though just short of breaking, was fearful. When about four miles west of the islands, and all danger of becoming involved in their eddies was passed, I considered the worst of the drift over for the present. But we were setting to the N.W. in the Turn Ness current, with apparently little hope of extrication, and the almost certainty, when the tide turned, of being drifted back in a course not of our own choosing.

June 17.—Having had very little sleep since we left Dover, and the last few hours having proved exceptionally trying, I left the mate and one hand on deck, with instructions to make for Dunnet Head if an opportunity presented itself, and, the better to be prepared for eventualities, went below at 2 A.M. for a little much-needed rest, and slept soundly until 7.30. At one time, with a light breeze from the southward, we had reached beyond Dunnet Head; but, the wind having again failed, had drifted back abreast of it. In this position I found her, and had only sufficient time to view the Firth, and note the movements of other vessels drifting more helplessly than ourselves, when we became enveloped in a dense fog that hid the land and everything else from view. With the roar of the sea breaking on the rocks at no great distance, and a motion scarcely less violent than the worst we had experienced, the situation was perplexing in the extreme. At 11 A.M., when the fog partially lifted, the tide was again in our favour, and the position of the early morning, alongside of Dunnet Head, regained. From this point, a course by compass, before a nice easterly breeze, carried us into Thurso Bay, the fog clearing away just in time to enable us to find temporary anchorage there at noon, half a mile from the shore, while the mate was landed in the dinghey to post letters home. Owing to the swell on the rocks, and want of acquaintance with the passage through which boats pass safely in and out, the landing was effected with difficulty, and attended by so much delay that, though only the head sails had been lowered, by the time the boat was stowed on board again, and the anchor aweigh, three hours of go-ahead weather had been consumed.

3.30 P.M., passed Holburn Head, the western point of Thurso Bay; wind E., fresh, and very fine. 5.30 P.M., set large foresail to windward as a spinnaker, and closed with the land—as much as the irregularity of its outline would permit—to enjoy the grandeur of the scenery, which inland is mountainous, and on the shore side rugged in the extreme. Though the wind was fresh and promised fair for the run to Cape Wrath, it soon reverted to the old style of dropping and reviving, preparatory to a shift to S.W. at 8.30, from which quarter it came faintly for a while, and then dropped entirely. Night calm and cold.

June 18.—The sun rose clear out of the sea, and soon became very warm. 7.30 A.M., commenced turning to windward against a light and variable breeze between W.N.W. and N.N.W. 8, tacked off Whiten Head (E. point of Loch Eiboll). 10 A.M., dense fog, atmosphere very chilly. Noon, wind W., very light; supposed position, near Cape Wrath. 12.30 P.M., fell in with a strong ripple from the northward, showing we were being drifted in that direction. What little wind there was being rolled out of the sails, we tacked with difficulty, and, heading S.S.W., eventually succeeded in making the land about a mile east of the Cape. Thence, guided by the whiteness of the breakers, which alone were visible at any distance, passed between the Stag Rock, on which the sea was breaking heavily, and Cape Wrath (400 ft. high), of which only sufficient was visible at the base to show that its remarkable formation corresponded with its picture on the chart. At 2 P.M. we ran almost suddenly into a lump of a race and a strong N.E. wind, which partially cleared the fog away, and, in half an hour, brought Bulgic Island into view. The next business was an awkward gybe, and we handed the big topsail, with difficulty, at 3 P.M.; set the large foresail as a spinnaker, and laid a course of 55 miles for Streanach Head (N. point of Loch Shell), intending thereafter, if possible, to keep the Hebrides Islands aboard, rather than run the risk of becoming entangled on a foggy night among the numerous islets and rocks that render the passage from the North to the South Minch so dangerous. 6 P.M., set second topsail. 9.30 P.M., off Streanach Head. Our rate of sailing, which had varied from seven to nine knots, declined to an average of six, wind puffy and dead aft, continually threatening us with a gybe. Midnight, passed Glass Island Light; night, tolerably clear for large objects at half a mile, sea rough.

June 19.—5.30 A.M., passed South Uist Lighthouse. Altered course to S. by W. ½ W. for twelve miles; and then to S.W. ¼ W., on a course of 115 miles for Tory Island, N.W. coast of Ireland. The run down the Hebrides should have been most interesting; but, with the exception of just so much here and there as partially assisted navigation, they were enveloped in fog. 10 A.M., fog dispersed, and Barra Head became visible about ten miles west. The weather for the rest of the day was perfect— bright sunshine, fresh breeze, and, though somewhat rough, not too much sea. At noon our distance for twenty-four hours was 163 knots, proving, notwithstanding the loss of an hour at Cape Wrath, and that the pace slackened to six during many hours of the night, we were capable of doing a satisfactory day's work when the opportunity was afforded. The great N.W. swell was again fallen in with when clear of the islands, interfering neither with our comfort nor with the run of the shorter sea raised by the prevailing wind. 2 P.M., shifted spinnaker for squaresail. 10.45 P.M., Tory Island Light visible S. by W. about ten miles, altered course to W.S.W. for ninety miles. Night gloriously fine; barometer 30·40. As compared with the worrying traffic of countless steamers and other craft on the east coast, to say nothing of 'drifters' and their nets, it was quite a treat to pass twenty-four hours without a single vessel being seen.

June 20.—At 3.30 A.M., called up to gybe, which, when the squaresail was set, could not be managed without an extra hand. The wind, after remaining pretty constant for forty hours, veered gradually to S.E., and the squaresail had to be taken in. The wind backed to E., and became very light, causing us to plunge and roll miserably on the swell, chafing the gear, and rendering any kind of work most troublesome. After breakfast, shifted second topsail and second mizen for first. 3 P.M., fresh breeze E.N.E. 9, abreast of Eagle Island. Midnight, becalmed about two miles beyond Blackrock, and two hours later were apprehensive of being drifted by the north-going tide upon some of the rocks that lie near it. Night fine and clear. The log of Sir Richard Sutton's yacht 'Genesta' shows she passed us here four miles farther to the westward, and that she continued to retain the breeze we had lost since early morning.

June 21.—6 A.M., becalmed three miles S.W. of Blackrock; weather clear at sea, but very hazy over the land, where Croghan, a precipitous mountain, near Achill Head, 2182 ft. high, with a cliff of 1800 ft. towards the sea, remained visible to us in outline the greater part of the day. It was impossible not to regret the grand sights, such as this one should have been, that were being continually lost to us through the abominable haze. 8 A.M., the 'Sleuthhound' cutter, in the Jubilee race, passed us under an enormous spread of canvas, and her crew labouring assiduously to take advantage of the variable and paltry airs.

Being 'Jubilee Day,' wine was placed on the companion at noon, and the toast 'Long life and honour to the Queen' proposed and responded to in right loyal fashion.

287

After a detention of sixteen hours, a light breeze from N.N.E. enabled us to set the squaresail and lay the course, W. by S., 118 miles, to clear the islands at Sybil Head. 11.30 P.M., handed squaresail and jib-topsail; wind puffy and heading. Saw Inishark Island at dusk, but no more land afterwards for nearly two days.

June 22.—Wind S.S.E., very paltry; sun hot. Set jib-topsail in early morning, and at 4 P.M. the squaresail. 8 P.M., handed jib-topsail. 11, gybed accidentally, without blame to helmsman or harm ensuing; wind N.E. by E., fresh. Night fine, and very mild. Moon, Venus and Jupiter beautiful.

June 23.—3 A.M., fell almost calm. 6, light air, E.N.E., set jib-topsail. 7.30, wind to E.S.E., handed squaresail. 10, tacked to eastward, having over-reached the islands in consequence of the miserable haze which continued to prevail, and that, even in sunshine, prevented land from being visible beyond a range of five miles. Away on the lee quarter sighted two schooners in the Jubilee Race, heading S.W. ('Gwendolin' and 'Selene'). Noon, passed about a couple of miles to windward of Vickillane Island, and tacked again, heading S., to pass between the Skelligs and the mainland. 6 P.M., saw, a long way off, and in line with the lofty cliffs of Bolus Head, what we believed to be a little fishing yacht, but which, on a much nearer inspection, proved to be a large Revenue yawl, bound in the same direction as ourselves. Having no large and light canvas suitable to the occasion, she stood in about the same relation to us that we did to the racers, and, in the haze, that increased as night approached, was eventually left out of sight. 11.30, it then being very hazy and calm, our proximity to land on the south side of the Kenmare estuary was made known to us by a faint smell of peat, no doubt from Dursey Island, and shortly afterwards, the Bull Rock (290 ft. high), towards which the tide was drifting us, became visible in faint outline ahead. After a time, which seemed terribly long, the stars opened one by one to the westward; but not until the big rock and its companions were well on the port quarter, at 2 A.M., did I feel really comfortable, or in the least inclined to sit down to supper.

June 24.—2.30 A.M., laid down and slept till 5, by which time the breeze had freshened from the eastward and the sea became so rough, that the big topsail, which had been so serviceable the last four days, had to be handed. 7, tacked to the eastward, and, having a strong spring ebb to contend with, stood in N.E. towards Blackball Head, north side of Bantry Bay. The weather was delightfully exhilarating, being, in fact, the only clear one over the land we had seen since the 17th, on the north coast of Scotland. While on this tack a large yawl, freely showing her bright copper, opened Dursey Head, and, for a time, was mistaken for a yacht in the Jubilee race; but, in reality, was the Revenue cruiser, which I now apprehended would give us a beating.

8.30 A.M., tacked off Blackball Head, and had a good view of the real Irish 'holdings'; wind strong. 10, becalmed, and knocked about violently by the swell; set first topsail and jib-topsail, but the work was scarcely completed before a breeze sprung up so strong from S.E. that they had to be handed again, the latter badly split at the head. Stood off until 1 P.M. into 60 fathoms water by the chart. The next tack was made at 3 P.M., in 32 fathoms, close to Sheep Head, when the colour of the sea was observed to be a beautiful emerald green. A good deal had been seen of the Revenue cruiser, but always at an increasing distance to leeward, until at this hour, and end-on in our wake, it was difficult to distinguish her at all. 4 P.M., with a strong flood tide and as much wind as was required for plain lower sail, passed Mizen Head much nearer than I have ever done before; its peculiar features and panoramic-like scenery furnishing us with quite an interesting entertainment—unfortunately the last of the day. The wind being unfavourable for our course, which was S.E. ¾ E. 175 miles to the Land's End, we worked the weather-going tide to Cape Clear, and finally stood off S. at 6.30 against a lumpy head sea. 8.15, heading S. ¾ E., set log; the position at that time being twelve miles on the true course, or four miles S.E. ¾ E. of the Fastnet Rock. Midnight, wind variable between E.S.E. and E.; way much impeded by swell from southward; set first topsail.

Barometer, 30·30, after having stood at 30·40 for several days.

June 25.—5.30 A.M., log 38 from Fastnet; wind E. by S., and little of it; colour of sea, dark blue. 11.30, standing part of topsail halyards chafed through; lowered topmast and repaired. For this we had to heave-to, on account of the confusion occasioned to the slackened wire and hemp gear by the swell, with which, while two hands were engaged at the heel rope, it was very difficult to deal. 1 P.M., resumed, heading S., wind S.E. by E. 4, set jib-topsail. 8, very light air, E.N.E.; night fine; swell, a perfect nuisance; course to Longships, S.E. ¼ E., 95 miles.

June 26.—Wind most paltry between N.E. and S.E. 1 P.M., fell flat calm, the great Atlantic, but for a trifling swell, looking like a millpond or a mirror. Saw the fins of several tunny fish during the day; temperature of the air in the shade 68°, surface of sea 66°; barometer 30·35. 11 P.M., fine moonlight and starlight night; light breeze W.; course to Longships S.E. by E. 60 miles.

June 27.—2 A.M., carried away jib-topsail halyards, and sail had to be handed. There was then a thick fog, which—considering the many hours they had lasted before, and that in 1863 I had seen one of three days in these parts—caused us no little anxiety about the steamers, the Seven Stones, and, apart from its perplexing currents, which 'no man can understand,' the general rocky nature of the Land's End. To lessen the risk of all but the first cause for apprehension, we steered a point to leeward of the course. 5.30, fog dispersed, and westerly breeze improved. 6.30, set squaresail; morning very fine and sunny; colour of the sea, dark blue, depth, 57–60; and at 10 dark green, depth about 40. Noon, though bright overhead, there was still so much haze that the land, which might have been visible at twenty miles, came suddenly into view, ahead, only at the distance of three. Having passed the Longships seven miles to the northward of our course, and made the land near Gurnard's Head, the squaresail was handed, sheets hauled aft, and the jib-topsail set, to turn to windward alongshore, which, while there is wind enough to render it safe, I consider the most interesting and instructive of all kinds of sailing. For a time we were successful, and weathered the Three Stone Oar; then, the wind falling light, drove back into the bight between the latter rocks and Gurnard's Head, where, it is difficult to say with what slender assistance in the light canvas aloft, we contrived to maintain our position alike out of the tide and the traffic until midnight. Night fine; fog on hills.

June 28.—2.30 A.M., rounded the Longships with a light air and favourable tide. 4, passed to windward of the Runnel Stone, blowing fresh from N.E.; handed jib-topsail not a second too soon to save the topmast, and, shortly afterwards, the topsail. 6.30, having cleared the high land, set first topsail again. 8, made the Lizard, but, in consequence of eddying puffs and calms, did not clear it till 9. Set log, and, luffing and falling off as the wind would allow, headed E. ½ S., on average, for the Start. What a glorious day it was! Sky, and sea, and land unsurpassingly clear; a steady breeze, and a lively motion, with very little spray, all combined, together with the hope of its continuance, to render it enjoyable in the extreme. In anticipation of a regular 'turn in' off Dover, the opportunity of a fine drying breeze to air my bedding, which had not been used since the 11th, off Yarmouth, was too good to be lost; two hours of such weather being equal to a dozen of that we had mostly seen. 5 P.M., passed the Eddystone to the southward, as near as possible, to have a good look at the new lighthouse and the remains of the old. It was a pleasing incident in the day's work, as all such close inspections are. 7, ran into a glassy calm that had been visible on the sea a long way ahead, but, assisted by light and fitful breezes from the same quarter as before, made good way, owing to the smoothness of the water. A splendid sunset, when drawing near to Bolt Head, ended a day that was felt by all hands to have been one of real pleasure.

From 9 P.M. to 11.30, when the Start Point was passed with a nice breeze N.N.E., there had been little puffs from so many points of the compass, alternated with calms, that the watch were almost continuously engaged in 'sheet trimming.' There were two redeeming features in this entertainment—that the heavens were grand with moon and planets and stars, and the breeze, when it came off the land, was deliciously scented with hay.

June 29.—Fine morning; wind light, but partly compensated for by absence of swell. 10 A.M., almost calm, sun hot, weather very hazy over the land; set jib-topsail. 1 P.M., light air, S.E. by E., putting us about, and to the northward of our course. 1.30, sighted Portland, when the wind veered to S., and enabled us to take such full advantage of the Race, which I have never seen so smooth, that at 3.45 our position was seven miles S.S.E. of the 'Bill' and four S.S.W. of the Shambles Lightship. Set log, and steered E. by S., on a course of forty miles, for St. Catherine's Point. 4.15 becalmed; air chilly, 61° in the shade; barometer 30·45, atmosphere hazy, and threatening fog. 7 to 8, breeze S. 8.30, Anvil Point E. by N. six miles; drifting back rapidly with the ebb tide. Midnight, ceased drifting; light breeze N.E., weather cloudy and hazy.

June 30.—5 A.M., Atherfield Point, I. of W., N.W.; drifted back several miles in a calm. 10, very gloomy and hazy; breeze, S.S.E.; handed jib-topsail. Noon, weather became bright and clear; hove-to off Blackgang Chine, handed topsail, lowered topmast, and put fresh seizings on backstays, set first topsail again. 12.45, passed St. Catherine's, and, later, tacked close in to Ventnor, as, when turning to windward, and, if not inconvenient, I do to all towns and other interesting spots, to relieve monotony, and impart a pleasing character to the day's proceedings. 3 P.M., strong breeze E. 4.30, calm. 6.30, light air N.W.; set jib-topsail. Another calm, followed by shuffling airs and much sail trimming, during which time Selsea Bill and Bembridge Ledge were rendered visible to us by a mirage which shortly passed away; then, a breeze from E.N.E. Night, fine and clear.

July 1.—3 A.M., handed jib-topsail. 7 to 9, almost becalmed off Brighton; then nice breeze S.; set jib-topsail; weather, very fine and clear. 1 P.M., tacked off Seaford; wind E., fresh. After a few boards, standing in as close as we dared, rounded Beachy Head at 3.30, wind E. by N. 4.30, handed jib-topsail, again blown away at the head. Made two long boards to Hastings; and, at 9, stood off from there S.E. by E., wind light. Repaired the jib-topsail by reefing it at the head, barge fashon, and set it again. The heavens were as attractive as on the previous night; and, in addition, the town of Hastings, with its numerous lights, backed by the high dark land, looked exceedingly pretty in the distance. Such scenes as these are very interesting to passers-by on clear nights; but here, as in other seaside resorts for pleasure, there is a growing disposition to gratify visitors by the exhibition of electric lights alongshore, which in the interests of the maritime population, unless screened by ground glass on their seaward side, should be forbidden by the Board of Trade.

July 2.—3 A.M., passed Dungeness Point, and very soon got becalmed. 8, a nice little breeze S.E. by E., with promise of a speedy arrival at Dover. Folkestone, and its nest of rocks, was fortunately well on the lee quarter when, at 9.30, the wind, such as it was, shifted to E., and brought a dense sea-fog with it. 10.30, though keeping a sharp look-out, narrowly escaped running ashore. 11.30, abreast of Shakespeare Cliff, the fog rolled away to the westward as suddenly as it had advanced, and enabled us to reach our destination shortly before noon.

On arrival at this point, which was that of our departure for the North, we fired a gun, to join the line; made a short board to windward to tie the knot; and—when the station it has been my custom for years to select was regained—let go the anchor in the bay.

Immediately the canvas was lowered, wine and glasses were placed on the companion, not only because it was the most appropriate moment for mutual congratulation at the completion of our task, but that it afforded me the opportunity of expressing to Detmar and the men how thoroughly I appreciated the unremitting exertions they had made, and the ability and cheerfulness with which, under all circumstances, they had supported me.

Sailing from Dover, June 10, at noon, the daily runs and canvas carried—giving only the maximum and minimum areas for each day in the order they were required—were as follows: (Note.—1200 square feet is the area of the plain lower sail.)

To noon	Place	Canvas in sq. ft.	Distance
June 11.	Shipwash Lightship . . .	1370–1705	59
„ 12.	4 m. N.E. of Cromer (Norfolk) .	1705–1595	58
„ 13.	Off Scarborough (Yorkshire) .	1595–1370	105
„ 14.	Off Bulmer (Northumberland) .	1030–1705	82
„ 15.	Parallel of Aberdeen . . .	1705–1110	105
„ 16.	36 m. N. by W. of Kinnaird Head .	1300–1530	74
„ 17.	Thurso Bay	1405–1630	47
„ 18.	Farout Head (near Cape Wrath) .	1635–1405	39
„ 19.	17 m. S. by W. of Barra Head (Hebrides)	1345–1535	163
„ 20.	62 m. W. by S. of Tory Island (N.W. Ireland)	1535–1710	130
„ 21.	Achill Head	1475–1700	48
„ 22.	31 m. S. of Inishark Island . .	1930–1475	44
„ 23.	Vickillane Island. . . .	1930–1475	76
„ 24.	5 m. S. by E. of Dursey Head .	1180–1700	36
„ 25.	On course from Fastnet . .	1180–1475	87
„ 26.	„ „ . .	1700	47
„ 27.	Land's End	1700–1475	51
„ 28.	16 m. E. by S. of Lizard Point (Cornwall)	1180–1475	45
„ 29.	35 m. E. of Start Point (Devon) .	1475–1700	83
„ 30.	St. Catherine's Point (I. of W.) .	1700–1475	55
July 1.	Off Newhaven	1475–1700	55
„ 2.	Dover	1475–1700	52

		1541
Extra distance sailed in turning to windward . . .		204

Actual distance sailed from Dover round to Dover . .	1745

16½ hours under way between Greenhithe and Dover; 26 hours under way between Dover and Greenhithe .   153

Number of miles for 24 days under way . .   1898

THE TRIAL CRUISE OF THE
'PERSEUS'
(6-TON LUGGER), 1890

SCARCELY three months had elapsed after the sale of the 'Orion' in 1889, when the novelty of being without a craft of any sort for the first time for thirty-nine years, instead of being deemed a relief as at first, came to be felt as a deprivation, and led to my planning a small carvel-built boat for single-handed work, rigged and internally fitted like the 'Procyon'—but without centre-board, such as a few years before I had advocated in the *Field*.

Considering the 6½-ton 'Procyon' too big, I set out with the idea of producing a boat of 5½ tons, Thames measurement, that would register about 3; but, as the use I contemplated making of her assumed a more definite shape, my requirements in respect of draught and freeboard and stowage necessitated an addition to the depth, which, without altering the nominal tonnage, resulted in her registering 4·75—with 2 ft. more mast, 100 sq. ft. more canvas, and over a ton more ballast than I had considered it needful to give to the 'Procyon.' The plans were submitted to the builder in this form, and no alteration was made after the building commenced; so that, viewed as a single-hander, the fault, which I admit can be found with her rather inconvenient size and weight, rests entirely with myself. The fact is, within the limits of a 5½-ton boat I had to choose between handiness, combined with cramped quarters, and dependence on the shore on the one hand, and thorough seaworthiness combined with appreciable comfort and independence on the other; and considering what a trying season 1890 proved to be for small craft, on looking back there is reason to believe it was fortunate I chose the latter.

The particulars and dimensions of the 'Perseus,' built by Holloway, 1890, are: carvel-built, oak frame, planked with

THE 'PERSEUS'

CARIM WAIST STEERAGE A.L.

BALLAST TANKS

SCALE OF FEET.

5 10 15 20 25 30 35 40

1½ in. elm; length, 27 ft. 2 in.; breadth, 7 ft. 4 in.; draught, forward, 3 ft. 3 in., aft, 4 ft. 6 in.; height from water-line to planksheer, forward, 4 ft., least freeboard, 2 ft.; ballast, 13 cwt. of lead on keel, a 20 cwt. cast-iron keelson, and 32 cwt. of kentledge, in all, 3¼ tons. The diameter of her mast, which is stepped 18 in. from the stem, weighs 2 cwt., and is self-supporting, is 6½ in., and its height from partners to head-iron 23 ft. The mizenmast, from deck to truck, is 12 ft.; and the bowsprit, a very substantial little spar, is 8½ ft. outside. In

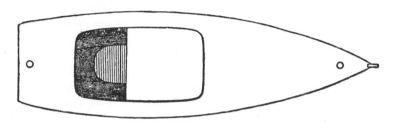

form, the midship section is that of the 'Orion.' Her topsides are kept 'bright' (that is, not painted), and, for economy of labour as much as for appearance, she is coppered. Though rather too heavy-looking at the quarters—the transom being slightly immersed—she is admitted by all who have examined her, professional and non-professional, to be a most substantial and beautiful structure, for which credit must be given to the builder; but whether the elm planking will stand as satisfactorily as it did in the 'Procyon' remains to be proved.

Finding it impossible to place an ordinary pump where it would not be inconvenient and unsightly, I ordered, at Blundell's, 23, West India Dock-road, a 3 in. force pump, of which the standard and lifting rod could be shipped and unshipped at pleasure, and fixed it under the waist platform in such a position that, in case of need, it could be worked while in attendance at the helm. The suction pipe has three branches, with a stopcock in each; so that water can be drawn from the well by a 1½ in. pipe, or from either bilge by an inch pipe; or, should the necessity arise, from all three together. Worked with a 4½ in. stroke (out of a possible six), and at the moderate rate of seventy-five strokes per minute, I ascertained, by pumping into a large iron pail suspended to a handy little weighing machine, that it threw 1 lb. per stroke, equal to 7½ galls. per minute. Though, for convenience, the result of the experiment is given here, it was not tried until I had been several days at sea.

As the launch, which was to have been about June 5, did not take place till the 25th, I went down a week prior to that date to expedite the work; and, because much time would have been wasted in passing to and fro if a lodging had been taken, decided to establish myself on board at once. Though the discomfort of the first twenty-four hours was considerable, the advantages derived from the adoption of this plan were numerous and important; since, besides the still further delay, and the omission of many things needful to my future comfort, which must have ensued if I had not done this, the effect of exposure, day and night, to the strong sea air was, that I lost, in less than three days, a persistent cold and cough that had troubled me for three months.

Notwithstanding the large amount of work that had been got through during the week, the number of odd jobs to be completed on the last day, and of packages put aboard at the last moment, would have resulted in intolerable confusion, had not a carefully revised list been prepared for the occasion.

Though in appearance and weight the hull of the 'Perseus' is rather that of a small and deep revenue cutter than of a boat in the sense the term is usually employed, she was not launched in the usual manner, but, the weather being favourable, was moved down the ways to a position whence the succeeding high water floated her off the blocks, when, after taking in the kentledge from a boat alongside, the jib and mizen were set, and she was sailed to an anchorage below the town. The services of a local man were indispensable for this, who, also, having helped to scrub down and to establish some degree of order, returned to the shore at my request; for the very sufficient reasons that he could not be accommodated in the cabin without depriving me of the few hours absolute rest and comfort, on which depended my ability to carry on the work, and that henceforth, according to a rule, I determined should admit of no exceptions, other than might arise from illness or accident; as everything, however difficult, would have to be managed by myself alone, the sooner a commencement was made the better.

The sails, by Lapthorn and Ratsey, subjected (in the bolt) to Burnett and Co.'s process for the prevention of mildew, are all of one material, viz., fully bleached 12 in. canvas, No. 6, double. Their areas, in square feet, are—mainsail, 336; stormsail, 225; mizen, 56; jib, 45; storm jib, 25. Weight of mainsail, with 13 ft. yard, 100 lb.; of stormsail, with 8 ft. yard, 70 lb.

Between the wing platforms, and resting on the top of the keel and deadwood, is the lower platform, occupied by eleven galvanised iron tank cans, 8½ in. square by 17½ in. high, with handles on top, and a 3½ in. neck closed with a bung. Each contains about 4½ gallons, and, when full, weighs 50 lb. By a strong batten on each side the space allotted to them, they are prevented from shifting, however great the list of the vessel may be. They were made specially to my order and drawing by Prior Bros., 92, Blackman-street, Borough, and, as an improvement on wooden breakers, or on one unhandy tank, gave me immense satisfaction. In practice, I kept ten below and one out, which, when empty, was exchanged for a full one.

On the same level as the steerage platform is the after locker, beneath which bottles of wine and spirits, and a large quantity of preserved provisions were stored. In the locker itself, which is almost a small cabin, the bulk of the stores were stowed, chiefly in boxes, labelled 'books,' 'tools,' 'boatswain's stores,' &c., of which those most likely to be in request were nearest at hand.

The riding light, side lights, binnacle light, and a fair-sized bulkhead light for the cabin were all adapted to burn the new patent illuminant called Cera, to which my attention was first directed by the receipt of a circular from the Cera Light Co., of

Glasgow. The material is a species of wax—made, I believe, from refuse petroleum—very clean to handle, easily cut, and perfectly free from smell. The chief advantage is, that, burning on the wick in the form of hydrogen gas, the wick is not consumed; consequently, there being no char to remove, the light retains its brilliancy for 12 or 13 hours without needing further attention. Both above and below I found it a great comfort, and would not be without it on any future occasion.

Objection has been taken to it on the score of trouble, which I attribute chiefly to the idle habit of neglecting the preparation of the Cera until the moment it is required for use, resulting, as it is almost certain to do, in non-compliance with the printed directions. In the absence of a kettle supplied by the patentees, the lamp-feeder, filled with cut up Cera, should be placed in boiling water until the Cera is melted; then pour in hot, and let a few drops fall on the wick to start it. After that, if the lantern be right, there will be no more trouble.

The Acme petroleum stove, of which the large flat reservoir was skilfully adapted to my requirements by Mr. Bruce, 90, Blackman-street, Borough, has two burners, placed wide enough to bake, boil, and stew or fry at the same time. To stop the waves of oil which, when the boat was in violent motion, would have rendered the stove a horrible, smoky nuisance, I had the reservoir divided into eight compartments, of which one end of each partition was left open one-eighth of an inch. The great use I made of the apparatus, even in the worst of weather, when not only the stove, but the kettle, coffee-pot, and everything else—myself being scarcely excepted—required to be firmly lashed, is a proof it left little to desire. To catch overflow or leakage of the oil I stood the apparatus in a baking-tin, large enough to accommodate it conveniently, and should never think of using an oil or spirit stove without taking that precaution. Provided they are carefully trimmed and kept thoroughly clean, the advantages of these stoves for small yachts are that they can be lighted or extinguished in a moment, do not generate inconvenient heat in the cabin, and, while light and clean to handle, the fuel occupies infinitely less space than coal.

The sleeping bunk, constructed to my draft, consists of stout canvas laced into a galvanised iron frame, 6 ft. 3 in. by 2 ft. 2 in., supported on one side by rests screwed to the vessel's side, and, on the other, by lanyards to the deck beams. A horsehair mattress and pillow, a feather pillow, and three fine blankets, rendered it as restful and comfortable a bed as any man could desire. When not in use, it is protected from damp by an oiled canvas cover, and turned up against the side, forming a convenient sofa back against which to recline.

The riding gear consists of three galvanised anchors, 43 lb., 37 lb., and 28 lb.; 35 fathoms $\frac{5}{16}$ in. galvanised chain, a $3\frac{1}{4}$ in. bass rope, 60 fathoms, and a $2\frac{3}{4}$ in. bass rope, 35 fathoms, besides shorter length of hemp rope for mooring to quays and buoys.

Though for a single hand the work of such a boat is excessive, it is possible to carry it on for a long period, not only with safety, but with a feeling of intense satisfaction, if a reasonable system of routine is adopted, and cleanliness and order are rigidly observed.

On *July* 5, by kind permission of the captain, the 'Perseus' was towed out of the creek by the boys of the training ship 'Arethusa,' moored to a buoy, and supplied with filtered water from the ship.

July 6.—Wind W.N.W., moderate, threatening rain. 4.30 A.M., sailed from Greenhithe, Kent, under stormsail, mizen, and jib, intending to anchor when pure sea water was reached, and spend a quiet day. But at 8.30, when the Nore was passed, in a fresh breeze from N.N.W., the weather looked so much like a repetition of the previous afternoon performance, that there was no alternative but to proceed. Noon, off Reculvers, paid out the bass warps and towed them for an hour, to lessen their extreme harshness, but this did not soften them much. However, it enabled them to be properly coiled, for which the boat had to be brought to the wind, and laid-to, as it was impossible to get an inch of them on board again

without doing so. 3.30 P.M., rounded the North Foreland.
8 P.M., anchored off Deal, about a mile from the shore; wind
very light; night fine.

July 7.—Wind W.N.W., light; weather, showery and unsettled. The barometer was steady at 30 degs., and, notwithstanding the wind was backing all day, and that the clouds
had for a long while assumed a very threatening appearance,
so remained until I turned in at night. In a depth of 3½
fathoms low water, under ordinary circumstances, 30 fathoms
of the bower warp was sufficient scope; but, with a view to
improve the condition of the warp itself, and not in the least
from apprehension, I paid out the entire 60, which was
fortunate, as at midnight a heavy gale set in from S.S.W. and
soon knocked up a big sea.

July 8.—4 A.M., the motion and the uproar were so great that
I turned out to see how matters stood. Noticing that the
barometer had fallen $\frac{3}{10}$, I proceeded to take a survey outside,
but encountered such a torrent of spray and rain that, after
hurriedly convincing myself the 'Perseus' was behaving well,
and that there was nothing to apprehend from the vessels
which were plunging and straining at their anchors in my
vicinity, I scrambled back into bed again without a moment's
needless delay. Though wind-rode, the lurches were so violent
that to sit or stand was impracticable, so that lying down,
snugged in the blankets, was the only tenable position in the
cabin at that time. Sleep being out of the question, with head
in the air one moment and heels the next, there was nothing
to do but listen with anxious curiosity and wonder to the roar
of the wind and the loud thud of the sea on one bow or the
other, according as she sheered, instantaneously followed by
a rush of water along the deck. To a certain extent this extreme
violence abated about six, when the wind veered to S.W., and
later, to W.S.W., which—though it was carried on under
difficulties—permitted the ordinary daily work to proceed.

July 9.—Wind W.N.W.; morning squally; afternoon fine.
Shifted anchorage nearer to the shore, and landed with the
intention of posting a letter, but meeting a gentleman on the

beach who kindly relieved me of the trouble, immediately returned. The gale was remarkable for the orthodox regularity of its changes. Starting from W.N.W. on the morning of the 7th, with showers at intervals, the wind gradually backed to S.S.W., from which point it blew hard and rained in torrents for six hours. Then, during thirty-six hours, veered point by point back again to the quarter from which it started, wind and rain gradually subsiding into squalls of decreasing violence until it became fine.

July 10.—Wind N., light and fine. Sailed to Dover, and anchored in the bay. Amongst articles brought off from the shore were fresh provisions, rope, crockery, and needles, for which I bargained that six for black thread and six for white cotton should be threaded with about a couple of yards in each. In one sense it was a harder bargain for me than for the tradesman, since the wear and tear of my clothes was great, and it left me without excuse for neglecting repairs.

Surprise was frequently expressed that I did not go into harbour—into which the privilege of free entry was accorded me by virtue of the flag. But, apart from my disinclination to be berthed in close company with a fleet of grand yachts, it was not contemplated; for the reasons that my work could be carried on with more regularity and with far greater satisfaction to myself in the freedom of an open roadstead, and that the canvas and gear, being new and exceedingly harsh, it was not improbable I might run end on into a granite quay, or into another vessel before the mainsail could be taken off. True, at the expense of a rule that was not established without a motive, I could have hired assistance; but to have my canvas trampled by a stranger who had no interest in its preservation was not to my mind; nor was it likely to be upon this or any other occasion, except in a case of dire necessity, judged to be so by myself.

July 12.—The appearance of the sky indicating a return of bad weather, and the anchorage of Dover Bay in southwesterly gales notoriously being not of the best, determined me to seek the more secure holding ground and less circumscribed anchorage of Dungeness Road. Accordingly, at noon, in a strong W.S.W. wind and rising sea, barometer 30·05, I sailed from Dover under the stormsail, made a long board to the southward, and, when about on the other tack, heading W.N.W. towards Dymchurch, left the 'Perseus' to sail herself while I had dinner, and cleared up below. On a twelve mile reach, with nothing in the way, there was plenty of time to do this and settle down again to the helm before closing with the land. A hungry individual in robust sea health may victual to repletion under such circumstances; but where exertion is needed to keep oneself right side up and the crockery from going to smash, in a strictly epicurean sense, it would be affectation to say that a dinner had been enjoyed. After another board off and on, during which frequent soundings were taken, the anchor was let go about a mile S. by E. of New Romney. Night, strong and rainy. Though only the stormsail is mentioned on this occasion, the mizen and the jib were also set, as, henceforth, I wish it to be understood they always were, unless otherwise stated.

July 13, 14.—Wind alternated between W.S.W., S.W., and W., strong to a gale, with much rain at intervals. The roadstead, within the line of the Roar Bank, being protected from S.W. by Dungeness Point, distant three miles, the sea, though rough enough to be a constant nuisance, and, at times, to send heavy showers of spray on board, was never of a character to cause apprehension, as it would have done in Dover Bay. On the afternoon of the 14th the weather became clear, and the sun shone for the first time for three days, followed by a calm and bright night, which was quite a treat.

Evidence of the extent to which ships now proceed direct to foreign ports to unload, is observable in the large number of foreign pilot vessels stationed at Dungeness. As the majority, if not all, are schooners of 100 tons and upwards, it is certain the demand for their services must have enormously increased since my attention was last directed to their 'big lettered' sails.

July 15.—4.30 A.M., sailed from Dungeness Road; wind W., almost calm. 8, when drifting astern, with an adverse tide, a breeze sprang up from W.S.W., which gathered strength all the forenoon, until it became very fresh with a troublesome head sea. 10, fell in with a fleet of fishing smacks, bound to windward, from Rye Harbour. In bright sunshine and clear weather the scene was interesting, and a little bit stimulating, as, by the constant luffing and trimming of sheets, it was evident that all within a reasonable distance were determined to have a go at the stranger. Though none could hold a better wind, two or three of the large cutters gradually forereached the 'Perseus' by sheer weight and power, while the others dropped farther astern. 2.30 P.M., fetched Hastings pier; thence, to avoid as much as possible an adverse tide, tacked about every half-hour—guided by the clock when standing off, and by the lead when heading inshore—and, at 8.30, in a roaring breeze, without which no way could be made against tide, anchored off Eastbourne.

An account of the day's proceedings, domestically and nautically, which, at least in the former respect, will be tolerably representative of all the others, will, perhaps, here not be out of place. 3.30 A.M., turned out, made toilet, and tidied cabin; 4.30, got under way, and while sailing with a light breeze towards Dungeness Point, watching course, and checking the helm, trimmed and lighted stove, cleaned down and tidied on deck; 6.30, early cup of tea; 8.30, substantial breakfast—pint of coffee, warm bread, bacon, &c., &c.; all articles used at this, and at all other meals, being immediately cleaned and stowed away.

At this time the breeze sprang up from W.S.W., and a turn to windward of nearly 30 miles commenced; 11.30, wine and biscuits; 2.30 P.M., cold dinner, with pint bottle of Bass; 6.30, another substantial meal, with pint of tea. When, in my prefatory remarks, I stated that, including the long business of preparing and stowing away, six hours of the day were consumed in this manner, it is clear that, where rules so necessary to the preservation of order are strictly observed, less time could not suffice. The opportunities chosen for these rather long absences from the helm were immediately after going in stays and when standing off the land; during which time, as before said, by carefully trimming and occasionally checking the helm, the boat displayed the most remarkable facility for sailing herself to windward I have ever observed in any vessel.

July 16.—Landed at noon to make a few purchases, post letters, &c. The day having been exceedingly fine, barometer 30·10, and the night calm and warm, I fell into the mistake of believing that summer had really set in at last, and took advantage of the stormsail being thoroughly dry to stow it below and get the mainsail on deck in its place. To prevent the luff of either of these two sails from roaching when the main-sheet is hauled aft for turning to windward, and the strain upon them very great, the reef cringles in the sail are bent to hoops on the mast. It is because they are working lugs tacked to the heel of the mast like a cutter's yard topsail, that this arrangement is necessary, and that they are spoken of as being 'bent to the mast,' which, in the case of an ordinary, or dipping, lug would be incorrect, and convey a wrong impression. To shift the lug under way would occupy about three-quarters of an hour, because the one removed would be made up only temporarily, and the other not at all. But in this instance, which occupied me from 8.30 to 11, the stormsail had to be uncovered, unmade, unbent, and made up and covered again; while the mainsail—a heavy and awkward parcel to move out of its confined space in the cabin and put on deck—had to be treated in a manner precisely similar to the above.

On *July* 17 remarkably heavy thunderstorms broke over London and South Devon, of which I did not hear until three days later. At Eastbourne the weather was cloudy and close, with a light air from the eastward, thunder occasionally rumbling in the distance, and the barometer 30 degrees. 2 P.M., got under way and reached down to Beachy Head, which had just been rounded when a spanking breeze from N.E. came off the high land, but in less than an hour the breeze faltered, puffed faintly from the northward, and then dropped entirely. 6, off Seaford Head, a light breeze sprang up from W.S.W. The breeze gradually strengthened until it blew hard from W.S.W., with rain and a fast rising sea. 9, hove-to, and took two reefs down. Midnight, tacked off Brighton, and shortly afterwards backed the jib and stood 'on and off,' without losing sight of the lights of the town.

July 18.—Being within the line of Channel traffic, the only craft of which I had to keep clear were fishing luggers, carrying a bright light, anchored about three miles and upwards from the shore; so that, apart from the discomfort which only an improvement in the weather could mitigate, the night's work was rendered as little irksome as circumstances enabled me to make it—which means that I had a good supper and an occasional pipe, and, so far as was consistent with a due regard to safety, sat aft, to be pelted as little as possible. 4.30 A.M., when about five miles out, the wind veered to the westward and rain ceased; let draw the jib, and stood in for the land. 6, in a fresh breeze, W.N.W., anchored about half a mile west of the entrance to Shoreham. After the duties of the morning were got through, I made sail.

Notwithstanding, the weather looked so fine, that I was sorely tempted to shake the reefs out of the mainsail; considering the large amount of extra labour it would have occasioned me, it was fortunate they were retained, since, in less than an hour, the wind backed to W.S.W., and became so extremely violent that, after tacking to the southward, off Worthing, at 1.30 P.M. I backed the jib, lowered the mainsail half down, and hove-to with the helm a-lee. The reason for so doing was a firm conviction that, with the barometer steady at 30 degrees, and such a recent blow from this quarter, it was a temporary aberration that would moderate at sunset. Shortly before this, a yawl yacht of about 8 tons—apparently of Hampshire build—which was also bound to the westward, passed near enough under my stern for me to hear, in reply to my hail, 'We'll have no more of it!' and proceeded in the direction of a few other small craft which were anchored S.E. of Worthing pier. At the time it caused me astonishment they should do so; but I have since learnt that there is a grass bank there, which has the effect of moderating the sea, much in the same way, I presume, as when oil is poured on the surface.

While heading off in the manner that has been described, I had dinner and a pipe, and busied myself in various other ways; but as hour after hour went by, and the prospect of a fearful night out increased, I decided, at whatever cost of inconvenience and labour, to take the third reef down and make a determined effort to gain some sort of anchorage on the Bognor or Selsea shore. The sea was terrible, and rendered the reefing job I had vainly endeavoured to avoid, of which a great part had to be done sitting or kneeling in a stream of water on the deck, protected only by a 3 in. rail, difficult beyond imagination; and it was because experience was scarcely needed to know that in a brand new sail, of stout canvas, saturated and stiff as millboard, the labour required to take the third reef neatly and effectively would be severe, I waited until no alternative remained before undertaking it. Nevertheless, when it was mastered, and the sail, with the assistance of watch-tackles, set like a board, the boat displayed such extraordinary power and capability that, if the day had been commencing, instead of drawing to a close, comparatively the situation would have been viewed with indifference. In three hours the boat had gained such an offing on her own account that, to my surprise, on the first board to leeward she made Littlehampton, where I tacked and stood off at 6 P.M., weather densely cloudy, and raining in torrents. There was only one vessel in sight, which eventually proved to be a 'ketch' I had seen flaring out of Shoreham at noon with topsail and everything set, but now, faintly visible through the haze, about three miles to windward, hammering along industriously under double-reefed mainsail, reduced foresail and mizen, and the storm jib.

Chilled through and through by wind and wet, which on these occasions no amount of clothing or of waterproofs will exclude, the necessity of having to abandon the shelter of the weather coamings to take soundings was a great nuisance; yet, consequent upon the darkness and haze rendering anything like a correct estimate of distance from land impossible, together with a wholesome dread of an extensive outlying reef called Bognor Rocks, a great many had to be taken. The clouds were so dense, that, at 7.30, the chart could not be read in the cabin, nor at 8—when I passed the ketch like a steamer, weathering and fore-reaching at the same time— could the course be ascertained without difficulty at the binnacle. In such a dangerous vicinity, and in the midst of such fury above and around, the little daylight that remained was far too valuable to waste in an endeavour to procure a light, even if the dripping wet plight I was in had not been certain to render the attempt fruitless; so I held on the tack to the W.N.W. until the lead warned me to go about, stood off again into three fathoms, low water, and at 8.30 lowered the mainsail and let go the anchor about 2½ miles S.S.W. of Bognor.

After the jib was hauled down and temporarily secured to prevent the anchor from starting, the remainder of the riding warp had to be paid out to the 60-fathom parcelling. While this was being done, a simultaneous heavy plunge and sheer dipped the bowsprit under the warp, which in its passage capsized the jib into the water, and pinned it there. At the same time, the wind lifted the upper part of the mainsail off the deck and—owing to the guys, which should have prevented it, having been carried away by pressure of the mainyard about two hours before—swung the yard square over the lee side, and half the sail with it. At the first attempt my efforts to get it aboard were unavailing; so I retired below to get a little much-needed refreshment, and think what course to pursue; but returned almost immediately, resolved, at any cost of time and patience, to succeed. Short as was the interval of relaxation, it was beneficial. Little by little, kneeling on every haul of a few inches gained against the power of the wind, the mainsail was eventually secured; and then attention was directed to the jib. Fortunately another deep plunge— presumably at the time when she straightened, or reversed the sheer, which had been occasioned by paying out the second 30 fathoms of the riding rope too hurriedly—had passed the warp back to its proper side; so that, by lying half out on the bowsprit—a position I should not have chosen if any other had been consistent with safety—the jib was gathered up and lashed with a long mainsail tyer, which had been taken out for the purpose of rendering the work as effective and expeditious as possible. When the head of the jib had been properly secured inboard, and the mizen furled, there being, happily, nothing more to do, I retired below, having left the drenched waterproofs (?) outside, lighted the candle lamp and the stove, and, when the reservoir had been warmed, the Cera cabin lantern, undressed, 'towelled' vigorously, and put on dry clothes. As to have boiled the Cera and got up the riding light would have cost me an extra hour and another drenching, I threw a strong light into the steerage and on the furled white sail of the mizen, drank a mug of hot tea, and, in a semi-prepared state for the deck, snugged between the blankets at midnight, after thirty-six hours' continuous employment as severe as it has ever been my lot to encounter.

July 19.—Though for some time the roar of the wind, the rush of water, and the tremendous tossing, kept me awake, I was fortunately unable to note the hour the storm began to abate; but at 6 A.M. the wind had veered to W.N.W., with rifts in the clouds, and only a troublesome short sea. After a jolly breakfast, for which abstinence since dinner the previous day had left ample space, a little smack, with four or five men in her, came dodging round with all sorts of suggestions for my benefit, if I would only consent to receive some of them on board, but their offers of assistance were declined.

As the 'Perseus' had not been pumped since her arrival at Eastbourne, it astonished me exceedingly, after such a heavy turn to windward, and so much rain, to find that the water (as after the gale in the Downs) only amounted to the small quantity of forty gallons, or less than, through inadvertence, might easily be shipped from a single green sea. Undoubtedly, this satisfactory result is due to the protection afforded the open waist and steerage by the high side she presents to the sea when heeling over; so that the harder it blows the greater is the tendency of the spray and rain to fly over to leeward without falling inboard.

After dinner, and when it suited me, I set the mizen and jib, to assist in getting the anchor, reached, close hauled, down to Selsea, and at 5 P.M. anchored off the village, about half a mile from the shore.

Sailing, close hauled, in moderate weather, the helmsman looks to windward almost exclusively, and, therefore, sees very little of the water on the lee side. But, in bad weather, when the vessel is heeling gunwale down, his eyes, when not on the compass, are perforce directed to the lee side, and the boiling sea, between which and his sight nothing then interposes. In these circumstances three-fourths of the steering is conducted by sound and feeling, and not by sight; in fact, by means that no amount of literary or oral instruction can possibly convey to another. If instruction on such a common sense point could be needed by anyone who contemplated taking the helm in stormy weather, it would be a recommendation never to allow his ears to be closed by the lugs of a sou'-wester, or by any other form of covering; since, when, by reason of darkness or violence, one is unable to keep a continuous look-out to windward, the approach of a breaking sea, at a distance which affords ample time to take precautions, is as often detected by its noisy surf as by sight. Similarly, when already hard pressed by wind, anyone with his ears open and on the alert will luff nearer, and infinitesimally nearer—even to the extent of throwing some of its power out of the sail by gentle lifting—just in proportion as its sound in the rigging attains a higher tone or key. The objects of this manipulation are, to hold on through the exceptional puffs that, during a gale, invariably accompany a densely clouded sky, without unnecessarily reducing canvas, and, while counteracting the tendency to heel excessively, to keep the vessel sailing at her best, and under fullest command. The reason for keeping her thus strictly in hand is, that at a moment's notice she may be brought head on to a breaking sea, and filled off again with but little loss of way; or, if the increase of wind should not prove temporary, be put in stays, which will enable the mainsail to be eased down, or lowered entirely, while she is rounding, and the jib to be thrown aback without handling the sheet, consequently, with least trouble or loss of time.

July 21.—Wind W.S.W., a nice breeze, and very fine. 1 P.M., sailed from Selsea at high water, and tacked out between the Mixon Rocks and the Bill; made two long boards, and at 5.45, having tacked west of Ryde Pier, was able to lay a straight course for East Cowes Point, which, under occasional supervision, the boat was able to accomplish by herself. Meanwhile, I boiled two small lobsters that one of my visitors of the previous day tossed on board while sailing past, and good-naturedly asked me to accept; had as good a tea as one could wish to sit down to; cleared all away in time to make a series of short tacks against a strong current into Cowes Roads, and at 8.30 anchored on the edge of Cowes Spit.

July 24.—Wind W.S.W., strong breeze and fine. 3.30 P.M., got under way, and had a difficulty with the anchor, which came up very foul, with turns of the chain and a mass of coarse seaweed. Hurried by the tide into the vicinity of the large yachts in the outer road, I had to control her drift in a rough sea, ahead of one and astern of another—first by the jib alone, and then by the jib and mizen combined, as the necessity of the case required—and was unable to turn my attention to the mainsail until arrival at the Lepe Buoy. Thence, it was a smart turn to windward, with a reef down, to Totland Bay, where, at 7.30, the anchor was let go for the night. In moderate weather pleasant and comfortable anchorage will be found here, out of the strength of the Needles Channel tide.

July 25.—Among the repairs that are constantly requiring attention, the bower warp had to be cut and spliced, consequent upon damage to one of the strands on the night of the 18th, which had been detected by the sharp eyes of a Selsea fisherman. Though the injury was too slight to attract the attention of less keen eyes, I shifted the 30 fathoms parcelling instantly, and did not again ride to the warp in open sea until it was placed beyond suspicion. A four-strand bass warp, on which one's safety may depend, cannot be spliced in a moment, as the strands require to be whipped, and great care taken that it does not unlay itself during the operation. 3.30 P.M., sailed from Totland, with a reef down, wind W., fresh and fine. Had a strong turn to windward, and, at 8.30, anchored in Swanage Bay. Remained over Monday, the 28th; weather variable, with smooth water in bay, but mostly stormy and rough at sea.

July 29.—7.30 A.M., sailed from Swanage, under whole mainsail, wind variable between W. by S. and W. by N., a moderate breeze and fine. 11.30, log 10, S.S.W. of Anvil Point, went about and headed N.N.W. seventeen miles to Portland Bill. 3.30 P.M., in a roughish sea, three miles W.S.W. of the Bill, re-set log. I had not found it necessary to put on waterproofs, but, just when the Race was supposed to be cleared, a massive spray came over that soused me handsomely, and rendered my working suit uncomfortable for the rest of the day. 5, having to bring out and fix the side-light screens, prepare Cera for the lamps, and get tea, besides attending to a score of other matters it would be useless to describe, I backed the jib moderately, trimmed the helm according to require-ment, and, as on similar occasions when there was nothing of which notice need be taken in sight, trusted the (intelligent) boat to make a good weatherly course by herself. At the same time, it must be clearly understood that neither now nor at any time was my supervision withdrawn for periods sufficiently long to permit any failure of duty to her owner. About this time I met a small yacht with five or six hands on board, which I believed had passed me under a great spread of sail early in the morning, running back to Portland. And they were right; for, with half-a-dozen jostling each other in a craft not much larger than my own, and night coming on, the confusion that must have ensued later in the evening, I, for one, would not willingly have consented to share. 8.30, took a reef down, wind W. by S., freshening ominously. The moon, then nearly full, was surrounded by a halo, while the cirro-stratus (or fish clouds), and cirrus, in its neighbourhood, were also tinged with colour; indicating a gale that, at first, I thought there was a chance might be postponed till next day; but which the appearance of low and fast flying scud, before another hour had passed, conclusively settled to be near at hand.

July 30.—12.30 A.M., in thick weather and a driving rain, sighted the red light of Lyme Regis, and, at 1, put about in haste, being startled by the loom of high land. Whether at the distance of more or less than a mile, it was not desirable to waste time in taking soundings on a lee shore to ascertain, as the wind was increasing, and the sea becoming heavier every minute. When round, with the jib aback, the second reef taken down, and the mainsail again trimmed to my satisfaction, I took the opportunity of being several miles to the northward of the Channel traffic, to allow the 'Perseus' to make an offing for herself, and forthwith commenced my term of release from constant attendance at the helm, by having supper and a pipe.

Notwithstanding the heavy sprays that came aboard, the side-lights—which were fixed by thumb-screws to the inner side of the gunwale at the quarters—burned with great power and brilliancy, the effect of their red and green rays on the foaming sea alongside and ahead being exceedingly pretty.

4 A.M., having resumed the hateful waterproofs, I settled down to business, and continued the course she had been making for herself until 5.30, at which time the position was about twelve miles S.S.W. of Lyme, when the wind backed a couple of points to S.W. by S., and enabled an advantageous tack to be made to W.N.W. for several hours. Though somewhat favourable to the course, the result, which invariably attends a backing wind in bad weather, was an increase of violence that caused me to regret the third reef had not been taken down at the same time as the second, off Lyme; but which, so long as its necessity could be fought off by sailing extremely 'fine' (luffing), was an extra bit of hard labour, in which it was not to my interest, either in point of speed, or fatigue, now to engage. Notwithstanding the drenching torrents of spray and rain, the violence of the motion, and the efforts that were needful to maintain my position at the helm, between 6 and 7, I had to contend with a fitful attack of

somnolency—a complaint well known to me by experience, and from which, so far as my observation extends, seamen who have been up all night are rarely, if ever, exempt at some early hour of the morning. Strange to say, while making almost superhuman efforts to retain consciousness, which, by reason of the motion, cannot be lost for longer intervals of time than the vessel happens to be nearly on an even keel, my instinctive appreciation of the surrounding circumstances and sense of hearing were sufficiently acute to enable me to luff in time to meet every comber that threatened to come aboard, and, without materially diminished speed, fall off again on the course when the crisis had passed. With me, the attack usually lasts about forty-five minutes, and does not return till a late hour of the night, or early the following morning.

When I started on the W.N.W. course at 5.30 there were three schooners on the same tack, of which the nearest was more than a mile to windward. I had too much sea to contend with to dare to give the 'Perseus' full play, but gradually drew into line with them, and eventually passed on to their weather side. Occasionally, a sea that was doubtful, but not threatening enough to require special precautions to be taken, had its equilibrium destroyed by the 'Perseus,' with the curious result that, when issuing in massive foam from her lee side, a small head welled up into the foot of the mainsail, and, with a loud thud, drenched me at the helm on my least protected side, like a fort attacked in the rear. It was a slight penalty for 'carrying on,' which, in a boat less completely protected by a waterway and an inner coaming, I should have thought it undesirable to endure for a moment.

7 A.M., hauled the jib sheet to windward, and partially hove-to, with helm amidships. The effect of this on a vessel that carries a weather helm is to deaden her way, and keep the mainsail on the verge of lifting, without the possibility of putting herself in stays. When standing off from Lyme Regis, I gave her sufficient weather helm to insure a fair speed being maintained; but, since then, the sea had become so much heavier that to have allowed her to gather way, except within

the narrowest limits, would have been unsafe. Under these circumstances, by the exercise of more than usual vigilance and care, I was able to perform the morning duties, beginning with the standard cup of tea, followed, when ready, by an excellent breakfast, and got all cleared away by 10. During this time her advance was about two knots per hour, on the most weatherly course that could be made. In all this there was no loss of time, but great gain; for, without proper meals—as well as without sleep—how could the work proceed! 10.30, rain ceased, and weather became clear, which afforded me a charming view of all the east coast of Devonshire, and, to my pleased astonishment—not having ventured to anticipate such a favourable landfall—showed Teignmouth only about six miles ahead. Shortly afterwards, a brief lull and a gleam of hot sunshine induced me to shake out the reefs, which had scarcely been done when, but for the smoothing of the sea as the weather shore was approached, they would have had to be taken in again. The result was a fine bit of sailing that kept me at the helm to the end of the passage, which, after a tack off Teignmouth, and another off Babbacombe, finished at 1.30 P.M. in a beautifully wooded little bay (unnamed on the chart), situated immediately to the north of Hope's Nose, and between it and Ansty's Cove. I cannot say how supremely delightful it was to get into smooth water on such a picturesque and delightful shore. Work there was of course, and plenty of it, but on an even keel, at leisure, and not to order, or under compulsion. My intention had been to anchor off Babbacombe, but as the number of boats out indicated an excursionist invasion, however tired and hungry, I preferred to pass on.

July 31.—South-westerly gale and a deluge of rain until 2 P.M., when the wind shifted to the westward and became less violent. Night fine; wind W., strong.

Aug. 1.—4 P.M., under way with a fine whole sail breeze from W. by S.; looked into the outer harbour of Brixham to see what it is like, and proceeded to Dartmouth. 8 P.M., wind light; anchored in the Range, being unable to enter against tide. Night fine.

Aug. 2.—4 A.M., had great difficulty with the riding rope, which had probably fouled a rock, but eventually got it in with a tackle. 6, anchored off One Gun Point, Warfleet Cove—having, with the exception of the call at the Isle of Wight, kept the sea since leaving home on the 6th ult.

Aug. 3.—Passed a delightfully quiet Sunday. Weather warm and fine.

Aug. 4.—Took advantage of a fine quiet day to rub down and varnish.

Aug. 5.—5 P.M., sailed from Dartmouth against tide with a nice westerly breeze, and at 8.30 anchored in Start Bay, which, while the wind remains anywhere in that quarter, I consider one of the most pleasant anchorages in the kingdom. Night fine, barometer 30·20.

Aug. 6.—3.30 P.M., got under way, with a fine whole sail breeze, N.W., and fortunately smooth water; as, at 4.40—notwithstanding the chart had that instant been consulted—when heading W. for Prawle Point, at the distance of from one to two cables outside the Start Rocks, I ran with great violence on a rock, then about twelve inches below the surface, but which is said to be awash at low water springs. Very shortly after striking, the 'Perseus' swung with her head to the northward and threw the jib aback—a movement I attempted to assist by bearing her head off with a spar; but failing to make any impression on her in that manner, I went aft and eased the mainsheet, when she slid off and, the breeze being strong, immediately gathered sufficient way to enable me to wear her short round and start afresh on an amended course. The time spent in this untoward performance could not have been long, as on resuming the course I found myself under the lee of a sloop bound to Plymouth, which had been following precisely in my wake until some fisherman shouted, 'The yacht ahead of you has struck.' While passing through his lee, and eventually on to his weather bow—which seemed to occasion some astonishment—I asked the master, 'Did you know of the existence of that rock?' To which he replied, 'Yes!' But I was of opinion that if the 'Perseus' had only grazed it and passed on he would have learnt more than he had hitherto been privileged to know concerning it.

From Prawle Point to the exceedingly picturesque harbour of Salcombe the wind was 'on end'; likewise, through the narrow, rocky entrance, and up to the town, where I anchored at 7.30. Though, after the bar was crossed, the navigation required anxious attention, being rendered all the more troublesome to a stranger by the eddying gusts from the cliffs, the little turn to windward in sunshine and smooth water, enlivened by numerous sailing boats, was a charming finish up to what might have been a rather too eventful day.

Aug. 7.—Laid the 'Perseus' ashore, to ascertain if any injury had been received, and observed that, for about twelve inches upwards from the iron band, the stem was rather deeply indented and ragged, proving conclusively that, if the band had not been turned up at the forefoot, the injury must have been far more severe.

Aug. 9.—Wind E.N.E., very strong, and fine. 1.30 P.M., sailed from Salcombe with one reef down, when at least there should have been two. Though between Bolt Head—two miles S.W. of the town—and Bolt Tail, only four miles had to be covered, I made an offing of more than a mile to procure a steadier wind than prevailed along the base of the lofty cliffs, where violent gybes without notice were certain to have occurred. As it was my first experience in the 'Perseus' of a hard run before wind and sea, and was a bit of accidental 'carrying on' that would not have been indulged in if the force of wind outside the shelter of the Salcombe hills had been ascertainable beforehand, I greatly desired to test her speed by the patent log—which by mere guess-work I assessed at 8 knots; but, owing to the difficulties of avoiding a broach-to, found it impossible to divert my attention from the helm for an instant, and therefore was unable to do so. However harmless on a wind, to leave the helm when running under a press of sail is very dangerous. 2.45, hauled aft sheets, and luffed round the Bolt Tail—a very picturesque and highly-coloured head-land, red predominating, honeycombed with large caverns and extensive fissures, it would have delighted me to explore. The wind being off shore in Bigbury Bay, and the sea smooth, I hove-to for dinner, jogged about for a couple of hours, and at 5, anchored in a small roadstead north of Borough Island— one of the dullest spots that can well be conceived. The reason for anchoring there was that the chief object of the visit to Devonshire was to inspect this part of the coast, and that it was a central point from which to start. 7 P.M., when tea was nearly ready, it blew so hard from the eastward, and the barometer was so unsatisfactory, that I paid out the bower rope to 60. While this was being done, a flash of lightning and premature darkness warned me that severe weather was at hand; and, as it was impossible to know if the off-shore wind would stand, I close-reefed the mainsail and covered it again—the motive for covering being not only to keep it clean, but preserve it in lighter condition for handling. This heavy work was scarcely out of hand when the rain began to descend, and, just because there was a sense of preparedness, and a feeling that nothing more could be done, I was able to sit down, comparatively speaking, in comfort, and make a hearty meal, though the din outside was fearful. The electric storm came from the east, and, as there was not likely to be a change, I could turn in at the usual hour without fear of being disturbed. The barometer fell two-tenths, to 29·80.

Aug. 10.—Morning fine, wind E.S.E., gradually veering S., at which point it fell calm till 10.30, when a light breeze sprang up from S.W. 11, hoisted the dinghey out, rowed round the bay to find a proper landing-place, and eventually beached with the assistance of the coastguard; but the breeze was so evidently freshening that I was ill at ease, and, judging that not a moment should be lost, hastened back to the beach, and, with the same efficient assistance in launching as in landing, contrived, by dint of hard pulling, to get back to the 'Perseus.' Having stowed the little boat below, my first idea was to have dinner; but the sea was rising fast, and the weather so thoroughly out of gear, that, at 1.30 P.M., I decided to get under way immediately, with one reef down, and dine in peace—freed from the anxiety of a lee shore—while heading in the direction of Plymouth. Long before reaching there the weather became densely cloudy and hazy, and the sea, though neither violent nor surfy, heavier than any I had yet seen; warning, unmistakably, of the near approach of a south-westerly gale. Being well to windward, I made for the western entrance to the Sound, for which several coasters and foreigners were also running, and, at 6, anchored in a clear berth under lee of the breakwater at the western (or lighthouse) end. 9 P.M., paid out bower warp to 60; wind S.W. blowing hard, with rain; barometer 29·75° F. When I heard the roar of the sea on the breakwater, and saw the great sheets of foam tumbling over its lee side, it contributed not a little to the enjoyment of the meditative pipe to know I had cleared out of Borough Island Road in good time.

Aug. 13.—In the vain hope that the weather might become more favourable, and permit me to return to the coast from which I had been driven by the S.W. wind, I remained till the morning of this day, and then decided to make towards home. For the convenience of the authorities, who had been 'sweeping' for the dropped moorings of a Government vessel, my anchorage had been shifted to a position from which, in the then state of wind and tide, it was dangerous for me to attempt to get under way. Thus awkwardly circumstanced, through no fault of mine, I requested the assistance of a boat's crew to tow me out, which was at once considerately and kindly granted. Notwithstanding the men removed much mud from the warp and the anchor before leaving me, their condition was so unsatisfactory that, out of regard for my white canvas, I hove-to in the Sound, cleaned them thoroughly by hand, towed the warps overboard, and after they were stowed had to finish up with a general wash down. This is but one instance out of the many of the extra or unforeseen work that from one cause or another was pretty constantly recurring. 11.30, cleared the breakwater, with one reef down, wind W., squally. 1.30 P.M., being unable to quit the helm for more than a minute at a time, I brought everything aft by degrees, rigged up a table on the grating seats, and had dinner there. Though in some respects more troublesome than dining below, it was a highly satisfactory performance. 3.30, off Bolt Head, had a miserably cold and heavy shower, that would have been less unpleasant if it had come after the sails were furled. 4, anchored in Salcombe.

While lying here on the 14th and 15th, the weather at the time being extremely bad, three large torpedo boats came in for shelter.

Aug. 16.—Wind W., blowing hard. 6.30 A.M., sailed from Salcombe with only one reef down—the least sail with which I could hope to get safely down to Bolt Head, owing to the heavy swell on the rocky shore to leeward, and to the eddying gusts, alternated with calms, which in westerly winds prevail about the entrance. The greatest inconvenience that attends leaving the harbour of Salcombe in bad weather, and which is not felt when quitting the extensive harbours of Plymouth and Falmouth, is that from the moment the anchor is weighed the navigation demands such careful and close attention that it is impossible to coil down or get into proper order before being hurried into a heavy sea. Immediately the line of broken water, occasioned by the clashing of the currents, is passed the sea becomes tremendous. Simultaneously with the crossing of this line, the partial protection afforded by the cliffs ceases, and the full force of the wind is encountered. Whereas, up to this point, the 'Perseus' would not have been under proper command with less canvas than a single reef, she was suddenly overpowered to an extent that necessitated the mainsail being lowered half down, as for a heavy squall; and, when a fair offing to windward of the surfing tide line (which is dangerous to small craft) had been gained, I bore up, dead before the wind, for Start Point. It has been said that the sea off Plymouth, on the 10th, though by no means the roughest, was the heaviest that had been encountered—but it was a bagatelle compared to this. Two or three times she gybed awkwardly, when being, as it were, hurled along by the high following sea; and once shipped a lump over the quarter, which, though it seemed rather much at the time, on pumping out at Dartmouth, proved to have been of no consequence at all. 8.15, rounded the Start, and expected to find more moderate weather; but, on coming to the wind, it seemed to be more furious than before, and converted the white tops of the sea into spoondrift. Off Beesands Cellars, in the central bight of Start Bay, I hove-to for awhile, tied up the second reef, and hoisted the sail only sufficiently to allow it to work clear overhead. Three reefs, smartly set, would have been an improvement; but, having the protection of a weather shore, with port in sight, for the reason before stated, my hands were not disposed to the extra work it would have entailed.

On arrival at Dartmouth Harbour, from which the tide was setting out strongly, I made several attempts to pass St. Petrox Castle. 2 P.M., succeeded in turning up to Warfleet Cove, and, at 3, had a grand breakfast.

Remained in Dartmouth four days, and passed a pleasant, quiet time.

Aug. 20.—Had to get two anchors in; the bower with 30 fathoms of chain, and the kedge with 32 fathoms of rope. Where the dinghey is too small for anchor work, my plan—especially, as in this instance, when the chain will probably be muddy—is to slacken the kedge warp as required and take up the bower first; then shorten in the kedge, and ride to it, while the canvas is being prepared. 4.30 P.M., sailed from Dartmouth, against tide; wind W., weather looking stormy. 7, anchored to the westward of Brixham, in Tor Bay; night fine, and quiet.

Aug. 21.—7.30 A.M., under way with a reef down. 8, cleared Berry Head, and set log. 11, wind W., light, with a tiresome swell which caused much chafing of gear. About twenty miles from land, fell in with the largest flight of gannet I have ever seen in the English Channel. 4.15 P.M., rounded Portland Bill, against tide; wind S.W., strong and cloudy, sea rough and racy, until the shelter of Grove Point was gained. Under lee of the high land, the wind came off in whizzing gusts that were exceedingly troublesome to deal with, followed, in turn, by a

roaring breeze inside the breakwater-heads, as much as the
'Perseus' could stand up to, against which, sailing in her best
style, I beat up, through a fleet of men-of-war, to the weather
shore of Portland Roads, and anchored at 6.15. Night, blew
hard from S.W., with rain.

Aug. 22.—Wind W.N.W., fresh and fine. 10.30 A.M., with a
reef down, weighed anchor, by a method I habitually resorted
to when the wind was too strong to enable the riding rope (or
chain) to be got in by hand, viz., by 'sailing' it out of the
ground. (At sea, I use rope; and in river harbours, like Dartmouth, &c., chain.) On this occasion, besides the strength of
wind and the large scope to be got in, there was the additional
reason, that hulks and other vessels were anchored under my
lee, of which it would have been possible to fall foul if, during
the process of shortening in by direct hauling, the anchor had
prematurely begun to come home. Under these circumstances,
I set the mainsail, carried the steering lines forward to be
within easy reach, and forthwith commenced a series of
gradually shortening boards to windward, which, I trust, the
following description of the manœuvre will sufficiently explain.
(For cutters and yawls, the jib is a necessity; but the mast of the
'Perseus' is so far forward that she will not lie head to wind
with the mainsail set, so that in her case a jib is not required.)

Being compelled by the mainsail, not too harshly sheeted,
to take a wide sheer from her anchor, the strain on the bow,
assisted by the helm, forces the vessel round on the other tack,
and, while sailing close hauled towards her anchor, allows the
rope or chain to be hauled aboard rapidly and with great ease,
until, having crossed the original line of her anchor, the
strain again begins to be felt, when care must be taken to 'bitt'
instantly and securely, and so enable the operation to be repeated while there remains any slack to be got in. The result
is that the vessel breaks the anchor out of the ground herself,
and, instead of falling to leeward while it is being hauled
aboard and stowed, continues to increase her distance to windward of any obstructions, whether vessels, sand banks, or
rocks, by which her safety might have been imperilled.

When at anchor on the coast in the 'Orion,' and surprised by strong on-shore winds, it has been my custom for many years to clear out of difficult positions by this method, which, if properly executed, lightens labour, and, as a manœuvre, is as interesting in the performance as I have invariably found it satisfactory.

11 A.M., cleared Portland Breakwater; wind W., freshening, 30° F. 4 P.M., after close shaving the honeycombed limestone cliffs from St. Alban's, which always interest me, passed suddenly into a rush of adverse tide at Durlston Head. 5.30, entered the Needles Channel, steering hard before a rough sea, wind S.W., dirty, and threatening a gale. Met a few yachts, under short canvas, bound to Weymouth regatta, of which one or two put back, while the others, notably a rather small white-painted racer, were evidently resolved to take their dose of salt like men. 7, anchored in Newtown Bay, too far out for comfort; the result was that towards morning, when the tide again set to windward, the motion in the trough of the sea was abominable. I should not have anchored there as a deliberate choice; but I was tired and hungry, and, being under an inconvenient press of sail, did not wish to make Cowes in the dark.

Aug. 23.—Barometer 29·80, blew hard and rained till noon, when the wind shifted to W.N.W., and moderated. Having wind and tide to contend with in getting under way, in this instance, the sailing-out process, if practicable, was not desirable; so as the 30 fathoms of rope could not be got in by hand alone, I used the mainsheet for a tackle, swifted it forward seven times, securing three fathoms each haul; then, as there was plenty of sea room, left her to fidget the anchor out of the ground for herself, which she very soon did, while I turned my attention to the mizen and jib for the little run up to Cowes.

On the 24th, a day of thunder, heavy rains, and much wind, the barometer fell to 29·50, the lowest reading since leaving home. The reason why the barometer was seldom much below or above 30° was because the atmosphere was 'electric'

324

throughout, so that no dependence could be placed upon it at all.

Aug. 28.—Dressed, lighted stove for early tea, got two anchors in, and under way with all sail set at 6.30 A.M., bound to Shoreham, and arrived before dark; wind W.N.W., a nice little breeze, and fine.

Aug. 30.—Wind N., a light breeze, and fine. Noon, sailed from Shoreham. 5.30, rounded Beachy Head, and, at 7.45, anchored in Pevensey Bay. Though the breeze was light from off-shore at the anchorage, a strong wind the other side of Dungeness sent a wretched swell down to Pevensey, directly on my broadside, which at times caused the 'Perseus' to roll as severely as in the S.W. gale at Newtown (I. of W.) on the morning of the 23rd.

Aug. 31.—Weighed anchor at 7.30 A.M., set the jib and mizen, and while I dressed and breakfasted, &c., allowed the boat to convey me to Hastings. It was a delightful little sail of three hours, with an off-shore wind and an exceptionally bright atmosphere, undertaken in the hope that the next night would prove less unquiet than the preceding. 'Pitching' occasions me only trifling inconvenience; 'lurching to leeward under canvas' can be provided against; but 'rolling excessively at anchor' capsizes everything that is unlashed, or, if in use, out of hand for a moment, and is an abomination.

Sept. 1.—Wind N.E., light, and very fine. 7.15 A.M., sailed from Hastings. Between Fairleigh and Winchelsea, fell into a calm, of which the tedium was considerably relieved by the beautiful views on shore. 2 P.M., passed Dungeness. 6.30, anchored in Dover Bay. Wind W.S.W., fresh; night cloudy and rough.

Sept. 2.—Sailed the anchor out of the ground, with a reef in the mainsail, wind S.W. strong, and went into harbour.

Sept. 3.—Left Dover 2 P.M., wind W. fresh. 6.30, anchored in a calm off Kingsgate; night very black and drizzly.

Sept. 4.—About 8 A.M., several large Rochester and Milton boats tacked within hail, whose employment I ascertained was 'shrimping' on the Goodwin Sand and landing their catches at

Margate. Probably but few persons imagined—and certainly I did not—that shrimps were ever sought for in such a dangerous place. 9.30, under way; wind N.W., moderate, rain at times. 4.15 P.M., wind light, anchored near East Spaniard buoy. Night calm and dark; sea remarkably phosphorescent; barometer 30·40.

Sept. 5.—Calm and foggy. 11 A.M. to 5 P.M., drifted up to the Nore and back to an anchorage, out of the traffic, off the Isle of Sheppey.

Sept. 6.—Dense fog, early morning, followed by bright sunshine and fitful breezes from all quarters. Afternoon, wind N.E., fresh and cloudy. 5.30, arrived and anchored at Greenhithe.

Time, 63 days; geographical mileage actually sailed, 835, or an average 13·2 *per diem*. Nights at sea under way, 2; nights anchored at sea, 33; and nights in harbour, 28.

Sept. 11.—Berthed the 'Perseus' in the Creek at midnight, there to remain for the winter.

MR. McMULLEN'S LAST CRUISE—THE 'PERSEUS', 1891

THE following are the entries Mr. McMullen made in his journal after setting out on his last cruise in the 'Perseus,' 1891, in the high spirits usual with him when setting out on a single-handed cruise.

June 8.—Went out of dock, and alongside pier (causeway), to scrub the copper and take in water. Hauled off during night to moorings.

June 10.—4 P.M., sailed from Greenhithe; wind high, N.E.; cool, but sunny. Off Northfleet the breeze freshened, and below Gravesend became strong; weather cloudy and hazy. With no jib, and towing the dinghey, she eventually beat every barge in a long turn to windward. 6.30 P.M., anchored in Mucking Bight.

June 11.—Sunshine. Turned out 4.15; had some trouble with the anchor. 5.30 A.M., set mainsail. 7.40, passed the Nore; weather very gloomy and cold; wind N., puffy. Noon, Re-culvers, S.W.; gladdened by a gleam of sunshine; touched both the Spaniards, but did not stay. 1 to 3, wind very light with swell. 3 P.M., tacked off Westgate; wind fresh, E.; large jib set; after rounding the North Foreland, wind fell lighter, with troublesome swell. 7, anchored with rope on Sandwich Flats; rolled dreadfully all night.

June 12.—Wind N.E., fresh and fine. 6 A.M., under way with mainsail only; very much work. Eventually got early tea. Set jib and mizen; washed, and prepared breakfast before reaching Dover. 9 to 10, hove-to in Dover Bay, had breakfast, &c., and sailed again. 10.30, set large jib. 11, off Folkestone, going grandly, but the wind soon fell light. 2.30 P.M., passed Dungeness against tide; wind E.S.E., light. 7 P.M., St. Leonards; wind S.S.W., light; boat making good way, owing to smoother water and the large jib. 8.30 P.M., anchored off Bexhill; night fine. (Bexhill is between St. Leonards and Eastbourne.)

In the morning of the 13th, Mr. McMullen landed and posted a letter at Eastbourne. After this he boarded the 'Perseus' again, and went on down Channel. The next heard of him was a telegram on June 16, saying he was found dead on the evening of June 15 by some French fishermen. He was sitting in the cockpit, with his face looking towards the sky, and the vessel sailing herself along. The doctor said he had been dead twenty-four hours when his body was found, the cause of death being failure of the heart's action. He must, therefore, have died in mid-Channel on Sunday night, the 14th of June. The weather was fine, the breeze light, and the young moon was shimmering on the placid sea. He was landed at Beuzeval (about six miles west of Trouville), and the Vice-Consul, Mr. A. O'Neill, at once communicated with his family and arranged for the funeral. Mrs. McMullen and his brother, Mr. J. McMullen, reached Beuzeval on the 18th, and Mr. R. T. McMullen was buried the next day in the cemetery at that place, after a simple service in the Protestant church.

THE END